Josiah Gilbert Holland

Miss Gilbert's Career

An American Story

Josiah Gilbert Holland

Miss Gilbert's Career
An American Story

ISBN/EAN: 9783337063160

Printed in Europe, USA, Canada, Australia, Japan

Cover: Foto ©Andreas Hilbeck / pixelio.de

More available books at **www.hansebooks.com**

MISS GILBERT'S CAREER

A

AMERICAN STORY

BY

J. G. HOLLAND

NEW YORK
CHARLES SCRIBNER'S SONS
1882

Trow's
Printing and Bookbinding Company
201–213 East Twelfth Street
NEW YORK

CONTENTS.

CHAPTER VIII.

CHAPTER XVIII.

MISS GILBERT'S CAREER.

CHAPTER I.

THE CRAMPTON LIGHT INFANTRY AND THE CHALK PLANETARIUM.

DR. THEOPHILUS GILBERT was in a hurry. He had been in a hurry all night. He had been in a hurry all the morning. While the village of Crampton was asleep, he had amputated the limb of a young man ten miles distant, attended a child in convulsions on his way home, and assisted in introducing into existence an infant at the house of his next-door neighbor—how sad an existence—how terrible a life—neither he nor the poor mother, widowed but a month, could imagine.

Dr. Gilbert had taken an early breakfast, and still the black Canadian pony, with his bushy head down, the long hair over his eyes, and his shaggy fetlocks splashed with mud, flew around the village of Crampton, bearing the doctor in his gig, and stopping here and there at the houses of his patients without the straightening of a rein, as if the pony knew quite as well as the doctor where the sick people were, and had a private interest in the business.

It was a familiar vision—this of the doctor and his

pony and his gig. They had been intimately associated for many years, and formed what the good people of Crampton called " an institution." If the doctor had died, the pony and the gig would have been useless. If the gig had broken down, the doctor and the pony would not have known what to do. If the pony had cast himself in his stable (he knew too much for that), and died of suffocation, the doctor and the gig could never have got along at all. The gig was very small—a little, low-backed, open chair—and how the doctor, who was a large, burly man, ever sat down in it, was a mystery to all the wondering boys of the village. But he did sit down in it a great many times in a day ; and the stout springs bore him lightly, while the wheels plunged into the ruts, or encountered the stones of the street, communicating to the rider a gently rising and falling motion as he sat leaning forward, eager to get on, and ready to jump off, like the figure-head of a ship, riding an easy-going swell.

Still Dr. Gilbert, borne by the pony and the gig, hurried about the village. He plunged from the street into the house of a patient, and then plunged from the house into the street, and repeated the process so many times in the course of the morning, that, had his limbs been less muscular, he would have dropped with fatigue. He paused but a moment at each bedside, and when he came forth from it, with his case of medicines under his arm, and a doubtful, aromatic atmosphere enveloping him, his strong eyes and firmly compressed lips expressed haste and determination, as if they said : " This work must be done at once—all done—done so that there may be no more to do during the day."

The doctor's business, on this particular morning, was not, it must be confessed, wholly in the line of his profession. In truth, it had not been for a week. He had patients, certainly, but they did not monopolize his interest and attention. The young man whose limb he had abbreviated the previous night was told by the doctor, in his most sympathetic tones, that he would lose a great privilege in not being able to attend the exhibition. The little girl who had convulsions was threatened, soon after recovering consciousness, with being kept away from the exhibition if she did not take her medicines promptly. Poor Mrs. Blague, with her baby on her arm—fatherless before it was born—was commiserated on the interference of the event of its birth with her enjoyment of the exhibition, and assured that if Mr. Blague were alive, such an exhibition would do his heart good. Every family he visited was adjured not to fail of attending the exhibition ; and the doctor greeted those whom he met in the street with "you are all coming out to the exhibition, of course."

Of course, everybody was going to the exhibition ; for the doctor was a driving man, and when he undertook an enterprise, everybody understood that it would go through. He was wilful, opinionated, industrious, indefatigable. The duties of his profession expended not more than a moiety of his vital supplies, and the surplus sought investment on every hand. He was a stirring man in the parish, in the church, and in all the affairs of the town. He was a stirring man in the public schools, and was, in fact, the leading spirit in them all. He made speeches at all the conventions of his town and county, with little apparent discrimination of their objects. In order to be always employed, he had studied a little law, obtained an appointment as Justice of the Peace. and. by degrees, had become a sort of general administrator of the estates of his more unfortunate patients.

The morning wore on, and the doctor at length turned in at his own gate, and. turned out the little black pony. Country wagons well loaded with women and children began to enter the village. Several ministers from

neighboring towns drove in, and alighted at the door of
the Crampton parsonage. First came Rev. Dr. Bloomer,
a very large man with a very large shirt-collar and a very
small wife, in a lop-sided wagon, weak in the springs.
Then came the Rev. Jonas Sliter, with Mrs. Rev. Jonas
Sliter, whose generous physical proportions produced a
visible depression of the wagon-spring over which she
sat, the Rev. Jonas Sliter meanwhile sitting very erect
and looking very severe behind his white cravat and
gold-bowed spectacles, as if he were dangerous, and had
been lashed by the former to the back of his seat, and
the latter had been put over his eyes for shutters. Following these, came the Rev. J. Desilver Newman, a
young sprig of divinity in brown gloves and a smart
black neck-tie, without any wife, although, judging by
his rather dashing toilet, not altogether unwilling to take
in weight sufficient to balance his wagon.

Barefoot boys from distant farms gathered upon the
steps of the old church, or assembled in the porch to
watch the sexton while he rang the bell. A smiling old
man with a bass-viol under his arm, and a grave young
man with a flute in his pocket, passed up the steps, entered the door, and were soon heard tuning their instru-
ments, and performing certain very uncertain flourishes,
in which the flute flew very high and the bass-viol sank
very low.

The bustle was increasing every moment. Little children, mysteriously bundled up, were deposited at the
door of a school-house across the common by men and
women who handled them carefully, as if they were glass,
or porcelain. Then Dr. Gilbert was seen to issue from
his house and to enter the house of his pastor, Rev. Mr.
Wilton. Then he was seen to come out with Rev. J.
Desilver Newman, followed by Rev. Dr. Bloomer and
wife, Rev. Jonas Sliter and wife, and Rev. Mr. Wilton
and wife, the last of whom closed and locked the door.

These dignitaries, instead of making their way to the church, crossed the common to the school-house, and disappeared within.

The church filled rapidly, in front of a stage temporarily erected, and covered with a carpet of green baize. The only occupants of the stage were the two musicians, the older one of whom relieved his embarrassment by drawing his bow forward and backward upon a piece of rosin, while the younger continually took his flute in pieces to wet the joints, and then put it together again, and squinted along its length to see if the holes were in range. There was a mysterious diagram upon the carpet, in French chalk, that taxed the curiosity of every eye, and provoked unlimited comment.

At length the bell began to toll, and the assembly, momentarily augmenting, and momentarily becoming excited with expectation, looked forth from the old church-windows, toward the school-house. The door of the school-house was opened as the bell closed its lazy summons, and the curiosity of Crampton was on tiptoe. First appeared Dr. Gilbert alone, as grand-marshal ; and he was followed by all the clergymen as aids. Then came little boys dressed in extravagant little dresses—crosses between trousers and petticoats—the stoutest of whom, a little red-headed fellow of five summers, bore a banner inscribed with the words :

" The Crampton Light Infantry."

The Crampton Light Infantry did not march very well, it must be confessed. It was all that mothers and the wives of the pastors could do to keep them in line. One little boy insisted that his mother should carry him, and ultimately carried his point. Some looked down upon their clothes. Some looked up, and around, to see who might be looking at their clothes. Others, with a grave thoughtfulness sadly beyond their years, seemed impressed with the proprieties of the occasion, and, among these, the little boy with golden curls, fair skin, and large, dark eyes, who brought up the rear of the male portion of the procession, and who bore a second banner with this inscription :

> " *There shall be no more thence an infant of days— for the child shall die a hundred years old.*"

Following this banner, came the little girls in pairs, their eyes bright and their cheeks flushed with excitement, looking like so many blossoms of silk and muslin. Last of all—driving her flock before her — came Miss Fanny Gilbert, a tall, slender girl of sixteen,—queenly, self-possessed, and triumphant.

It was thirty years ago that this very sweet and simple pageant moved across the Crampton common, under a bright, August sun ; and nothing more beautiful has been seen upon that common since. It was during the Infant School Epidemic of the period, that Dr. Gilbert, going from town to town, had taken the infection, and communicated it to all Crampton ; and he had selected his daughter Fanny as the best instrument upon which he could lay his hand to effect his purposes. He planned, and she executed ; and this, the great day of exhibition, had been looked forward to by the doctor with intense interest for many weeks. He should now demonstrate his own foresight, and the capacity of the youngest minds to receive and retain instruction. He should inaugurate a new epoch in the history of education. There should be no more an infant of days—of years, at most—in Crampton.

The procession now reached the church, and moved up the broad aisle. There was brisk cheering through the house, and waving of handkerchiefs, and fluttering of fans, as the little creatures mounted the stage—a place to which they had become accustomed by several visits for rehearsal. The limited orchestra (already alluded to) had intended to receive the procession with appropriate musical demonstrations, but the confusion quite confounded them, and they shrank from the attempt.

Order was at last secured. Some of the little boys had been set down very hard, as if it were difficult to make them sit still unless they were flattened. Others were pulled out from among the girls, and made to exchange seats with girls who had inadvertently strayed off with the boys. All were perched upon benches too high for them, and the row of pantalets in front looked very much as if they were hung upon a clothes-line.

Then Dr. Gilbert came forward, and, rapping upon the stage three times with his cane, called the assembly to order. They had gathered, he said, to witness one of the distinguishing characteristics and proudest triumphs of modern civilization. It had been supposed that the time of children less than five years old must necessarily be wasted in play—that the golden moments of infancy must be forever lost. That time was past. As the result of modern improvement, and among the achievements of modern progress, it had appeared that even the youngest minds were capable of receiving ideas, and that education may actually be begun at the maternal breast, pursued in the cradle, and forwarded in the nursery to a point beyond the power of imagination at present to conceive. It was in these first years of life that there had been a great waste of time. He saw children before him, in the audience, older than any upon the stage, who had no knowledge of arithmetic and geography—children, the most of whom had never heard the word astronomy pronounced. While these precious little ones had been improving their time, there were those before him whom he had seen engaged in fishing,

others in playing at ball, and others still, little girls, doing nothing, but amusing themselves with their dolls!
He had but a word to add. There were others who
would address them before the close of the exercises.
He offered the exhibition as a demonstration of the feasi-
bleness of infant instruction. He trusted he offered it in
a humble spirit; but he felt that he was justified in
pointing to it as an effectual condemnation of those
parents who had denied to their infants the privilege of
attending the school.

Administering this delicate rap upon the knuckles of
such parents as had chosen to take charge of their own
"infants," the doctor turned to Rev. Mr. Wilton, and
invited him to lead the audience in prayer. Like many
prayers offered to the Omniscient, on occasions like this,
the prayer of Mr. Wilton conveyed a great deal of information pertinent to the occasion, to the Being whom
he addressed, and, incidentally of course, to the congregation.

It was now Miss Gilbert's office to engage the audience; and her little troop of infantry was put through
its evolutions and exercises, to the astonishment and
delight of all beholders. They sang songs; they repeated long passages of poetry in concert; they went
through the multiplication table to the tune of Yankee
Doodle; they answered with the shrill, sing-song voice
of parrots all sorts of questions in geography; they re-
cited passages of Scripture; they gave an account of the
creation of the world and of the American Revolution;
they told the story of the birth of Christ, and spelled
words of six syllables; they added, they multiplied,
they subtracted, they divided; they told what hemi-
sphere, what continent, what country, what state, what
county, what town, they lived in; they repeated the
names of the Presidents of the United States and the
Governors of the Commonwealth; they acted a little

drama of Moses in the Bulrushes ; and they did many other things, till, all through the audience, astonishment grew into delight, and delight grew into rapture.

" Most astonishing ! " exclaimed Rev. Dr. Bloomer.

" Very remarkable ! " responded Rev. Jonas Sliter.

" Perfectly—ah—beats every thing I ever saw ! " said Rev. J. Desilver Newman, very flush of enthusiasm and very short of adverbs.

Dr. Gilbert calmly surveyed his triumph, or turned from one to another of the pastors upon the stage, as some new and surprising development of juvenile acquisition was exhibited, with a nod of the head and a smile which indicated that he was indeed a little surprised himself. He had never been so proud of his daughter as then. Rev. J. Desilver Newman was also receiving powerful impressions with regard to the same young woman. In fact, he had gone so far as to wonder how much money Dr. Gilbert might be worth ; but then, he had gone as far as this with a hundred other young women, and come back safe.

The musicians, who had been kept pretty closely at work accompanying the children in their songs, moved back their chairs at a hint from Miss Gilbert, and took a position behind the pulpit. There was a general moving of benches and making ready for the closing scene and the crowning glory of the exhibition—a representation of the solar system on green baize, by bodies that revolved on two legs.

The mystery of the chalk planetarium was solved. Out of a chaos of frocks and juvenile breeches, Miss Gilbert proceeded to evoke the order of a sidereal system.

" The Sun will take his place," said Miss Gilbert ; and immediately the red-headed boy, who bore the banner of " The Crampton Light Infantry," stepped to the centre of the planetarium, with a huge ball in his hand, mounted upon the end of a tall stick. Taking his stand upon the chalk sun, and elevating the sphere above a head that would have answered the purpose of a sun quite as well, he set it whirling on its axis; and thus came the centre of the system into location and into office.

"Mercury!" said Miss Gilbert; and out came a smart little chap with a smaller ball in his hand, and began walking obediently around the chalk circle next the sun.

"Venus!" and sweet little Venus rose out of the waves of muslin tossing on the side of the stage, and took the next circle.

"Earth and her Satellite!" called forth a boy and a girl, the latter playing moon to the boy's earth, revolving around him as he revolved around the sun, and with great astronomical propriety making faces at him.

Mars was called for, and it must be acknowledged that the red planet was very pale and very weary-looking.

"Jupiter and his Satellites!" and the boy Jupiter walked upon the charming circle with a charming circle of little girls revolving around him.

So Saturn with its seven moons, and Georgium Sidus, otherwise Herschel, otherwise Uranus, with its six attendant orbs, took their places on the verge of the system, and slowly, very slowly, moved around the common centre. But there was one orbit still unfilled, and that was a very eccentric one. It was not all described upon the green baize carpet, but left it, and retired behind the pulpit, and was lost.

The system was in motion, and, watching every revolving body in it, stood the system's queen, indicating by her finger that Uranus should go slower, or Mercury faster, and striving to keep order among the subjects of her realm. The music meantime grew dreamy and soft, in an attempt to suggest what is called "the music of the spheres," if any reader happens to know what kind of music that is. Heavenly little bodies indeed they were, and it is not wonderful that many eyes moistened with sensibility as they mingled so gracefully and so harmoniously upon the plane of vision.

Still the eccentric orbit was without an occupant, and no name was called. At last, a pair of large dark eyes appeared from behind the pulpit, and behind the eyes a head of golden hair, and behind the head a wreath of floating, golden curls. This was the unbidden comet, advancing slowly toward the Sun, almost creeping at first, then gradually increasing his velocity, intent on coming in collision with no other orb, smiling not, seeing nothing of the audience before him, and yet absorbing the attention of every eye in the house. The doctor's eyes beam with unwonted interest. Miss Gilbert forgets Mars and Venus, and looks only at the comet. At last, the comet darts around its perihelion, and the golden curls are turned to the audience in full retreat toward the unknown region of space behind the pulpit from whence it had proceeded.

The house rang with cheers, and the doctor was prouder than before ; for this was his little son Fred, the bearer of the banner with the long inscription, Miss Gilbert's darling brother, and the brightest ornament of the Crampton Light Infantry.

Miss Gilbert clapped her hands three times, and her system dissolved—returned to its original elements—and stepping forward to her father, she announced that her exhibition was closed.

Rev. Dr. Bloomer was then informed that there was an opportunity for remarks. He rose, and addressed the assembly with much apparent emotion. "We have seen strange things to-day," said Rev. Dr. Bloomer. "We have seen a millennial banner waving in Crampton, and a millennial exhibition within the walls of the Crampton church. There shall be no more hence—you will observe that I say hence, not thence—an infant of days, for the children of Crampton shall die a hundred years old."

Dr. Bloomer said that he did not feel authorized to speak for others, but he felt that he had learned much from the exhibition. He felt that he should go away from it a wiser man, with new apprehensions of the powers of the human soul, and the preciousness of time.

The hour was coming, he doubted not, in the progress of the race, when knowledge would be so simplified, and the modes of imparting it would become so well adapted to the young mind, that the child of five would begin his process of education where the fathers left off theirs. These little ones had already taught him many things, and God would perfect his own praise out of the mouths of babes and sucklings.

Then turning to Miss Gilbert, he thanked her for himself, and assumed to thank her on behalf of the audience, for the great gratification she had given him and them, and for the example of usefulness and industry she had set those of her own sex and age in the community. "Young woman," said Rev. Dr. Bloomer, with an emphasis that brought the tears to Miss Gilbert's eyes, " you have a career before you. May God bless you in it!"

Then Rev. Jonas Sliter rose to make only " a few little remarks," as he modestly characterized them. He had been particularly struck with the other banner; and, while his Brother Bloomer was disposed to take the millennial view of the subject, he was inclined to the military. These children were undertaking the battle of life early. They had enlisted under a captain who had already led them to a victory prouder than any ever achieved by a Cæsar or a Napoleon—an American Joan of Arc, whose career of usefulness, if she should keep her sword bright, and her escutcheon untarnished, would far surpass in glory that of the world-renowned heroine whose name he had mentioned. Heaven forbid that he should flatter any one. He despised a flatterer ; but he felt that he was honoring Cæsar and Napoleon and Joan of Arc in their graves by mentioning their names in connection with such achievements as he had witnessed on that occasion.

It is true that Rev. Jonas Sliter rather mixed things, in his more ambitious rhetorical flourishes, on all occasions ; but the language sounded well, and, being accompanied with appropriately magnificent action, it was accustomed to bring down the house. It did not fail before the Crampton audience ; but the rounding of his period left him vacant. Standing back, as if to wait for the subsidence of the applause, his mind retired behind his glasses, and thrust out its antennæ in every direction to feel for his theme, but he could not find it.

In his desperation he turned, at last, to the children, and said in his blandest tones : " Little children, can you tell me who Cæsar and Napoleon and Joan of Arc were ? "

" Cæsar is the name of my dog," responded the little golden-haired comet.

" Napoleon is the name of *my* dog," cried Mars.

There was an awful pause—a suppressed titter—when precious little Venus, in a shrill voice, with an exceedingly knowing look in her face, said that " Joan of Arc was the name of the dog that Noah saved from the flood ! "

What wonder that Crampton roared with laughter ? What wonder that Rev. Dr. Bloomer shook with powerful convulsions ? What wonder that Mrs. Bloomer and Mrs. Wilton nudged each other ? What wonder that Dr. Gilbert and Miss Fanny Gilbert bit their lips with mingled vexation and mirth ? What wonder that Rev. Jonas Sliter grew red in the face ?

But Rev. Jonas Sliter was up. The sole question with him was how to sit down. What should he say ? He waited until the laughter had subsided, and then he told the children they had not got to that yet, but their excellent teacher would doubtless tell them all about it the next term.

"The next term!" The speaker had found a theme; for he deemed it his duty to "improve" all occasions of public speech for giving religious instruction. From the next term of school, he easily went over to the next term of existence, and told the Crampton Light Infantry that, in order to make that a happy term, they must all become Soldiers of the Cross, and fight valiantly the battles of the church militant. Then Rev. Jonas Sliter generously declared that he would occupy the time no longer, but would "make way for others."

Rev. J. Desilver Newman rose, and came forward. He was very red in the face and very shaky in the knees. He regretted that he was left without a banner, there having been but two in the procession, and those having been appropriated by the gentlemen who had preceded him. He took it as a hint that he should say but little, and he should say but little. The children were tired, and were eager for their refreshments. He would not detain them. He owed it to himself, however, to say, that no man could be more sensible than he of the splendor of the achievements of these children, and of their accomplished instructress. Though he had no children himself, he was interested in the rising generation, and was a convert to infant schools. He should have one organized immediately in Littleton on his arrival home. He would further gratify his sense of justice by saying that he fully agreed with the gentleman who had preceded him, in the opinion that the young lady who had shown such remarkable ability in training and instructing these children, had the power of achieving a great career.

Mr. Newman sat down, having said a great deal more than he expected to when he rose. Half a dozen children had fallen asleep upon their benches. Two or three had begun to cry. The remainder were tired and in confusion. Rev. Mr. Wilton, a quiet, sensible man, had intended to say something, but, seeing the condition of things, came forward and pronounced a benediction upon the audience, and the exhibition was at a close.

Of the gorging of fruits and sweetmeats that followed in the grove back of Dr. Gilbert's house, nothing needs to be said. As evening came on, the throng separated, and the little ones went cross and very weary to their homes.

The ministers and their wives, the minister without a wife, and the doctor and his daughter, took tea quietly at the parsonage after all was over, and one by one, the clerical wagons, still very badly balanced, were driven out of the village.

Miss Gilbert had commenced her career.

CHAPTER II.

MISS GILBERT VISITS THE SKY, AND LITTLE VENUS TAKES UP HER PERMANENT RESIDENCE THERE.

WHERE was Fanny Gilbert's mother during the exhibition? What could keep the mother of little Fred away? She was asleep—she was resting. She had been asleep for two years. She had rested quietly in the Crampton graveyard during all this time, "making up lost sleep." She had been hurried through life, and hurried out of life. She had bent every energy to realize to Dr. Gilbert his idea of a woman and a wife. She had ambitiously striven to match him in industry—to keep at his side in all the enterprises he undertook ; but her stock of strength failed her in mid-passage, and she had fallen by the way. She had known no rest—no repose. There was not a room nor a piece of furniture in her house that did not give evidence of her tireless care. Her Sabbath was no day of rest to her. She taught, she visited the poor, she managed the village sewing-circle, she circulated subscription-papers for charities, she attended all the religious meetings in sunshine and storm; and, what with maternal associations, and watchings with the sick, and faithful care of her own family, she wore herself quite away, and faded out from Dr. Gilbert's home, and from the sight of her children.

Everybody mourned when good Mrs. Gilbert died, but everybody drew a long breath of satisfaction, as if it were pleasant, after all, to think that she was resting, and that nobody could wake her.

Her death shocked Dr. Gilbert, but it did not stop him. On the contrary, he seemed to plunge into the work of life with fresh energy. He could not pause for an instant now. New schemes for the employment of his time were devised. The temporary paralysis of grief terrified him. To stand still, to cherish and linger about a sorrow—this he could not bear. He must act— act all the time—or die. People who looked on said that Dr. Gilbert was trying to "work it off." He fancied that there was no way by which he could so appropriately show his grief for her as by following her example.

"Aunt Catharine," sister of the sleeping wife and mother, kept house for Dr. Gilbert, and did what she could for the children. This was very little, for the doctor had his own ideas about their training, which he allowed no one to interfere with.

It was supposed by the gossips of the village that Dr. Gilbert would ultimately marry Aunt Catharine; but it is doubtful whether he ever dreamed of such a thing. She was a woman who, if we may credit her own declaration, "never loved a man, and never feared one." It was pretty certain that she did not love the doctor, and quite as certain that she did not fear him. She held his restlessness in a kind of contemptuous horror, and felt herself irresistibly drawn into antagonism with him. She loved his children, and served them affectionately and devotedly for the mother's sake ; but the doctor always aroused her to opposition. If he spoke, she contradicted him, or felt moved to do so. If he acted, she opposed him, or desired to oppose him. She was neither cross-grained nor malicious ; but a will that acknowledged no ruler, and that did not recognize her existence any more than if she had been a house-fly, bred an element of perverseness in her character.

Of course, Aunt Catharine was not an admirer of infant schools. She had not attended the exhibition. Possibly she would have liked to see Fanny and Fred, but she would not humor Dr. Gilbert. Accordingly, when he and Fanny walked into the house, after bidding the people of the parsonage good-night, they by no means anticipated a cordial greeting.

Aunt Catharine had very black eyes, set in a sharp, honest, sensible face, and they looked very black indeed that night. Now there was an infallible index to the condition of Aunt Catharine's mind, which both father and daughter perfectly understood. When she was knitting very slowly, and rocking herself very fast, they knew that a storm was brewing in the domestic sky ; when she was rocking very slowly, and knitting very fast, the elements were at peace.

When they entered the parlor, the rocking-chair was in furious action, and the knitting-needles were making very indifferent progress.

"Well, I'm glad it's done, and over, and through with," exclaimed Aunt Catharine, decidedly.

"Done, and over, and through with, eh ? And fin-

2

ished, and performed, and consummated, I suppose," responded the doctor with a pleasant sarcasm.

" Well, I'm glad it's done, then."

" Done ? " said the doctor with emphasis. " Done ? It's only begun."

" You'll find it's only begun, I guess, before the week is out," replied the woman. " Do you suppose the little babies you've been tormenting in church all day will get through the week without being sick ? There was poor little Fred, who was so tired that he could not go to sleep, and cried for an hour before he shut his eyes."

" A little natural, childish excitement," said the doctor, a shadow of apprehension coming over his face unbidden. " He will be rested and all right in the morning."

" Dr. Gilbert," said Aunt Catharine, laying aside her knitting, and raising her forefinger excitedly, " I have been longing to speak my mind for a month about this business, and now I am going to speak it, and I want Fanny to hear me."

" Well, be quick about it," said the doctor impatiently, " for I have a good deal of writing to do to-night, and time is short. Besides, Fanny is tired, I imagine."

" Yes, you always have work to do, and time is always short, and Fanny is always tired. It was always so when your wife was living, and it is about her that I'm going to speak. You had as good a wife, Dr. Gilbert, as a man ever had, if she was my sister ; and she might just as well be alive now, and sitting in this room, as to be lying in the graveyard yonder. I don't say you killed her, but I say the life she led killed her, and the life she led was the life you marked out for her, and encouraged her to lead. Mind you, Dr. Gilbert, I don't say this to taunt you. What's done can't be helped. I can't bring her back, and if it were to recall her to her old restless life of work, work, work, I wouldn't bring her back if I could. She's better where she is. No, sir, I wouldn't lift my finger to call her from the grave, if that would do 'it. What I say, I say for her children. They are going on in the same way. Fanny is working herself to death. If she had not your constitution, she would be lying by the side of her mother now. Think of a girl of sixteen, with her education finished, and the work of her life begun! It's awful, it's shameful, it's outrageous. And there is your precious little boy, only five years old —his mother's boy. He's just as sure to die before his time as you keep on with him in the way you have begun—heating his brains with arithmetic and geography and history and comets, and all sorts of stuff, that children have no more business with than they have with your medicine-case, and showing him up to a church full of people, and getting him so excited that he can't sleep, and keeping him shut up in a school-room all day, when he ought to be at home playing in the dirt."

Aunt Catharine said all this impetuously, with tears that came and went in her eyes without once dropping.

" Is that all? " inquired the doctor coolly.

" It's God's truth, what there is of it, any way," replied the excited woman.

What he would have said if Fanny had not been present, he did not say ; so, with forced calmness, he simply responded : " Well, well, Catharine, we'll not quarrel ; but I think I understand these matters better than you, and I propose to manage my children, and conduct their education as I think best."

Aunt Catharine had " spoken her mind," and, as usual on such occasions, was aware that she had made no impression—produced no effect. But she felt better. The fire was spent, and, turning kindly to Fanny, she told her that she was looking very weary, and had better retire.

Then, gathering up her knitting, she went up-stairs to her own room.

Father and daughter sat a while in silence, the latter waiting for the former to speak; but he turned to his little desk, and was soon busy with his papers.

As Fanny rose and bade him " Good-night," he said, without lifting his head : " You had better look in and see how Fred is."

The fatigues of the day showed themselves plainly in the girl's heavy eyes, pale lips, and languid motions, as she left the room, lamp in hand, and climbed the stairway. The excitement that had held her up for weeks was gone, and the natural reaction, with the warning words her aunt had spoken, and the reawakened memories of her dead mother, filled her with the most oppressive sadness. Vague dissatisfaction, undefinable unrest, took the place of ambitious aspiration, and the delight of strong powers in full exercise.

In accordance with her habit, not less than in obedience to the suggestion of her father, she took her way to her room through the chamber of little Fred. He lay moaning and feverish upon his pillow, his fair cheeks flushed, and his hands tossing restlessly. She was too weary to sit by him, so she unconsciously repeated the words of her father : " A little natural, childish excitement. He will be rested and all right in the morning." Then she kissed his hot lips, and passed into her own chamber.

She was so weary that she could hardly wait to prepare for her bed ; but, when she lay down, sleep came quickly—a kind of half sleep, half swoon, that went almost as quickly as it came. After a time, which seemed very long, but which was, in fact, very short, she found herself, almost instantaneously, painfully wide awake, as if sleep had snatched and strained her to its bosom, and then thrown her hopelessly off.

Then all the scenes and all the triumphs of the day thronged her mind. She was again in the church. Admiring eyes were upon her; she heard the applause again; and again the flush of gratified pride warmed her heart and her cheeks, as she recalled the words of praise that were spoken to her in the presence of her associates. Again the little children were revolving around the chalk planetarium, obedient to her will. Noiselessly, beautifully, they swam around in her waking dream, to the rhythm of ideal harmonies. The little comet went and came, and went and came again, and still her ears rang with the applause of the admiring assembly.

She lay thus, the events of the day re-enacting themselves in her brain, careless of sleep, but locked in a delicious and half-delirious repose. In retiring, she had neglected to extinguish her lamp, and was glad to have it burning. At not infrequent intervals she had heard her little brother moaning and muttering in his sleep. At last the clock struck twelve, and soon afterward she heard the sound of footsteps in the hall—a delicate, measured tread, light as the step of a fairy—jarring nothing, awaking no resonance, but constant—now approaching her door, then receding and fading away till its velvet fall almost escaped her strained and sharpened sense.

Her mother! What wonder that the words her aunt had spoken should call up the well-remembered form? What wonder that her quickened imagination at this midnight hour should conceive the presence of the loving spirit around the beds which her feet, while living, had visited so fondly and so frequently?

Fanny heard the little parlor clock faintly strike the half-hour before she thought of stirring. She was not superstitious. Her father's spirit was in her, and when it was roused, she was calm, self-poised, and courageous. She rose from her bed, determined to learn the cause of the footsteps which she still heard. Taking the lamp in her hand, she opened the door into the hall, and holding the light above her head, peered into the passage. At its farther end she saw a small white object approaching her slowly, and knew at once that little Fred was walking in his sleep. She did not dare to speak to him, for he was near the stairway. As he came nearer to her, she saw that his eyes were open, in an unwinking, somnambulic stare, and further, that he was still enacting the part of the comet in his dream. He came up, gradually increasing his speed, then suddenly he darted around her, and started on another circuit out into the unknown spaces. Fanny followed him, took him by the hand, and quietly led him to his bed, and lay down by his side, afraid to leave him.

Now she did not dare to fall asleep. She could not risk her little brother again to the danger of walking off the stairs. Now she must think, to keep herself awake. The most exciting thoughts would be the most welcome.

Of all the words spoken to her, or spoken within her hearing, during the day, there was one which had left the deepest impression, and was charged with the most grateful suggestions. There were words of praise that had been appropriated for immediate consumption ; this was kept sacredly for future use, as a precious morsel to be devoured in secret. There were words which had settled like a flock of singing birds among her fresh sensibilities ; this had wheeled and hovered alone above her, waiting till the others had gone before it would come down and nestle at her heart.

A career! Dr. Bloomer had told her, with abundant emphasis, that she had a career before her. Rev. Jonas Sliter had yoked her name with a woman famous in history, as one to whom a great career was possible—one, indeed, who had already commenced a career. Even

Rev. J. Desilver Newman had been compelled, by his sense of justice, to accord to her the power of achieving a great career. She had caught the taste of public applause, and it was sweet—sweeter than anything she had ever known. Her inmost soul had been thrilled by its penetrating flavor, and she became conscious of a new hunger, a new thirst, a new longing. A new motive of life was born within her, and she must have a career that she might win more praise, and drink more deeply at the fountain which the day and its events had opened to her.

Her soul was on fire with a newly kindled ambition. Life grew golden and glorious to her. Projects of achievement rose like fairy palaces in her imagination, and ran out in glittering lines to its farthest verge. She would be an authoress. She would write books. She would reveal her life in poetry, the music of whose numbers should charm the world, and compel the world to give her homage. She would hold the mirror up to life in fiction, and win the plaudits of the nations, like women of whom she had heard. She would become a great painter. She would cross the seas, and gather from the masters their secrets, and then she would return and glorify her name and her nation by works of unequalled art. She would become a visitor of prisons, and a minister of mercy to the abodes of infamy and of misery, and win immortality for a life devoted to works of charity. She would be a missionary, and, on " India's burning sands," plant the standard of the Cross. She would stand before public assemblies, and there assert, not only her own womanhood, but the rights of her sex. She would have a career of some kind.

In one brief hour of dreaming, all the charm of domestic home-life had faded. The thought of marriage, its quiet duties, and its subordination of her life and will to the life and will of another, became repulsive to her.

Even Crampton was become too small for her, and the
praise of the humble country pastors, that had so elated
her, grew insignificant, almost contemptible. One thing
was certain — she could never keep an infant school
again.

Gradually the period of wakefulness passed away.
Little Fred became more cool and quiet, and slept
sweetly. Already she had launched out into the sea of
sleep on a vessel under full sail, and was waving her
handkerchief to the crowd of friends on shore, whom she
had left for an indefinite term of years, for a pilgrimage
to the shrines of classic art, when the door-bell was rung
violently, and she was startled into consciousness again.
She heard her father's prompt step in the hall, and then
she listened for the errand of the messenger. The voice
was that of a boy, evidently very much out of breath
with running.

"Please, Dr. Gilbert, come down to our house just as
quick as you can," said the boy.

"Whose house is our house?" inquired the doctor
gruffly, unable to make out the boy in the darkness.

"Why, you've been there forty times. You know Mr.
Pelton's, don't you?"

"Oh! yes ; who is sick at Mr. Pelton's?"

"Not anybody as I knows of," said the boy, taking a
long breath. "It's the next house—Mr. Tinker's."

"Well, who is sick at Mr. Tinker's?" inquired the
doctor impatiently.

"You know Ducky, don't you?"

"Ducky who? Ducky what?"

"Why, don't you know little Ducky Tinker? You've
seen her forty times," exclaimed the boy in a tone of indignant astonishment.

"Look here, boy," said Dr. Gilbert, "if you know
who is sick, tell me."

"Well, you know little Venus, *don't* you?" exclaimed

the boy, in a tone that said, "if you don't know her, it is beyond my power to go further."

"Little Venus?"

"Yes, little Venus. Of course you know her. You saw her in church forty times to-day."

"Oh! yes; I understand. I'll be down there directly," said the doctor, and slammed the door in the boy's face.

Fanny, amused with the lad's cool oddity, and pained to hear of the sickness of one of her little pets, rose and went to the window to make further inquiries. Putting out her head, she saw him sitting on the door-step, and overheard him talking to himself.

"Spiteful old customer, any way. Wonder if he thinks I'm going home alone. No, sir—you don't catch me. I'll sit here and blow till he comes round with his old go-cart, and then I'll hang on to the tail of it, and try legs with that little Kanuck of his. Hullo! Who's there? Tell me before I count three, or I'll fire. *One—two——*"

These last words were addressed to a dark figure that appeared at the gate to interrupt the boy's soliloquy. "I want the doctor," said the figure, just in time to save himself from the boy's fatal "three."

"You can't have him," said the boy promptly.

"Can't have him? Who are you?"

"Don't you know me? You've seen me forty times. I know you like a book."

"Well, why can't I have the doctor? Isn't he at home?"

"Yes, he's at home, but he's spoke for."

"But I must have him," said the man decidedly.

"Why, what's the row down to your house? Mars sick?"

"Mars sick? Who's Mars?"

"Why, don't you know Mars? Well, that is funny. Didn't go to the exhibition, did you?"

"Oh! yes. It is Mars. He is very bad, and the doctor must see him now. Where is the doctor?"

"Well, if you think Mars is very bad, I wonder what you would think of Venus," said the boy, intent on diverting the man's attention from the doctor. "Screaming all night, folks all up, poultices all over her, paregoric no use. Don't know a thing."

At this moment the doctor drove round, having harnessed his own horse, and was hailed by both messengers at the gate. The messenger of Mars made known his errand, and the doctor promised to visit that planet immediately after his return from Mr. Tinker's. In the meantime, the messenger of Venus had secured his hold of the tail of Dr. Gilbert's gig, and was soon on his way, half running, half riding, and trying his legs very successfully with the little black pony.

Fanny went back to her bed, fearful and distressed, wondering if all her little planets were going to fall. Examining little Fred once more, and finding him still composed, she surrendered herself to her pillow, and, when she awoke again, it was not only daylight, but the sun was shining brightly in at her window.

She rose, and dressed little Fred and herself, and descended to the breakfast-room. The boy had little of the elasticity of his years, and she felt languid and miserable. Aunt Catharine received them with anxious eyes, and was evidently relieved to find them both able to be upon their feet.

"Where is father?" inquired Fanny.

"Out, looking after his men in the field, as usual," replied Aunt Catharine. "I don't believe that man slept two hours last night, and he was up all the night before. I wonder he lives."

It was the breakfast hour, and promptly on the stroke of the clock he entered the room. He looked at little Fred anxiously, but he did not speak to him. There was a cloud upon his face which Fanny understood, but which Aunt Catharine could not interpret.

"Who called you up last night?" inquired Aunt Catharine.

"That's more than I know," replied the doctor evasively, while an expression of hard pain passed over his face.

Fanny regarded him with marked apprehension, and on the impulse inquired, "Are they very sick, father?"

Dr. Gilbert looked in her face, and saw that she knew what Aunt Catharine did not.

"Both have been very sick, but both are relieved. Your little Mars is much better. Your little Venus, Fanny——"

Dr. Gilbert paused. His daughter noticed his hesitation, turned pale, and dropped her knife and fork. He could not bear to speak the word in presence of little Fred.

"Little Venus——" suggested Fanny, repeating the commencement of his broken sentence.

"Little Venus," pursued the doctor, "has taken her place in the sky."

Little Fred looked up, with his eyes full of wonder, and said, "Has she really, and truly, papa?"

"Yes, really and truly, my boy."

"Well, I want to take my place in the sky, too. Can't I take my place in the sky with Venus? I won't run against her," said the boy with eager enthusiasm.

"Little Venus is dead, my boy," said the doctor, his eyes filling with tears.

"Dead? dead?" inquired the little fellow, his eyes wide with solemn wonder. "Who killed her? What made her die? I don't believe it was right that little Venus should die; was it, papa?"

"Yes, it was right, my child, for God took her away."

Aunt Catharine moved uneasily in her chair. It was all she could do to maintain silence. It seemed to her straightforward, honest mind, almost blasphemy to attribute to God an event occasioned by the excitements and exposures to which the delicate childhood of little Venus had been subjected.

Fred's brain was sorely puzzled, and, as his young reason found no way to grasp and adjust the event, he burst into an uncontrollable fit of weeping. The doctor could not withstand this, and, starting as if he had been smitten in the face, he rose and left the room.

CHAPTER III.

HUCKLEBURY RUN AND ITS ENTERPRISING PROPRIETOR.

NEW and important characters wait impatiently for an introduction to the reader, and why pause to relate events that occurred as a matter of course, after the death of little Venus? Why pause to tell of Aunt Catharine's further exposition of "her mind;" of the touching funeral of the little girl, attended to her grave by the entire corps of the "Crampton Light Infantry," in procession; of each little member going up and tossing flowers into her grave; of the prayers and preachings of the good pastor over the "mysterious providence;" of the reaction against infant schools among the people of Crampton; of the disgust of Dr. Gilbert with the ignorance and superstition of those whom he had striven to benefit; and of the freedom in which Miss Fanny Gilbert was left to dream of a career?

A few weeks after the events which have been narrated, Dr. Gilbert had a long interview with Mrs. Blague, in her snug back parlor. That little lady, pale with her recent sickness, and dropping tears freely under the stress of present gloomy reflections, sat rocking the cradle of her little boy, and rocking herself at the same time.

"You must cheer up," said the doctor, with a voice so sonorous that it seemed to jar the floor.

"Ah! doctor, you say it very easily; I find it very hard."

"Well, you must stir about, you must get out doors and see people, and—and—get strength. That was always Mrs. Gilbert's way."

"Poor Mrs. Gilbert!" responded Mrs. Blague, with an involuntary sigh. "How much comfort she would be to me, if she were living!"

Aunt Catharine's recent remarks upon Mrs. Gilbert had made the doctor sensitive, and he changed the direction of the conversation.

"Well, to come back to business. We may as well look all our troubles in the face. I find, on examining your husband's accounts, that, after paying all the debts, you will only have this house left. Now the practical question is, how you are going to live. You are not able to earn anything, and you will not be, while this child is young. You have but one resort, and that is Arthur. He is eighteen years old—smart and strong— able to earn his own living and yours too; and if he is a boy of the spirit I take him to be, he will devote himself to you gladly."

"But it will be such a disappointment to him to be obliged to relinquish study; and I had set my heart on his going through college. It was the strongest wish of his father that he should be an educated man, and have a chance to rise in the world. I would willingly give up the house——"

"It cannot be done, madam," said the doctor, interrupting her. "You've got a house—keep it over your head. You've got a son able to earn money enough to support you in it. Let him do it. It is as plainly God's providence for you," said the doctor, rising, and walking back and forth across the room, "as if he had told you so in so many words. Let Arthur be called, and let us find out what he thinks about it."

Arthur is in his chamber writing up accounts; and while Mrs. Blague goes to call him, let us engage ourselves with a bit of history which is passing through the busy mind of Dr. Gilbert. Mr. Blague had been a humble country tradesman, industrious and frugal, but not prosperous. He had lived comfortably and reputably, but he had lived a life of sorrow. His first child, Arthur, had thriven, but he had had many children, all of whom he had lost. Some taint of constitution had attached to all in turn, and just as they were blossoming into childhood, one after another had sickened and died. These repeated blows had so stricken the feeble mother that she had become what strong people call a "broken down woman." For her, there were no bright skies, no green fields, no pleasant melody of birds, no beautiful flowers, no life-inspiring breezes; and, when the last blow came, and he who had been her constant friend, and her one stay and support, was taken from her, her spirit was crushed into a helpless grief from which she did not even care to rise. The birth of another boy, after the death of her husband, was but an added grief, for she had lost all hope now, that any child of hers might live.

So, when Dr. Gilbert told her to "cheer up," it only made her the more sensible that she was beyond the ability of cheerfulness. When he bade her "stir about," she comprehended no motive for the effort. She could cheer no one; she could be cheered by no one. Vital elasticity there was none within her. Her life had become a passive, grieving, plaining thing.

There is a sound upon the stairs, and Dr. Gilbert, growing impatient with a few minutes' delay, looks at his watch. Arthur Blague opens the door, and respectfully steps aside for his mother to enter. He is tall enough and strong enough to lift her in his arms like a child. His hair is black, his eye is dark—there is something manly beyond his years in his bearing—yet the down of manhood hardly darkens his lip. Shaking Dr. Gilbert's hand, he advances to the cradle, and, taking it up, he removes it to another room. The mother follows passively, and he shuts the door after her. Dr. Gilbert clears his throat, and forgets what, in his hasty promptness, he was going to say. Arthur is not a boy any longer, and there is something in his presence—felt but undefinable—that gives Dr. Gilbert the consciousness that he has will and character to deal with.

Can streams rise higher than their fountains? They can, and they do. There was more power, more character, more life, in this boy, than either his father or his mother possessed—nay, more than both together possessed. He was of a more generous pattern, physically and mentally, than either. Where did he come from? What germ of a feeble life enclosed the germ of this large life? Philosophy tells of great hereditary qualities stepping proudly over the heads of many generations, and entering into life again. Philosophy tells us that family life is like a garden vine that repeats the parent root at long intervals, and pushes on with new vitality. Philosophy is a cheat. God makes new Adams every day.

Arthur Blague took a chair in front of Doctor Gilbert, and calmly looked him in the face. The doctor cleared his throat, and began : "As the administrator of your father's estate, and as his old friend, I am, of course, much interested in the future comfort and welfare of his family."

Dr. Gilbert paused, uncertain how to proceed, and drummed upon the arm of his chair with his finger-nails. Arthur still looked in his face, and simply responded " Yes, sir."

" Well," pursued the doctor, entirely breaking down on his preamble, " to make a long story short, we can only save this house from the estate ; and some means are to be devised for supporting your mother, her little one, and yourself."

" Yes, sir," responded Arthur again.

" I am aware," continued Dr. Gilbert, getting easier, " that you have entertained high aims in life, and you know, Arthur, that I sympathize with you in them. It will be very hard for you to relinquish them, I know ; but you see how it is, and I have no doubt you will be ready to make the sacrifice."

" I suppose," replied Arthur, " that I can change my plans, without changing my aims."

Light dawned on the doctor. He would encourage the boy to entertain a pleasant delusion, though he was entirely at a loss to imagine how a man could become eminent without first attaining, in the regular way, what people are accustomed to call " an education."

" A very proper distinction," said the doctor, rubbing his hands. " Keep your aims and change your means. Keep your eye on the goal, and, if circumstances make it necessary to change the path by which you have chosen to reach it, then adopt a new path. A good distinction—very good. I'm glad you thought of it, because it will help you, and make a change in your plans comparatively easy."

" Easy ! " exclaimed Arthur, a half-contemptuous twinge in his lip, and added : " I take it that the simple question with me is, what is right, and what is best."

" Very well, how do you decide that question ? "

" I decided, before my father was laid in the grave,

that it was right and best for me to support my mother and myself, and that it would be a shame and a curse to me to relinquish her, or submit myself to the charity of friends, in order to attain my own selfish ends."

"A brave decision, Arthur Blague!" exclaimed the doctor with a hearty smile. "Now what do you propose to do? Will you teach a school this winter?"

"I think not."

"Why not?"

"Because I wish to undertake some employment which I can follow constantly, and which will give me a regular income throughout the year. It must be near my home, for my mother cannot be left alone. It must be an employment of promise, in which I can feel that I am learning that which will be of more value to me than my wages."

"I don't know where you'll find it," said the doctor, shaking his head dubiously. "There isn't much going on in Crampton. Wagon-making is down. I had to take one for a debt last week, and sacrifice on it. Brooms are very uncertain. Brush is high now, and nobody makes anything. Ketchum & Fleesum are doing a good deal with palm-leaf hats, I suppose. They make considerable noise about it, at least. What do you say to going into their store?"

"I've had enough of stores," replied Arthur decidedly.

"Well, there's old Ruggles, down at Hucklebury Run. He is about the only man in Crampton who is making any thing. Cotton and sugar are high now, and the market for linsey-woolsey was never better at the South. He employs a great many hands, and pays good wages."

Arthur cast his eyes, which he had held steadily on the doctor's face till this moment, upon the floor. His face grew red, and a mingled expression of pain and disgust passed over it.

3

The doctor noticed the change, and added : "I know that they tell hard stories about matters down at the Run. Old Ruggles, as we call him, isn't exactly a popular man. I suppose he does the best he can for himself, like the rest of us, but he's a driving fellow, and brings a great deal of money into the place. He's a member of our parish, you know, and pays something for the support of the Gospel."

"And starves what he pays out of his operatives, unless they lie," replied Arthur.

"Well, well, we can't always tell about these things. Men who have so many people to manage have a great many trials we know nothing about. I'm inclined to think he is a little hard, but he will do as he agrees to do ; and the question which you have to settle is, whether you can earn enough in his employ to support the family, and still be learning something that will enable you to get up in life."

"Dr. Gilbert," said Arthur warmly, "you know that old Ruggles did my father more injury than any other man he ever dealt with. He always over-reached him, and always abused his confidence. I have quarrelled with him myself, and he hates me. I have no respect for him, and can have none."

"Very well, if you can do better, I have nothing to say ; but you see how it is. I confess that I see nothing for you to do, unless you can find it in his establishment."

Arthur rose, and walked the room in undisguised distress. It was torture to think of being under the control of one whom he knew to be mean-spirited and tyrannical. Then the humiliation of coming upon a level with those who had been the slaves of their employer for years, and who, for bread, had forfeited their manhood in a craven sycophancy, chafed his pride almost beyond endurance. The loss of caste with his associates in the village—young men with whom he had hoped to dispute the honors of a higher grade of life—he could bear better than this, but it helped to make his cup more bitter.

" You see," suggested the doctor, watching him close-ly, " that you will not be obliged to stay at the Run at night. You can breakfast here, take your dinner along with you, and come home to sup and sleep."

Arthur did not need the suggestion. He had strug-gled with himself, and he had conquered. Brushing tears from his eyes that the conflict had cost him, he calmly seated himself again, and said : " The matter is settled. I shall go to the Run, if I can get employment there."

He had hardly finished his sentence when the doctor rose from his seat, hurried to the window, raised it, and shouted to a man passing along the street in a wagon, behind a half-fed horse. Having just then received a swinging cut with the whip, the animal was not readily checked. So the driver gave him another cut to make him stop, and as the horse did not understand that way of doing business, he gave him another cut to make him understand it, shouting " Whoa then !" so savagely that he could be heard from one end of Crampton common to the other.

The doctor beckoned him to return. Arthur trembled from head to foot, not with apprehension but with indig-nation. It was old Ruggles himself, on his regular morn-ing visit to the post-office. As he came back to the win-dow, his horse, half-crazed with pain and fear, was not readily pulled up, and he was whipped again, and then he was driven round and round a circle in front of the house, and whipped all the way. At length the poor brute stood still.

" I'll teach you," said old Ruggles. spitefully, and then, seeing for the first time who had called him, whined out by way of apology, " The fact is, doctor, the women drive this horse so much that he isn't good for anything. I hate to whip a horse."

"I never whip a horse," said the doctor.

"Well, you can't always get along without it. Horses are like folks. You have to straighten them out once in a while. He! he! he!" and the proprietor of Hucklebury Run tried to smile amiably.

"Have you a few minutes to spare now?" inquired Dr. Gilbert.

"Well! yes—always enough to do, you know. We are working folks down to the Run. Can't stop long. What is't?"

"A little matter of business. Suppose you tie your horse, and come in."

Old Ruggles looked down upon his rusty satinet suit, perfectly conscious that he was out of place in a decent house and good company.

"I ain't fixed up any, you see," said he, "but handsome is that handsome does, as they say. He! he! he!" and he tried to smile again. Arthur was burning with disgust. His sensitive nature revolted from contact with the man, but he stepped to the door and admitted him. He took Arthur's unresisting hand, and remembering that he was in a house which death had recently visited, he drew on a very long and a very sympathetic face, and told Arthur he was glad to see him looking well, and inquired how his mother "stood up under it." Then he blew his nose, a tough organ, accustomed by long usage to that process, and on the present occasion blown as an expression of sympathy for the bereaved family, and as a signal for the commencement of business.

"We were talking of you the moment you drove past the window," said the doctor preliminarily.

"Saying nothing bad, I hope," replied Ruggles, looking from the doctor to Arthur, and from Arthur to the doctor again, with his small, shrewd, gray eyes.

Arthur blushed, but the doctor, intent on business, paid no attention to the remark, and proceeded.

"Perhaps you know, Mr. Ruggles, that Mr. Blague's affairs do not turn out so well as we had hoped, for the sake of his family, they might."

Ruggles nodded his head, and said that he had heard something to that effect.

"Which," continued the doctor, "will make it necessary for our young friend Arthur to relinquish some of his plans, and to devote himself to obtaining a support for himself and the family."

Ruggles nodded his head again, evidently puzzled to know why all this should be said to him.

Dr. Gilbert proceeded : "Arthur and I have been considering the matter, and have come to the conclusion that a situation in your establishment would perhaps give him the best opportunity he could have for earning reasonable wages, and, at the same time, of acquiring knowledge of a business that would enable him at some future day to realize a competence."

Arthur's eyes were riveted upon the face of his future employer. The gray eyes twinkled with a new light, the thin, long lips twitched with unwonted excitement, and the hard, wrinkled cheeks, black as ink with a three-days beard, seemed to hug more tightly the bones beneath them. The thought that the son of the old tradesman—that Arthur Blague, who had defied him, and who had proudly expressed his contempt of him to his face, should become his dependent, was one which gratified everything that was malignant in his nature. Arthur, with his keen instincts, read the hard face as if it were the page of an open book.

Old Ruggles looked about the room, wrinkled his forehead as if in a brown study, and whistled to himself. He was at home now. He forgot his rusty suit of satinet. He forgot the dissonance of his breeding with that

of the quiet house in which he sat. He was the lord of
a favor and a destiny, and, as a fitting expression of his
new dignity, he put his dusty feet in a chair, and
whistled again.

"Well, I don't know hardly what to say about it. I've
got all the help I care about, and I'm afraid that Arthur
ain't quite used enough to work to be contented with us.
We are working folks down to the Run, you know;"
having said which, old Ruggles subsided into another
whistle.

"I'm not afraid of work, sir," said Arthur.

"Well, I'm glad to hear you say it. Pluck is everything, but I—I—don't exactly like to have you do it.
It's a kind of—sort of—coming down, ain't it?" The
proprietor of Hucklebury Run grinned maliciously, and
thought he was looking amiable and sympathetic.

"If you are particular about knowing my opinion on
that point," replied Arthur sharply, "I think it is."

"Now that's jest the trouble I expected. You see
we are all alike down to the Run. I work jest as hard
as any of my hands, and we can't have anybody round
that feels above his business. You can't learn my business, and learn it so that it will be of any use to you,
unless you begin at the foot of the ladder, and work up.
I began at the foot of the ladder, and I make 'em all
begin at the foot of the ladder. Hucklebury Run is the
last place to have high notions in."

"I suppose a man may have such notions as he
chooses, provided he does his work well," said Arthur,
and added, "but if you don't want me, there is an end
of it. I shall try somewhere else."

"I s'pose I can make a place for you, but I couldn't
give you much the first year."

"How much?"

"Let's see!" and the manufacturer ciphered it out
with his eyes on the ceiling. "Ten times twelve is a

hundred and twente-e-e—ten times twelve is a hundred and twente-e-e—fifty-two dollars—fifty-two quarters—fifty-two quarters—sixty-five—wages and board. Well, a hunderd and eighty-five dollars for the first year. That's—ah—ten dollars a month for twelve months, and a dollar and a quarter a week for board."

" Is that all you can give ? " inquired Dr. Gilbert, very much disappointed.

" It's all that it's safe to offer, I assure you, doctor. The fact is he may not like, and I may not like. If he should earn more, why, of course, I would increase his wages."

" But the board," replied the doctor, " is very low. A young man of Arthur's age cannot live on it."

" A dollar and a quarter a week is all I ever pay at the boarding-house, and my hands live just as well as I do. We are all alike down to the Run. We work hard, and live economically."

Old Ruggles comprehended his advantage perfectly. He knew there was no other steady employment in Crampton procurable, that would pay Arthur as good wages as he had offered him. So he blew his nasal horn, as a hint that he was in a hurry.

" We will let you know," said the doctor, " and will not detain you longer this morning."

The manufacturer rose to his feet, so intent on new and pleasant thoughts that he forgot to bid his friends good-morning. His horse shrank from him as he approached, and was sharply jerked in the mouth as a punishment for his apprehensions. As the jerk brought the raw-mouthed creature back almost upon his haunches, he kicked him in his side to bring him up again.

" I'll teach you," spitefully exclaimed the lord of Hucklebury Run again, as if he were addressing an equal, or one of his operatives. Then he added, as a piece of information that it would be well for the horse to know, that he "hadn't got a woman hold of him now." The animal understood the information, and went off down the street at a rattling pace.

Arthur said not a word, but stood exploring vacancy through one of the parlor windows. Dr. Gilbert said not a word, and drummed with his fingers upon the other.

"Well, Arthur, what do you say?" inquired the doctor, breaking the silence at last.

"I shall go, I suppose," he replied with a sigh that was almost a groan.

"I think I would try it."

"If I try it, I shall go through it," said Arthur. "I know what I shall have to encounter. I know the man; I know his men, and I know his place. I am to be insulted, humiliated, and overworked."

"Oh! you exaggerate. You must not be too sensitive. The world is all rougher than you have supposed it to be, Arthur; and Mr. Ruggles is not so much worse than everybody else as you imagine. Do your work well, be quiet, learn all you can, improve all your spare time, and keep up your high aims, and all will come out right in the end."

Having said this, in his most encouraging tone, Dr. Gilbert looked at his watch, and said he must go. The moment he crossed the threshold, and closed the garden gate behind him, the subject was dismissed from his mind for the time, and he plunged into the business of the day as if a young and unperverted nature, struggling with destiny, were a matter of the smallest consequence. Arthur's life was only one of the things that engaged his attention, and, as soon as it was disposed of, other things came in turn. Mrs. Blague's house was to be saved, and the family was to be supported, more or less ably and respectably, by Arthur. On the establishment of his plans with relation to these affairs, he left Arthur to himself.

Dr. Gilbert had not been aware, during his interview with Arthur, of the struggle for self-control that the young man had been carrying on all the time. The moment Arthur was left alone, the reaction came. He thought of the sneers of his old companions, the mean satisfaction of those whose position had made them jealous of him, the society into which he should be cast at the Run, the humiliations which his employer would be sure to visit upon him, and then he gave himself up to a nervous frenzy. He walked the room, he swung his arms with uncontrollable excitement, and exclaimed in a hoarse whisper which he meant should escape the ear of his mother, "Oh! I cannot do it! I cannot do it! I cannot do it!"

Then there arose a little wail in the next room, and the clenched hands, wildly swinging, fell at his side; the rapid feet, pacing up and down the parlor, were stayed, and a gush of tears came to the relief of the excited brain. He heard the appeal of a little helpless life, placed by Providence in his hands. Should he, could he, be faithless to the trust? As he stood listening to the feeble cry of the infant, his mother's voice broke into a plaintive lullaby, to which the cradle kept time — a sweet, dreamy melody, not of joy, but of ministry — which recalled to him sweet faces of little brothers and sisters long since turned to dust. Still the little voice wailed on, still the mother sang her plaintive lullaby, still the gently rocking cradle kept time, and still Arthur stood where the baby's voice arrested him. Under the influence of the two voices, he learned in a few minutes to front calmly the life before him. Into his hands God had given a helpless woman — that woman his mother — a helpless child — that child his brother. God had honored him by a great confidence, and he felt his heart springing up into heroic resolution. He would devote himself to them, trusting God to take care of and prosper him. He would outlive humiliation, contumely, and hardship. Outside of the realm of love and of duty, he would know no life.

Strong, and at peace with himself once more, he lifted the latch of the door that divided him from his mother, and approached her with a smile. The cradle was empty, and the baby was sleeping on her bosom. She lifted her desponding eyes to Arthur, and heaving a sigh, asked him what had been decided upon.

"I am going to work for wages, mother, and shall board at home with you," replied the young man.

"Who has been in the room with you? I heard a strange voice."

"That was Mr. Ruggles, of Hucklebury Run."

"What could he want here?"

"We called him in. I am going to work for him."

"In the factory?"

"In the factory."

"O Arthur!" and the poor woman hid her face in her handkerchief, and sobbed as if her heart would break.

"What is there to cry about, mother?"

"To think that you should be called to suffer so for me," and his mother renewed her sobbing.

Gently the tall boy dropped upon his knees, gently he took his mother's hand, gently he bent over and kissed the soft cheek of the sleeping baby, and then he said, "I want to tell you, mother, all about what I am going to do, and what I wish you to do. I am going to work for Mr. Ruggles. I do not like him, and I expect a great many hardships, but I am young and strong. I can get along with my work, and with him, if I can have you happy at home. Now you must not worry about me, nor ask me questions. I shall go in the morning and come at night, and I shall do this until I find some better way to do. You must be as cheerful as you can, and if you feel badly about me, don't tell me of it. It will fret me, and do more to make me wretched than all that old Ruggles can do. One of these years it will all be right, and I shall have a business, and we can live together, and be happy. It will be lonely here, but the neighbors will be kind, and you can visit here and there, and little Jamie will grow and be company for you, and —and—you will be cheerful, will you not, mother?" and he kissed his mother's forehead.

She could not take her handkerchief from her eyes; she could not speak. She only pressed his hand.

CHAPTER IV.

ARTHUR BLAGUE GETS HIS HAND IN, AND THE PRO-
PRIETOR MEETS WITH AN UNEXPECTED REVOLU-
TION.

ARTHUR still had writing to do in finishing up his father's accounts, and a few weeks were passed in this employment before he was ready to begin work at the Run. In the meantime, he had visited Ruggles, and entered into a formal engagement with him.

On a frosty morning toward the last of October, he rose before daylight, quietly crept down stairs, made a fire in the kitchen, and cooked for himself a simple breakfast. He found his dinner already snugly packed in a little basket—the timely work of his mother on the previous evening. The daylight had just begun to tinge the sky, as he stepped forth from his home, and only here and there in the village rose the smoke from the early kindled fires. The Run was a mile from the vil- lage, and only farms and farm-houses lay between. He supposed he should be early at the mill, so, though the air was brisk, he loitered thoughtfully along the uneven highway, recalling the past and revolving the future. Unmindful of the passage of time, he found himself suddenly within sight of the tall chimney of the mill. The buildings were still buried in the valley.

For the first time since he had fully decided on this step of life, his heart sank within him. He shrank from the eyes that would be fixed upon him, the sneers that would reach his ear, and the subjection of his will to that of a man whom, in his inmost soul, he abhorred. At length, he discarded these details ; and a dull undercurrent of dread took their place, while he endeavored to engage his mind with the most insignificant observations and incidents. There was a long golden cloud in the east, which only lacked a fin of being a model salmon. He walked under a maple whose foliage frost had changed to amber, and dropped ankle-deep upon the ground, and wondered what he should do with those leaves if they were all golden eagles. He picked up an apple in the street, tossed it into the air, caught it in his hand, bit into it, and then threw it at a cat sneaking under a fence.

Lingering in this aimless kind of way, and pausing to hear any sound that struck his ear, he was still a hundred rods from the mill when the sun rose, fresh and bright, above the eastern hills. The tall chimney was vomiting forth thick masses of black smoke, the hum of machinery with the pulsating din of many looms filled the air, and a few minutes' walk brought him to the brow of the hill, at the foot of which lay the factory and the little hamlet of Hucklebury Run.

Young men and young women, and boys and girls, were pouring out of the door of the large boarding-house, and crowding into the mill. Arthur waited until all had disappeared within the black door, and then boldly pushed down the hill. As he entered the yard, he became conscious of many eyes at the windows. Dirty-looking wenches, with arms bare to the elbows, were tittering behind the dirtier glass. Frowzy-headed men passed him in the yard, and gave him an offensively familiar greeting. What struck the young man with peculiar force was the perversive spirit of old Ruggles in all these people. They acted like him, they looked like him, they all seemed to have sold themselves to him. He understood old Ruggles' remark now—" We are all alike down to the Run."

Uncertain where to look for his employer, he approached the door, and hailed a boy—barefoot, and with no clothes upon him but shirt and trousers—and inquired if he knew where Mr. Ruggles was.

" He ain't very fur off," replied the boy with a grin, and in an undertone that showed that he was afraid to speak louder.

" I wish to see him," said Arthur.

" Stand right where you be then, " said the boy. " That's the quickest way. You can't find him afollerin' him ; he's too fast for that. Old Gabriel will blow his horn afore you've stood here five minutes," and the little wretch looked around him carefully and cunningly, to see if he were overheard.

Arthur understood and smiled at the allusion of the boy to his employer's nasal note, and felt that possibly it might announce the day of doom to him.

The boy cocked his eye suddenly, shrugged his shoulders, and was out of sight in an instant. He had detected the signs of the old man's coming, and was hardly in the mill before that individual ran down the stairs at the foot of which Arthur stood, taking three steps at a leap, and blowing his nose at the landing.

" On hand, eh ? " was his greeting of the new operative.

" On hand," was the response.

"Little late this morning, but never mind—it's the first day, and we won't be particular to start with."

"Late!" exclaimed Arthur in astonishment, "why, I saw the hands just go in."

"Oh! yes, they've jest had their breakfast. They work an hour before breakfast, by candle-light, you know." The old man grinned as he said this, and looked at Arthur curiously, to see how he took it.

"Do you expect me to be here an hour before breakfast every morning?" inquired the young man.

"Well," replied old Ruggles, "we'll be as easy with you as we can, you know, but we can't show many favors. I'm here an hour before breakfast myself. That's the way we get our living, and we all fare alike down here to the Run. I work jest as hard as my hands, and my hands are jest as good as I am."

This, by the way, was the method by which the low-bred proprietor of Hucklebury Run settled all the complaints of those in his employ. They worked no more hours and no harder than he ; they fared as well as he. That was true, and, if a workman were not content with that, he had the alternative of leaving, provided he could raise money enough to get away.

Arthur was not to be frightened away from the Run without a trial ; so he said : "Mr. Ruggles, I am ready for work, and will conform myself to your rules so far as I can."

"Well, I really haven't anything for you to do in the mill this morning," responded Ruggles, scratching his head. "Let's see—let's see. What do you say to going out into the pasture and mowing bushes with Cheek?"

"That's what you call the foot of the ladder, I suppose," said Arthur, with poorly disguised contempt.

"Very well," said old Ruggles. "Stay here, and do my work, and I'll mow bushes. I had rather be out of doors than in."

This of course settled the matter. The practicability of Arthur's stepping into the shoes of the manager of the mill, and sending that gentleman out to clean up a shrubby pasture with Cheek, one of his hopeful operatives, was entirely evident to the young man, but he was too polite to avail himself of the offer. So he said : "Set me to work where you will, and let me have a place in the mill as soon as you can."

The old man took down a bush-hook that hung upon a post near the mill, and then called Cheek, who straight-way appeared from the basement, coming up the stairs through a cloud of steam that issued from the passage.

"Cheek, you're to mow bushes in the mountain-pasture with this new hand to-day. Show him how it's done, and do a better day's work than you did the last time you were up there, or I'll show you how it's done. Do you hear?"

Cheek heard, nodded his head a great number of times, took off a very dirty striped apron, rolled down a very dirty pair of shirt-sleeves, put on an old cloth cap with the visor turned up, took down another bush-hook, and said, "Come on."

The young men were of about equal age, though Arthur was much the taller of the two. Old Ruggles stood and watched them as they passed out of sight, with a grin of satisfaction, then blew his nose and plunged into the mill.

As soon as they were out of sight and hearing of the master, Cheek exclaimed : "I vow, Blague, you're the last feller I ever expected to see in this hole."

"This is the last hole I ever expected to be in," responded Arthur ; adding, "how did you know my name was Blague ?"

"Oh! I've heard all about you. The old man has been bragging that he'd got hold of one of the Crampton

aristocracy, and was going to put him through a course
of sprouts."

" Those that grow in the pasture are the first of the
course, I suppose," said Arthur drily.

Cheek laughed, and said that was good.   Then he
threw down his bush-hook, and cried, " Halt ! Now,
Blague," said he, coming up and laying a hand on each
of Arthur's shoulders, " don't you remember me ? "

" I think I've seen you before, but I cannot tell when
nor where. Possibly I have seen you in my father's
store."

" Not often, but you knew me when I was a shaver "
(by which term Cheek meant a very small boy), " and I
knew you when you was a shaver. You remember old
Bob Lampson—drunken old coot—he was my father.
I'm Tom Lampson, and you gave me a pair of shoes
once. Do you twig now ? "

" Oh ! yes, I remember you. What do they call you
Cheek for ? "

" Look here," said Tom Lampson ; and lifting his
long hair with one hand, and pulling down his shirt-
collar very low with the other, he displayed a cheek very
black with gunpowder. " I got blowed up one Fourth
of July, and did this ; and ever since, the boys have
called me Cheek. I don't mind it now. I vow I b'lieve
I like it better. They never call me Tom Lampson
now, but I think of old Bob Lampson—old scamp—my
father, you know."

" Don't talk so about your father," said Arthur. " I
don't like to hear you."

Cheek shrugged his shoulders, as if the unpleasant
memory of his father had got under his jacket. " I
guess," said he, "you don't remember him very well.
If he had tanned you, and swore your head off, and
abused your mother till he used her up, you wouldn't
like him any better than I do—old—well, never mind ! "

At a motion from Arthur, Cheek resumed his implement, and both moved on toward the pasture. Arthur comprehended the character of Cheek very readily. He was a good-natured fellow, whom no amount of bad treatment could thoroughly demoralize. He was garrulous and shallow, but he had a kind heart and a degree of genuine sensibility. He had always remembered Arthur Blague with affectionate respect. This morning he pitied him, because he saw that his mind was troubled, and knew there was sufficient reason for it. He wondered what he could do to make him feel better.

"Blague," said. Cheek (and when he called him Blague, instead of Arthur, he intended it as the more respectful and pleasant style of address), "Blague, you'll find that you and I ain't exactly like the rest of 'em, and now I want always to be your friend, and you shall always be my friend."

"Certainly, Cheek, we shall always be friends, of course," responded Arthur with a smile.

"Well, I mean," said Cheek earnestly, "that I will always stick to you, and you shall always stick to me. Give us your hand on that," and Cheek seized Arthur's outstretched hand, and shook it violently. The act seemed to give his affectionate nature a great deal of satisfaction, and he burst tunefully into "Away with melancholy," the name of that sombre passion sounding very much in Arthur's ears like "melon-colic."

When the song had subsided, Cheek turned to Arthur, and said : "What do you suppose is the reason you're so much bigger than I am?"

Arthur replied : "I'm sure I don't know."

"It's because," said Cheek, "that you've always had enough to eat, and I haven't. I haven't seen what you've got there, of course (looking at Arthur's dinner-basket, and alluding to its contents), but I'll bet a goose I haven't seen so much good, wholesome victuals in three months

4

as you've got in your basket there. I am always hungry
—hungry from one year's end to the other. I'm hungry
now—hungry enough to eat a jackass, and chase the
driver a mile."

Arthur laughed long and loud, which pleased Cheek
very much. So he repeated the statement, that Arthur
might get more satisfaction from it, if possible, and then
added that it was "a true fact, and no mistake."

"You ought to see the boarders skin that table once,"
continued Cheek, "regular grab game. Every thing
comes on together, and the pie goes first. Sometimes
we put it into our pockets, so's to be sure of it, and eat
it when we get ready. You might carry one of them
boarding-house pies in your pocket for a year, without
hurting the pocket any, or the pie either any more than
if it was a whetstone. But you ought to see the old man
when he comes in to weigh the victuals, to see if he isn't
feeding us too much."

"But he doesn't do that?" said Arthur incredulously.

"Don't he, though! I've seen him weigh every mouthful that went on to the table, and sit and look at us, and
figure with his little black pencil all dinner-time. Then's
the time we put in. Didn't I have a time with him one
day? I vow, wasn't that a time!"

Cheek shrugged his shoulders again, as if another very
unpleasant memory had got under his jacket.

"Tell me about it," said Arthur.

"It was when I first went there," said Cheek. "I
shouldn't dare to do it now. We all get afraid of the
old man after we've been with him a while. You see he
came in one day, and we all heard a jingle, and knew
the steelyards were round. So we all dipped in strong,
and said nothing. I saw what they were up to, so I stuck
my fork into a chunk of corned beef as big as your two
fists. The old man was mad enough, I tell you. 'Cheek,'
says he, ' you're a pig, to take such a piece of beef as

that.' Says I, ' Not as you knows of.' Says he, ' You're a pig.' Says I, ' I ain't a pig;' and I took up the chunk of meat on my fork, and held it where all the boarders could see it, and says I, ' Do you s'pose a pig would eat such a piece of meat as that? Smell of it, Mr. Ruggles!' Everybody at the table looked scared, but I hadn't learned him then. He came straight toward me, and I held out the piece for him to smell of, and just as he got his nose to it I gave it a little dab, and he jumped as if something had hit him. I s'pose it was a little hot. Wasn't he mad? He knocked my fork out of my hand, and then he kicked me clear into the yard. I think I've got a little place somewhere on me now that has been numb ever since ;" and Cheek felt around upon his back to see if he could find it.

"Here's the place," said Cheek at last ; and, lifting some clumsy bars, he turned Arthur into the field of his day's labor—a barren, rambling pasture, more friendly, apparently, to the growth of scrub-oaks and blackberry-bushes than to grass. Arthur soon got the swing of the hook, and laid about him right lustily.

"You'll get sick of it before night," said Cheek, "if that's the way you pitch in." Cheek then illustrated the manner in which he proposed to perform the labor of the day.

"I shall work faithfully, Cheek," replied Arthur ; "you will do as you choose, of course."

"Well, you're right, I s'pose," said Cheek, "but I can tell you one thing—the more you do for old Ruggles, the more you may do. We old hands all understand it."

Arthur had worked half an hour vigorously, when his hands began to feel sore, and, drawing on a pair of gloves for their protection, he proceeded. Straightening up, at length, for a little rest, he turned to Cheek, and inquired what he meant by saying that everybody became afraid of the old man after living with him a while.

"Why, you see, he haunts us," replied Check, leaning upon his hook. "He's always 'round. If three heads get together in the mill, off goes his nose right over their shoulders. If anybody laughs, off goes his nose again. He's always within ten feet of everybody, and—I don't know, we kind o' dread him, and then we get to hating him, and somehow we all settle down at last into being afraid of him. There's Big Joslyn — strong enough to lick a regiment of him—he'll swing a hundred-and-sixty-spindled jack like a feather, but he's as afraid of old Ruggles as if he was a tiger. The old man will abuse him up hill and down, and he'll stand and take it as meek as Moses. Somehow or other he gets 'em all."

"What do you mean by get's 'em all?"

"Well, take Big Joslyn now. He's got a wife and children, and he doesn't get wages enough for 'em all to live on, so the old man lets him get in debt, and he never lets him get out of debt. There isn't a hand in the mill who isn't in debt in the same way; and when the old fellow gets a chap there, it's all day with him. He never expects to leave Hucklebury Run, unless he cuts stick, or goes out on wheels in a black box that smells of vinegar. Them that have families can't peep, you see, and the old man makes 'em take things out of the store, and pays 'em in all sorts of ways."

"Out of what store?" inquired Arthur, very glad indeed to be placed on his guard.

"Oh! he's got a store up in the mill, and you ought to see it. You see he sells some of his nigger-cloth for goods, so as to accommodate his hands, he says. I bought this old cap there, when it was new" (Check touched it with his finger), "and it smelt so strong of codfish that it kept my mouth watering for a month. You see everything goes in together, and the thing that smells the strongest gets the lead. If you've a mind to try it," pursued Cheek, anxious to impress the truth of his assertions upon Arthur, and handing his cap toward him, " I shouldn't wonder if you could find a little codfish about that now."

Arthur laughed, and told him he would take his word for it.

" I tell you," said Cheek, recalling the hopeless condition of Big Joslyn, " that when a feller gets tied to a wife, and has a lot of little chickadees around him, there's no help for him if he once gets into old Ruggles's hands."

" How do the girls get along with him ?" inquired Arthur.

" Well, they wilt to it," replied Cheek. " I know every girl in the mill, and they get along a mighty sight better'n the men. Some of 'em will put on their sunbonnets and cry all day. There are girls there that have regular crying days. I always know when there's a shower coming. A girl sits down to the table in the morning with the corners of her mouth drawn down, eats just a bite of breakfast, then on goes the sun-bonnet, and just as soon as she gets her looms running, and all ready for it, she begins to cry, and cries till the mill stops. I used to kind o' pity them at first, but I've got used to it now, and don't mind it so much."

" What do they cry for ?" inquired Arthur.

" Oh ! I don't know. I don't s'pose they do. They feel bad promisc'usly, I reckon, and don't know what else to do. They all come out bright enough next day, if nobody says any thing to 'em. It's a kind of a fashion at the Run for girls to have crying days. All of 'em cry, but them that have long hair."

" Long hair !" exclaimed Arthur with a smile, " what has long hair to do with it ? "

" Well, they all have to get something to take up their minds, you know—kind of amuse them, you know," pursued Cheek, in explanation. " If a girl has long

hair, she takes in a comb regular when she goes to work,
and her hair isn't done up all day. She gets her looms
going, and then she draws her comb down through her
hair, and keeps doing so till there's a bobbin out. Oh!
I tell you, combs and sun-bonnets are thick some days;
but they work first-rate when they cry, for they're always mum then. When old Ruggles comes in and sees
the sun-bonnets thick, he knows its all right for one day,
so he just blows his nose and leaves 'em."

At this instant the young men were interrupted, by
the accustomed note of warning, that their employer
was with them. They had not seen where he came
from, and did not know how long he had been near
them.

"How are you getting along?" said old Ruggles.
"You find Cheek very good company, don't you, Arthur?"

Cheek had no sooner become aware of his master's
presence than he began to lay about him with great dili-
gence. Arthur understood the taunt, but replied quietly,
that Cheek seemed to be a very good fellow, indeed.

Old Ruggles, accustomed to no replies from his workmen, looked up and down Arthur's cool front in astonishment. There was no servile fear in that eye, no
nervous apprehension. Failing to look him into activity,
he broke into a low, sneering laugh, and said, "Well,
that is very fine!"

"You seem amused," said Arthur.

"Amused!" exclaimed Ruggles. "Cheek, look
here!"

Cheek feared a scene, and came up trembling and
afraid.

"Cheek, here's something you never see afore in
your life. It's worth looking at. Here's a young man
at work for me in gloves!"

Arthur's face burnt for a moment with intense anger,

for the words were said in the most insulting way possible. Then he recalled his good resolutions, and checked the hasty response that sprang to his lips.

"My hands are not used to this work," said he, "and they are already blistered. I shall wear gloves as long as they do not interfere with my work." Having said this, he coolly turned his back on his employer, and resumed his labor.

Old Ruggles did not know what to say. In his establishment dependence always walked hand in hand with servility. Somehow, the spirit of the young man must be broken, but he could not decide how to undertake the task.

He watched Arthur for a few minutes in silence, then he stepped up, and, taking his bush-hook out of his hands, he worked actively a while, and handed the implement back to him with an air that said, "You have done nothing to-day ; work as I do."

Arthur smiled, and said: "You mow bushes very well, Mr. Ruggles. You must have had a good deal of practice."

The old man replied not a word, but went off, muttering something about "upstarts." As soon as he was out of sight and hearing, Cheek dropped his hook, mounted on a stump, slapped his hands upon his thighs half a dozen times, and crowed like a cock. Then he threw his old cap into the air, and caught it, and then he came up to Arthur, and said: "I vow, Blague, give us your hand. You are a trump. There ain't another man at the Run that would dare to do it ; but he's after you now. He won't stop until he's got you under his thumb."

"Cheek," said Arthur coolly, "I shall do for Mr. Ruggles just as well as I can, and I shall never be afraid of him."

That was a tedious day for Arthur Blague. Long before night he was tired and sore ; but he labored on faithfully until after sunset ; and then, in company with Cheek, walked back to the mill. The old man was away, and, without waiting for dismissal, he walked home. He was glad that the evening covered him from observation, for he was sad, and almost disheartened. His mother greeted him on his return with a very feeble attempt to smile ; but her eyelids were red with weeping. She sat and watched him as he devoured his supper, and wondered at his overflow of spirits. Whatever might be his hardships, he was determined that his mother should know nothing of them ; and as she obeyed his wishes, and refrained from asking him any questions, he got along very easily with her.

He went to bed early, and the next morning breakfasted and was off before his mother awoke. He found old Ruggles ready for him—waiting to set him to work in the mill. He could not help noticing a marked change in the expression of the faces which greeted him on all sides. The truth was, that Cheek had been full of Blague all night. The scene between Ruggles and Arthur in the pasture had been described in Cheek's best style, with all the exaggerations that were necessary to make an impression. The men had all got hold of it, and talked it over. The girls had heard the story, and rehearsed it to one another until they had become surcharged with admiration of the young man. There were none but kind eyes that greeted him among the operatives that morning. All wondered what Ruggles would do to tame him. Cheek's opinion was, that Blague would whip the old man in less than five minutes, if it ever came to that.

" How are your hands this morning ? " inquired Ruggles, as Arthur presented himself before him.

" They are very sore, sir," replied the young man.

" That's **too bad**, ain't it ? " said the master, " be-

cause I was going to set you to dyeing, and it might
make 'em smart some.   Besides, it ain't work where you
can wear gloves very well."

"I beg you not to consult the condition of my hands
at all," replied Arthur.

"Oh! very well!   You can go down stairs, and
Check will show you what to do."

Arthur went down through the same column of steam
out of which Check issued the previous morning, and
found that young man in a very lively state of mind, and
up to his elbows in a dyeing vat.   The atmosphere was
hot, heavy, almost stifling.   The room was full of the
noise of heavy gearing, and the constant plash of water
in the near wheel-pit.   Objects a few feet distant could
not be seen in consequence of the steam that rolled out
of the vat.

Check explained to Arthur the nature of his labor,
and set him to work.   The moment his hands were
bathed in the poisonous liquid they became as painful as
if they had been bathed in fire.   This was what he anticipated, and he was prepared to endure it.   By degrees,
however, sensibility was benumbed, and he worked on
with tolerable comfort.   He was disturbed by the frequent visits of the master, who would stand by him
sometimes for several minutes, and tell him how well
he took hold of business.   "When I want to take the
starch out of a man, I always put him in here," said old
Ruggles with a grin.

Arthur took no notice of these taunts, but kept on
with his work, until the bell rang.   The ponderous
wheel in the pit stood still, and the snarling, grinding
din of the gearing was hushed.   The world never
seemed so still to Arthur as it did then.   The noise of
the ever-revolving machinery had seemed to crowd out
of his consciousness all the rest of the universe ; and
when it stopped, it seemed as if the world had ceased to

move. Putting on his coat, and taking his dinner-basket in his hand, he ascended the stairs, and sought a quiet place in the mill where he could eat his lunch undisturbed. This he had hardly succeeded in doing, when old Ruggles, making a rapid passage through the mill, discovered him. " I've been looking for you, sir," said the master.

"Well, sir," responded Arthur, rising and brushing the crumbs from his lap, " you have found me, and I am at your service."

The old man had really begun to feel very uncomfortably about Arthur. He saw that the young man was determined to do his duty, and to serve him faithfully. He had become indistinctly conscious that there was nothing in Ruggles, the master, to inspire fear in Arthur, the hired workman. He had found a character which he could not overtop nor undermine; and he knew, too, that he was an object of contempt to a young man whose heart was pure and true. He had begun to find that his attempts to wound the young man's feelings reacted unpleasantly upon himself. He was the man whose pride was wounded, and not Arthur.

Therefore, when Arthur rose so readily, and so respectfully, and told him he was at his service, the old man hesitated, and became half-ashamed of a trick that he had planned for Arthur's humiliation. Then he stammered and lied. He thought, he said, that perhaps Arthur would like a little relief from his confinement in the basement, and he wanted to have him take his horse and go to the village for him. His object was simply to have him shown up to the village of Crampton as the servant—the errand-boy—of old Ruggles of Hucklebury Run. Arthur told him he would go very willingly (and thereby was guilty of a lie, with such a blending of all the colors of the spectrum of truth in it, that it was white), and inquired what his errand was.

At this moment the bell for the recommencement of work sounded, and the men and women came pouring into the mill. Seeing the old man and Arthur in conversation, they paused, as if anxious to overhear what was passing between them.

"You will go first," said the master, in a loud and insolently dictatorial tone, "to the post-office, and get the newspapers, and then down to old Leach's, and get a barrel of soap."

Arthur smiled.

"Well, sir, what are you laughing about?" inquired the old man savagely.

"I was only thinking," replied Arthur, "what a suggestive combination newspapers and soap were."

The very dirty audience tittered, and the dirty proprietor looked daggers.

"Do you mean to say that we need newspapers and soap here, sir? Do you mean to insult me and my hands?" and the proprietor grew white with anger.

"I never insulted anybody in my life, Mr. Ruggles. As for the soap and the newspapers, I think the combination an excellent one anywhere, and I suppose you need the articles here, or you wouldn't send for them."

The old man turned angrily round upon the gaping operatives, and said: "Go to your work; don't you know the bell has stopped ringing?"

They went off smiling, and exchanging significant looks with each other. Arthur looked out of the window, and seeing the horse and the accustomed truck-wagon waiting for him, he took out his gloves, drew them on over his stained hands, and asked his employer if the soap and the newspapers were all. The old man could hardly speak for anger, and the state of his mind was not improved at all by the success that Arthur had achieved in covering with gloves the mark of servitude which the dye had left upon his fingers.

" Nothing else," said the old man, answering Arthur's question snappishly. " Get what I tell you, and be quick about it."

Arthur left the mill, and as he stepped into the wagon was greeted by a voice coming out through the steam that poured from the basement window, with something that sounded like, " Hit 'im ag'in, Blague—I'll hold your moccasins."

Arthur drove off toward the town, feeling, on the whole, very pleasantly. He comprehended perfectly the trick of his employer, but the two days of his experience at the Run had given him strength. He had not been humiliated. He had not been crushed. On the contrary, he had risen to the point of laboring where God and duty had placed him, without being ashamed of it. He became conscious of a new power in life, and a new power over his destiny. Instead, therefore, of riding through the village of Crampton with a sense of shame and mortified vanity, he rode as self-respectfully and as confidently as if he had been a king. He greeted the old acquaintances whom he met with his accustomed freedom and cordiality, and was greeted in the old hearty way by all. There were some silly people who thought it must be very " trying" to Arthur, " brought up as he had been ; " but all the sensible people said that Arthur Blague was a brave, good fellow, and was sure to " work his way in the world."

Arthur visited the post-office and got his newspapers, and then he went to the soap establishment of old Leach, and procured the soap, and turned his horse toward Hucklebury Run. He caught a glimpse of his astonished mother as he drove by his home, and kissed his hand to her merrily, when she, poor woman ! sank into a chair as despairingly as if she had seen him in his coffin.

Returning to the mill, he delivered his package to

the master without a word, helped to unload the soap, and then went down to his work again among the vats.

Old Ruggles was very busy that afternoon. He was angry, irritable, baffled. Every thing went wrong. First he was in the weaving-room, then in the spinning-room, then in the carding-room. He went up-stairs three steps at a time; he plunged down-stairs three steps at a time; and blew his resonant nose at every landing. If he saw two men or two women talking together, he was at their side in an instant. If he caught a boy out of his place, he led him back by the ear. There was not a sun-bonnet nor a comb in use that afternoon, for the girls, illustrative of the ingenious theory of Cheek, had found something "to take up their minds." He was particularly attentive to the dyeing-room, so that Arthur and Cheek contented themselves with monosyllables, and only spoke when necessary.

The day wore on slowly, and it had become almost late enough for lighting the lamps. Still the old man was omnipresent. Arthur worked diligently, and his thoughts were as busy as the feet and eyes of his employer. The ceaseless noise in his ears wearied him. The constant plash of water in the wheel-pit, the grinding, metallic ring of the gearing, the prevalent sense of motion everywhere—the buzz, the whirr, the clashing overhead, the stifling atmosphere which enveloped him, all tended to oppress him with sensations and emotions utterly strange.

In an instant, every sound was swept from his consciousness by a cry so sharp—so full of fear and agony—that his heart stood still. The steam was around him and he could see nothing, but he noticed that Cheek escaped past him like lightning, and rushed up-stairs. In a moment more, the gate of the water-wheel closed with a sudden plunge, and the mill stood still. Another moment, and a dozen men came down-stairs with lamps in their hands, and the first one, walking a few steps into the darkness, exclaimed, "It's old Ruggles himself!"

Arthur approached the group as they held their lamps over the prostrate form of the master of Hucklebury Run.

"He's been round that shaft, the Lord knows how many times," exclaimed Big Joslyn, casting his eyes upward.

Not another word was spoken for a minute. All seemed to be stupefied. Arthur had stood back from them, waiting to see what steps they would take, and feeling himself quite too young to assume responsibility among his seniors ; but they seemed so thoroughly paralyzed, and so incapable of doing any thing without direction, that he pushed through the group, and, kneeling by the old man's side, placed his fingers upon his pulse. The prostrate master presented a sickening aspect. His face was bruised and bleeding, his clothes were nearly torn from his body, his whole frame seemed to be a mass of bruises, and one leg was broken, and fairly doubled upon itself.

"He is not dead," said Arthur ; and a gasp and a moan attested the truth of the announcement. "Now, lift him up carefully, carry him to his house, and take care of him till I send the doctor."

The young man waited only long enough to be sure that the master would be carefully looked after, and then he put on his coat, and, taking his basket in his hand, ran every step of the mile that lay between the Run and the house of Dr. Gilbert. He found the doctor at home, delivered his errand, watched the little gig as it reeled off toward the mill at the highest speed the little black pony could command, and then, tired and sore, and shocked and sad, entered his own dwelling.

CHAPTER V.

DR. GILBERT AND HIS DAUGHTER "COME TO AN UNDERSTANDING."

DR. GILBERT was a thrifty man. He held petty mortgages on half the farms in town, and carried on a large farm himself. Sometimes, when a sudden death brought forcibly to his mind the uncertain tenure of life, he became uncomfortable with the thought that his affairs were so extended and so complicated, that no one but himself could ever settle them safely and advantageously. At the close of the day on which he held his interview with Arthur Blague, and that young man determined to enter the mill at Hucklebury Run, he drank his tea, and, taking a newspaper in his hand, subsided into a brown study.

The occasion was the sudden revolution that had taken place in Arthur's plans of life in consequence of his father's death. Would his own little boy ever be brought to such a trial? He must not be. He would set apart now, while it was possible, a sum that should be sacredly kept from all danger of loss, so that, in any contingency, little Fred should not miss his education.

Having fully determined upon this, and arranged the plan by which the end should be effected, he called Fred to him, and took him upon his knee. Aunt Catharine was washing the silver, sitting high and trim in her tea-chair, and Fanny sat near the window reading.

"I wonder what we shall make of this little boy," said the doctor, with one big arm around him, and the other fondling roughly his white little hand.

"Oh! I know what I'm going to be," said Fred, with a very wise and positive look, and a tone that indicated

that he had never yet divulged his convictions to anybody.

"Tell us all about it, then," said the doctor.

"Oh! I know—I know. You can't guess," responded
the boy, with a smack of the lips that showed it must be
something very delightful indeed.

"I guess," said the doctor very thoughtfully, "that
you're going to be a great lawyer."

"No:" and the boy looked wise, and smacked his
lips again, and said it was "something better'n that."

"A minister?" suggested Aunt Catharine.

"Something better'n that." (A shake of the head,
and a wise look out of the window.)

"A doctor," Fanny guessed.

"I hope it's better'n that," said the disgusted young
gentleman—"nasty old pills."

"Tut—tut, Freddy! Your father is a doctor," said
Dr. Gilbert with mock severity.

"Well, I don't think it would be a good plan to have
two Dr. Gilberts ; do you, papa ? "

"Why not ? "

"Because the people would be always making mistakes, and getting the wrong one."

The doctor joined Aunt Catharine and Fanny in a
laugh over Fred's ingenuity, and then said : "Now I
can guess what my little boy is going to be. He's going
to be a great scholar first ; and then, after a while, he is
going to be a great man, and go to Congress, and make
splendid speeches, and then perhaps he'll be President
of the United States. That's it, isn't it ? "

The boy was not to be won from his first secret choice
by any eloquent description of the glory of scholarship,
or the grandeur of political elevation, and so made his
old reply, that it was something "better'n that." Then
all gave it up, and declared they could not guess at all.
He must tell them, or they should never know.

"I'm going to be a cracker-peddler," said Fred, in a tone of triumph.

"A cracker - peddler!" exclaimed the astonished father. "Dr. Gilbert's little son a cracker-peddler? What could put such nonsense into your foolish little head?"

"Yes, sir, I'm going to be a cracker-peddler," persisted the boy. "I'm going to have two splendid horses with long tails, and a cart painted red, and I'm going to stop at the tavern, and have all the baker's gingerbread I want to eat, and give Aunt Catharine and Fanny all they want to eat; and I'm going to have a beautiful whip with my name worked into the handle, and a spotted dog with a brass collar on his neck, to run under the cart; and fur gloves, and a shiny cap, and ——"

Here the little boy was interrupted by such a hearty and long-continued laugh from his three fond listeners, that he could proceed no further. As he looked with surprise upon the different members of the group, his sensitive nature took umbrage at the inexplicable merriment, and he turned his face to his father's breast, and burst into a fit of violent weeping. It took many words of tender assurance from all the offending parties to restore the child's composure, and when, at last, the smiles shone out through the tears, Dr. Gilbert was ready to tell him—a baby in years and thought—what he proposed to do with him.

"I wish to have my boy," said Dr. Gilbert, with a new tenderness which the child's tears had engendered, "be the best little scholar in Crampton. He must study very hard, and improve all his time, and learn just as fast as he can. By and by, when he gets a little older, and begins to fit for college, we shall have him recite to Mr. Wilton, and Mr. Wilton will teach him Latin and Greek, and a great many things that he doesn't know any thing about now; and then, after a while, he will go away to college, and be a grand young man, and study very hard, and be the best scholar in his class; and, when he has been there four years, he will graduate, and deliver the valedictory address, and his papa will be on the platform to hear him, and perhaps Aunt Catharine and Sister Fanny will be there too. Won't that be splendid, now? Won't that be a great deal better than to be a cracker-peddler?"

The boy was sober and thoughtful for a few minutes, and then inquired: "Shall I be in the college alone? Will nobody that I know be there with me? Won't Arthur Blague be there?"

"Arthur Blague will be too old then, my son," said the doctor. "Besides, poor Arthur Blague can't go to college at all. He has lost his father, and has not money enough. Poor Arthur is going to work down at Hucklebury Run, to get money to support his mother and little Jamie."

"Why, father!" exclaimed Miss Fanny Gilbert.

The doctor looked up, struck by the peculiar tone of surprise and pain that characterized his daughter's exclamation. Fanny blushed, then she grew pale, and trembled in every fibre of her frame.

Aunt Catharine's eyes flashed fire. "I think it's a sin and a shame," said Aunt Catharine, "that the noblest young man in Crampton should be allowed to waste his life in a factory under such a man as old Ruggles, when there are so many here who are able to help him."

"He wouldn't accept help, if it were offered to him," said the doctor drily.

"Then I'd make him," said Aunt Catharine decidedly.

"You'd work miracles, doubtless," responded Dr. Gilbert; and then, the conversation promising to lapse into an uncongenial channel, he put down his little boy, rose from his chair, and left the room.

"I think it's the most shameful thing I ever knew

your father to consent to," continued Aunt Catharine, addressing herself to Fanny.

Fanny would not trust herself to speak ; so, to avoid conversation, she left Fred with his aunt, and ascended to her chamber ; and now that we have the young woman alone and cornered, we will talk about her.

It has already appeared in these pages that she was tall and queenly in her carriage, that she was ambitious, that she had been crowded into early development, that she had been moved by public praise, that she had dreamed of a public career. Whatever there was of the strong and masculine in her nature, had, under her father's vigorous policy, been brought into prominence ; yet there was another side to both her nature and her character. If she had a masculine head, she had a feminine heart. If she felt inspired by a man's ambition, she was informed by a woman's sensibility. If, in one phase of her character and constitution, she exhibited the power to organize and execute, in what the world would style a manly way, in another phase she betrayed the possession of rare susceptibility to the most delicate emotions, and the sweetest affections and passions. The question as to Miss Gilbert's life was, then, simply a question as to which side of her nature should obtain and retain the predominance. In a woman of positive qualities like hers, this contrariety must inevitably be the basis of many struggles, and, in a world of shifting circumstances and various influences, she would have difficulty in achieving a satisfactory adjustment of herself.

When Fanny Gilbert entered her chamber, she closed the door and locked it. Then she went to her mirror to see what and how much her face had betrayed. The mirror gave her no answer. It only showed her a face in which the color went and came, and went and came again, and a pair of eyes that would have been blue had they not been gray, or gray had they not been blue. The double nature discovered itself hardly less in her physical than in her mental characteristics.

Fanny Gilbert did not love Arthur Blague. So far as she knew, he did not love her. They had, as neighbors, as early playmates, and, at one time, as school-mates, been much associated. Her father and Arthur's father had been excellent friends. Her mother and Arthur's mother had been intimately neighborly. But, though she had never loved him, she admired him ; and as he was the superior of any young man of her acquaintance, in manly beauty and all manly qualities, it is not strange that, quite unconsciously, her life's possibilities had yoked themselves with his life's possibilities. One thing was certain : her beau ideal—and by this is meant, of course, her ideal beau—had marvellously resembled Arthur Blague ; and when that beau ideal stepped down from its height of splendid possibilities, into actualities of life that were not only prosy but repulsive, she was sadly shocked.

"Humph !" (A fine nasal ejaculation of impatient contempt, accompanied by a decided elevation of the organ used on the occasion.) "What do I care for Arthur Blague ?" followed the ejaculation ; and her eyes, in which the gray and blue were struggling for the mastery, flashed proudly in the mirror.

Certainly ! Of course ! What did she care for Arthur Blague ? Nobody had accused her of caring any thing for him. Besides, how could a girl be in love who was going to have a career ? Love meant marriage at some time. Love meant subordination to somebody. So the heart, with its petals all formed and ready to be kissed into bloom (had the kiss been ready), was coolly tied so that it could not bloom at all. The head passed the string around the opening bud, and half-pitied the restraint of its throbbing life. The blue eyes looked softly into the mirror no longer; there was no longer any clash of colors; they had changed to gray.

Miss Gilbert, having discarded all thoughts of Arthur as a man whose life sustained any relation to hers, proceeded to think of him simply as a human being of the masculine gender, and an indefinite capacity for improvement. Could one like Arthur Blague become a slave? Arthur was a young man, and should have a young man's will. Would he—could he—bend that will to the will of a mean and sordid man, for bread? She was nothing but a woman, and she would not do it. No: she would starve first. Must there not be something mean and weak in a character that could so adapt itself to the shifting exigencies and paltry economies of life? He had always been gentle; now he had become quite a girl. He had consented to become the servant of an inferior—to place himself upon a level with inferiors.

"There's something wrong about Arthur Blague," soliloquized Miss Gilbert, "or he never could do this. Never!"

What a wise young woman! How wise all young women are at sixteen!

Having decided that Arthur Blague was nothing to her, and gone still further, and decided that there was a fatal defect in the young man somewhere, Miss Gilbert sat down in calm self-complacency, and commenced to read some loose leaves of manuscript. They were not old letters; they were not new letters. They were not even school-girl compositions. They were something of much more interest and importance. Fanny read page after page, while the daylight lasted, and then lighted her lamp, and read on until she had completed them all.

When she had finished them, she pushed them from her with a sigh, and, burying her face in her hands, subsided into deep thought and a deep chair at the same moment. While she is thinking, a few words about the manuscript. Perhaps a marked passage in a country newspaper which lies on the table before the young woman, will the most readily introduce us to the character of these interesting pages, in Fanny's own handwriting :

"We trust that we shall be deemed guilty of no indelicate breach of confidence, in giving publicity to a statement that by some means has found its way out of the private circle to which it was originally communicated, to the effect that a young lady, *not a hundred miles from the neighboring village of Crampton*—the highly accomplished daughter of a distinguished physician—is now busily engaged upon a work of fiction. The fair authoress, we are assured, has not yet exhausted the delicious term of ' sweet sixteen,' though she has already, in another field of effort, demonstrated the possession of those rare gifts and aptitudes which will enable her to succeed abundantly in the arduous career which she has chosen. We shall anticipate the essay of this new candidate for public honors with unusual interest. In the mean time, we beg her pardon, and that of her friends, if this early announcement of her intentions shall be deemed premature or unwarranted."

So this manuscript was Fanny's new " work of fiction," and so Fanny had chosen a literary career. How the fact that she was engaged in writing ever found its way into the Littleton *Examiner*, she was utterly at a loss to imagine. It was true that she had spoken of the matter to an intimate friend—a young woman, who knew another young woman who was very well acquainted with Rev. J. Desilver Newman, who, of course, knew his neighbor, the editor of the *Examiner*, and who, in fact, had the credit of writing the articles for that paper ; but it was hardly possible that the news should have got out in that way. One thing was certain : she had been indiscreet. She should have told no one, and then no one would have known any thing about it. She should have written all the time with her gray eyes ; for the blue eyes sought for sympathy and communion. She had told one friend, because the woman in her demanded that she should tell one friend. Was the public announcement distasteful to her? Fanny Gilbert with blue eyes shrank from it offended ; but afterward, when Fanny Gilbert with gray eyes began to think about it, she gloried in it. She would be re-marked upon, and pointed out as the young woman who was writing a novel. Admiring and wondering eyes would be upon her, whenever she walked through the street, or appeared in a public assembly. A romantic personal interest would attach to her. Ah ! yes. Gray-eyed Fanny Gilbert was pleased in spite of herself.

But the work of writing was a very weary and a very perplexing work. Sometimes she could not make her characters stand up to be written about. Her life had not been sufficiently varied to afford her a competent range of incidents. With the consciousness of the possession of sufficient power for her work, she had also the con-sciousness of poverty of materials. It was of this pov-erty that she was thinking so very deeply in her very deep chair.

It is not to be denied that she was also vexed with the thought that the hero of her story bore a striking resemblance to Arthur Blague, and that, although that young man had ceased to be a hero in her eyes, she could not change him for any other young man she knew. There were other uncomfortable thoughts that came to her with this. She had never communicated her designs to her father, and she was not certain that he would regard them with favor.

Her reverie, which had been somewhat protracted, was disturbed at last by the sound of feet upon the stairs, and then by a strong rap at her door. She rose hurriedly, thrust her manuscript into the desk, and then admitted her father and little Fred.

" Fred wishes you to put him to bed," said her father, " and Catharine says you have received a late Littleton paper," he added. " Ah! here it is ; " and the doctor laid his hand upon it.

Fanny put out both her hands in pantomimic deprecation.

" You can have it again, of course," said the doctor; " I only wish to look at the probate notices :" saying which, he bade Fred " good-night," and walked down, stairs.

There were some very stupid and very tremulous fingers engaged that night in undressing the little boy, and when he said " Our Father who art in heaven" to her, she was thinking only of her father who was down-stairs reading " probate notices," in the Littleton *Examiner.* The sweet little " Amen" was just breathed when she heard her father's steps in the hall, and his voice calling " Fanny," at the foot of the stairs.

Fanny looked in the glass again, and then went slowly down-stairs. Every part of her varied nature was awake and on the alert. A gentle, sympathetic word would win her into tenderness and tractableness ; while harsh dealing would arouse her to opposition the most positive. She would like, of all things the most, to have her father talk encouragingly and sympathetically of her new enterprise. The woman and the daughter were delicately alive to any gentle word or kind counsel that the strong man and the father might utter ; but the ambitious aspirant for public applause was sensitive in an equal degree, and, firmly throned, was prepared imperiously to defend her prerogatives and pleasures.

Miss Gilbert entered the drawing-room with any thing but the air of a child or a culprit—not defiantly, but as if she were prepared for any event, and rather expected the event to be unpleasant.

" Have you seen that paragraph ?" inquired the doctor excitedly, extending the copy of the Littleton *Examiner* to Fanny, with his thumb half-covering the familiar lines.

" I have, sir," replied Fanny, coolly.

" What does it mean ? " The doctor's eyes flashed, and he spoke loudly and harshly.

" I don't know, sir."

" You don't know, eh ? I know."

" Perhaps you will tell me, father."

" Fanny, Fanny, this will not do. You must not speak to me with such a look and tone. You know very well that this paragraph can refer only to you. Have you ever given authority to any one to publish such a paragraph as that ? "

" I certainly never have," Fanny replied, very decidedly.

" Have you ever," pursued her father, " said to any one any thing from which this impertinent paragraph could be made ? "

" I suppose I have, to an intimate friend."

" Were you hoaxing her, or telling her the truth ? "

" I told her the truth."

" To an intimate friend, eh ? To an intimate friend, and not to me, eh ? Why not to me ? "

" Because I feared that you would not favor my project."

" You are very frank, upon my word. So far as you could guess what my will would be, you would disobey it. What have you been writing ? "

Miss Gilbert was angry. She did not look into her father's face, but studied the paper on the wall.

" Fanny, tell me what you have been writing."

Still looking at the wall, Fanny replied, " I have begun to write a novel, and only begun. I have not been without the hope that it would please my father—that it would be a happy surprise to him. I have not been—I

have never been—a disobedient daughter. I have followed your wishes all my life, and no being in the world
has had so much to do in bringing me to the undertaking of this enterprise as you have. I am ambitious, because you have fostered ambition in me. I have been
kept before the public in one way and another ever since
I can remember. I have been taught to regard public
applause as a very pleasant and precious thing. To ex-
cel in study, to shine in examinations and public exhibi-
tions, to win praise for wonderful achievements, has been
the aim of my life for years, and to this you have always
pushed me. You have heard me publicly praised here
in our own church, and you were pleased. I feel now
that I can never be content with the common lot of woman, and I declare that I will not accept it. I will not
live a humdrum, insignificant life of subordination to the
wills and lives of others, save in my own way. I will
have a career."

Dr. Gilbert was utterly astonished. He had watched
his daughter with painful interest as she revealed herself to him in her first open attempt to cut loose from
his will and to assert herself, and, when she closed, he
could only echo her closing words—"a career!" A
woman with "a career" was something he could not
comprehend at all; or, if he comprehended it, he did
not comprehend the motives of his daughter's ambition.
That he had ever contributed to this ambition he did
not admit for a moment; but he was puzzled as to what
course to pursue. He saw that his daughter might be
easily exasperated; so the bright thought occurred to
him that perhaps this desire for a career might possibly
be a sort of mental small-pox or measles, which must
run its course, and would then leave her free from the
liability to a recurrence of the disease.

"Then you have determined to write this novel?"
said Dr. Gilbert.

" It would be the saddest disappointment of my life to be obliged to relinquish it."

" And to publish it ? "

" I have no motive for writing a book that is not to be published."

" I did not know," said the doctor, " but you would do it for your own improvement. It would be a very fine diversion, you know, in case you take up German and Hebrew, and the higher mathematics, this winter."

" Must I forever be doing something for my own improvement ? Must I be forever studying ? I am tired of always taking in ; I wish to do something, and to be recognized as a—as a—power in the world." Fanny said this very fervently, but the last words sounded very large, and she knew they seemed ridiculous to her father, who smiled, almost derisively, as the hot blood mounted to her temples.

The half-amused, half-pitying contempt which Fanny saw in her father's face roused her anger. She rose from her chair impetuously, and stamping one foot upon the floor, exclaimed : " I wish to God I were a man ! I think it a curse to be a woman."

" Why, Fanny !" exclaimed Dr. Gilbert, greatly shocked.

" I do think it a curse to be a woman. I never knew a woman who was not a slave or a nonentity, nor a man who did not wish to make her one or the other. A woman has no freedom, and no choice of life. She can take no position, and have no power, without becoming a scoffing and a by-word. You have been talking to Fred ever since he was in the cradle about a career ; you have placed before him the most exciting motives to effort, but you have never dreamed of my being any thing more than Dr. Gilbert's very clever daughter ; or a tributary to some selfish man's happiness and respectability. I say that I will not accept this lot, and that I do not believe my Maker ever intended I should accept it."

All this Miss Gilbert uttered vehemently, and enforced with sundry emphatic gestures, and then she turned to leave the room.

" Fanny, sit down ! " The doctor's will was rising.

" I can listen without sitting, sir ; but I should like to retire."

" Sit down, I say."

Fanny altered the position of her chair very deliberately, placed herself before it very slowly, and settled into her seat very proudly indeed.

" Fanny Gilbert, never speak such words to me again, while you live. I will not allow it ; I will not permit you to insult me, and disgrace yourself, by such language. I am astonished. I am confounded. I am—ah—who has been putting such mischievous, such blasphemous notions into your head ? "

" Women never have any notions, except such as are put into their heads, I suppose, of course."

" Do you use this tone of irony to me ? Hear what I have to say, and do not speak to me—do not speak to me again to-night. You have begun what you call a career, and have begun it just where such an inexperienced girl as you would naturally begin it. I understand your case, I think, and I shall not interfere with your purpose. Nay, it is my will that you go on and satisfy yourself—that you prove the utter hollown ss of your notions. I will go further than this. If, when you have finished your book, you will submit it to Mr. Wilton, and he decides that it will not absolutely disgrace you, I will find a publisher for it. But by all means be as diligent as you can be with your work. Do with your might what your hands have undertaken to do, and do not leave it until it shall be finished. You can go."

Browbeaten, but not subdued, Miss Gilbert rose and sailed out of the room. Her heart was in a tumult. Her eyes were full of tears. Her head ached almost to bursting with the pressure of rebellious blood. The moment she left the presence of the strong will that had roused her, the woman's want of solace and sympathy swept through her whole nature. Meeting Aunt Catharine in the upper hall, she cast herself, sobbing, and soft as a child, upon the spinster's bosom, and was led by that good woman into her room. Then Aunt Catharine sat down upon Fanny's bed, and took Fanny's head upon her shoulder, and passed her arm around her waist, and sat in perfect silence with her for half an hour, while her niece enjoyed unrestrained the " luxury of grief."

" There, dear, have you got down to where you can pray ? " inquired Aunt Catharine, putting off the young head.

Fanny smiled faintly, said, " Thank you, aunt, it has done me so much good," then kissed her affectionately, and bade her " good night."

Fanny's prayer was a very broken and unsatisfactory one that night, and the doctor's, it is to be feared, was hardly more consolatory. A long reverie followed the retirement of his daughter from his presence. At the close of this, he took up the copy of the Littleton *Examiner*, and re-perused the offensive paragraph. It had changed somehow. It did not seem so offensive as it did at first. Then he subsided into another reverie, in which the possibilities of Fanny's career were followed very far—so far, that Dr. Gilbert had become a very noted man, for having a famous daughter, who had contributed richly to the literature of her country. He began, before he was conscious of it, to sympathize with his daughter's project. Many excellent women had written books, and why not " the highly accomplished daughter of a distinguished physician ?"

Ah! if Fanny had possessed more tact, if her eyes had been just a shade bluer, she could have made her peace with her father that night, and sapped the will of the strong man through the weak point of his character, and made him essentially her servant.

CHAPTER VI.

THE MISTRESS OF HUCKLEBURY RUN AND HER AC-COMPLISHED DAUGHTER.

ON the evening of the accident at the Run, Arthur did not retire to bed until late, anxious to learn from Dr. Gilbert the fate of the proprietor. He called at the house of the doctor several times, but that gentleman had not returned. He knew that the casualty was a serious one, and one that would be likely to have important relations to his future life. It would inevitably thwart all his plans, or modify, in some unlooked-for way, his destiny. His despondent mother felt that it was only a new misfortune added to her already extended list, and declared that she had expected something like it from the first.

At last Arthur relinquished the expectation of seeing the doctor that night, and went to bed. The next morning was dark and rainy. An eastern storm was raging when he rose, and the walk was covered with deciduous foliage. Large trees that had borne into the night abundant wealth of mellow purple and scarlet and gold, greeted the gray light of the morning in shivering and moaning nakedness. The clouds sailed low and fast upon an atmosphere of mist, and tossed overboard their burden in fitful and spiteful showers. The ground was soaked and spongy, and every thing, above and below, looked sad and forbidding, as Arthur left his door for the scene of his daily labor.

He had accomplished possibly half of the distance to the mill, running rather than walking, when his ear caught the sound of wheels ; and soon afterward Dr. Gilbert and his gig showed themselves through the misty twilight. Arthur hailed the doctor, and inquired for his employer.

"He is at death's door," replied the doctor, "with the bare possibility of being saved. He wants, too, such care as only a man can give him. His family are worse than nothing, and I see no way but for you to become his nurse, and take the charge of him until he either dies or recovers. I have been with him all night, but I cannot be with him to-day. Go directly to the house, and I will be there in the course of a few hours, and give you my directions."

Saying this to Arthur, who was so much impressed by this new turn of events that he could not reply, Dr. Gilbert chirruped to the little black pony, who stood uneasily in the storm, with his ears turned back very savagely, and away rolled the gig into the mist, leaving the young man standing with his face toward Crampton. A moment of indecision was followed by the active resumption of his way to the Run. Arriving at the mill, he found every thing in confusion. The early breakfast had been eaten, and the operatives were assembled in the mill, as if there had been no other resort ; but the wheel was not in motion. Gathered into knots here and there in the different rooms, some of them were discussing their master's calamity with unbecoming levity, and others, less talkative, were looking solemn and apprehensive.

Why was it that all these men and women regarded Arthur Blague, as he entered the mill, with an expectation of help and direction ? He was but a boy, and knew nothing of the duties of the establishment ; but they turned to him just as naturally as if he had been their master for years. They were " all alike down to the Run." They were all men and women who had been governed, who had had their wills crushed out of them, who had lived and moved only in cowardly dependence. The bell had controlled them like a flock of sheep. Their employer's presence had been their stimulus to labor, and his mind and will were in them all. As soon as that mind and will and presence were withdrawn, they were helpless, because they had long since ceased to govern and direct themselves. There was no leader among them. They had all been conquered —" they were all alike down to the Run."

The moment Arthur stepped into the mill, the knots of men and women were dissolved, and all flocked around him. " Have you heard from old Ruggles ? " " Have you seen the doctor ? " " What does the doctor think ? " were questions which poured in upon him from every side. Arthur told them what the doctor had said, and asked them what they were going to do. Nobody knew ; nobody assumed to speak for the others. All were dumb.

Arthur waited a moment, looking from one to another ; when Cheek, standing on a bale of cloth, shouted : " This meeting will please to come to order."

As the meeting happened to be in a very perfect state of order at the instant, it of course immediately went into the disorder of unnecessary laughter.

" I motion," said Cheek, assuming all the active functions of a deliberative assembly, " that Arthur Blague, Esq., be the boss of this mill till somebody gets well, or somebody kicks the bucket. All who are in favor will say ' aye.' "

The " aye " was very unanimous, whatever may have been intended by it.

" All those opposed will shut their clam-shells," continued Cheek, " and forever after hold their peace."

In the midst of such merriment, Cheek handed to Arthur, with a profound bow, an old hat which belonged to the proprietor, and then put his own under his arm, in token of his readiness to receive orders.

Arthur was about to decline the honor conferred upon him, and to say that the occasion was hardly one that admitted of levity, when his eye detected, among the girls of the group, an earnest face, back from which fell the familiar sun-bonnet. The moment the woman caught his eye, she beckoned to him. Making his way through the group, he followed her aside, and then she turned upon him her full blue eyes, and spoke.

" Mr. Blague," said the young woman, with a low, firm voice, and with an air of good breeding, " these people are in trouble, and do not know what to do. Advise them frankly. Do not be afraid of them because you are a comparative stranger to them. Tell them what to do, and they will do it. Leave me, and act at once."

All this was said rapidly, and in a tone that no one heard but he. The words were those of command ; the voice was one of respectful entreaty. Arthur turned to the assembly, whose eyes had followed him, while his mysterious counsellor took her station at her looms.

" We do not elect our master in this mill," said Arthur, pleasantly. " It is not in accordance with the constitution of Hucklebury Run ; therefore, I beg leave to decline the honor you have conferred upon me ; but there is one thing we can all do."

" What's that ? what's that ? " inquired a dozen voices.

" Each person can do his own work, and his own duty, in his own place, and be his own master ; and if each one does this, there will be no trouble, and the work will all be done, and done well. If Mr. Ruggles recov-

6

ers, then his business will suffer no interruption ; if he dies, you will have pay for your labor."

The question, so difficult to these people, who had lost the idea of governing themselves, was solved. He had not ceased to speak, when a strong hand raised the gate, and the big wheel was in motion. In five minutes the mill was in full operation. A sense of individual responsibility brought self-respect, and awakened a sentiment of honor. They were happier, and more faithful in heart and hand to the interests of their employer, than they had been in all the history of their connection with the establishment. Arthur looked for the girl who had spoken to him. She met his eye with a smile, bowed slightly, as if acknowledging his service, and turned to her work.

Half-bewildered by the events of the morning, in which he seemed to have played an important part, without comprehending how or why he had done it, and with the strange, low voice of the young woman still lingering in his ears, he turned from the mill to seek the dwelling of his employer, in accordance with the wishes of Dr. Gilbert.

Old Ruggles lived in a little dwelling on a hill that overlooked the mill. It was hardly superior in size and architectural pretensions to the tenements occupied by the men, among his operatives, who had families. Arthur rapped softly at the door, and was admitted by a woman, whom he recognized at once as Mrs. Ruggles. She was coarse and vulgar-looking, very fat, with large hands, small, cunning eyes, and floating cap-strings. Every thing she wore seemed to float back from her anterior aspect, as if she had stood for a week facing a strong wind. Her cap flew back at the ears, and the strings hung over the shoulders ; the ends of her neckerchief were parallel with her cap-strings ; her skirts were very scant before, and very full behind, as if, which was the fact, she always moved very fast, and created a vacuum in her passage, which every light article upon her ponderous person strove to reach and fill.

She greeted Arthur with a very dolorous face, but called him " Arthur " quite familiarly, and affected an air of polite condescension, as she inquired if he would sit down and have a cup of coffee. " We are trying, Leonora and me," said Mrs. Ruggles, " to take something to support natur', because, as I tell Leonora, it's a duty to bear up under the strokes of Providence, and be able to help them that needs us."

Mrs. Ruggles said this as she pointed Arthur to a chair at the table, by the side of Leonora, and went to the cupboard for a plate, cup, and saucer. Leonora, the daughter, was an old acquaintance of the young man's, and he shook her listless, lifeless hand in silence.

" The coffee doesn't look very well this morning," said Mrs. Ruggles, as she poured out a cup for Arthur, " but I s'pose it's more nourishing than as if it was settled. I always told father," by which reverential term the lady intended to designate her husband, " that if coffee was nourishing at all, the grounds was the best part of it. You know how it is with porridge ? " And Mrs. Ruggles looked at Arthur as she handed him the cup and the suggestive illustration together, as if the two articles were sufficient to floor the strongest prejudices.

" Will you have another cup, dear ? " said Leonora's mamma, to that young woman. Leonora did not reply, save by a contemptuous twist of her features, and a shake of her head.

" I don't think Leonora loves coffee very well," pursued Mrs. Ruggles.

" I love coffee, but I don't love slops," responded the young woman, pettishly.

" Now, dear, don't speak so," said mamma depre-
catingly ; " this is what we get for sending you to boarding-school. Oh ! girls are brought up so different from
what they was when I was young. Now, dear, you
know that we never settle our coffee with eggs after they
get to be over a shilling a dozen. Father and me has
always been obliged to be equinomical, and to look after
odds and ends, and if you have got extravagant notions
into your head, you didn't git them to home. You know
it, dear, jest as well as I do."

Leonora breathed a little gust of irritation through her
nostrils, as if a fly were upon her lip.

Arthur was sufficiently amused with the mother, but
he was honestly concerned for the father, and he wondered how the face he met at the door could so suddenly
lose its longitude. He ventured to change the direction
of the conversation by inquiring into Mr. Ruggles' condition.

The fat face gathered incalculable solemnity on the
instant. " Father has took sights of laudlum—sights of
laudlum !" Mrs. Ruggles shook her head, as if the " laudlum " were the big end of the calamity.

" I hope it has quieted him," said Arthur.

" Yes, he's asleep now, and Joslyn is setting up with
him. Joslyn is a very still man, you know, for one that's
so heavy as he is. I s'pose he's got used to going tiptoe
by always having a baby to home. It would be an awful
stroke to Joslyn if father should be took away." Mrs.
Ruggles' own woe seemed to be entirely submerged by
her sympathy for Joslyn.

" But we all hope he will live," said Arthur cordially,
" and I know Dr. Gilbert hasn't given him up."

" Oh ! such a sight—such a sight ! " exclaimed the
wife, as the sound of the doctor's name recalled the
painful scenes of the night, " every rag of clothes torn
off of him, and his leg broke, and his body no better

than so much jelly ! It's the greatest wonder that he's alive now. It seemed to me as if I never should live through it ; and it wouldn't be strange if he should be took away, after all. But it isn't our doings, and we must be resigned to the stroke, if it comes."

The last portion of these remarks was accompanied by appropriate sighs, but it somehow seemed to Arthur as if resignation would not be such a difficult duty, after all. The small, cunning eyes of the woman read as much as this in the young man's face, and she continued : " It's a duty to be thankful for our comforts, whatever comes. If he should be took away, I shouldn't be like them that have no hope."

" Is Mr. Ruggles a religious man ? " inquired Arthur.

" It depends on what people calls religion," replied Mrs. Ruggles. " Some thinks it's one thing, and some thinks it's another. Some is professors, you know, and some is possessors. Father and me never made so much fuss about our religion as some folks do. He always give something for supporting the Gospil. I've seen him give twenty-five dollars to once, and he was forever taking down a codfish or something to Mr. Wilton. Father and me has always been equinomical, but we never stole the Gospil, never. Then father has always provided for his own family, which is more religion than some folks have. Folks that don't provide for their own families are infidels, the Bible says."

During all this conversation, Leonora had sat in perfect silence, expressing only by her lazy features the contempt she felt for her mother, and for the meal before her. Her eyes gave no evidence of tears, past or present. She was annoyed, to be sure, but she was always annoyed. With a father and a mother wholly absorbed by worldliness, she had grown up in indolence—the insipid, ungrateful recipient of every loving ministry of which her parents were capable. Arthur turned his eyes upon her in astonishment, wondering that the nature of any woman could be so apathetic.

Mrs. Ruggles noticed Arthur's observation of her daughter, and continued : " As I was saying, father has looked out for his own family, and Leonora is provided for. There isn't any girl in Crampton that is any better edicated than she is, and there isn't one that will have such a setting-out. Of course, she will have all we have got, at last, when we are both took away, but I mean she shall always hold it in her own right. I don't think it's right for folks to tug and tug all their lives to get money together to spoil their children's husbands with. When I married father—you know I married him out of the mill—I had my own bank stock that I had earned myself, and I've always held it in my own right. I think it's such a comfort for a woman to have bank stock, if her husband's took away."

Even Leonora could not withstand this. " Mother," said she, " Mr. Blague thinks you are a fool ; I'm sure I do."

" Don't speak so, dear," responded the mother tenderly. " You are not yourself this morning."

" That's a blessing : then I'm not your daughter ; " and without asking to be released from the table, Leonora rose, and lounged out of the room.

Arthur thought it time for business. " I am to nurse Mr. Ruggles, Dr. Gilbert tells me," said he, recalling Mrs. Ruggles from the admiring contemplation of her daughter's retiring figure.

" I know it," she replied, " and I should have spoke of it before, but I knew father was asleep, and that Joslyn would call us if any thing happened. I s'pose " (and Mrs.. Ruggles sighed) " that because I talk, and eat my victuals, you and Leonora think I don't feel this stroke, but little do you know ! I *have* to talk, for my mind's distracted, and I think of every thing ; and I *have* to eat to support natur' and bear up. Arthur, I forgot to inquire about your mother. How is she?"

Arthur's eyes filled with tears in an instant. "She can neither talk, nor eat, nor bear up, as you say," he replied.

"She was always kind o' weakly," said Mrs. Ruggles, musing. "Dear me! How well I remember her when she felt too big to speak to me! She was mighty crank when she married the storekeeper; but some goes up and some goes down; and isn't it strange, now, that her boy should come here and wait upon father!" Mrs. Ruggles said this without the remotest suspicion that her remarks were utterly offensive.

"My mother is a lady, Mrs. Ruggles, and never treated you in any other than a ladylike way. I beg you never to mention her again."

"Well, of course, I didn't mean to hurt your feelings," replied the woman, wondering at Arthur's impudence. "I'm very sorry, of course, for your mother. I ra'ally hope she's got something in her own right, and that she'll chirk up, and git along comfortable."

Arthur bit his lip, vexed at the woman's stolid pertinacity, and amused in spite of himself with her lack of sense and sensibility. He rose, and said : "Will you call Joslyn, Mrs. Ruggles?"

The floor creaked, and shook, as the large woman went on her errand ; and soon afterward Joslyn appeared—a white, tallowy-looking, middle-aged man, with a large, flat face, faded eyes, and a bald spot on the top of his head over which the hair was braided.

"How is Mr. Ruggles?" inquired Arthur.

"I don' know," replied Joslyn in a whisper.

"Does he suffer?"

"I don' know, I'm sure."

"Did Dr. Gilbert set his broken leg?"

"I don' know. He did something to it."

" Are you to stay here ? "

" I don' know, I'm sure."

" What are you doing for him ? "

" I don' know. Dr. Gilbert told me to set by him, and give him his drops once in two hours if he was awake. If he wasn't, I wasn't to wake him up."

" Well," said Arthur, " tell me about the drops, and then go home, and go to bed. I will look after Mr. Ruggles."

" Just as you say, of course," said Joslyn.

Then Joslyn explained the doctor's directions, and hoped Arthur would stand between him and all harm, if the master should wake and be offended because he had left him. " I feel particular about keeping in with him," said Joslyn in explanation, " for I have a good many to look after." Having said this, the humble and fearful man spread a spotted bandanna handkerchief over his head, and went off through the storm toward his little tenement on tiptoe, as if the street were lined with babies in profound slumber.

Arthur entered the room where the proprietor lay. Pale and haggard—the more so in seeming for the blackness of his beard—he lay moaning in a narcotic dream. Arthur took a seat by his side, and, in doing so, made a noise with his chair. The eyes of the sleeper were instantaneously wide open. Wild, glassy, and apprehensive, they gazed into Arthur's face with an expression that sent a shudder through his frame. It was an expression of hate, astonishment, and inquiry. The master tried to rise, but his muscles refused to lift him an inch.

" What am I here for ? What are you here for ? " whispered the man.

" You have met with an accident," said Arthur, stooping over him. " You are very badly hurt, and must be quiet."

" Who says I'm hurt ? Who hurt me ? Why ain't you

to work ? " Old Ruggles gasped with the exertion which the words cost him.

Then Arthur told him all about his injury, and what had been done for him, and furthermore informed him that he must obey all directions, or he could not live. As the meaning of Arthur's words sank slowly into his benumbed consciousness, the fierce look faded out of the master's eyes, and gave place to an expression of fear and anxiety.

" Don't let me die," said he, with a pitiful whine. " Don't let me die. I can't die."

" We shall do all we can for you, but you must not talk," said Arthur.

" I didn't mean you any harm," whimpered the master, evidently recalling his treatment of Arthur, and afraid that the young man would revenge himself upon him in some way. " I didn't mean you any harm. Don't lay up anything agin me." And the cowardly man cried like a helpless baby.

Arthur reassured him, and then without further parley commanded him to be silent. So the proprietor of Hucklebury Run, subdued by fear and helplessness, put himself into the hands of his new apprentice. Arthur watched him through the long morning, and as the reaction from the terrible nervous shock came on, he hung over him, and fanned him as faithfully as if he had been his own father. With the reaction came insanity. The master was in his mill, scolding his hands, and raving about Arthur. He accused one of wasting, and another of idling, and threatened another.

At noon, Dr. Gilbert's little pony came pounding over the bridge that crossed the Run, and the gig reeled up to the door, the doctor touching the ground before the vehicle had fairly stopped. He found his patient quite as well as he expected to find him ; and giving Arthur full directions as to his management, he told him that he had provided company for his mother, and that she would not expect him home until it should be proper for him to leave his charge.

Convalescence, with the proprietor, was very slow in its progress, and frequently interrupted by relapses. It was for many weeks a matter of doubt whether he would ever permanently recover. In the mean time, Aunt Catharine had taken it upon herself to see that Mrs. Blague was not left alone, and that she needed no essential service which Arthur's absence deprived her of. Business at the mill went on entirely through the medium of Arthur Blague. He was nurse, accountant, confidential clerk, salesman at the store, factotum. He was the only man competent to do the business correspondence for his employer; and as the latter was clear-headed after the first few days of fever, he made the young man his right arm in every department of his affairs.

It had been one of the pet boasts of old Ruggles that he had never been sick a day in his life, and had never paid a doctor's bill. All his business he had done himself. There was not a man at the Run in his employ who had a particle of his confidence, or who had ever known anything of his business affairs. He never expected to be sick. It had never entered into his thought as among the possibilities of life that he should be disabled and dependent. To suppose that such a man should take such restraint and such dependence patiently, would be to expect miracles. To Arthur he was exacting to the last degree of forbearance—giving him hardly time for sleep, and allowing him only a moment occasionally to drop in upon his mother and little Jamie, on the way to the post-office.

There was one shrewd pair of eyes that watched all these proceedings with great speculative curiosity. Mrs. Ruggles, relieved by Arthur from a serious burden of care, was aware of his importance to her husband, not only as nurse, but as business executive. Arthur's quiet assumption of entire social equality, and his actual personal superiority, had impressed the woman very decidedly ; and when she saw how well he took hold of affairs, how much her husband depended upon him, and how necessary he would be to the business in the event of a fatal termination of the master's injuries, she had come to the conclusion that a permanent partnership between him and dear Leonora would be a very profitable and a very desirable thing. The business at the Run could go along without difficulty. Arthur would come there to live, and the Widow Ruggles, not without her comforts, would pass her days in prosperity equal to her previous lot, and in peace quite superior.

Conveniently without the slightest sensibility, she had no difficulty in approaching the subject which occupied her thoughts, in her interviews with Arthur; and it must be confessed that, foolish as the girl thought her mother to be, she lent herself to her schemes. Bred to feel that money was the grand requisite for social position and personal power, she believed that she was mistress of her own matrimonial destiny. She had but to indicate her willingness to link her fortunes with those of any poor young man, to secure that young man's everlasting gratitude. It had been drummed into her ears by the repetitious tongue of her mother, even from young girlhood, that the ultimate mistress of Hucklebury Run, and heir presumptive of Madam Ruggles' bank stock, held in her own right, could marry whomsoever in Crampton, or in the towns thereunto adjacent, she might choose.

Whether eggs had gone down materially, soon after Arthur's advent into the family, the young man did not know, but he noticed a very decided improvement in the quality of the coffee. Leonora, too, grew from day to day more careful in her dress, and was always, at certain times, to be found sitting in Arthur's way. Wholly preoccupied, the honest-hearted, unsuspicious fellow did not notice these things at all. The possibility of a wife and daughter setting themselves seriously at work to entice a young man into a matrimonial alliance, at a moment when the husband and father lay in an adjoining room, trembling between life and death, was something alike beyond his suspicion and his comprehension.

One morning, Arthur was detained from his breakfast some minutes after it was announced to be ready. On entering the room, he found the mother and daughter waiting. Arthur took his accustomed seat at the head of the table, with Leonora at his right hand, robed in a very comely morning wrapper, and a mingled atmosphere of sassafras-soap, and sour hair.

Mrs. Ruggles looked radiantly across the table at Arthur, as if she were sighting a cannon, the top of the coffee-pot serving as the initial point in the range. " Leonora and me has been talking about you," said the lady. " You see we couldn't get along without you at all, and I don't know but we should have starved to death if you hadn't come. It seems just as nateral to have you to the head of the table somehow, as it does to have father, and that was what Leonora and me was saying. Leonora, says she, ' How well Mr. Blague looks to the head of the table, setting up so tall and handsome ! ' "

" Mother Ruggles ! " Leonora simpered, shocked purely as a matter of conventional propriety.

Mrs. Ruggles giggled. " Look at her, Arthur, and see how she blushes," said the fond mother, pointing to the impassive face of her daughter. " You needn't blush so, for it's just what I've said myself. But we don't make ourselves ; it's nothing for us to be lifted up about." The lady drew on a pious look, as if she were

the last person who would be guilty of feeding Arthur's
vanity. and the first decently to remind him of the great
Author of all beauty. " No, we don't make ourselves,"
continued Mrs. Ruggles, " but we know that some looks
well to the head of the table, and some don't. Some
seems calculated to be the head of a family, and some
seems ridiculous when we think of it. If there's any
thing that I hate, it is to see a little man to the head of
the table, particular if his wife is a sizable woman, and
he isn't big enough to say, Why do ye so ? I was saying to Leonora, only a day or two ago, says I, Dear,
when you get married—and I hope you don't think of
such a thing for the present—do you look out for a husband not an inch shorter than Arthur Blague, for I've
seen you together, and there's just the right difference
between you. That's just what I said to her—wasn't it,
dear ? "

." You say a great many foolish things, mother," said
Leonora, lazily.

" Now, dear, don't say so. Young folks always thinks
old folks is fools, but when I see your father lying dangerous, and the only child I have to my back in a way
of being left alone without any pertector, it's nateral for
mothers to think of the future, and to calculate on what
they'd like to see brung about. Don't you think so,
Arthur ? "

Arthur thus appealed to, responded as the lady apparently desired.

" S'posing every thing suits, and every thing should
be brung about just as it might be, and no damage
done to nobody," pursued the woman mysteriously,
" what is your notion about a woman's holding her property in her own right ? I mean after she gets married,
of course."

Arthur replied coolly, that he trusted all married women who desired to hold property in their own right,

would do so by all means. As far as he was personally concerned, while he would not blame a woman for 'having property, he should altogether prefer that she should depend upon him for support, rather than be independent of him.

"I think those notions is good, and honable," responded Mrs. Ruggles. "A husband always ought to support his family, and then if a woman has any thing in her own right, she can keep it. When I was married, I had bank stock, and I've always kept it in my own right, and father never has had a cent of it, and it's always been a comfort to me to think that if he should be took away, or any thing should happen, I hold my bank stock in my own right, and nobody can say, Why do ye so? Oh! I think it's such a comfort to a woman to have bank stock, if her husband's took away; don't you, Arthur?"

Arthur was polite enough not to tell her that there were some women who, he believed, would very much rather lose their husbands than their bank stock, but he thought so, and hurried through a meal made repulsive by the worldly Mrs. Ruggles' conversation, and her insipid daughter's presence. But one breakfast was the pattern of many others; and as Mrs. Ruggles saw how important Arthur was becoming to her husband, and how desirable an element he was in the society of Hucklebury Run, she became only the more pertinacious in her persecution of him on her daughter's behalf. Arthur could readily bring his mind to bear with his master's petulant exactions, but the flattery of the mistress, and her daughter's patronizing and familiar airs, were more than he could abide.

In truth, there was a reason for his disgust with Mrs. Ruggles and her daughter, beyond the repulsive nature of their advances. He had never forgotten the expression of those blue eyes that looked into his on the morning after the accident to the proprietor. He had never forgotten those low-spoken, well-spoken words, and the unconscious compliment which they conveyed to him. He had visited the mill every day—often many times in a day. Always, of course, he had sought for the mysterious young woman who seemed so different from all her associates. The sun-bonnet was always upon her head. She seemed to hold communication with no one, and to be not unfrequently in tears. He was thrown into no relations with her that warranted him in extending conversation, and he could ascertain nothing about her from others, beyond the facts that she had been in the mill for six months, always kept her own counsel, was well educated, intelligent, amiable, and religious ; was sadhearted, and bore the name of Mary Hammett.

If Arthur was abundantly employed during the hours in which he was upon his feet, he was also abundantly employed in his hours of retirement. The fever that so frequently attacks young men at nineteen was upon him —a fever invariably excited by a woman superior in years and experience. Mary Hammett was twenty-two, and had the maturity of a man of twenty-five ; but to Arthur Blague the earth soon came to hold no such divinity as she. The factory became a charming place because she was in it. Hucklebury Run was heaven, because hallowed by the residence of one of heaven's angels. Arthur had not been without his school-boy fancy for Fanny Gilbert, but she had never possessed the power to stir his deeper nature. Only the mature woman could do this, and all his boyish likings were swept out of mind by his new and all-pervading passion.

Autumn deepened into winter, and winter was softening into spring, before the health of the proprietor was so far re-established as to allow his young assistant once more to become permanently a resident of his mother's home. In the mean time, Aunt Catharine in person, or by the assistance of sympathetic friends, had ministered to Arthur's lonely mother, and little Jamie had grown into healthy and comely babyhood.

But Arthur had become too important to the proprietor to be lightly spared. It was a loss to old Ruggles in many ways to allow him to lodge at home. The old man could never again be in his business what he had been. His broken limb was shortened, and he could only get about upon his cane. His nerves were shattered, and he could not write. He could not live without Arthur. In the measure of his dependence upon the young man, he had grown careful not to offend him. Thoroughly selfish himself, and incapable of appreciating any thing higher than selfishness as a motive of action, he had addressed himself in all possible ways to Arthur's personal ambition and desire to get forward in the world. He had hinted vaguely at a partnership, possible in the future— at a great increase of wages when some desirable changes in his business should be accomplished — at a sale of Hucklebury Run entire to Arthur, when that young man should arrive at his majority, etc.

The aim of all these magnificent promises was to induce Arthur to leave his mother's roof, and become a resident of the Run. At length, uncomfortable weather and most inconvenient walking determined him to consider the master's desires, and to cast about for some one to take his place as nightly society for his mother.

It would not do to depend upon Aunt Catharine again, and, to tell the truth, he would not have thought of doing it had it been the most practicable thing in the world. He had conceived a project, and he would not be content until it should be fulfilled. On the same day during which he had come to his determination, circumstances opened a door to favor its fulfilment.

CHAPTER VII.

IN WHICH THE CENTRE SCHOOL OF CRAMPTON IS HANDSOMELY PROVIDED FOR.

ARTHUR divulged his new plan to his mother, kindly bore with her scruples, or very kindly bore them down, and quite inspired her, for the moment, with his own overflowing enthusiasm. That was the initial step in the business ; the next was to see Dr. Gilbert.

So he left the mill early one evening for the purpose of making the visit. He rang the bell at the physician's dwelling, and was invited into the parlor. Aunt Catharine was rocking herself very slowly and knitting very fast, showing thereby a peaceful condition of mind, and, on the whole, a pleasant state of things in the family. Fanny, looking weary and sleepy, was reading a novel. Little Fred sat at his sister's side, his head in her lap, asleep.

Aunt Catharine, who indulged in a great admiration of Arthur, greeted him as if he had been a favorite nephew ; and Fanny's face lost its weary look entirely. The doctor, whom Arthur inquired for, was not at home, but was expected every moment.

" How is your mother to-night ?" inquired Aunt Catharine, in her crisp way, her needles snapping as if they were letting off sparks of electricity.

" She is as well as usual," replied Arthur, " but you know how it is with her."

" Miserable, I suppose, of course," said Aunt Catharine. " She always is miserable, and I presume she always will be, and it's a blessed thing that it is so. I sometimes think that she is so used to misery that happiness would shock her. I've seen a good deal of her this winter, and it's my candid opinion that misery, if she has a good chance to talk about it, is the only solid comfort she has. I think it would seem so unnatural for her to be comfortable, that it would make her——"

"Miserable," suggested Fanny; and the young woman laughed at her aunt's philosophy.

"It's just so," pursued Aunt Catharine, "and you mark my word, Arthur—your mother will live to be an old woman."

"I'm quite delighted," said Arthur.

"As for me, trouble kills me," resumed Aunt Catharine. "Oh! if I could only wilt down like your mother when trouble comes, and get so used to it as not to expect anything better, I could get along; but dear me! I've no doubt that some day will bring along a great tribulation that will break my life off as short as a pipe-stem."

This was altogether the most cheerful view of his mother's case that Arthur had ever seen presented. It was not offensive to him, because he knew that it came from as sympathetic and friendly a heart as Crampton contained.

"How have you enjoyed being in Mr. Ruggles' family this winter?" inquired Fanny, archly.

Arthur, poor simpleton, did not know how much there was in this inquiry; so he replied that he had "enjoyed it as well as possible, under the circumstances"—a very safe and comprehensive answer, that might mean much or little, in either direction.

"Miss Ruggles, I understand, is quite accomplished," said Fanny.

"Is she?"

"Is she, indeed! Is it possible you have been three months in the family, and her mother hasn't told you?"

There was a delicious bit of malice and jealousy in this, that would have excited any man but one who was wholly preoccupied ; so, while the hit appeared admirable, he did not understand his own relations to it.

" I've been told she was very expensively educated," pursued Fanny, " really, now ! "

" So have I."

" You're a sweet pair of slanderers, upon my word," exclaimed Aunt Catharine.

" At least," said Fanny, " she must present a very strong contrast to her father and mother."

" I think she does, very," responded Arthur.

" Oh ! you do ! I presumed so." Fanny nodded her head and smiled very shrewdly, as if her suspicions were fully confirmed. " Perhaps," she continued, " you will tell Aunt Catharine and me some of the precious particulars of this contrast."

" I should say," replied Arthur, " that her father was not lazy, and that her mother was not extravagant."

" Upon my word ! " exclaimed Aunt Catharine again. " Arthur Blague, apologize to me this instant for slandering one of my sex."

" It's the old story," replied Arthur. " The woman tempted me, and I did eat."

" And who tempted the woman, pray ? " said Fanny.

" A little serpent with very green eyes," responded Aunt Catharine.

" Aunt Catharine ! Arn't you ashamed ! " Fanny was vexed, and blushed charmingly.

" Arthur has a right to be just as much pleased with Miss Leonora as he chooses to be, my dear," said Aunt Catharine in her spicy way. " I confess that I do not see what right you have to question him."

" Of course, he has," responded Fanny. " I hope you don't imagine that I have any fault to find with any fondness he may have for her."

" Oh ! not the least, my dear," Aunt Catharine responded, thoroughly enjoying Fanny's poorly dis-

guised annoyance; "girls are so generous toward each
other!"

Fanny was delighted to hear her father's footsteps
at the door and to have a change in the current of conversation.   Dr. Gilbert came into the parlor, greeted
Arthur with bluff heartiness, and then, with whip in
hand and buffalo coat still unbuttoned, inquired if there
had been any calls for him. There had been none.
The coat was thrown open, and the doctor sat down before the fire and warmed himself.

There was something in the conversation which preceded his advent, that made Arthur shrink from pre-
senting his errand in the presence of the family; but it
seemed quite as hard to ask him for a private audience
as to state his wishes in the hearing of Aunt Catharine
and Fanny. He felt half-guilty, and he knew not of
what. His heart beat thickly, and his hands and feet
grew cold.

"Well, Arthur," said Dr. Gilbert, still looking into
the fire, "how do you and Ruggles get along together?"

"Pretty well," replied Arthur.

"Glad to hear it. The old fellow is not quite so bad
as he is represented to be—is he, now?"

"Possibly not; though to tell the truth, he is quite as
agreeable to me when he is disagreeable as he is when
agreeable."

"Father, you don't know how absurd these people
are to-night," said Fanny, glad to find her tongue again.
"Aunt says that Mrs. Blague is never so happy as when
she is miserable, and Arthur thinks that Mr. Ruggles is
never so agreeable as when he is disagreeable."

"And Fanny has been anxiously inquiring of Arthur
about a girl for whom she does not care a straw," responded Aunt Catharine. "Very absurd, indeed!"

Arthur laughed feebly with the rest, but felt desperately pushed to business. Dr. Gilbert removed his

overcoat, and hung it with his whip in the hall, and the young man renewed the conversation with : " Speaking of Mr. Ruggles—he wishes very much to have me give up boarding at home, and to become more thoroughly a fixture of his establishment. I have so much to do for him, that it really seems necessary to be there all the time, and the walking, you know, is very bad now."

" Who is to take care of your mother ? " inquired the doctor.

" That is precisely the question which brought me here to-night. I wish to get your advice, and possibly your help."

" What are your plans ? Have you any plans ? "

The young man fidgeted. He knew Fanny's eyes were upon him, and was half afraid that they read every thing that was in his heart.

" Anything definite to propose ? " and the doctor wheeled about, and looked him in the face.

" I understand," said Arthur very clumsily, " that— that the, ah—centre school is soon to be without a teacher."

" Another sad case of matrimony," said Fanny aside to her aunt.

" Yes, there'll be a vacancy at the centre in a week," replied the doctor.

" You are the prudential—prudential—"

" Prudential committee," slipped in the doctor in a hurry. " Of course I am, and have been these twenty years."

" Have you secured anybody to fill the vacancy ? " inquired Arthur.

" No, I suppose not," replied the doctor, half-spitefully. " I should be glad to have Fanny take the school, but she is engaged in something that suits her better, I suppose."

" Oh ! of course, I haven't anything to say if Fanny wants the school," said Arthur, bowing to the young woman, and wishing from the bottom of his heart that she would take it, and relieve him of his embarrassment at once.

"Father knows that I will never willingly take the school," responded Fanny, her face grown hard with determination.

"I was thinking," said Arthur, trying to assume a business tone, "that perhaps you would be willing to engage some one who would board with my mother, and be society for her in my absence."

Fanny was mystified, but eager. Her quick insight had detected a secret motive in Arthur's strange embarrassment, that shaped his policy quite as powerfully as his wish to provide for his mother's comfort.

"Do you know of a teacher whom your mother would like to have in her family?" inquired the doctor.

"She would take any one whom I would recommend," replied Arthur evasively.

"Then I take it you have some one in mind whom you can recommend," responded the doctor. "Tell us who she is."

"There's a young woman at the Run," replied Arthur, his face glowing with the consciousness that the eyes of Aunt Catharine and Fanny were upon him, "who, I think, would make an excellent teacher of the school, and a very pleasant companion for my mother."

"At the Run? How came she at the Run?"

"I never inquired," Arthur replied.

"Does she work in the mill?"

"Yes, sir."

"What do you know about her?" inquired the doctor.

"I know very little," replied the young man, getting very hot in the face. I know she is a lady, that she seems very different from the other girls, that she associates with them but little, that she is intelligent, and that she ought to be somewhere else."

" But where did she come from ? "

" I don't know, sir."

" How old is she ? "

" She is not old ; that is all I know about her age."

" What is her name ? "

" Mary Hammett."

" Mary Hammett—Mary Hammett." The doctor pronounced the name two or three times to see if it would recall the face of any one, dead or living, whom he had known. " Mary Hammett. What makes you think she is intelligent ? "

" She looks and talks as if she were."

" Does she desire the place ? "

" I'm sure I—I don't know," replied Arthur. " I never have spoken to her about it. I should think she would like it very much."

" Ha! ha! ha! " roared the doctor. " I like this, Arthur, it's excellent." And the doctor laughed again. Then Arthur laughed, though he did not know exactly what he was laughing about ; and Aunt Catharine and Fanny laughed, because the doctor and Arthur laughed ; and little Fred awoke from his nap, because they all laughed.

" I think Miss Mary Hammett had better be consulted on the subject before we dispose of her," said the doctor.

" That is precisely what I came to ask you to do," replied Arthur.

" Well, I'll do it. I'll do it to-morrow," said Dr. Gilbert. " I'm quite anxious to see this marvel."

" Now you shall tell us all about her," said Fanny, speaking with that cordial sweetness which a young woman, just a little jealous, can assume when she tries very hard. " Is she beautiful ? "

" I think so. She seems so," replied Arthur.

" Hum! seems so! Feeling as you do toward her,

she seems so! You are not entirely certain whether she be so or no. Seems so!" (Turning to the doctor, and attempting to laugh :) "Father, this is a dangerous case. Treat it very carefully."

"The green-eyed serpent again," said Aunt Catharine.

"Aunt, you are insufferable. I really feel very much interested in Miss Hammett already. It's quite a romance."

Arthur was embarrassed, and felt very uncomfortable. He called Fred to him, and took him upon his knee. The little fellow had always been a favorite with Arthur, and had been famous for asking "leading questions." Some further conversation was had, when Fred looked up in Arthur's face and said, "Do you love Miss Hammett better than you do Sister Fanny?"

This terminated the conference, and in the midst of much merriment Arthur rose to take his leave. Aunt Catharine lifted her forefinger to him, and said, in her good-natured, emphatic way: "Arthur Blague, don't you think of getting married before you are thirty—not a day; don't you dream of such a thing!"

When Arthur had retired, and closed the door after himself, Fanny said to her brother : "Why, Fred! don't you know that it is very improper indeed for you to ask such a question of Arthur Blague ?"

"I thought you acted as if you wanted to know," replied the boy, "and I wasn't afraid to ask him. He always tells me."

"Well, I think you had better go to bed. You are a very dangerous young man."

"Don't be afraid, Fanny, I won't hurt you," responded Fred.

Dr. Gilbert was thinking, and drumming with his fingers upon the arms of his chair. "How fortunate it would be," said the doctor, "if Miss Hammett should prove to be a good teacher for our little boy here ; " and he thought on, and drummed till the little boy went to bed.

When Arthur went to his room that night, he felt that he had done a very unwarrantable thing. What would Miss Hammett think of him for daring to propose such a step before consulting her ? What was he—what was his mother—that they should presume to dream that so angelic a being as Mary Hammett would deem it a privilege to find a lodging under their humble roof ? She would refuse, of course, and that would be the last of his intercourse with her. She would detect all his motives — read the mean record of his selfishness — and despise him for a desire to entrap her.

The purer and the more exalted a young lover's love may be, the more unworthy and insignificant does he become in his own self-estimation. His fine ideal becomes, with the growth of his passion, a finer ideal, until he stands mean and poor and contemptible in the presence of perfections which his own sublimated imagination has builded. This is one of love's sweet mysteries, and if Arthur did not comprehend it, it must be remembered that he was hardly nineteen, and that he was in love with a woman some years his senior.

He dreamed of Mary Hammett and Dr. Gilbert all night, and awoke at last in the height of a personal altercation with that gentleman, resulting from the doctor's treacherous attempt to secure the consent of the young woman to take the place of Mrs. Dr. Gilbert, deceased.

When it is remembered that up to this time Arthur Blague had never exchanged a word with Miss Hammett upon the subject of his passion ; that their interviews had always been brief, hardly extending, in any instance, beyond the simplest and most commonplace courtesies, it will be understood that he got along very fast, and was a great distance in advance of the young woman herself. In truth, she had not the remotest suspicion of the condition of his heart. She understood, respected, nay, admired, his character, and whenever she had mentioned him, she had very freely and frankly praised him, and this was all.

According to his promise, Dr. Gilbert drove to Hucklebury Run the next day. Alighting at the boarding-house, he sent to the mill for Mary Hammett, and was soon in a very interesting conference with her. Half an hour—three-quarters—a whole hour—passed away, and still her looms did not start. Old Ruggles, hobbling feebly about, was in a fidget at the end of the first half-hour, and in a fever at the end of the second. Arthur saw the little gig standing outside, knew what business was in progress, and cursed his own temerity a hundred times within the hour.

At length a messenger came into the mill from the boarding-house, and said that Dr. Gilbert wished to see Arthur Blague. Old Ruggles, even more irritable and exacting than before his sickness, was enraged. He would " teach Dr. Gilbert to let his hands alone ; " and that was what " came of having help that had high notions." He did not undertake to interfere with Arthur's immediate response to the doctor's summons, however, for he could not afford to offend him now; but he laid up a grudge against the doctor which he never forgot.

Arthur entered the boarding-house with great trepidation, and found the doctor cosily cornered with Miss Hammett in the large dining-hall, and talking as easily with her as if he had known her from childhood. His self-possession in the presence of such divinity was something entirely beyond Arthur's comprehension. The young woman rose as Arthur entered, gave him a pleasant greeting, and pointed him to a chair with as much quiet ease as if she were the accustomed queen of a

drawing-room, and were receiving her friends. Arthur
returned her greeting with rather an unnatural degree of
warmth, the doctor thought ; and then the latter said :
" We are getting along pretty well, but Miss Hammett
declines to close any bargain with me unless you are
present."

" You have been kind enough," said Miss Hammett
to Arthur, "to recommend me to Dr. Gilbert as a fit
person to take charge of the centre school. He tells me,
also, that you desire to have me become a member of
your mother's family. You know that I cannot be otherwise than thankful for this mark of your confidence and
respect, but there are some things that must be considered before I enter into your plans. I wish to have you
withdraw your recommendation of me entirely."

" But I cannot do that," said Arthur, puzzled by the
nature of the request.

" Very well ; then you will, of course, tell Dr. Gilbert and me what you know about me."

" I know nothing but what you have taught me," said
Arthur.

Miss Hammett smiled. " That is very little," said
she, " and I wish to remove from you, in the presence of
Dr. Gilbert, all responsibility for me. I did not suppose
you had a competent reason for recommending me, and
I wish the doctor to know it. You have thought it strange
that I am here, I suppose."

Arthur colored, and said that he had.

" Has there been any gossip about me at the Run ? "
inquired Miss Hammett.

" None of any consequence—none that has done you
harm."

" Yet I am a mystery, I suppose."

" They wonder where you came from, why you are
here, what your history is—it is very natural."

" Possibly, though I do not see how. I have never

assumed any thing. I have never sought, as I have never shunned, society; and I presume there are many here whose histories are unknown to the rest. like my own. You are sure that, if I go to Crampton, no rumors will follow me to injure my good name, and those who befriend me?"

The doctor had spent all the time he could, and rose to his feet. "I see what you wish," said he to Miss Hammett, "and as my shoulders are broad, I will release Arthur from all responsibility. I don't care where you came from, what your history is, or what you are here for. I have seen something of men and women in my life, and I say to you frankly, that I thoroughly trust you."

Miss Hammett's blue eyes grew luminous with sensibility. "I thank you, sir," said she, "and now promise me that you will always trust me. I will not say that I am unworthy of your confidence, for I should belie myself; but I must remain to you just as much of a mystery as I am now. Only believe this, Dr. Gilbert, that if you ever learn the truth about me, by any means, it will bring disgrace neither to me nor to those who may befriend me. Will you promise me?" Miss Hammett looked in the doctor's eyes, and gave him her hand.

"It does not seem difficult," said Dr. Gilbert, "to promise you any thing; and now we will consider the engagement closed. I bid you a very good morning." There was something so uncommonly complimentary, nay, gallant, in the doctor's tone and bearing, that Arthur was annoyed.

When the doctor left the room, he left the young man not only annoyed, but oppressed with an uncomfortable sense of youthful insignificance. The self-possessed and easy style in which Dr. Gilbert had borne himself in Miss Hammett's presence, the calm tone of the young woman, the quiet manner in which she had shown him

the valueless and boyish character of his recommendation of her, all tended to dwarf him. He could not
realize at all that he was six feet high, or that he had
risen above his initial teens. Oppressed by a crushing
sense of his insignificance, he blushed under the frank
blue eyes with the thought that he could ever have had
the audacity to love the exalted being who owned them.

"The doctor seems to have a strong, hearty nature,"
said Miss Hammett, resuming conversation.

"And a strong and hearty will within it," responded
Arthur.

"I judge so," said Miss Hammett, "and do not object to it. I think I shall like him."

"I'm afraid you—yes, of course, I think you will,"
said Arthur.

Unsuspicious of Arthur's feelings, Miss Hammett
thanked him for his thoughtfulness, and told him that
her situation at the Run had become almost insupport-
able to her. "I knew that Providence would open a
door for me," said she, "and somehow I felt, when I
first saw you, that you were sent to do it. I think I shall
like your quiet home and your quiet mother very much."
Then she went to the mill to find the proprietor, that
she might give him notice of her intention to leave, and
Arthur returned to his employment, thankful, at least,
that he was considered by Miss Hammett worthy to be
the doorkeeper of Providence for her benefit. He
hoped that Providence would allow him to open doors
for her gentle feet in the years before him, a great many
times.

CHAPTER VIII.

MRS. RUGGLES SPREADS HER MOTHERLY WINGS OVER ARTHUR, AND IS UNGRATEFULLY REPULSED.

THE proprietor would receive no notice from Miss Hammett, but told her angrily that she could go at once. She accordingly made no delay in exchanging her unpleasant quarters at the Run for the comfortable, quiet, and tidy home of Mrs. Blague. Arthur's mother received the new-comer very cordially, for Dr. Gilbert had reassured her. As for Aunt Catharine and Fanny, they were in a state of great excitement about her. The doctor had shown more enthusiasm with relation to Mary Hammett than any woman had excited in him for years. He could not stop talking about her, and could not be stopped even by Aunt Catharine's sharp rallying.

The women can safely be left to make each other's acquaintance and Miss Hammett to commence her school, while Arthur's first experiences as a regular resident of the Run are chronicled.

The life of Mrs. Ruggles and her daughter Leonora had never been more delightful than during the illness of the husband and father, and Arthur's detention in the family. He had introduced a fresh element of life, and it was in accordance with their desire that old Ruggles had invited him to board in his family. The charge would be the same, and the bedding, at least, much more desirable. Arthur shrank from coming in contact with the mother and daughter again; but his duties would be out of the house, and he could shun them pretty effectually, he thought.

Very little did the young man know of the resources of his ingenious landlady. Leonora was always wishing to do a bit of shopping, and Arthur must take her along when he went to the post-office; or she wanted very much to attend an evening meeting, and would walk to Crampton, if Arthur would go for her after factory hours; or she was out at a neighbor's house, and the mother, worrying about her, wished that Arthur would walk over and bring her home. Always, when Arthur returned, the mother had retired, and there was a nice fire to be enjoyed by those who might come in out of the chilly air. Mrs. Ruggles said but little when her husband was present; but when he happened to be absent from a meal, the old range of talk was resumed, and often became almost unendurable.

One afternoon Leonora came home from Crampton, whither she had been on a three days' visit to a boarding-school acquaintance, and brought back to her mother her first knowledge of Arthur's agency in the removal of Mary Hammett, and the stories to which it had given rise in the village. The account which she gave of Miss Hammett's sudden popularity, and the attention shown to her by everybody, filled the mother with utter dismay. Something would have to be done, and done at once; but the matter was delicate, and must be delicately managed. It was managed very delicately—in Mrs. Ruggles' opinion.

Mr. Ruggles went to New York—his first visit after his long confinement—and this was Mrs. Ruggles' golden opportunity. She did not often visit the mill now. Time had been when she would go in and weave all day to help her husband along; but she had gradually got above this kind of amusement, socially, and grown too large for it, physically. Occasionally she waddled into the different rooms, when her husband was away, and held long conversations with those whom she knew, and then went away very proudly, her cap-strings, neckerchief points, and a great deal of woollen yarn following her. No sooner was her husband out of sight, and on his way to market beyond the possibility of turning back to look after something which he had forgotten, than the ponderous woman made her appearance before Arthur Blague, who was endeavoring to regulate matters in the store, so that codfish might be made to assume that subordinate position among dry goods which the nature of the article and good popular usage had designated as legitimate and desirable.

Mrs. Ruggles was very amiable. " Slicking up, eh, Arthur?" said she, with her most amiable and patronizing expression, and looking around upon the shelves in admiration. " I always tell Leonora that I love to see a young man that keeps things slick around him; 'for,' says I to Leonora, 'a young man that keeps things slick around him, and does not leave hair in his comb, but throws it out of the winder, and keeps the dander all off his coat-collar, and scrapes his feet before he comes into the house, always makes a good husband.'"

" I'm afraid I stand a very poor chance," said Arthur.

" You musn't be so modest," continued Mrs. Ruggles, looking Arthur in the face very encouragingly, and endeavoring to convey a great deal of meaning in her look. " 'Now,' says Leonora to me, when I had got through, says she, 'I know who you mean;' says she, 'you are thinking about Arthur Blague.' Dear me, how hot it is in here!" Then Mrs. Ruggles helped herself to a palm-leaf fan, and sat down upon a tea-chest, that creaked as if it were going straight through the world to the place where it came from.

Arthur had no reply to this talk, and was about to leave her on some plea of necessity, when she said, " I come down to the mill a purpose to ask you to come to supper early to-night, for we are going to have something real good. I want," continued Mrs. Ruggles, " that you should feel yourself to home to our house, because you have always had a mother to look after you, and to pervide for you, and, as I tell Leonora, it is my duty to be a mother to you, and to make you feel to home." Mrs. Ruggles looked in Arthur's face with a beaming maternal tenderness that must have won Arthur's heart, if he had trusted himself to look at her.

"Do you love rye flapjacks, Arthur?" inquired the maternal Ruggles, "rye flapjacks, baked in a pile, with the butter and sugar all on?"

Arthur thought he did.

"How much that is like Leonora," resumed the voluble woman. "Says Leonora, says she to me, 'I don't believe but what Arthur Blague loves rye flapjacks, and you shall have some for supper to-night,' says she. 'Arthur shall set to the head of the table, but you shall cut them up,' says she to me, 'for when you cut them up, your hand is so fat, and the cakes is so fat, that when your knife comes down through, and hits the plate, it sounds good and hearty, like the cluck of a hen.' Says I to Leonora, 'It isn't because my hand is fleshy; it's the eggs; the cluck is in the eggs, my dear.' Oh! you ought to have heard Leonora laugh when I said that. Says Leonora, says she to me, 'Mother, I believe you'll kill me.' How hot you do keep it here!" exclaimed Mrs. Ruggles, wiping her face, "I'm getting real sweaty." Then she rose from the tea-chest, which sprang back with a creak of relief, and giving Arthur a parting injunction to "be to supper in season," she sailed out of his presence and out of the mill with a grandeur equal to her gravity.

Arthur did not know what shape the torment of the evening would assume, but he knew very well what its character would be; and when the supper hour arrived, he started off to meet the maternal yearnings of Mrs. Ruggles in any thing but an amiable frame of mind. On entering the half-kitchen, half-parlor, that served as the Ruggles' dining-room, he found Leonora dressed more elaborately than usual, and wearing upon her tame and tiresome features a sad and injured look that was intended to be very touching.

"You must take your old place to the head of the table, Arthur, and perside," said the hearty hostess, overflowing with good-nature and hospitality. She had been pent up within herself so long by the presence of "father," between whom and herself there was no more communion than between the north and south poles, that it was a great treat to be free. Arthur took his seat, and Leonora sat down at his right, but did not bestow upon him a smile—not even a look of gentle patronage.

"Leonora, dear, what makes you so kind of down in the mouth?" inquired the affectionate mother.

"Nothing," replied the young woman, her face inflexibly doleful.

"What ails you, dear? Don't you feel well?"

"Feel well enough."

"Well, well, dear, you must chirk up, or you won't enjoy your flapjacks."

"Flapjacks!" exclaimed Leonora contemptuously, a gust of annoyance escaping from her nostrils, which were always open for the delivery of her miserable emotions.

"I know," said Leonora's mother, sympathetically, "that flapjacks doesn't cure every thing."

Arthur could not help smiling at the fancy which sprang in his mind of a very hot flapjack tied over Mrs. Ruggles' mouth, and another bound upon Miss Ruggles' heart. Miss Ruggles lifted her languid eyes in time to see the smile, and sighed.

"You should remember, dear," suggested the mother, "that you have gentleman's company to-night, and that whatever sufferings you have, you should cover up, so's to make it pleasant. We're making company of Arthur to-night, you know, and you musn't look on him as a boarder. I've been thinking all the afternoon, how pleasant it would be to see you and Arthur eating flapjacks together."

" A good deal Arthur cares for us, I guess," said Miss Ruggles, taking in a large mouthful of the unctuous staple upon her plate.

" Now, my dear, you shall not talk so," declared the mother very emphatically; " it's just like a young girl like you to believe all the stories that's told you. You shan't go down to Crampton again, and get your head full of things to distress you. You see," Mrs. Ruggles explained to Arthur, " Leonora has been down to Crampton village, and she heard all about that Hammett girl's being to your mother's, and she heard it was you who got her away from father's mill, and what else she heard, I don't know; but she thinks now that you don't think so much of your old friends as you used to. ' Nonsense ! ' says I to Leonora. ' Do you suppose that Arthur Blague would take up with a poor creature that he don't know nothing about, and that there don't anybody know nothing about ? Nonsense,' says I."

" It's very romantic, mother," said Miss Ruggles, whose spirits were improving. " She might be a princess in disguise, you know."

Arthur's " flapjacks " stuck in his throat, and he felt conscious of growing angry. He would not trust himself to speak.

" Leonora," said Mrs. Ruggles, in a tone of reprimand, " you are letting your feelings run away with you. Arthur Blague is a sensible young man, and he has feelings ; and because he thinks he's called upon to help a poor outcast girl, that hasn't any friends, and is a suspicious character, and wants to take her away from temptations, and give her a chance to get along in the world, it isn't for us who's more favored, to pick flaws with him, or to say, Why do ye do so ? "

Human nature, as it existed in Arthur Blague, could stand no more. "Who says that Mary Hammett is a suspicious character?" said he, his eyes burning with anger. "Who dares to breathe a word against her?"

Mrs. Ruggles giggled. "Now you look handsome," said she. "Look at him, Leonora. I never see you when you was mad before. I said to Leonora once, says I, 'Arthur Blague has got it in him, you may depend. Them eyes of his wasn't given to him for nothing,' says I. Have some more flapjacks, won't you? Your cup is out, I declare. Why didn't you pass it? Leonora, you should have seen that Arthur's cup is out, you know my eyes is feeble."

Arthur looked her steadily in the face till she had finished, and then said : "Mrs. Ruggles, the woman of whom you have been speaking is not without friends, and will not want a friend while I live ; and I will not sit anywhere quietly and hear her spoken against. A woman's good name is not a thing to be trifled with, especially by a woman ; and if you have anything to say against her, I will leave your table."

The maternal brain was puzzled, but the maternal ingenuity was not conquered. "It's a very kind thing in you, Arthur, to take up for those that ain't in persition to take up for themselves. If there's one thing that I've always stood up for, it's my own seck. I ought to know," continued Mrs. Ruggles, "how easy it is to say things, and how hard it is to prove it ; but don't you think that this Hammett girl is—well, I don't mean but what it's all right, you know—but don't you think she is kind of artful? They say Dr. Gilbert is quite took up with her, and that folks think she wouldn't have any objections to being his second wife."

"I say I will not hear Miss Hammett abused," said Arthur, rising from the table in uncontrollable excitement. "She is a noble woman, and no decent man,

young or old, can help admiring and respecting her.
There is not a woman in Hucklebury Run, or in all
Crampton, who is her equal, and if you have any thing
more to say against her, I will leave the room."

Leonora heard the young man's declaration, and,
rising from the table, bounced out of the room. The
maternal Ruggles watched her as she retired, with fond
and painful solicitude. Then spreading her handkerchief over her fat palm, she put it to her eyes, and exclaimed : " You have broke her heart ; Arthur, you've
broke her heart."

" Whose heart ? " inquired Arthur.

" Oh ! no matter now," sobbed Mrs. Ruggles. " This
is the thanks we get for helping poor folks, and making
much of them that can't appreciate what's done for
them. But the world is full of disappointments. Little
did I think, when I took you in, that I was ruining the
peace of my own heart's blood."

" What do you mean ? What under heaven are you
talking about ? " said Arthur excitedly.

" Oh ! no matter now ! It's too late," continued Mrs.
Ruggles, holding her handkerchief over her eyes with
one hand, and attending to her nose with the other.
" Go on, ruining hopes, and—and—scattering firebrands.
It's woman's lot, but I did hope that my own flesh and
blood would be spared."

" If you mean to say or intimate," said Arthur,
" that I have ever, by thought, word, or deed, intended
to make your daughter believe that I love her, or wish to
marry her, or that she has any legitimate expectation
that I shall marry her, you are very much mistaken ;
for I do not love her, never did love her, and I never
will love her."

" Oh ! that's always the way, when peace is gone and
the heart is broke ! " sobbed Mrs. Ruggles.

" Mrs. Ruggles," said Arthur, losing all patience, " I

wish you to understand that I consider you and your daughter a pair of fools, and that I always considered you so."

On the announcement of this very decided and very uncomplimentary opinion, the young woman whose heart was broken and whose peace was ruined reappeared, having previously so far compromised her determination to retire to her room as to stop upon the opposite side of the dining-room door, and listen at the keyhole.

"Pretty talk before ladies, Mr. Arthur Blague, I should think," said Miss Ruggles, resuming her seat at the table.

"These is Crampton manners, I expect, dear," said Mrs. Ruggles sarcastically, forgetting about her eyes, and dropping her handkerchief in her lap. "O my dear! we've had such an escape—such an escape!"

"I'm sure I wish Miss Hammett much joy," said Miss Ruggles tartly.

"Help yourself to more flapjacks, dear," urged the mother, "and finish out your supper. We s'posed we had a gentleman to the table, didn't we, dear? But we s'posed wrong, for once. Some folks is brung up perlite, and some isn't, and them that isn't we must make allowances for."

Then Leonora giggled, and the mother giggled, and grew amazingly—almost alarmingly—merry. Arthur looked at them in quiet contempt, and rapidly determined upon the course it was best for him to pursue. He knew that he had been hasty, but he could not bring himself to believe that he should not repeat the same indiscretion under the same circumstances.

"I bid you good-night," said Arthur, when the laughter of the mother and daughter had subsided sufficiently to allow him to be heard. "I presume it will not be your wish that I remain longer in your house, and I will look out for other lodgings to-night."

"Suit yourself, and you'll suit me," responded the old

woman. "The quicker you and your duds are out of this house, the better I shall feel. Young men that takes factory girls out of the mill, and keeps them to his home, don't make this house any safer when the head of the family is gone abroad."

The idea of being dangerous society for Mrs. Ruggles and her daughter was so ludicrous to Arthur, that he could not help smiling, and turning on his heel, he took his hat, and without more words went to the mill. His first business was to find Cheek, and to reveal to him the necessities of his condition. Cheek scratched his head with great perplexity. "We can feed any quantity of people at the boarding-house, but we can't sleep 'em," said Cheek. "I sleep," continued he, "with Bob Mullaly, the Irishman, and if I can only get him to take to his old hammock under the roof again, you can sleep with me."

This Bob Mullaly was an old sailor, and by no means an unpopular item of the population of Hucklebury Run. He told yarns to the boys, every one of which they believed, and was always trying to deceive himself with the idea that he was on board ship. His brief mornings he spent in splicing ropes. Sundays he devoted to weaving hammocks, whenever he could provide himself with the necessary twine. Occasionally, a window of the mill directly over the pond would be raised, and out would fly a bucket at a rope's end, which would very certainly go straight into the water, and dip itself full, and then Bob Mullaly would haul it in as if he were leaning over a ship's side, and were dipping from the sea. He sang sea-songs in the minor key, and with a very husky voice, all day, while at his work.

"We've been trying to get rid of the old cock this ever so long," said Cheek, "and this is a first-rate chance, because he likes you, and will be glad to do you a good turn."

"Oh! I won't deprive Bob of his bed," said Arthur.

"He might just as well sleep in a hammock," said Cheek, "such sleeping as he does, as not. He's always agrunting, and agroaning, and chawing, and spitting, and gritting his teeth, and snoring. Lord! you'd think he was fighting, and dying, and eating his dinner all at once. I'd just as soon sleep with a highpoppytaymus. You don't know any thing about it," continued Cheek. "You wouldn't sleep any for three nights if he was within ten feet of you. Oh! I tell you, he has the nightmare, and the nighthorse, and half a dozen colts, and a yellow dog sometimes."

Under this representation of Bob Mullaly's terrific nocturnal habits, Arthur consented that Cheek should apply to the old salt for the desired favor. Accordingly, that young man sought him out in his room, and succeeded very speedily in his object. Arthur then returned to the Ruggles mansion, entered the door, and was surprised to find awaiting him in the passage, his valise, packed and locked, and ready for transportation. Leonora was not visible, but Mrs. Ruggles met him, candle in hand, and told him she "wasn't going to have him running all over her house." "Your things is all in the portmanter, there," said the old woman, "and all I've got to say is, good riddance to bad rubbidge!"

Having finished her happily limited speech, and Arthur having taken the valise in his hand, she turned, and left him to find his way out in the dark and alone. As the young man left the house, he heard mother and daughter laughing loudly, and thought that, for women whose hearts had been so terribly dealt with, they were very merry indeed.

Leaving his valise in the mill until the close of the labors of the evening, Arthur resumed his duties, which he continued long after the bell had dismissed the operatives. Cheek came, and sat quietly down near his desk to wait for him, and introduce him to the lodging-rooms of the mill. As Arthur closed the ledger, and wiped his pen, Cheek said : " Blague, you musn't expect any thing very grand now. I stand it well enough, because I'm used to it ; but you have been in another line, you know. You haven't slept in an ash-hole to keep away from old Bob Lampson, and been tucked in with a pair of tongs, as I have."

Arthur said that he thought he could live as other people did, if he should try ; and taking down his hat, and taking up his valise, he announced himself ready for bed. They went out of the mill, leaving the watchman making his ceaseless round of the rooms, and crossed a spongy patch of garden to reach the lodging-room. The building which contained this room was constructed originally for a wood-shed. It was narrow in proportion to its length, and all the lower portion was open to wind and weather. The necessities of the boarding-house had induced the proprietor to construct and finish off, in a rough way, a hall running the entire length of the shed, with a room at one end as a general depository of trunks and clothing. Into this hall as many beds were crowded as it could contain, and at the same time allow the lodgers sufficient room to dress in. In the winter, the carpetless floor gave free passage upward to the wind that swept through the open wood-shed beneath ; and in the summer, the hot roof imparted to the atmosphere a stifling power, that rendered sleep well nigh impossible, while the idea of ventilation was lost sight of entirely.

Arthur and Cheek entered the wood-shed, and climbed the dark stairway. On entering the hall, they found a few dim lamps burning, and the atmosphere pervaded by the stench of unclean breath and unclean clothing. Sitting on his trunk, surrounded by half a dozen boys, one foul-mouthed fellow was singing an obscene song. Another was on the floor, near the stove, greasing his boots. Others, still, were already in bed, cursing those who would not permit them to sleep. Old men of sixty, and boys of almost tender years, were crowded into this dirty hole, where there was no such thing as privacy, or personal decency, possible. All heard the same foul songs, all listened to the same obscene stories, all alike were deprived of the privilege of reading and meditation; nay, of prayer itself, had such a privilege been desired. It was a place where health of body and of mind was impossible, and where morals would inevitably rot. Arthur thought again, as he had many times before, of old Ruggles' boast—" We are all alike down to the Run ; " and he comprehended, as he had never done before, how the levelling process had been accomplished.

As Arthur spoke to one and another in a cordial and respectful way, the confusion subsided by degrees, and a new sense of decency and dignity seemed to find its way into the hearts of all. Perceiving that he wished to retire, all suddenly concluded that it was time to go to bed; and in a few minutes the motley crowd were stretched upon their hard and dirty lodgings. Arthur noticed that, as Cheek lay down, he took a position directly upon the outer rail of the bedstead, leaving to his new bedfellow nearly the entire bed. Arthur expostulated, but Cheek declared that he always slept so, and could never close his eyes in the world if he were obliged to do it in the middle of a bed. If Arthur liked the middle of a bed, he had better take it. If he could have his way, he would never have a bed more than nine inches wide, and he would be willing to bet any reasonable amount of money that he could sleep on the ridgepole of the building without rolling off. Arthur read the good fellow's motives, and was, on the whole, too weary to refuse to indulge him in self-sacrifice.

There were too many weary bodies and restless dreams
in the hall that night to allow an unaccustomed lodger
more than a few disturbed and unrefreshing snatches of
sleep. Bob Mullaly, swung up in his hammock between
the wall of the room and the eaves of the building, had
a great sea-fight that night, in which not only immense
navies were engaged, but, judging from the sounds which
found their way through the wall, a large number of sea-
monsters took part.

The night was a long one to Arthur ; but, before a particle of daylight made its appearance, the first morning
bell was rung by the watchman. Everybody seemed to
awake angry ; they cursed the bell, and cursed the watchman who rang it ; but still it rang, persistently, torment-
ingly, outrageously, until it became impossible to sleep
another moment. One after another tumbled out of
bed. Little boys that slept like logs were shaken violently by the men, or pulled bodily out upon the floor
and set upon their feet. Arthur lay and watched them
for a time, by the dim light of the lamps. Half a dozen
boys near him dressed themselves without opening their
eyes, and went stumbling, dirty, and unrefreshed, out of
the room to their places in the mill.

" Sich is life !" exclaimed Cheek with a comical sigh,
as he turned and shook Arthur's shoulder.

" God pity those who cannot take it easily, like you,
Cheek," said Arthur.

Cheek's toilet was very quickly made ; and, as the
second bell was ringing, he left Arthur to dress at his
leisure. The young man was at last alone, and full of
the thoughts which such a night's experience was calculated to excite in such a nature as his. Here was a little
world of misery, set off from the consciousness of the
great world around it, without a redeeming or purifying
element in it. There was no hope—no expectation of
any thing better. It only sought for the lowest grade of

enjoyments; it had no emulations; it pursued no object higher than the attainment of food to eat, and clothes to wear; it was ruled by an exacting will, and kept in essential slavery by the fear of the loss of a livelihood. Then he thought of his own misfortunes and hardships, and thanked God for showing him how greatly above the lot of multitudes of men he had been blest. He thanked Him also for enlarging the field of his sympathies, and for giving him an intimation, through the pity inspired by his contemplations, of that divinely tender consideration which the Good Father bestows upon the outcast and the oppressed, the ignorant and the degraded, wherever human souls look out from human eyes.

Arthur Blague was getting his education, and we will leave him for a while.

CHAPTER IX.

MISS GILBERT COMPLETES HER NOVEL—A GREAT SUCCESS, IN THE OPINION OF HER FRIENDS.

THE snow had passed away, and Spring, shy-faced, and shivering under sheltered rocks, had breathed the sweet arbutus into bloom, and sky-born bluebirds came down on the air of wondrous mornings, with throats full of fresh and fragrant melody. The days grew still and long. On the hills around the village of Crampton, the sugar-fires were smoking; and in the yards of the quiet dwellings the sturdy chopper's axe was swung all day long above the winter-gathered piles. Sounds came from a great way off, startling the universal stillness. Dogs basked all day on southern door-steps, and cattle, turned out from dark stalls, tried horns and heads with each other, or frisked in ungraceful, elephantine play.

There was a sound in the earth, as if myriad fairies were at work preparing juices for the grass and fruits and flowers—a sound of tiny footsteps and multitudinous bells, deep down in caverns and dingles ; and here and there a bank smiled back in downy green the sun's first radiant favors.

On one of these beautiful spring days, Miss Fanny Gilbert, grown weary and thin with her hard winter's labor, sat in her room, giving the finishing touches to her novel. It had been a task of far greater magnitude than she had anticipated. Oftentimes she had been quite discouraged. Animated by no purpose but to win popular applause, the day of repayment for all her self-denial and labor seemed so far distant that not unfrequently she felt tempted to throw her manuscript into the fire. Had she been at work for money, or had she been animated by a desire to accomplish some great reform, or had she been engaged in doing some work of duty, as one of God's willing laborers, then she might have been content. But always the eye of the public was upon her. What will the critics think of this ? What will the world think of this ? What shall be the reward, in popular praise, for all this tax upon the heart and brain, and all this toil of hand ? These were the questions that were always before her. Frequently her pen dropped from her fingers, and her imagination flew away like a bee to nestle among the flowers and suck the honey that were not yet hers.

Dr. Gilbert had been too decided in his opposition to Fanny's project, to betray any anxiety to make himself acquainted with its progress ; yet he was very curious to see the new book, or to hear it read. It had been enough for Aunt Catharine that the doctor opposed his daughter to secure her sympathy for the young authoress, and as Fanny felt praise to be absolutely necessary to her, she had read every chapter to her aunt, and had been very much inspired by the good woman's comments. Aunt Catharine said there was a great deal more love in it than she cared any thing about, but it was "real good, every bit of it." Fanny had not a very high regard for her aunt's literary judgment, but she got the praise, and the praise answered its purpose.

Fanny laid aside her manuscript, and raised the window of her room, upon which the sun shone warmly, and looked upon the scene. Her weary brain and heart sought for refreshment. She remembered the springs that had come and gone during her childhood and girlhood, recalled the golden time when a perfect spring-day flooded all her sensibilities with sunshine, and crowded her heart to overflowing with a sweet, exultant joy. She recalled the pervasive spirit of poetry that informed and enveloped the rudest objects, warmed by the sun of spring, and longed, in forgetfulness of self and of care, to bathe her heart in it once more. Oh! for the fresh, innocent, careless gladness in existence that had once held its honeyed centre in her soul!

She looked out, saw the sun and the deep blue sky, heard the carol of the bluebird, marked the smoke slowly curling up from the sugar-groves, listened to the awaking murmurs of the season, watched the uncouth gambols of the rude forms of life in the farm-yard; but the old joy would not come back to her. **Her** heart seemed dry and dead—only living in an unsatisfied yearning. Her sensibilities, kept tense through the long winter, and overwrought among scenes of fictitious joy and woe, refused to respond to the simple influences of nature. There was no spring for her. She had stood so long in a false attitude with relation to a true, natural life, and had labored so long in obedience to an illegitimate motive, that nature could find no open passage to her soul—no responsive chamber within it.

It was noon. Across the common, the door of the old

school-house opened, and forth poured a chattering throng of boys and girls. They seemed like so many senseless dolls to her. Their noise annoyed—almost disgusted her. She preferred, after all, her own insensitive isolation to joy that had no meaning in it, and pleasure that could not reason of itself. Soon the form of Mary Hammett made its appearance. She passed through the group, and every eye seemed to turn to her in love. With a calm step, looking up and around, and apparently drinking in with fulness of delight the influences of the day, she crossed the common and entered the dwelling of Mrs. Blague. Fanny watched for her appearance at her window, separated from her own by two or three patches of garden. Miss Hammett entered her room, raised her window, looked out without seeing her friend, and then turned back. But Fanny could not keep her eyes from the window of her neighbor, whom, in one or two interviews, she had learned to respect profoundly. At length she caught the sound of a low song, rising and falling in Miss Hammett's room; and then there burst out, sweet and clear as the notes of the blue-bird on the elm that drooped over the house, the words:

> " Thou art, O God! the life and light
>   Of all this wondrous world we see;
> Its glow by day, its smile by night,
>   Are but reflections caught from Thee."

Ah! yes. Fanny's heart was greedy for the praise of men—thirsting for the adoration of the world—and it was dry. Her neighbor's heart was overflowing with adoration and praise of the paternal fountain of her life, and it was as fresh as if it were beaded with the dew of childhood. For the moment, the massive manuscript upon her table looked utterly meaningless and worthless to her. Had the paper been blank, it would have seemed of higher value. She recalled her mother's pious counsels, her neglect of her own higher duties, and then she closed the window and wept. How happy are those, thought Miss Gilbert, who have no ambition, who have never tasted the world's praise, and do not feel moved to great achievements to secure it! Would God she were like others! The womanly nature was, for the moment, predominant within her, and she longed for sympathy—longed to pour out her heart to Mary Hammett.

If Miss Hammett would hear her book, and advise her, would it not be well? She would go and see her. But if the young woman should not like her book, and should tell her so, how would she receive the criticism? Her whole nature, she felt, would revolt against the adverse judgment at once. If Miss Hammett should be pleased, it would be very well; if displeased, she would turn upon her heel and rely upon herself.

Nightfall came, and with it the close of Miss Hammett's school for the day. When Fanny saw the teacher enter Mrs. Blague's dwelling, she threw a shawl upon her shoulders, and walked over to call upon her. Miss Hammett invited Fanny to her room, and after a brief conversation the latter said : "Miss Hammett, I have been doing a very foolish and a very indiscreet thing."

"The first, I presume, in your life," said Miss Hammett with a smile ; "but confession half-atones for it."

"You cannot guess what it is."

"I am a very indifferent guesser," said Miss Hammett. "You are not engaged ? "

"No," and Miss Gilbert laughed almost derisively.

"You haven't kissed the cat ? "

"No."

"Nor your father ? "

"No," and then Miss Gilbert laughed merrily.

"You see I can never guess," said Miss Hammett, "and you may as well tell me at once."

" I have written a book."

Miss Hammett held up both hands in astonishment, that had quite as much of the genuine as of the fictitious in it. " There is only one thing worse than this that I know of," said she, and shook her head with mock seriousness.

" What is that?" inquired Fanny.

" To publish it."

Fanny's eye flashed, the color mounted to her forehead, her lip quivered, and her tongue refused its office. Miss Hammett was on her knees in a moment, and throwing her arms tenderly around Fanny's waist, exclaimed : " Dear! dear! what have I done? Tell me, Miss Gilbert—have I offended you? Have I wounded you?"

Ah! how the woman in Fanny melted before this delicate demonstration ! She bowed her head on Miss Hammett's shoulder, and there in a precious embrace she poured out her heart, revealing all her hopes, ambitions, expectations. When it was all over, both rose to their feet, and, with their arms around each other, paced back and forth in the apartment. Miss Hammett, whose quick sensibility and insight had enabled her to read her companion's heart at once, was pained. " We are very different to each other," said she. " To me, the idea of making my name public property—of permitting it to go abroad as an author, subject to criticism, and to unjust and frivolous judgments—the thought of being talked about in private parlors and public places, and of coining my heart's best emotions and my sweetest imaginations into words which the world can use as a glass by which it may read my life, is very terrible. If I could write books, I might possibly do so ; but I could only be induced to allow them to be published by the assurance that I should never be known as their author."

" And have you no desire to be admired, to be loved,

9

to be praised by the world ? " inquired Miss Gilbert warmly.

" By my world, yes ; " and Miss Hammett's eyes filled with tears. " Miss Gilbert, the time will come when even one soul will be more than all the world to you — when you would give all the praises of the world's thousand millions — when you would give the sun, moon, and stars, if they were yours, to monopolize the admiration, the love, and the praise of one man. A woman's true world is a very small world in its dimensions, yet it is the heart's universe. The great world is fickle, and must be so. It lifts its idols to their pedestals, and worships them for an hour ; then it kicks them off, and grinds them into ruin, that other and fresher objects of worship may take their places. Besides, a woman cannot be content to be a sharer. She claims monopoly, and, in the richest world she ever knows, she has it."

Fanny made no immediate response, and the pair walked back and forth in silence for a minute. At length she said : " And has fame positively no charms for you ? Do you never envy those kings and queens in the realm of intellect, who walk, in the sight of the people, with crowns upon their heads ? "

" Envy them, Miss Gilbert ? I pity them—rather, perhaps, I am grateful that God did not impose upon me their responsibilities, their labors, their isolation, and their sad temptations to envy each other. I have no experience to inform me, and no direct testimony from the experience of those I have known ; but my heart tells me that the sweetest reward of great achievements is the excitement to a tenderer love, and a more thorough devotion of the one heart and the little circle of hearts with which the author holds direct personal communion. A great man, without a loving heart at his side, or a circle of loving hearts around him, must, it seems to me, have a love for all mankind, such as only a great Christian heart can know, to keep him from committing suicide. My heart tells me, too, that we can only find reward in working for those we love. A woman, working for the world's praise, will always have to measure the satisfaction she finds in that praise by the same cup that holds her love. How much do you love the world, Miss Fanny ? "

" I don't know—I haven't thought—it is all new to me," replied Fanny, convinced for the moment of her selfishness.

" Now," said Miss Hammett, kissing her companion, " I will stop preaching. I am sure I did not mean to let my tongue run on so. But you shall preach to me now. Do me the favor to read your book to me, will you ? It will be delightful employment for half a dozen evenings."

" I came here on purpose to ask you to hear me read it," replied Fanny.

" You are very kind."

" On the contrary," said Fanny, " I am entirely selfish. I wish to have you tell me what you think of it, and to suggest alterations where you see opportunities for improvement."

" Ah ! Miss Gilbert, I'm afraid," replied Miss Hammett, shaking her head, and looking pleasantly into Fanny's eyes. " I'm afraid, I'm afraid."

" Really, now," said Fanny earnestly, " I want your opinion on my book, and I promise to be reasonable, and tractable, and patient."

" I can deny you no service," replied Miss Hammett, " but if I engage to criticise your book, I cannot enjoy it. Criticism and enjoyment never go hand in hand. If I had undertaken to criticise even this beautiful morning, it would have shut out all the joy it brought me. So you see that I am very selfish, too."

" You do not decline ? " said Fanny.

"No, I do not decline, but you must promise me some things first. You must promise to regard me as an elder sister—one who loves you, and has a real interest in your happiness and your success—as one whose pain it would be to pain you—as one whose love and truth to you can only be vindicated in a matter like this by the most thorough faithfulness. Further than this, you shall promise that, whatever may be the result of our interviews over your book, it shall never interfere with our friendship."

"I promise—in token of which I hereby—" the act took the place of the word, the act being performed by organs that could not speak and kiss at the same time.

So Fanny promised that after tea she would bring in her book, and begin the task agreed upon. As she left the door of Mrs. Blague, she felt that she had been shorn of some very comfortable delusions. She had caught a pretty distinct glimpse of her own heart, and of the worthless nature of its ruling motives. Her book, that had looked so large to her, and had seemed to fill so much of the world, had become almost contemptible. She was about to commit it to the critical eye of the village schoolmistress—lately a factory-girl—at most, a very insignificant portion of that great public for which the book was written; yet her heart sank within her. Miss Hammett loved her, and would be kind, yet she shrank from her judgment. How would she fare with the great world that did not love her, and would not be kind?

The story of the subsequent interviews between the authoress and her gentle critic would be tedious, and needs not to be told. With the tact of a truly kind heart, Miss Hammett praised the excellencies of the book, and pointed out its defects. When alone, Fanny often quarrelled with the judgment that had been rendered—rebelled against it—but ended by adopting it, and profiting by it. Many pages she rewrote entirely, but her self-love was grievously wounded during the process, and it was only by the severest self-discipline that she was kept from entertaining bitter and unworthy thoughts of the kind woman who had humiliated her. It was not pleasant to think that the book was better for Miss Hammett's ministry. It was not agreeable to remember that her own good judgment had been called in question, and that she had been obliged, as a rational woman, to yield the point.

But there was another ordeal, lying between Miss Hammett and the public. Her father had not heard the book read, and she knew that he would not allow it to be published until he should become acquainted with its contents in some way. Though shaken by the arguments and the sentiments of the schoolmistress, she had never for a moment relinquished the idea of publication. Her overweening desire for public applause had slept at intervals, but it had only slept to awake with new vigor. As she passed out from Miss Hammett's immediate personal influence, the old dream of fame and a career filled her and enveloped her.

She was shrewd enough, and knew enough of her father's character, to detect the real gratification he felt, when, with assumed coolness, he received the announcement that her book was concluded. It belonged to a class of books, he said, that he never read, and he felt himself incompetent, in many respects, to judge of its merits. Would it not be well to invite in Mr. and Mrs. Wilton? Both were people of taste and culture, and he should rely much upon their judgment.

Fanny declared herself ready for any arrangement, and the doctor walked over to the parsonage, and talked up the matter with the good pastor and his wife. They were ready for the proposition of the doctor. They always were ready for any proposition of the doctor. He ruled the parish, and they had a profound respect for him, partly from that fact, and partly from the fact that he was honestly worthy of it.

Fanny approached this ordeal without a particle of trepidation. Miss Hammett had helped her to a more just appreciation of her book than she had before possessed. She knew where it was strong, and she felt, furthermore, that those who would listen to her were more in sympathy with the motive which actuated her than Miss Hammett had been. The evening for the reading was set, and, at the appointed hour, Miss Fanny Gilbert had her audience about her. Aunt Catharine, who had heard it all piecemeal, wished to hear it entire, and was in her seat. Fanny began, and as, occasionally, she looked out upon her auditors, the eager look, the expression of undisguised interest, filled her with proud satisfaction. Mr. Wilton gave frequent exclamations of delight, and the reader gathered new excitement with every page. Her eyes flashed, her cheeks glowed, her voice grew round and full and flexible, and her audience looked on and listened in astonishment. Dr. Gilbert, as he became aware of the impression produced upon the others, forgot his resolution to be cool and reserved, and took no pains to conceal his gratification. Mr. Wilton was amazed. Mrs. Wilton was overwhelmed. The voice of the reader flowed on and on, never faltering, never pausing. The little clock with its tiny bell struck the hours, but no one heard it. " Eight—nine—ten—eleven —twelve— " articulated with silver sound the silvery-sounding revelation ; and then the last page was tossed from Miss Gilbert's hands. Mrs. Wilton threw her arms around Fanny's neck, and kissed her again and again. Mr. Wilton, inspired about equally with the book and the pretty scene enacted between his wife and Fanny, jumped to his feet, and clapped his hands wildly. Ah, Dr. Gilbert ! Dr. Gilbert ! Why can you not sit still ?

What are you doing? Shaking hands with Aunt Catharine, and laughing like a madman, to keep yourself from crying! Ah, Dr. Gilbert! what a fool!

And what did Fanny do? What did Fanny say? Nothing, but she thought this : "If I could only get the ear of the world as I have got the ears of these! If I could only get the praise of the world as I get the praise of these!" The evening's triumph was only significant to her as an earnest of a prouder triumph to come, and an assurance of the co-operation of her father in her schemes. She received his congratulations amiably, but in that queenly kind of way which showed that she regarded them as her right, rendered to her as a matter of course.

"It's getting rather late," said the doctor, pulling out his watch and winding it, "but you would oblige us very much, Mr. Wilton, by advising us with relation to a publisher."

Fanny smiled at her father's ready assumption of partnership, and recalled the scene in which he played so different a part in the early history of her enterprise ; but she said nothing, while Mr. Wilton rubbed the spot on his head where he had apparently laid aside a list of publishers, and prepared his opinion of their respective merits.

"There's the great house of the Kilgores," suggested Mr. Wilton. "They have a larger list of publications, and a larger correspondence, than any other house in the country."

Dr. Gilbert frowned, and drummed on the arms of his chair. "Is it not possible," said he, "that, in consequence of such a range of business, they would fail to give to the work that degree of consideration which our interest, not to say any thing of its merits, demands ?"

"Possibly," responded the pastor, adding, "then there is the enterprising house of Kapp & Demigh. They are famous, you know, for advertising freely, and pushing things. I should say the Kilgores, if you can get them, and Kapp & Demigh if the Kilgores decline —an event which, I confess, does not seem very likely to take place."

" I have no fears," said Fanny proudly, " if they will read the book."

" I'm sure you need not have any, my dear," responded Mrs. Wilton warmly.

" Well, perhaps we had better write to both," said the doctor, with a shrewd twinkle of the eye, " and if they should both want the book, it may help us to get more favorable terms."

So it was settled, and the Wiltons took their leave. The doctor then advanced to the table, and copied into his note-book the name of the volume which he had decided to offer through the mail to the great publishing firms of Kilgore Brothers, and Kapp & Demigh, and this was the record :

TRISTRAM TREVANION;

OR,

THE HOUNDS OF THE WHIPPOORWILL HILLS :

A Novel,

BY EVERARD EVEREST, Gent.

" Why do you choose the name of a gentleman for your *nom de plume*, Fanny ? " inquired the doctor, spelling over the name slowly, to see if he had got it right.

" Oh ! a fancy," replied Fanny languidly. " Besides, it seems to me to be written in a masculine style."

" But I—I should think you would like to have your own name associated with the book," suggested the doctor.

" If it should prove to be a success," replied Fanny, " there are ways enough, I suppose, for securing such an association. Meantime, a little mystery will hurt nothing, and may help a great deal."

The doctor, wholly unsophisticated in matters of authorship, did not see through the whole of his daughter's plan, but he saw that she had a plan with which she was satisfied, and thought best to trust her. Fanny gathered up her manuscript, and, bidding her father " Good night," retired to her room.

It was impossible, of course, for Dr. Gilbert to go to bed with work undone, that it was possible to do. So he took his pen, and addressed to the great publishing house of the Kilgores in New York the following letter, a duplicate of which he also wrote and addressed to Messrs. Kapp & Demigh :

" GENTLEMEN :—Will you allow me to call your attention to a novel, just completed by my daughter, Miss Fanny Gilbert, entitled, ' Tristram Trevanion, or, The Hounds of the Whippoorwill Hills, by Everard Everest, Gent. ? ' I am not, perhaps, a reliable judge of its merits. Paternal partiality and exclusive devotion to scientific and business pursuits may, in a degree, unfit me to decide upon the position in the world of art and the world of popular favor it is calculated to achieve. In fact, I have not relied upon my own judgment at all. The book has been read to competent literary friends, and their voice is unanimous and most enthusiastic in its favor. The impression is that *it cannot fail to be a great success.* With your practical eyes, you will recognize, I doubt not, in the title of the book, the characteristic poetic instincts of the writer and her power to clothe her conceptions in choicest language. We have concluded to offer this book to your celebrated house for publication. It is our desire that it may come before the public under the most favorable auspices—such, in fact, as your imprint alone would give it. I think I can promise you the undivided support of the local press, as I certainly will pledge all the personal efforts on behalf of the volume which my relations to the writer will permit me to make. I may say to you, in this connection, that I have a large medical practice, extending throughout the region, and that I know nearly every family in the county.　Please reply at once, and oblige, &c., &c.

"THEOPHILUS GILBERT, M.D.

"P.S.—How shall we send the manuscript to you ?

"T. G."

Dr. Gilbert re-read his twin epistles carefully, folded and sealed them, and went to bed.

CHAPTER X.

DR. GILBERT AMONG THE NEW YORK PUBLISHERS.

IT seemed an age to Dr. Gilbert and his daughter before the responses from the New York publishers reached the Crampton post-office.　When, at last, both letters were delivered at the wicket, the doctor confessed to himself a greater degree of excitement than he had felt for many a day.　As he walked home with them in his pocket, he busied himself with framing an apology to Kapp & Demigh for giving the book to the Kilgores, for he could hardly doubt that both had accepted his proposition.　"I've got something for you, Fanny," said he, as he entered the house.　Fanny followed him into his office, and took a seat.　Then the doctor broke the seal of one of the letters, unfolded it, and read :

"DR. G. :

"DR. SIR—Yours about book Tristram, &c., rec'd.　Novels except by well-known writers not in our line, and we must decline.

"Permit us to call yr attention to catalogue of professional books wh we mail with this.　Shall be happy to fill any orders.

"Yours respectfully,

"KILGORE BROTHERS,

"pr RUDDOCK."

"Impertinent cub!" exclaimed the doctor, as he finished this brief and business-like production, his face swollen with sudden wrath. "You may depend upon it, Fanny," said he, without venturing to look in her face, "that not one of the Kilgores has ever seen my letter—not one—no, not one. This understrapper, Haddock, or Hemlock, or Ruddock, or whatever his name is, has not only replied on his own responsibility, but has had the impudence to stick his catalogue in my face."

While the doctor was excitedly delivering himself of these words, his daughter sat perfectly silent, with cheeks as pale as ashes and a heart that thumped so violently against its walls that her whole frame was shocked by it. He sat for a minute, and looked at the letter of Kapp & Demigh, hardly daring to take it up. At length he opened it, and read it silently. Fanny watched him, and assured herself that its contents were no more favorable than those of its predecessor.

"We are disappointed here again, Fanny," said the doctor with a mollified tone, "but these fellows are gentlemen, and attend to their own business. Will you hear it?"

Fanny said, "Of course," and her father read:

"To Dr. Theophilus Gilbert:

"My Dear Sir—Your favor, relating to the manuscript novel of your daughter, is at hand, and has been carefully considered. The title of the book seems to us to be exceedingly attractive, and, in a favorable condition of the market, could not fail of itself to sell an entire edition. Unfortunately, the market for novels is very dull now, and, still more unfortunately for us, our engagements are already so numerous, that were the market the best, we should not feel at liberty to undertake your book. We could not possibly make room for it and do it justice. Thanking you for your kind preference of our house, we remain,

"Yours faithfully,
"Kapp & Demigh."

"P. S.—Have you tried Ballou & Gold?"

Father and daughter sat for some time in reflective disappointment, but neither was discouraged. It was not the habit of Dr. Gilbert to undertake an enterprise and fail of carrying it through ; but he comprehended the fact, at once, that he could do nothing by mail. The process was too slow and indirect. He must attend to the matter personally. He must go to New York.

Fanny had great respect for her father's personal power and efficiency, and received the announcement with evident satisfaction. The preliminary arrangements for the journey were entered upon by both with much spirit. Fanny, with unusual readiness, took upon herself the preparation of her father's wardrobe, while he and the little black pony busily attended to such affairs as were necessary to be looked after out of doors. It was quite an event in the history of Crampton—this departure of everybody's family physician, and his indefinite period of absence. The postmaster had duly reported to the villagers the arrival of the two important-looking letters, and they had found it very difficult to decide whether he had been summoned to some great case in consultation, or whether he had been invited to a chair in one of the medical colleges.

As father and daughter kept their own counsels on the subject, the question was open for discussion during his entire absence. All agreed that Dr. Gilbert was a man who knew what he was about, and had a distinct comprehension of the side upon which his bread was buttered.

The day set for his departure came at length, and the little Crampton mail-coach started out from the little Crampton tavern for the doctor's door, and the little driver blew his little horn to inform the doctor that it was time for him and his baggage to be ready. The coach came up to the gate with a pretentious crack of the whip, and a rate of speed which the reputation of the establishment upon the road did not at all warrant.

In fact, the doctor found that the fiery little pair of horses that made the coach rattle so merrily about Crampton, underwent a serious change of character immediately after leaving the village.

The Crampton line of public travel and mail carriage was only one of the many tributaries to the great trunk lines that traversed the Connecticut valley from the northernmost point to the commencement of steam navigation at Hartford ; and it was not until late in the afternoon that the Crampton basket was emptied into the trunk-line bin that came along behind six smoking horses, covered with passengers, and piled with baggage. The doctor was obliged to take an outside seat. It was an unwelcome shock to the gentleman's dignity, and as he was a heavy man, the seat was reached by an outlay of physical exertion that cost some temper and more breath. His state of mind was not improved by the stimulus supplied to his efforts by an irreverent young man in sea costume, who reached down his hand, and shouted, " Now, old feller ! Yo-heave, O ! "

The stage-coach started off with a fresh team at a smashing speed, and the doctor felt that he was getting into the whirl of the great world. There was something in the thought that exhilarated him. Floating along in one of the arteries of business life, it seemed to Dr. Gilbert, as a business man, a very splendid thing ; but his satisfaction was marred by the fact that the broader the stream of life grew along which, and into which, he was gliding, the smaller grew Dr. Gilbert. Out of Crampton, the great man of Crampton was of no more account than anybody.

At the next grand station of the route, the passengers had accumulated in such numbers that another coach was put on, and the doctor was favored with an inside seat. He left Greenfield at nightfall, the coach plunging down the hill upon which the town stands at what he thought to be a dangerous rate of speed, rattling over Deerfield River bridge, and sweeping along the skirts of the Deerfield meadows. It was a glorious evening, and the fresh phase of life which it presented to our Crampton passenger would have been refreshing beyond expression, if the burden of care which he had taken on could have been lifted. As he realized, more and more, the great and clashing interests of the world, the little bundle of manuscript in his trunk seemed to lose its importance. What would this great world care for a country physician? What, particularly, would it care for the productions of a country physician's daughter?

At Bloody Brook, the passengers took a late supper, connected with which the only thing that Dr. Gilbert remembered was a picture in the dining-room, of the celebrated massacre from which the village had derived its name. Some very stiff-looking people, whom he had read of as " The Flower of Essex," were represented as picking grapes upon very high trees, and receiving deadly arrows from very low Indians, who seemed to have grown among the bushes. He entered Northampton and a dream about the same time, and left both without any distinct notions of their respective characteristics. Half-sleeping, half-waking, and uniformly uneasy and uncomfortable, he passed the night, and the towns through which his course lay, and came in sight of the spires of Hartford just as a brilliant sun was rising into a cloudless sky.

Here the stream of life was swelling again, and again Dr. Gilbert's proportions, as a man of mark and importance, consciously shrank. The coach rolled in upon the paved streets, and even at that early hour found many astir. Hackney-coaches were actively pushing about, collecting passengers for the New York boat. Loads of stores and light freight were pressing to the river bank, where lay the splendid steamer Bunker Hill. The coach

which bore him and his fellow-passengers was only one
of a dozen that came in and deposited their passengers
and luggage. Everybody was in a hurry. A score of
stevedores and deck hands were trundling boxes and
barrels on board. Black porters were dodging here and
there, collecting baggage, of which they proposed to take
the charge for a consideration. The bell of the Bunker
Hill introduced its tongue among the Babel voices of the
hour. The hurry every moment increased. Men came
running down the street with umbrellas and satchels
under their arms, and rushed on board as if life depended on their crossing the plank ten minutes before the
steamer swung off.

Of much of this active life the doctor was a quiet
observer from the upper deck of the Bunker Hill. The
great man of Crampton had at this time come to be exceedingly insignificant. He saw elderly, portly, dignified gentlemen come on board, attended by ladies of
stylish appointments and a demonstrative air of high
breeding, all smacking of a loftier grade of life than he
had been accustomed to. He could not help acknowledging to himself that Dr. Theophilus Gilbert of Crampton, accompanied by his accomplished daughter, the
authoress of " Tristram Trevanion," would make, anywhere, a less impressive figure. Then the question
again occurred to him—" What does all this world of
life, full of high enterprises, grand pursuits, headlong
business, and unresting competitions, care for the offspring of a country girl's brain ? What possible relation has the book which stirred such enthusiasm in the
Crampton pastor and his wife to the life that I see before me ? " The doctor grew timid. The doctor was
actually frightened. He wished that Fanny Gilbert's
" career " had taken another direction, and that Fanny
Gilbert's father had been less a fool.

At length the bell of the Bunker Hill began to toll,

and then a dingy mulatto, in dingy satinet, went back and forth in the boat, warning with a professional twang all those to "go ashore that's going," and ringing a hand-bell to attract attention to his message. The wheels began to move, the last straggler crossed the plank, the lines were cast off, and the boat wheeled into the stream, and was soon under full headway.

Dr. Gilbert's quick, observant eyes had scanned every passenger he met. He was alone, bound to a great city, which, though a man of experience, he had never seen. He longed for companionship. Among those who had most impressed him was a tall gentleman of middle age, in spectacles. He seemed to be alone, and had the appearance of being a literary man, just the kind of man whose acquaintance he would like to make. This solitary gentleman soon came to monopolize all the doctor's attention. He had an air of profound reflection; and when he made remark upon the scenery to any person near whom he might be standing, it was always accompanied by some new and striking attitude, and by a gesture of the hands at once so graceful and natural, that the doctor concluded that he must be some great public speaker.

The gentleman seemed to be aware that he had attracted the doctor's eye, and came up and took a position near him, with his thumbs in the armholes of his waistcoat, his left foot finely thrown out in advance, and his eye evidently drinking in the beauties of the scene.

"This seems to be a fine country," suggested the doctor.

"Rich, sir, rich in all the elements of fertility, and, as a poetic friend of mine would say, redolent of sweets," responded the gentleman.

The doctor was struck by the language, and hardly knew how to continue conversation. The tones of the gentleman's voice were deep and rich, and the gentleman himself seemed to rejoice in them. He did not change his position ; so the doctor said, " We have quite a large company on board to-day."

" Yes, sir, yes," responded the stranger.

" Many very interesting-looking people."

" Yes, to me the human face divine is the most interesting vision of nature. I turn from fields to faces, as I turn from earth to heaven."

The doctor was almost stunned. At length he ventured the suggestion that the boat seemed to be a very fine one, and a great improvement upon the stage-coach.

" Yes, sir, yes," responded the stranger with magnificent emphasis ; " fit emblem of human life, bearing us down to the bosom of the mighty ocean."

Having delivered himself, the stranger turned and moved grandly away, but Dr. Gilbert had no intention of parting with him thus. So he resolved that he would not lose sight of him, and followed him at a distance. He saw him engaged with another passenger, and went up behind him. The fresh interlocutor was overheard to remark upon the filthy condition of a landing they were passing.

" Rich, sir, rich," responded the magnificent stranger, " in all the elements of fertility, and, as a poetic friend of mine would say, *not* redolent of sweets."

" You are hard on 'em," said the astonished fellow, with a peculiar smile.

" I hate towns," said his highness. " I turn from towns to faces as I turn from earth to heaven."

" Well ! you'll find faces enough on the boat here, I should think," said the fellow.

" Aye, the boat ! the boat ! fit emblem of human life, bearing us down to the bosom of the mighty ocean."

Having redelivered himself of these splendid sentences, the stranger turned gracefully away, leaving his companion puzzled and dumb. The latter caught the

10

eye of Dr. Gilbert, and came up to him with the inquiry, " Know that feller ? "

The doctor replied that he did not, but would like to find him out.

" He *is* rather numerous, ain't he ? " responded the man.

Dr. Gilbert, preferring magniloquence to slang, turned away still unsatisfied, and determined to see more of the man who had interested him so much. Keeping at a decent distance from him, he heard him for half an hour ringing his changes on the beauty of the human face divine, the richness of nature in all the elements of fertility, and the steamer Bunker Hill as a fit emblem of human life, bearing him and the rest of the company down to the bosom of the mighty ocean. Then the bell of the steamer rang, and the boat ran in and threw out her lines at the Middletown landing. A number of passengers came on, and a number debarked. Among the latter, much to the doctor's surprise, was the stranger with the spectacles, carrying in one hand a diminutive carpet-bag, and in the other a little oblong case, that looked very much as if it contained a violin.

" Found out who that feller is," said a voice in the doctor's ear—the voice of the man who thought the stranger so " numerous."

" Ah ! " responded the doctor. " Who is he ? "

" Well, he's a rovin' singin'-master, by the name of Peebles," replied the man ; and then added, " they call him the pasteboard man round here. You see he thinks he's a man, but he's nothing but pasteboard. He sort o' stands round, and spreads, and lets off all the big talk he hears. Ain't he rather numerous, though ? "

" I have never been so disappointed in a man in my life," responded the doctor, with equal gravity and earnestness.

" You come from up country, I guess," said the man,

taking in a fresh quid of tobacco. "That wasn't the only pasteboard man on this boat, by a long chalk."

"What do you mean, sir?" inquired the doctor, suspecting that the fellow was quizzing him.

"Well, see that old feller with the gals there?"

"The old gentleman with an eye-glass? Yes."

"Take him for a member of Congress, wouldn't you?"

"I confess," replied the doctor, "that it had occurred to me that he might be in public position."

"Well he does look numerous, that's a fact; but he keeps tavern, and spells breakfast b-r-e-c-k, breck, f-i-r-s-t, first, breckfirst. Fact—saw it on a bill. Lots of 'em all around here in the same way. I come from up country myself, and I s'pose I know how all these slick fellers look to you, but three-quarters of 'em are pasteboard, jest like Peebles. Now you don't know it, but you are the most sensible-looking old cove there is on this boat, and these pasteboard fellers know it, too. Goin' to New York?"

"I am on my way to New York," replied the doctor, ignoring the compliment.

"Where do you put up?"

"I have not determined."

"Lucky," responded the man, drawing a card from his pocket. "That's the house for you—City Hotel. I always stop there—right in the centre. You may keep that card if you are a mind to. It's one I brought away, but I know the street."

The doctor received the card gratefully, and the accommodating fellow turned away, and was soon busy in conversation with a group of countrymen, to each of whom he handed a card, that looked very much like the one which the doctor put in his pocket.

Dr. Gilbert began to open his eyes. He was not so insignificant a man after all. Very much encouraged, he began to make conversation with one and another, and before the day expired, he had established friendly relations with quite an extensive circle of men and women, with whom he discussed politics, religion, education, and all the leading subjects of general interest, proving himself to be quite the equal of the most intelligent of the company.

The long day wore away, and nightfall found the gallant steamer ploughing the waters of the Sound. It was not until midnight that the lights of the great city showed themselves, and the boat, with its freight of life, ran in among a forest of masts, and was made fast to the wharf. The doctor was anxious. He had secured his trunk, and stood firmly by it while beset by the crowd of importunate hackmen. At length his acquaintance of the card appeared, and calling to a rough-looking fellow, said : " This gentleman goes up to the house." Then, slipping his arm through that of the doctor, and ordering the porter to carry out his trunk, he conducted him to the City Hotel carriage, already full and piled with baggage, and managed to get him in.

The doctor awoke the next morning with a dull, heavy roar sounding in his ears, and then rose and looked abroad from his high window upon housetops and chimneys, and busy streets and sidewalks, thronged with early passengers going to their daily employments. The vision was a novel one, and would have been very agreeable, had not the thought of his unfinished and unpromising errand constantly intruded itself. What could Tristram Trevanion do in such a place as that? Who would care for the Hounds of the Whippoorwill Hills?

Dr. Theophilus Gilbert shaved himself very carefully, put on the best linen that Crampton ever saw, and robed himself in a black broadcloth suit, made by the Crampton tailor, and only brought out on very pleasant Sabbath days, or great secular occasions. He descended to

breakfast, and was exceedingly pleased with the attentions bestowed upon him by the waiters. It really
seemed to him that he was securing a larger share of
attention than anybody else, and that those less favored
must look upon him with a measure of envy. Breakfast
concluded, he devoted half an hour to the Directory,
copying the names of the principal publishing houses,
with their street and number. Then he held a long
conversation with a fat bar-keeper (who, in his shirt-
sleeves and a paper cap, was polishing off the outside
and filling the inside of his bottles), with relation to
the locations he wished to find, and then he started out,
with the manuscript novel under his arm, to attend to
his business.

He had not given up the Kilgores. He was entirely
faithless as to their having seen his letter. So he made his
way to the great house of the Kilgores, and entered it
with assumed courage, though, to tell the truth, he felt
more like a beggar than a gentleman in easy circumstances. He inquired of a clerk, whom he had some
difficulty in apprising of his presence, for "the head of
the house."

" The old man, I suppose," said the young man, listlessly.

The doctor said, " Yes, sir," at a venture.

"Oh! he won't be down town these two hours," replied the clerk. " You'll have to wait."

The doctor waited. He was bound to see Kilgore
the elder, before any other publisher. He walked up
and down the long salesroom, looking at the shelves
deeply packed with books, and the cases full of the pets
of the public, dressed in gorgeous gold and morocco,
and wondered what kind of a figure his manuscript
would make in such brilliant society. Alas! how could
room be made in such a crowded establishment for Tristram Trevanion?

He had begun to tire of his thriftless employment, when the clerk, to whom he had originally spoken, came out from behind the counter and, inviting him into the elder Kilgore's private office, told him that he could sit there quietly and read the papers, until the head of the house should make his appearance. He accepted the invitation, and was conducted back to a little room, carpeted and neatly furnished. At a desk sat a lean, middle-aged man, engaged with bills and letters. At his side were piles of proof-sheets, waiting for examination.

At a window, stood a seedy-looking man of fifty, in brown clothes, with his hat on, gazing out upon a dead-wall, and apparently absorbed by reflection. The clerk looked up, nodded, waved the doctor into a chair, pointed to a newspaper, and went on with his work.

As the doctor took his seat and the newspaper, the seedy looking man in brown turned around, and came toward him. Dr. Gilbert noticed the wildness of his eyes and the dingy pallor of his face, and, with professional readiness, perceived the malady that afflicted him. The stranger seized the doctor's hand, and, shaking it warmly, said : " This is Mr. Kilgore. May the Lord bless him, and cause his face to shine upon him ! "

" You are mistaken," replied the doctor. " My name is not Kilgore. On the contrary, I am waiting to see Mr. Kilgore, as I presume you are."

" Then you are not Kilgore, eh ? Who are you ? "

" My name is Gilbert," replied the doctor.

" Your Christian name ? "

" Theophilus."

" Theophilus, I salute you. All the saints salute you. What are your views of the millennium ? "

" I can't say," replied the doctor, " that I have any very distinct views of the millennium. I suppose everybody will be very good and very happy."

" Yes, but how are they to be made good and happy ?

That's the grand secret, sir, and that secret is hid in me, an unworthy vessel. You behold in me, sir, the forerunner of an epoch—the John the Baptist of the Second Coming."

The doctor was amused, and asked him to declare his secret.

"It's soon to be published to the world. The Kilgores have had it all night. In the mean time, I have no objection to saying to you privately that it's flesh. You know how it was with the children of Israel when they gathered quails in the wilderness, ten homers apiece. While the flesh was yet between their teeth, ere it was chewed, the wrath of the Lord was kindled against the people, and the Lord smote the people with a very great plague. God made man upright, but he has been eating dead animals so long that he has lost the divine image, and become a beast. All we have to do to bring about the millennium is to stop eating dead animals, and to refrain from drinking the blood of beasts. The cattle upon a thousand hills are the Lord's, not ours, sir ; and when the blessed thousand years shall dawn, and these cursed slaughter-houses are shut up, even the animals of the forest will be partakers of the benefit, for the lion shall eat straw like the ox, and the cow and the bear shall feed together."

Dr. Gilbert might have been held a listener to the crazy reformer's scheme for the regeneration of the race for an uncomfortable period, but, at this moment, the elder Kilgore appeared, and in company with him a gentleman exceedingly well dressed, carrying a cane. Mr. Kilgore removed his hat from his high, bald head, and laid it upon the window-sill. "Positively now," said he continuing a conversation with the young man which had been interrupted by his entrance, "you must give us something in the fall. The public expect it, you know. You have had a great success, and the market is wide open for you. Just a little less religion, eh? You must positively bend to me in this. I think I know the market; not quite so much religion. People are not fond of it. Sermon on the Mount, spread rather thin, goes very well—but not too much—not too much."

The young man laughed jocularly, twirled his cane, and said: "Perhaps I did spread it on rather thick the last time; but really, now, Mr. Kilgore, I think there is a religious vein that will pay for working."

"Undoubtedly! But, to make a marketable book, religion must be sprinkled in, in about the proportion that we find it in the world. Then it goes very well, and offends nobody. In fact, I think irreligious people like enough of the article to give a book a kind of flavor or smack of piety, and that is usually enough to satisfy the church."

"Well, I'll think of it," responded the young man.

The doctor had listened to this business conversation in silent astonishment. The reformer watched the pair with burning eyes, and coming up to the young man, he extended toward him his long, thin finger, and said: "Through covetousness shall they with feigned words make merchandise of you, whose judgment now of a long time lingereth not, and their damnation slumbereth not. There's religion for you, clean and solid, right out of the Bible; no sprinkling about that."

"Ruddock! Ruddock!" called Mr. Kilgore, excitedly. "Who is this person? What does he want here?"

"I am the Prophet of the Second Coming," answered the man for himself.

"This is his second coming," replied the clerk, "and I shall be glad to see his second going."

"What is his business, Ruddock?"

"He is the man who left the manuscript on the millennium yesterday," replied Rudduck.

"Oh! yes. Well, sir, our engagements are such that we couldn't think of undertaking it. Besides, its contents are not of a popular character. Nobody cares anything about the millennium, and you, I judge, are not the man to treat upon it. Ruddock, give this person his manuscript."

Ruddock handed out a small, dirty roll of paper, and the reformer pocketed it.

"Ruddock," said Mr. Kilgore, "be kind enough to open the door, and show this person out."

The man stood irresolute, and commenced to speak, when Ruddock laid his hand upon his shoulder, and he retired shaking the dust from his heels, or trying to, and distributing anathemas right and left. The young author, whom Mr. Kilgore had been courting and counselling so daintily, pleaded an engagement, and soon followed the author of the work on the millennium.

"You have business with me, sir?" said Mr. Kilgore, turning to the doctor.

"I have," replied Dr. Gilbert, and added : "Perhaps this note, which I received from your house, will introduce it."

Mr. Kilgore took the note, and ran his eye over it.

"Did you ever see the letter before?" inquired the doctor.

"I think not," replied Mr. Kilgore.

"Did you ever see the letter from me to which this is a reply?"

"I presume not. Ruddock attends to these things. By the way, Ruddock, I see we are out of blanks. You've had to write the whole of this. How long have we been out of blanks?"

"Not long," replied the confidential clerk ; "I didn't have to write more than a dozen complete. I have plenty now."

"Do you mean to be understood, Mr. Kilgore, that

you have blank replies to such applications as mine? " inquired the doctor, in undisguised astonishment.

" Certainly, sir," said Mr. Kilgore. " You see we have an average of three such applications as yours a day. Three hundred working days in a year makes it necessary to send nine hundred letters. Well, we have so much to do that the blank saves time, and affords a nice little chance for advertising. It's really quite a matter of economy."

" Of course, then," said Dr. Gilbert, " you have decided on my daughter's book without giving it any consideration. I wish you to see it, and personally to become acquainted with its merits."

The great publisher laughed. Mr. Ruddock overheard the remark, and laughed too. " Bless your soul, sir," said Mr. Kilgore, " I never read a book; I haven't time."

" Somebody reads, I suppose," continued the doctor, " and I wish my daughter to have a chance."

" My literary man," said Mr. Kilgore, would read it if it were of any use, but my engagements are such that I cannot take the book. Besides, the novel market is perfectly flat. I think, perhaps, Kapp & Demigh might do something for you."

"What class of books does the young man who has just left you produce? " inquired the doctor.

" Oh! that was young Fitzgerald, the most popular and promising novelist of the day. Great faculty for hitting the popular taste just in the bull's eye,—just—in —the—bull's—eye." And Mr. Kilgore rubbed his hands pleasantly together, and told over a package of letters, as if they were a pack of cards.

" I see your engagements are not such as to prevent you from making a new one with him, nor the novel market so flat as to fail of responding to him," said the doctor, with a bitter tone.

Mr. Kilgore smiled. Mr. Ruddock looked up, and smiled also. " You are sharp," said Mr. Kilgore. " You are hard on me."

" You will allow me to return the compliment, and repeat the accusation," responded the doctor, rising angrily to his feet.

" We profess to understand our business here," said Mr. Kilgore, entirely unruffled. "Ruddock and I manage to get along very well ; eh! Ruddock, don't we ? "

" In our small way," responded the clerk, with pleasant irony, not stopping for a moment in his work.

" Yes, yes, in our small way," repeated Mr. Kilgore ; and then he began to bustle about his desk in a way that said, " I wish this old fellow would take his leave ; why don't he go ? "

Dr. Gilbert was not accustomed to being treated in this way at all ; and it irritated him exceedingly. He turned lingeringly toward the door ; then hesitated, and then said calmly : " Mr. Kilgore, do you think this is treating my daughter fairly ? "

"Why, bless your soul, my good friend," exclaimed Mr. Kilgore, " I've been treating you very politely, to save your feelings, I have told you that my engagements are such that I cannot take your book, and that the novel market is flat. Now, if you want the truth, it is that a publisher's engagements are never such that he cannot take hold of a book that will sell, and that the novel market is always flat to new-comers. There, you have the whole of it, and as you are probably going the rounds here in New York, I'll pay you something handsome if you find a single publisher who will give you the real reason he has for refusing your manuscript."

" I thank you for your present frankness, at least," said the doctor.

" Well, come back and sit down," said Mr. Kilgore warmly, as a new thought seemed to strike him. " Ruddock, be kind enough to leave us till I call you. Sit down, sir, sit down!"

The confidential clerk looked up surprised, took up some of his papers, and retired.

" You say," said Mr. Kilgore, drawing his chair close to Dr. Gilbert, " that this novel is written by your daughter. Is she an obedient daughter?"

" Well," replied the doctor, a good deal puzzled, " she has a strong will, but she is mainly obedient. Fanny is a good girl, and not without genius, I think."

" D—n the genius! Is she obedient? That's the question. Is she willing to honor your judgment in every thing?"

" I can't say that she is; in fact, this book of hers was written against my will, and I am only sorry at this moment that I had not enforced my wishes."

" That's enough," replied Mr. Kilgore, while his eye flashed angrily. " I wouldn't publish her book if I knew I should sell a million copies of it."

" You are strangely excited," said Dr. Gilbert ; " and you will allow me to say that you greatly exaggerate my daughter's disposition to disobedience."

" Yes—excited—yes! I've seen something of disobedient daughters. When your Fanny snaps her fingers in your face, and raises the devil with all your arrangements, as she's sure to do, sooner or later, you'll be excited—very strangely excited. Yes! By the way, whom are you going to now with your book?"

" I have Kapp & Demigh, and Ballou & Gold, on my note-book," replied Dr. Gilbert.

" Good houses, both of them," said Mr. Kilgore, " but don't go beyond them, or you'll get into trouble. At any rate, keep out of Sargent's hands—the ripest young scoundrel that ever wore a sanctimonious face, or whined at a prayer-meeting. I know him. He used to be a clerk of mine."

The doctor laid the name of Sargent carefully away in his mind, left the strangely acting publisher as soon as he could, and went directly to the City Hotel, to think over his morning's adventures, get some dinner, and lay out his work for the afternoon.

From the moment Sargent's name was mentioned, Dr. Gilbert had felt that Sargent was his man. He could not fail to detect in Mr. Kilgore a strong personal enmity toward this young publisher. His mind, too, had in it that perverse element which rebelled against all dictation, whether intended for his good or not. He did not like Mr. Kilgore at all ; and as the probability was that Mr. Sargent did not like him at all, they would be apt to like one another, and get along together very well. Besides, Dr. Gilbert had had sufficient experience with first-class houses, and was ready to try a little lower down.

Accordingly, after dinner, Dr. Gilbert held another examination of the Directory, and another conversation with the fat bar-keeper in paper cap and shirt-sleeves, and issued out to find the unpretending establishment of young Sargent. This he succeeded in doing ; and inquiring for Mr. Sargent, he was directed to a young man in a brown linen coat, engaged in nailing up a box of books—a lithe, springy, driving fellow, with a bright, open face, and an unmistakable air of business about him. The doctor loved him at once. All the Kilgores in Christendom could not frighten him from such an apparent impersonation of good nature, determined enterprise, and laborious activity.

The doctor waited until the publisher had nailed his box, and then told him he would like to see him privately. The young man doffed his brown linen, and donned a more dignified article, and then invited the doctor into what he good-humoredly called his " den."

Mr. Frank Sargent was frank by nature, as by name,

and when Dr. Gilbert made known his business, he said : " Well, sir, I suppose you have been the rounds. They all do before they come to me."

" On the contrary, I have been to but one concern," replied the doctor.

" Whose was that ? "

" The Kilgores'."

" The Kilgores' ? *They* didn't tell you to come to me ! " exclaimed Mr. Sargent in astonishment.

" Not at all ; they warned me against you."

" And why do you come ? "

" Because I thought I should like a young man whom the elder Kilgore did not."

Mr. Frank Sargent tried to smile, but his lip quivered, he put his hand to his forehead, and exclaimed, " God forgive him ! " Then he pushed out his hands impatiently, as if warning away a crowd of unwelcome thoughts and memories, and said : " Well, let's talk about the book."

The first thing Mr. Sargent did was to tell Dr. Gilbert all about his business—what disadvantages he labored under—what lack of capital he suffered from— what treatment he was constantly receiving from heavy houses that could undersell him, or give longer time on accounts. Gradually he came to the book, and revealed to the doctor the fact that he could not alone run the risk of publishing it, even if he should like it. The doctor would have to agree to share any loss that might attend its publication ; and it was concluded, after a full and free conversation, that Mr. Sargent should read the manuscript, and that Dr. Gilbert should return home and await the result.

Mr. Sargent obligingly conducted the doctor back to his hotel, treated him with a great deal of consideration, came for him in the evening, and walked with him to some of the principal points of interest in the city, was

at the boat on the following morning to see him safely
off, and then he bade him good-by. The doctor started
for his home quite satisfied—determined, in fact, that
he would pay for the publication of "Tristram Trevanion" entirely, rather than have Mr. Frank Sargent
poorer for it by a dollar.

CHAPTER XI.

TRISTRAM TREVANION IS ACCEPTED, AND DR. GILBERT IS REJECTED.

DR. GILBERT accomplished his whole trip in less than
a week, and arrived at Crampton in the evening, just as
his family were retiring to bed. Fanny met him with
the very unusual demonstration of a kiss, and Aunt
Catharine shook his hand cordially, declaring she was
"right down glad to see him," for she had had no one
to quarrel with since he went away. He was glad to get
home; and for the first ten minutes busied himself with
inquiries for his patients, his pony, his farmers, his boy
Fred, and everything and everybody bearing any direct
relation to him.

"And how is our friend, Miss Hammett?" inquired
Dr. Gilbert, at last.

"She has not been herself at all, since you went
away," replied Fanny. "When I told her that you had
gone to New York to get the book published, she turned
very pale, and came near fainting."

"Hem!" from Aunt Catharine.

The doctor could neither help smiling nor feeling a
great deal more gratification than he was quite willing
to manifest.

"All I ask," said Aunt Catharine, with mock seriousness, " is, that you give me suitable notice to quit, so that I can have time to get a new home."

" Oh ! nonsense ! Catharine," exclaimed the doctor, yet he could not look displeased. The thought that the gentle Mary Hammett cared for him was exceedingly precious to him. It brought back with a wild sweep through his heart the tides of youth, and seemed to open to him another life.

" I suppose you and Fanny wish to get rid of me," said Aunt Catharine, " so, good night."

After her obliging withdrawal, father and daughter held a long conversation on the subject which the latter had most at heart. The doctor told the story of his journey, of his interview with Kilgore the elder, and of his final arrangement with Mr. Frank Sargent. Closing the narrative of his enterprise and adventures, he said : " And now, Fanny, this is the last time I shall ever consent to be engaged in anything of this kind. You see that your career is very much my career, and that you were utterly powerless to do any thing alone. I have neither time nor disposition to do this kind of business. It does not pay in any way. It has already cost both you and me more, tenfold, than it will ever return to either of us, in money or reputation. It is all very well for us to dream pretty dreams up here in Crampton, but the world does not care for them, nor for us ; so what is the use of our caring about the world ? "

Fanny was under too many obligations to her father for his assistance to multiply words with him concerning her future course ; but he read, in her silence, her firmly compressed lips, and the gray coldness of her eyes, the strength of unrelinquished purpose.

The next day Dr. Gilbert was abroad early, looking after his affairs. The little black pony had rested a longer time than since he had been in Dr. Gilbert's possession, and the little gig rattled and reeled along behind him so merrily that the doctor quite forgot the excitements and vexations of the week, in the pleasures of his business. But he was working against time quite as evidently as when he was first introduced to the reader, on the morning of the great exhibition of the Crampton Light Infantry. He had always been faithful in visiting schools, and the pony and gig understood their way to the school-house door quite as well as to the doors of half a dozen patients who had been on the doctor's hands for twenty years. In fact, they seemed to regard it as a hopelessly chronic case, and to turn up regularly whenever they came that way.

At mid-afternoon, Dr. Gilbert, with feelings very new and peculiar, knocked at the door of the centre school-house, and was admitted by Miss Hammett, who seemed to be possessed by feelings quite as new and peculiar as his own. After the exchange of the routine of civil inquiries, she went on with her recitations, alternately flushed and pale. Her appearance was so unlike what it had previously been, that Dr. Gilbert was puzzled. What was the matter with Miss Hammett? It was not joy, but apprehension, that she manifested when he met her. Pleasure was not the parent of such pallor. The flush of delight did not burn the forehead.

"I am not well," said Miss Hammett, at last, "and with your leave, Dr. Gilbert, I will dismiss the school."

"Certainly. Do so at once," responded her visitor. "I will send Fanny over to see you, and, if you get no relief, I will attend you."

The doctor felt that she wished to get rid of him, and lost no time in leaving her. Going directly to his home, he bade Fanny visit the schoolmistress, and went about his affairs oppressed with an unsatisfied, uneasy feeling, that he could neither explain to himself nor shake off.

Fanny made the visit, and while Miss Hammett reclined in her chamber, entertained her with a long account of her father's adventures in New York and by the way. The story seemed to possess almost miraculous powers of healing. Miss Hammett listened with the profoundest interest, and made a great many inquiries, particularly with relation to the publishers visited, and seemed to be interested in the minutest particulars. Then she rose from the sofa, and sat with her hand in Fanny's, and told her how much good she had done her. " Tell your father," said Miss Hammett, " that his prescription has wrought wonders, and that if he will visit my school again, I will not turn him out of doors."

Fanny went away very much puzzled, after promising Miss Hammett that she would faithfully communicate to her the result of the negotiations with Mr. Frank Sargent.

A few days passed away after the usual fashion, and then came the anxiously looked for letter. Dr. Gilbert read it, made no comment, and handed it over to Fanny. Fanny read it, made no comment, and went directly to Miss Hammett's room with it ; and there she read it carefully to the schoolmistress. We will look over her shoulder, and read it also :

" Dr. Gilbert :

"Dear Sir—I have carefully read your daughter's manuscript novel, ' Tristram Trevanion,' and find it quite interesting, though I doubt whether it can ever achieve much success. I should say that it is a very young novel—written by one who has seen little of life, and much of books. The invention manifested in the incidents is quite extraordinary, and displays genius, though the characters are extravagant. But I do not write to criticise the book. Worse books have found many buyers. I accept it on the terms upon which we settled, *as it is ;* but there are one or two points touching which I wish to make some suggestions. The hero, Tristram Trevanion, does not marry Grace Beaumont, as he ought to do. I think I understand the public mind when

I say that it will demand that this marriage take place. It could be done by altering a few pages. Again, I think that the public will demand that the Jewish dwarf, Levi, be made in some way to suffer a violent death at the hand of Trevanion. One word about the title. I confess to its music, but it seems to me to be so smooth as to present no points to catch the popular attention. Besides, I find that the ' Hounds of the Whippoorwill Hills ' make their appearance but once in the story, and have no claim upon the prominence given them on the title-page. Your daughter will think it very strange, no doubt ; but I believe that the sale of the book would be increased by making the title rougher—more startling. How does this look to you—' Tristram Trevanion, or Butter and Cheese and All ; ' or this—' Tristram Trevanion, or The Dwarf with the Flaxen Forelock ' ? There is another course which is probably preferable to this, viz.: that of making a title which means nothing, and will puzzle people—a title that defines and explains nothing—bestowed in a whim, as we sometimes give a child a name. What would your daughter think of ' Rhododendron,' or ' Shucks ' ?

" I can imagine the horror with which your ' Everard Everest, Gent.' will look upon these suggestions, but they are honestly made, with a view to securing the highest success of which the book is capable. You will remember, of course, that I presume to dictate nothing ; I only suggest. In regard to the title, I feel less particular than with relation to the marriage of Trevanion and the violent death of the dwarf. The public demands that the issues of a novel shall be poetic justice ; and that the devotion of Trevanion and the diabolism of the dwarf deserve the rewards I have indicated, the public cannot fail to perceive.

" Awaiting your reply, I am

" Yours very truly,
" FRANK SARGENT."

When Fanny concluded the reading of this epistle, it was with a most contemptuous curl of the lip, and a general expression, upon her strong and handsome features, of disgust. " Did you ever hear of any thing so ridiculous as this in your life, Miss Hammett ? " inquired Fanny.

Miss Hammett could do nothing but laugh. She seized the letter, re-read portions of it, and laughed again uncontrollably—almost hysterically. Miss Fanny Gilbert did not know what construction to put upon this merriment. She tried to join with her at first, but the joke would not seem pleasant to her. First came upon her face a shadow of pain, then her eyes filled with tears, and she rose and walked to the window to hide her emotion. Her companion was sober in an instant, and following her, put her arm tenderly around her, and led her back to the sofa. "You know," said Miss Hammett warmly, "that I would not wound your feelings for the world, but one has fits of laughing sometimes that one cannot account for at all. I don't know what I have been laughing at, I'm sure."

If Fanny had been looking at Miss Hammett, she would have seen that that young woman was having the greatest difficulty in restraining herself from a further outburst.

"It seems so mercenary," said Fanny.

"And so professional," said Miss Hammett.

"And so careless of an author's feelings."

"And so ridiculous."

"And so servile to public opinion. As if everybody must be married or killed, because the precious public demand it! Who cares what the public demand?"

"Tut, tut, Fanny! Take care!" said Miss Hammett, looking archly into Fanny's face. "Are you sure that you do not condemn yourself in your condemnation of this young publisher? Unless I have misunderstood you, the book was written for fame—for public applause —and Mr. Sargent is only endeavoring to assist you to accomplish your ends."

"But I wish to accomplish my ends in my own way," said Fanny, imperiously.

"But suppose the public will not be pleased with your way?" suggested Miss Hammett. "People who work for public applause are not so independent as you think. What do you care for the marriage of your man, or the death of your dwarf, if it help you to obtain your object ? "

" But the title ! Who ever heard of any thing so preposterous as ' Rhododendron,' or ' Shucks ' ? "

" Everybody has heard of titles quite as ridiculous as those, adopted for no reason in the world but to catch the public eye. As for the first one suggested, ' Tristram Trevanion, or Butter and Cheese and All,' it seems to me to have a charming mingling of the ideal and the real in its structure."

" Miss Hammett, you are laughing at me," said Fanny, in a tone of vexation.

" Indeed, I'm not. Now tell me why you chose the title you did."

" Because it was musical. Because — because — I thought the public would like it," said Fanny, blushing, and biting her lips.

Miss Hammett broke into a low musical laugh. " Ah ! Fanny, Fanny," said she, " we are not so much elevated above the motives of our publishers as we might be, are we ? Let me advise you to be very just toward Mr. Frank Sargent. You are both laboring for one object— the popularity of Tristram Trevanion ; and if you put your heads together—I mean by mail, of course—your hero will make the better headway in the world for it. For my part, I see no objections to the marriage and the murder proposed. As for the title, I think you have the advantage ; so you can compromise by keeping that, and changing the issues of the story."

" I wish Mr. Frank Sargent could know what an advocate he has here," exclaimed Fanny.

" Fanny," said Miss Hammett with undisguised alarm, " you must promise me that you will never mention my name, or say one word about me, in any communication you may make to Mr. Sargent. I am really very much in earnest, as you see."

Fanny did see this, but, with girlish perverseness, said: "I positively cannot allow such disinterested service to go unrewarded. Mr. Sargent must be informed, in some way of his indebtedness to you."

Miss Hammett grasped Fanny's wrist, and said, almost fiercely, "Fanny Gilbert, if you do not promise me, before you leave this room, that you will never mention my name, nor allude to me in any way in your letters to New York, I will leave Crampton to-morrow."

"Why, Miss Hammett!" exclaimed Fanny.

"Yes, to-morrow; and I shall go where you will never see me again. I beg you to promise me, because I am happier here than I have been for many months, and happier than I can be elsewhere."

"Of course, I promise you," said Fanny; "but it's very strange—very strange."

"Oh! I thank you! I thank you a thousand times," said Miss Hammett; "but you must stop thinking how strange it is. I cannot explain any thing to you now; but some time—some time. There, dear, let's talk no more about it. Please do not mention this to your father. By the way, Fanny, leave me that letter for half an hour. I wish to look it over, and think it over."

The young women kissed each other, and Fanny took her leave. Miss Hammett accompanied her to the street-door, then locked it, then entered her own room, and locked herself in, and then she took the business letter of Mr. Frank Sargent in her hands, pressed it to her heart, and walking back and forth in her apartment, kissed it a hundred times. It does not become us to linger, while she kneels and pours out her thanksgiving and her prayer. Eonugh for us now that there was something in the letter that touched the deepest springs of her life, and startled its sleeping secrets into intense alarm.

In the interval between Dr. Gilbert's call upon Miss Hammett at her school-room and the reception of the letter from Mr. Frank Sargent, the doctor had seen her more than once, and was glad to find her equanimity quite restored. She treated him in the old frank way, which had always been a way exceedingly charming to him. He found himself more and more attracted to her, and more and more significant did life look to him, as he came to associate it with her life. He had very honestly loved the mother of his children, and when she passed away it seemed to him that there was nothing but work that could fill the vacant life she left. Now he dreamed of this new, sweet presence in his house, of a wise and sympathetic companion for his daughter, of a mother for little Fred. Aunt Catharine, whose shrewd eyes had read everything, had noticed that he was more careful about his linen, and took more pains with his toilet than usual; and the neighbors thought that the school had never been so closely looked after by the committee before.

Still, there was this mystery about Miss Hammett. Would it be prudent for him—a man of position and influence—to marry an unknown woman, picked out of so dirty a factory as that at Hucklebury Run? What would the people say? Would it not compromise his respectability? Again and again he recalled the assurance she gave him in her first interview with him: "Only believe this, Dr. Gilbert—that if you ever learn the truth about me, by any means, it will bring disgrace neither to me nor to those who may befriend me." He did believe it; yet caution said, "This is what a guilty woman would say quite as readily as an innocent one. Be on your guard, Dr. Gilbert. You are too old a fellow to be taken in by a sweet face and plausible words." Miss Hammett, of course, was entirely unaware of the nature of Dr. Gilbert's feelings and the character of his cogitations. She regarded him almost as a father—at least, as a reliable counsellor and friend

—one to whom she might go with all her trials, and one in whose protection she might thoroughly trust. She took great pains to please him, and to satisfy all his wishes in the arduous position she had assumed. They held frequent consultations in the school-room, and at the doctor's own tea-table, at which she was always a welcome guest. In these interviews, the young woman's unassuming manners, rare good sense, and charming modesty and vivacity, won more and more upon the doctor's heart, until he found that a day passed without seeing her, and hearing her voice, was tasteless and meaningless.

A matter like this could not be long in coming to maturity in a mind like that of Dr. Gilbert. To feel that Mary Hammett was desirable, and to will the possession of her hand, were one, so soon as he could satisfy himself that Mary Hammett was indeed what she seemed to be. How could he satisfy himself? Alas! There was but one who could inform him, and her lips were sealed, and he, as a man of honor, was bound to respect their silence. For once he was forced to trust to Providence, or chance, and to leave his own action to impulse.

When Fanny returned home, after reading Mr. Frank Sargent's letter to Miss Hammett, her father, who guessed where she had been, inquired what the young woman thought of the publisher's missive. Fanny made a hurried, unsatisfactory reply, and went to her room. This was excuse sufficient for Dr. Gilbert to call upon the schoolmistress, and talk over the affair. Accordingly, Miss Hammett had hardly composed herself after the emotions excited by the letter, when Mrs. Blague came to her door, and told her that Dr. Gilbert waited for her in the parlor. Hurriedly thrusting Mr. Frank Sargent's letter into her bosom, and giving a glance in the mirror to see if her face were telling forbidden tales or not, she descended, and met her fatherly friend with her usual frankness and cordiality.

" Fanny has been to see you ? " said the doctor.

" Yes."

" And read to you Mr. Sargent's letter, I suppose."

" Yes."

" What do you think of it ? "

" It seems to me to be the letter of a man who has a sharp eye for business, and a shrewd insight into the popular taste," replied Miss Hammett.

" Hem ! I hope you advised Fanny frankly in the matter," said the doctor.

" I can hardly say that I advised her at all."

" Well, I am sorry you did not," responded the doctor. " Fanny needs womanly counsel. Poor child ! Since her mother died she has had little sympathy from her own sex, and has grown up a little unfeminine, I fear."

" I have been very happy in her society," said the young woman, cordially, " and have always given her such advice as I felt competent to give her."

" Hem! I thank you. It has always been a comfort to me to know that you were together. By the way, how is my little boy getting along with his books ? "

" Only too rapidly," replied the schoolmistress. " I sometimes tremble when I see how eagerly the little fellow pursues his tasks, and how frail he is."

The doctor's eyes sparkled with pleasure, and he rubbed his hands with satisfaction as he said, " Ah ! Freddy is a rare boy—a rare boy ! I think we shall be able to make something of him."

" But you must not force him, doctor. I'm afraid he has too much study."

" Well, I suppose," said the doctor, " that I'm unfit to manage him ; " and then he blushed to think that he had lied. He wanted somehow to say that the boy needed a mother, but he was certainly unable to manage that.

Dr. Gilbert found that the relations which existed between him and Miss Hammett, though intimate and cordial of their kind, formed almost an impassable gulf between him and his wishes. How could the fatherly Dr. Gilbert come to a declaration of his love for a woman who, as she sat before him, seemed never to have dreamed of any other relations as possible? The gulf must be bridged, in some way—if not by artifice, by violence—by main strength.

Dr. Gilbert cleared his throat again. "I have noticed the intimacy between you and my daughter with great pleasure," said he, "and have been delighted with the manner in which you have managed to secure the affections of my little boy; of course, the thought has naturally been forced upon me, that if this intimacy and affection could be found at home, in one who would bear the name of mother, it would be every way desirable. You will pardon my abruptness, Miss Hammett, when I say to you that you are the first woman I have met, since the death of my wife, whom I would be glad to see in her place."

It was out. The gulf was bridged, and the doctor was relieved to think that he had established a basis for negotiations. But what was the impression upon the young woman? As the nature of the declaration gradually found its way into her consciousness, she grew deathly pale, and sat speechless, with her eyes upon the floor.

"I have believed," continued the doctor, "that you were not altogether without respect for me, and have hoped that you might come to entertain a more genial sentiment. There is difference of age between us, I grant; but, if I know my own heart, I offer you an honest affection, as I certainly offer you my home, my protection, and my position. There are some mysteries connected with your life which I have not, as you will bear me witness, sought to probe. I have trusted you, and of course I trust you still. My proposition, I see, surprises you, and if you wish for time to consider it, I will leave you, and take your answer at some other time."

During all this speech, delivered in a low, firm tone of voice, Dr. Gilbert had closely watched the young woman. He saw the pale cheek and lips redden into crimson. He saw tears forming slowly in her downcast eyes, and then drop unheeded upon her hand. He saw a tremor like a chill pass over her frame, and then, as he concluded, and spoke of a future answer to his proposals, he saw her lift her head, and heard her say, " Do not go."

The temptation to seize her hand and kiss it was irresistible. The doctor grasped it, and bent his head toward it, but instantly Miss Hammett had withdrawn it, and was upon her feet. " Dr. Gilbert," said she, " that hand is sacred. It is not mine. It cannot be yours. I will be your servant. I will do any thing for the happiness of those you love that it is consistent for me to do —but I cannot be your wife. I asked you not to go, because my answer was ready."

It was now Dr. Gilbert's turn to be surprised. He could not realize that he—Dr. Gilbert—who had hesitated to offer himself to an unknown woman, should be so peremptorily rejected.

" You are hasty," said he. " I beg you to consider the matter. I have set my heart upon it; it must be so; I—I cannot take your answer."

Miss Hammett stood with her hands folded and pressed to her heart. " Dr. Gilbert," said she, " I should be entirely unworthy of the place to which you invite me, if I were to give one moment's entertainment to your proposition. Were I to consent to be your wife, I should become a perjured wretch, fit only for your loathing and your abhorrence."

"My God!" exclaimed the doctor, the veins of his forehead swelling fearfully, "and is my case with you so hopeless? Why! woman, it darkens my whole life."

"Dr. Gilbert," said Miss Hammett with assumed calmness, "if I were my own, I could give myself to you, but I am not, and why should we exchange further words? You know that I would rather suffer much than wound you, and you know, too, that I have never invited this proposal from you. You have been always a generous man toward me ; I ask you to be so still, and never to allude to this subject again. I am alone ; and if, after what I have told you, you persist in pursuing the matter, I have but one remedy, and that is to flee. I beg you to treat me generously."

"God knows I thought I was treating you generously, when I offered you my heart and my hand," said Dr. Gilbert, bitterly ; "but it seems that a strapping, unfledged boy is more esteemed, and I must e'en take my offer in my teeth, and walk home with it."

"Can you, Dr. Gilbert—a man—old enough to be my father—talk to me like that without blushing? I bid you good evening ; " and, suiting the action to the word, she bowed, and left Dr. Gilbert standing in the middle of the parlor, alone.

An obstruction placed in the channel of a strong will, and abruptly checking its flow, raises, by the reflux, a power that climbs and plunges till the current of life becomes turbid and unwholesome. It goes thus madly back to sweep the obstruction away, and when it finds it unyielding, it dashes over its verge with broken voice and volume, and ploughs up the filth that sleeps in the beds of the purest streams. It was thus with the strong will of Dr. Gilbert. He had made up his mind to the step he had taken. All the strong currents of his life had, for the time, taken this new channel ; and when the irrevocable word was dropped into it, the tide of a powerful life was stopped. It swelled and piled, and then plunged madly over it, and lost, at once, its music and its purity. But as streams thus stopped and thus started, though still complaining, grow pure again, so Dr. Gilbert's anger and mean jealousy subsided at length, and left him subdued, sad, ashamed, and acquiescent. If he could not have Miss Hammett's love, he must not lose her respect. If her hand could not be his, her society should not be sacrificed, and she should see that he could not only be generous, but chivalrous and brave.

Mrs. Blague had been made aware by Miss Hammett's rapid passage through the hall that Dr. Gilbert was alone, and, as he lingered, she walked into the parlor, and found him standing where Miss Hammett had left him, with the marks of strong emotion still upon his features.

" Madam," said the doctor, " you will oblige me by never alluding to what you have witnessed, and by bearing a message to Miss Hammett." He knew he could rely upon his old friend, and, without waiting for her reply, he advanced to the table and wrote, in pencil, a note to the schoolmistress. It was brief and characteristic : " Miss Hammett : Whatever you deny me, I know you will not refuse me the privilege of apologizing for my inexcusable rudeness. Come down, and permit me to bear away with me a measure of self-respect."

Mrs. Blague took the note to Miss Hammett's chamber, and the lady immediately appeared in response. Her face was clothed with an expression of pain, and her eyes were full of tears. The doctor advanced to meet her, and held out his hand. " Miss Hammett," said he, " I have been mean and unmanly. Will you forgive me ? " Her cold hand was in his strong grasp, and, smiling sadly and looking gratefully and trustingly in his face, she answered, " Yes." As the doctor looked into her deep, honest, blue eyes, down into the true soul which shone through them, and thought in one wild moment of the treasure forever swept beyond his winning, his frame shook with powerful emotion. Oh! rare intuition! The small, cold hand grew uneasy, and was slowly withdrawn, and again folded over her heart.

"Will you be seated, Dr. Gilbert?" said the young woman, pointing to a chair, and taking one herself. "As between ourselves, Dr. Gilbert," she continued, "every thing is settled. You know my wishes, and respect them. I take your apology very gladly, for I do not wish to part with you, so that we might not meet again; but you have made an allusion to some one as a favorite of mine, and, that no other person may suffer injustice, I think I should know to whom you allude, and be allowed, for his sake and my own, to set you right."

The doctor blushed. In fact, he was never so thoroughly ashamed in his life. "Miss Hammett, I beg you not to humiliate me further," said he. "I spoke wildly and meanly—outrageously, if you will. Will not that do?"

"I think I have a right," pursued the young woman, "to be more particular. You could not have said what you did without some conviction, and I wish to put your mind forever at rest on the subject. Tell me, Dr. Gilbert, do you imagine that my hand belongs to any man here in Crampton?"

The doctor fidgeted. "We talk in confidence, of course," said he. "I knew that Arthur Blague was interested in you, very deeply. I knew that, at his susceptible age, he could not be much under the same roof with you without being impressed by you. I did not know how far the matter had gone, and very naturally thought of him when you so readily and so decidedly replied to my proposals. It irritated me, of course, to feel that an undeveloped youth, without means and without position, should be able to win that which was refused to me."

The doctor stumbled through his explanation, and Miss Hammett received it with a smile of amusement, touched with sadness and apprehension. When he closed, she said : " I thank you, for myself, and on behalf of Arthur Blague. I confess to you that he is a young man whom I very warmly esteem. It seems to me that he possesses the very noblest elements of manhood, and yet there is nothing that would give me more pain than to know that he has other feelings toward me than those of friendship. He has been very kind to me, and I pray God that nothing may happen in our intercourse to make my residence with his mother unpleasant te either of us."

Dr. Gilbert rose to his feet. The reaction had come, and it was a healthy one—honorable to the rugged nature in which it had taken place. Whether a lingering memory of the shipping in New York harbor, or a reminiscence of some great naval battle that he had read about in history, rose to him on the moment, under the spur of association, will never be known ; but he said : " Well, Miss Hammett, the deck is cleared, I believe ; the dead are thrown overboard, and the wounded are taken care of, and doing well." Then he laughed a huge, strong laugh, that showed that his physical system, at least, was unshaken.

Miss Hammett smiled — glad that the battle was over, and particularly rejoiced that the " wounded " were doing so well. She gave him her hand at the parlor door, and shaking it heartily, he said : " Let the past be buried. We shall get along very well together."

As he turned to leave her, he saw, standing in the street door before him, Arthur Blague in his working dress. He knew that Arthur had overheard his last words. The poor fellow stood like one paralyzed, and gave the doctor his hand as he passed out in a state of the most painful embarrassment. The doctor knew what it meant, and went away (what an exceedingly mean and human old fellow!) glad from the bottom of his heart that the young man had got to pass through the same furnace that he had.

It was Saturday night, and the young man had come home to pass the Sabbath. Miss Hammett met him cordially, but saw at once that there was something in the words of Dr. Gilbert that oppressed him. In her sweet endeavors to erase this impression, she only drove still deeper into his heart the arrow by which he had long been wounded. Ah! what charming torture was that! What a Sabbath of unsatisfactory dreaming followed it! How he listened for her steps in her chamber! How like the singing of an angel sounded her morning hymn! How her face shone on him as he sat near her at the table! How did heaven breathe its airs around him as he walked by her side to the village church! How did he lean back for hours in his easy-chair at home, with his eyes closed in delicious reverie! Arthur Blague was nineteen. Poor fellow!

CHAPTER XII.

ARTHUR BLAGUE IS INTRODUCED TO A NEW BOARD-ING-HOUSE, AND DAN BUCK IS INTRODUCED TO THE READER.

WE left Arthur Blague, some chapters back, sitting on his bed in the long lodging-hall at Hucklebury Run, having the previous evening left his bed and board at the house of the proprietor, under circumstances that forbade his return. The lodgers had all turned out, and were commencing their work in the mill. The more Arthur thought of the uncomfortable night he had passed, and of the low and degrading associations of the human sty into which circumstances had forced him, the more unendurable did his position seem. There were others at the same moment thinking of, and endeavoring to contrive for him, and when, at his leisure, he entered the mill, he found three or four men, including Cheek, gathered around Big Joslyn, and apparently urging upon that eminently cautious and impassive individual some measure of importance. As Arthur came up, they made room for him, and then Cheek, as the readiest spokesman, announced the matter in hand. "We've been trying," said he, "to make Joslyn take you into his house, and board you."

Joslyn was overshadowed by a great doubt. He "didn't know what the woman would say;" and the setting up of his will over hers was a thing he never dreamed of. Like gentlemen with delegated authority, acting under instructions, he found great difficulty in appearing to act on his own personal responsibility, and, at the same time, keeping within the limits of his power.

"I'll agree to any thing that the woman will," said Joslyn; and it was at last arranged that Arthur should walk home and breakfast with the discreet husband and father, and make his application in person.

On this conclusion, Cheek took Arthur aside, and, touching him significantly over the region of the heart, said, "Are you loose here?"

"What do you mean?" inquired Arthur.

"Have you hitched on anywhere yet?" said Cheek.

"I don't understand you," replied Arthur.

"I mean have you got a girl?" exclaimed the young man. "You see," continued he, "all we factory fellers have a girl. We may marry 'em, and we may not; but we are all kind o' divided off, and when we go out anywhere, we have an understanding who we are going to wait on."

Arthur smiled, and said that, so far as he knew, he was without any incumbrances of the kind.

"Well, all I want of you is not to go to hitching on to Joslyn's oldest girl," said Cheek. "She belongs to me. She isn't grown up yet, but I spoke for her when she was a little bit of a thing. You see, when I was a boy, I used to hold her in my lap, and have all sorts of talks with her, and then she told me she was going to wait for me ; and, by George ! I've always stuck her to it ! I tell her of it now, whenever I get a chance, and she's got so big that she begins to blush about it. Oh ! she's right, I tell you, and she's got one of the mothers —regular staver."

"I give you my pledge," said Arthur, "not to interfere with any of your rights."

"That's the talk," said Cheek. "If I was going to be cut out, I'd rather have you do it than any of these other fellers ; but I've set my heart on it, and I'm bound to win. Now mind—none of your tricks," said Cheek, with a good-natured shake of the finger ; and then he went off down-stairs whistling to his work.

When the breakfast bell rang, Big Joslyn rolled down his sleeves, took off his apron, and intimated to Arthur that he was ready. All the way to his house Joslyn did not speak a word. He felt that he was running a great risk in taking a stranger to his breakfast-table, without first consulting "the woman," as he always called his wife. As he raised the latch, Arthur heard from the inside the caution—"Sh-h-h-h !" Instantly the husband and father rose to his toes, and entered his door as noiseless as a cat. Arthur had seen Mrs. Joslyn before, and shook her hand in silence, as if he had come in to attend a funeral. "The woman" gave him a polite greeting, and then directed to her husband a look of inquiry.

Arthur's eyes hastily surveyed the breakfast apartment. Every thing was as neat as wax, and as orderly as the little clock that ticked in the corner.

" I have brought him home to breakfast, and he wants to talk with you about board," said Joslyn, in an undertone.

" Jenny, get another plate, and another knife and fork," said Mrs. Joslyn, and straightway the little girl that was " waiting " for Cheek—a second edition of her spirited and enterprising mother—obeyed the command, and the family at once sat down to their meal. Jenny was the only one of the large family of children visible ; the remainder were not allowed to wake up until Mr. Joslyn could be got out of the way for the morning, and she was only permitted to open her eyes because she could assist her mother.

Mrs. Joslyn was one of those high-strung creatures that are occasionally met with in humble life, endowed with quick good sense, indomitable perseverance, illimitable endurance, administrative faculty sufficient to set up a candidate for the federal presidency, and abundant good-nature whenever she could have every thing her own way. Besides, she was good-looking, and only needed to have been born under kinder stars, into a more gentle and refined circle of society, to make a splendid woman. Gods! What an apparent waste of valuable material there sometimes is in such places !

Now the moment her husband announced the nature of Arthur's errand, she had scanned the possibilities of her little dwelling, rearranged the beds of the children, got a room cleared in imagination, fixed upon the exact number of palm-leaf hats that the price of Arthur's board would relieve her from braiding, and was ready with her answer before her phlegmatic husband had helped Arthur to a plate of the humble morning fare.

"If Arthur Blague can take us as he finds us, we can take care of him," said Mrs. Joslyn decidedly.

"Just as you say," responded Joslyn, greatly relieved; and so the matter was regarded as settled.

Joslyn and his wife ate their breakfast, Arthur thought, with unexampled rapidity, and pushed back from the table, leaving him alone. "Don't you mind any thing about us," said Mrs. Joslyn. "I've got to attend to this man's head, and this is the only time in the day I have to do it." So she drove her husband back into a corner, ran a wet cloth over his bald crown, wiped it dry, and then brought the hair up over it from the temples, and braided the ends together in an incredibly short space of time.

"I do hate to have my husband look like a great, bald-headed baby," said Mrs. Joslyn, " and it all comes of his wearing his woollen cap in the mill. I wish men knew any thing. There! Off with you! The bell is ringing. Sh-h-h-h!"

Mr. Joslyn went out on tiptoe, leaving Arthur to arrange matters with his wife. She wished to have him understand, definitely, what the size of his room would be, what privileges he could have in the family, how late he could be admitted at night, and how much she expected for his board. While she was talking, her children, who seemed to understand exactly when they were expected to wake up, came tumbling in, one after another, in their night-dresses, until the room seemed to be full. The last fat little fellow that appeared came in crying. He was hardly old enough to walk, yet the enterprising mother said, "Sh-h-h-h! don't wake the baby!"

"Do you like children?" inquired the prolific mother.

"I like them—yes. You know I have not been much used to them," replied Arthur.

"I was going to tell you that there's but one way to

do in this house," she continued, " if you don't like 'em, and that is, not to pretend to like 'em. They'll be all over you like leeches when you've been into the river, if you make much of 'em. Less racket! Sh-h-h-h!"

Arthur departed, uncertain as to whether the place would be entirely to his liking and convenience, but quite certain that he would be more comfortable there than in the house of the proprietor, or at the short commons of the boarding-house, with the accompanying lodgings.

While these operations were in progress, there was an animated and angry consultation going on between Mrs. Ruggles and her hopeful daughter Leonora. " I tell you we want to get father real wrathy over this," said Mrs. Ruggles. " The more I think about it, the madder I get. I never took such imperance from anybody in my life, and to think that that great saucebox that we took in, and tried to do for, should presume to set himself up to put us down, and then to say that both of us was fools! As for that Hammett girl, if we don't make Crampton too hot to hold her, then it'll be because she's got brass enough in her face to make a kettle, that's all. I tell you, I won't be put down—not by a couple of factory hands, I tell you. I know what belongs to my persition, and I'll allow no understrapper to call me a fool, nor to say, Why do ye so?"

Leonora was quite as angry as her mother, but, when thrown directly upon her own resources, was wiser—at least more cunning. She had made up her mind to write to her father, in New York, a discreet account of the occurrences which we have recorded, insisting particularly on the wound which Arthur had inflicted upon her feelings by calling her a fool. She would not mention the fact that the same epithet had been applied to her mother, because she knew that that would rather please than offend him, and because she knew that the more she mixed her mother's name with the affair the more reason he would have to suspect that Arthur's insult was not altogether without excuse.

The letter was written and despatched—decidedly the most powerful and well-considered literary missive that had ever left Miss Leonora's hand. The shot told admirably, and produced the precise effect desired. Old Ruggles, as he sat in the little dirty hotel which he always lived in when in New York, read the letter, and was very angry. The result of his anger made itself manifest in a letter he wrote to Arthur, directing him to meet the Crampton stage-coach on a certain day, with two seats in the wagon.

Eight or ten days after Arthur had become a member of Mrs. Joslyn's family, he started for town with the two-seated wagon to meet the returning proprietor, and such individual or individuals as he might bring with him. He arrived at the Crampton hotel just as the stage came in. The coach was not wont to be crowded, and it was not overburdened on this occasion. Mr. Ruggles enjoyed a monopoly of the inside, while a highly dressed, stylish-looking young man occupied the box with the driver. Arthur watched the alighting of the young man with a good deal of interest. There was nothing about him of the Crampton stamp. He wore a sort of jockey cap, and downward, as if carrying out an idea begun in the cap, a jaunty coat, under which flamed a very jaunty waistcoat of red velvet. In his hand he carried a bamboo cane with an ivory top, carved in the form of a pointer's head. His face was not offensive, nor was it prepossessing. The chin was heavy, and the nose Hebrew, while the eyes were of that undefinable color that is sometimes found in connection with the finest characters, and sometimes with the coarsest—a kind of dirty gray,—but they were small, uneasy, and wicked.

Ruggles did not affect delight at meeting Arthur.

The old, taunting manner that he was accustomed to wear when angry with him, he was either too tired to assume, or he thought it of too little consequence. Yet Arthur would have been glad to shake hands with him, and approached him, ready to respond to any greeting that the proprietor might extend. Ruggles was cross; in fact, the long ride had half-killed him. He had travelled directly through from New York, without stopping, according to his old custom; and the event had shown him more than any thing else how much his shock and sickness had shattered him.

The young man on the box dropped his glossy boot to the wheel, and leaped to the piazza of the hotel, and then walked up and down, whipping his trousers with his bamboo cane, and sucking the pointer's head, and surveying Crampton common.

"Both of those trunks go," said Ruggles to Arthur, and both of them Arthur lifted to the wagon. As between himself and the young New Yorker, Arthur felt that he was at a decided disadvantage. He was not well-dressed, and the consciousness of the fact somehow stole away, for the time, half of his manhood. There is nothing that will so disarm and depress certain sensitive natures as conscious inferiority of dress. Until a degree of familiarity with the world has been acquired, and a man has learned that he has a recognized place in it, his dress either holds him up in his own self-respect, or compels him into abject self-contempt. There was nothing in the young stranger's face that indicated the gentleman, yet his dress was something to be respected, and Arthur felt so shabby by his side that it seemed as if the stranger must look upon him as an inferior.

"Come, Buck, get in," said old Ruggles, sharply.

"Ah! This is your dog-cart, eh? Gad! How lame I am!" exclaimed Mr. Buck, as he raised himself slowly into the wagon, and took his position by the side of the proprietor on the back seat, and stuck the pointer's head into his mouth. "Now, two-forty! Hold him in, and let him trot," said he, by way of announcing that he was ready for the ride to Hucklebury Run.

The "two-forty horse" started off at any thing but an ambitious pace, and Mr. Buck had sucked his cane but a short time, when he said very familiarly, "Driver, how much can you get out of him?"

It was the first time that Arthur had ever been addressed by this title, and he did not deign a reply. "Ruggles," said Buck, "what is this driver's name? Introduce me to him."

"Mr. Arthur Blague," said old Ruggles with mock politeness; "this is Mr. Dan Buck, of New York."

"Plague, how are you? How's your ma'am?"

"Buck, how are you? How's your doe?"

"Eh?"

"How's your doe?"

"Don't hear you," responded the imperturbable Buck, and then burst out pleasantly into the familiar refrain, "Speak a little louder, sir; I'm rather hard o' hearin'."

"Plague! I say! Plague!" called out Mr. Buck. Arthur made no reply.

Old Ruggles chuckled. "Blague," said he in a low voice. "His name is Blague."

"Blague! I say! Blague! Who made your boots?"

"None of your business. Why?"

"Speak to a gentleman like that again, and I'll knock your hat off," said Buck, without the slightest show of anger. "I was only going to ask you if you supposed he would have any objection to your kicking that horse with 'em. Kick him smart, and I'll give you a cent."

"I'll kick you for half the money," said Arthur.

"Eh?"

"I'll kick you for half the money," said Arthur again, without turning his head.

"Speak a little louder, sir; I'm rather hard o' hearin'," responded Mr. Buck, with another tuneful explosion; and then, subsiding for a moment, he burst out with, "Blague! Hullo! Blague! Where did you get your manners?"

"I borrowed them," replied Arthur, "of a fellow just in from New York."

"Well, you'd better return 'em then," said Buck.

"I'm doing it as fast as possible," replied Arthur.

"Good boy! Good boy!" exclaimed Mr. Dan Buck, tapping Arthur on the shoulder with the tip of his cane. "You're some, that's a fact; but tell me, oh! tell me before I die, what's the price of putty?"

"Ask Mr. Ruggles," replied Arthur. "He has just brought home a very large piece."

"Who the devil have you got on this front seat here?" said Mr. Dan Buck, turning to the proprietor, who had sat very quietly, enjoying the low impudence of his companion, and wondering what new spirit was in possession of Arthur. "Who the devil is this?" said Mr. Dan Buck. "I shall have to lick him, positively; sorry to do it—great sacrifice—but necessary."

"He's the fellow," replied Ruggles in a low tone that did not escape Arthur's ear, "that I told you about."

"S-h-o!" responded Dan Buck, with a look of surprise.

For the remainder of the ride to Hucklebury Run, the young man devoted himself entirely to Mr. Ruggles. Although he had made nothing by his onslaught upon Arthur, he was as cool and self-satisfied as if he had annihilated him. There was no sensitiveness—no sense of shame—that could possibly find manifestation through the mask of brass that encased his face. Arthur was amused to hear him pour into the proprietor's ear the tales of his exploits by flood and field. He had sailed as the captain of a packet, with no end of perquisites;

won five thousand dollars on a horse-race ; was on familiar terms with Washington Irving ; had slaughtered
innumerable buffaloes among the Rocky Mountains ;
had been partner in a large jobbing firm, and, on one
occasion, when hard pushed, had said grace at table.
This last achievement seemed to strike him as one of
the funniest pieces of business he had ever been engaged
in. " Gad ! " said he, " I never was so near floored in
my life. Lot of women, you know, all round the table,
with their heads down, and the whites of their eyes
rolled up. I sat at the head, you know, and the old
woman of all down to the foot. ' Mr. Buck,' says she,
putting down her head lower, and rolling up her eyes
higher, ' Mr. Buck, will you ask a blessing ? ' Well, I vow
I didn't know what to do. There they were, you know
—heads all down—eyes all rolled up—and every darned
one of 'em with a sort of squint on me. So, says I to
myself, ' Dan Buck, where's your pluck ? go in !' Well,
sir, I went in—didn't say much, you know, but it answered. All I could do to keep on a long face. Oh! I
vow, I never had such a time in my life. I thought I
should have died laughing after I got out. Wasn't it
great, though ? " and Mr. Dan Buck laughed uproar-
iously with the memory of the rare and eminently funny
exploit.

How much of this stuff old Ruggles believed, did not
appear, but as Mr. Dan Buck had flattered him on all
convenient occasions during the journey home, he felt
bound to appear as if he believed the whole of it. As
for Arthur, he knew that Dan Buck was lying, and Dan
Buck knew that Arthur understood him perfectly, though
he was entirely undisturbed by the fact.

Arriving at the factory, the proprietor alighted, and
told Arthur to go on to the house with Dan Buck and
the trunks. As the horse slowly climbed the hill, Dan
leaned forward to Arthur, and pointing over his shoulder

with his ivory pointer's head, said, " Cussed old hunks, how shall we manage him ? "

" How will he manage us ? is the question, I believe," replied Arthur.

" Gad ! when I can't manage my boss, I leave, I do," said the young man decidedly.

" You'll find this one a hard customer," said Arthur.

" Soap's the word, my boy ; soap's the word. Lord ! I can stuff his old carcass so full that he won't know his head from a bushel-basket. I've tried it, and got his gauge."

" What are you going to do here ? " inquired Arthur.

" Well, I'm going to sort o' clerk it, I suppose," responded Dan Buck. " Ruggles says you've been abusing his dry-goods, and he's going to promote you."

" You are to take my place, I presume," said Arthur, " and I am to go back into my old tracks. I understand it."

" I reckon that's it. Now tell a feller : is there any chance to knock down ? "

" Knock down ! " repeated Arthur with a tone of inquiry. " I don't know what you mean."

" Ah ! green's the color, eh ? very ! I understand. By the way, who is that fat old lollypop in the door yonder ? "

" That is Mrs. Ruggles—your landlady, and the wife of the proprietor."

" Come to my bosom, my own stricken deer ! " exclaimed the young man in a low tone, and with such a feint of an embrace, that Arthur laughed in spite of himself, while Mr. Dan Buck's face had never been longer than at that moment. " Now," said Buck, in an undertone to Arthur, " see me do it."

As the wagon drove up to the door, Mr. Dan Buck leaped from it, and rushing up to Mrs. Ruggles, seized her hand, and shaking it very heartily, exclaimed :

" Why, Mrs. Cadwallader ! How did you come here ? I'm delighted to see you—perfectly delighted."

Mrs. Ruggles was quite overcome. The greeting was so unexpected, and so violent, that, to speak figuratively, she was fairly carried off her feet. All she could say was : " You've got the advantage of me."

" You don't pretend to say, Mrs. Cadwallader, that you don't remember me ? That's too cruel ; " and Mr. Dan Buck looked as if he were about to wilt utterly under the crushing disappointment.

" You've made a mistake," said the woman amiably. " My name's Ruggles—Mrs. Ruggles. I never was a Cadwell."

" Is it possible that two ladies can look so much alike, and not even be sisters ? I would have sworn you were the wife of my friend, General Cadwallader. Then you are Mrs. Ruggles, and I'm to be a member of your family ! It is very pleasant, I assure you, for me to meet a face that so much reminds me of one of my dear friends, here among strangers."

" Be you the young man that's going to live with us ? " inquired Mrs. Ruggles, with patronizing sweetness.

" Yes, I be," replied Dan Buck, with the pointer's head between his teeth, and his eye half-shut, looking over his shoulder at Arthur Blague.

" Well, walk right in, then, and make yourself to home," said Mrs. Ruggles, heartily ; and turning about, she sailed into the house, calling, " Leonora ! Leonora ! "

Dan Buck gave Arthur a comical look, followed her in, and was introduced to Leonora, who received him with a most profound courtesy. In the meantime Arthur had deposited the trunks upon the piazza, and driven off.

" Who is this insolent fellow that drove us over ? " inquired Mr. Dan Buck.

" Now you don't say," said Mrs. Ruggles, in alarm,

" that he has been treating you to any of his imperance, do you ? It ain't possible, is it ? "

" Never was treated so in my life—thought the fellow
was drunk or crazy. I cut one man all to pieces with a
bowie-knife once, on a smaller provocation than he gave
me to-day ; but Mr. Ruggles was in the wagon, you
know, and I would not make him witness such a scene.
But, gad ! I'll chastise him—I'll lick him before I've
been here a week, if he gives me any more of his jaw."

" I wish you would," said Leonora savagely.

" You leave me alone for that. Don't bother your
little head about it, now ! I'll take care of him."

Mrs. Ruggles' heart was full. Leonora felt attracted
to the gallant and stylish stranger at once.

She would achieve a grand triumph over Arthur
Blague through him, or die in the attempt.

Dan Buck was delighted with his new home ; and before Mr. Ruggles had made his appearance within his
own door, he had succeeded in establishing the most
cordial relations between himself and that portion of the
family which he had collectively designated as the "dry-
goods." The mother reminded him more and more of
Mrs. Gen. Cadwallader, as the acquaintance grew. The
peculiar smile—the tone of voice—the manner—the style
of carriage—each brought forth from the enthusiastic
young man an exclamation of wonder, that two women
who were not only without blood relation to each other,
but without any knowledge of each other, could be so
much alike. The measure of "soap" was filled, at last,
by his assurance that " in her day, Mrs. Gen Cadwallader was the most splendid woman in New York."

Leonora was a *fac-simile* of his own sister Carrie, of
whose personal charms and accomplishments he bragged
as if she had been a favorite horse. " Gad ! " exclaimed
Dan Buck, " don't the fellers open their eyes when she
comes out ? But they know me—they do ; and they

know I won't stand any of their humbug. Oh! you ought to see 'em hang round, and try to get introduced. I was counting 'em over the other day, just before I started, and I'll be darned if I wasn't surprised to find ninety-five bottles of brandy that these fellers had sent to me to get me to introduce 'em to my sister. No, you don't, says I. I'll take your liquor, but visitors are requested not to muss the goods unless they wish to purchase."

Mr. Dan Buck expected that he should call Leonora "Carrie" half the time; and he begged her not to be offended if he should do so. If she would only regard him as a brother, his happiness would be complete. When supper came on, and all sat down at the table, the young man began and executed a series of romances, in which he invariably personated the central figure, that quite eclipsed any thing of which the Ruggles family had ever heard. He laughed immensely at his own wit, and as every thing he uttered was interlarded with choice bits of flattery, tossed in about equal proportions to father, mother, and daughter, the meal was one of the most delightfully memorable ever enjoyed in that little mansion. Arthur Blague was lugged in on all convenient occasions, to illustrate some ludicrous point of a story; and the voluble drollery of the fellow kept the whole family in irresistible laughter. Finally, Mrs. Ruggles assured him that she regarded him as a "valuable accusation to the society of Hucklebury Run," at which he said "Very," with a wink at Leonora, which made that young lady spill her tea with giggling.

The next day old Ruggles undertook to introduce the young man to his duties. It is not to be denied that the proprietor had very serious misgivings about his new clerk, who was altogether too talkative—too familiar— too presuming. He did not like being called "Ruggles" by any one in his employ, or to have any assumed superiority over himself among his dependents. He saw that the fellow who had palmed himself off upon him in New York as a "struggling young man, ready to undertake the humblest employment for the sake of honestly earning his bread," had no element of reverence in his composition, and that he could not be "snubbed." In vain were all his endeavors to establish any distance between the young man and himself. It was—"Look here, Ruggles," "What do you say, Ruggles?" or, "Hadn't *we* better do so and so,"—as if he had just become a partner in the concern, and had brought in and invested a hundred thousand dollars in the business.

Mr. Ruggles was irritable and sick. His journey had overtasked him; and when he saw how orderly matters had been conducted by Arthur in his absence, he cursed his stupidity in yielding to the importunities of his daughter. He was the more vexed and disgusted because he felt that his old energy was gone—that he was in a great degree a broken man—that he could not be again the omnipresent, all-sufficient power in his own concern that he had been. He found no difficulty, however, with Arthur's assistance, in making Mr. Dan Buck acquainted with the details of his business. The young New Yorker was ready with his pen, and though apparently without a great degree of business education, possessed a quick and ready insight into business affairs, that gave him a command of his duties at once.

Arthur at once resumed, with a degree of cheerfulness which he did not himself anticipate, his old duties as a regular operative in the mill. It was a relief to be less confined to the society of the proprietor. Though their relations to each other had been greatly changed, he had never learned to respect the man whom accident and helplessness alone could make tolerable, but always felt oppressed and uncomfortable when in his presence.

CHAPTER XIII.

DAN BUCK GOES TO CHURCH AND RECOGNIZES AN OLD ACQUAINTANCE.

WEEKS came and went over the busy hamlet of Hucklebury Run, and Mr. Dan Buck had become not altogether an unpopular member of that little community. The boys delighted in his stories, and he said such droll things to the girls that they could talk of little else. He had disseminated the idea, among the operatives generally, that he was the son of a merchant of immense wealth, and that, being a little wild in New York, his father had consigned him to old Ruggles for reformation. If " the governor " would only send him his horse and his dogs, he might go to the devil, and New York with him : he could get along.

It was Mrs. Ruggles' special ambition to get the young New Yorker to go to the Crampton church with her and Leonora. Mr. Ruggles found himself so tired and so weak, that he had no disposition to take his naps under the soothing effects of Mr. Wilton's eloquence, and had relinquished church-going altogether. For this, the wife and daughter would not have cared at all, if Mr. Dan Buck had not been quite as averse to accompanying them as the proprietor himself. The young man always dressed himself elaborately, took his cane, and walked off into the woods, and spent the day as lazily as possible. At last, Mrs. Ruggles took him seriously to task for his delinquencies. Dan Buck assured her that there had been a time when he was constant at the ministrations of the Gospel, and a member of the Sunday-school ; but on one occasion he had a very dear aunt who dropped dead in church, and since that time he had found it very difficult to bring himself to enter a sacred edifice. He could not sit down in a church, in fact, without thinking about the death of his aunt, and constantly suffering from the apprehension that he should meet with a similar fate. " I know," said Dan Buck, " that lightning never strikes twice in three places, but I can't help my feelings."

At last, however, his anxiety to see Miss Mary Hammett, of whom the operatives had told him much, and against whom Mrs. Ruggles and her daughter were constantly uttering their slanders, overcame his fear of sudden death, and he announced his determination to " try it on once." It was a very happy Sabbath morning for Mrs. Ruggles. The old carryall was brought out—a heavy vehicle, with two seats and a top—and the double of Mrs. Gen. Cadwallader took the back seat to herself, while Leonora and Mr. Dan Buck occupied the other. Dan was in very high spirits, considering the character of the day, the capacity of the horse, and the apprehensions which the death of his aunt so powerfully excited in him. He turned out of the road occasionally, and frightened Mrs. Ruggles with the idea that the carriage was about to be overset. He whipped the horse into a run, and then, winding the reins around his hands, and leaning back as if he had in hand something immense in the way of animal power and spirit, shouted, " Take care! take ca-a-a-re! wan't to kill another man, don't you ? "

Poor Mrs. Ruggles suffered pitifully. She declared she was never so " scat" in her life, while Dan Buck and Leonora had the pleasant part of the ride all to themselves, and seemed to understand each other perfectly. Leonora was, in fact, very wild. Her mother declared that she " acted as if she was possessed." She laughed at all Dan Buck's drolleries, declared herself ready to be turned over, hoped the horse would run away, and performed various most unladylike feats,

13

simply because her conduct amused Dan Buck, and frightened and vexed her mother.

In the church, the young man was the impersonation of gravity. Of all the solemn faces that greeted the Crampton pastor that morning, there was none of greater length—certainly none of greater sanctimoniousness—than that which rose above the shoulders of Dan Buck; yet for some reason Miss Leonora could hardly behave decently. When the hymn was given out, the young man drew a plump song-book from his pocket, and politely handed it to Leonora, opened at "Betsy Baker." He whispered "Amen" and "Hallelujah" to all the pastor's emphatic utterances, so that none but Leonora could hear him; and the girl had not self-command enough to keep within the bounds of decent behavior.

The sermon was almost finished, when he seemed to be suddenly arrested by the turning of a head, not far before him. For the first time since he had arrived in Crampton, there was an expression of surprise upon his face. Leonora caught the expression, and, directing her eyes to the object which had so absorbed him, found it to be nothing less than Mary Hammett herself. Leonora was, of course, disturbed. That something had produced a profound impression upon the young man was very evident. After observing her intently for some minutes, and moving in his seat to obtain a better view, he leaned over to Leonora, and asked her who she was.

"She is that Hammett girl," said Leonora, with a sneer.

"The Devil!" said Mr. Dan Buck.

When the service was completed, and the congregation crowded from their pews into the aisles, to the utter consternation of Mrs. Ruggles and her daughter, Dan Buck left them abruptly, and, rushing to the side of

Mary Hammett, took her hand with much apparent respect, and greeted her as an old acquaintance. They saw Mary Hammett's face grow ashy pale, and noticed that it was with great exertion that she kept herself from falling. They saw him leaning down, and talking to her in a low tone, intended only for her ear. They saw that she made no reply, but that she listened for every word, and paid no regard to any one else. Then they saw her lift her pale face to his in silent appeal, which, as he continued to talk, reddened into an expression of indignation. As they came out of the church, he glided away from her, and she, joined by Arthur Blague, walked off to her home.

Mrs. Ruggles and Leonora were dumb with astonishment and vexation. The horse and carryall were brought before the door, and Dan Buck helped the women to their seats, and drove off. Not a word was spoken until they had passed the bounds of the village, when Mrs. Ruggles, unable to restrain herself longer, burst out with, "What *was* you doing with that Hammett girl?"

"One of my cussed blunders," replied Dan Buck. "You know how I thought you were Mrs. Gen. Cadwallader, when I first saw you. Well, I got into just such another mess as that. I would have sworn she was a cousin of mine—a poor girl that got deceived, you know —feller took advantage of her—you understand. Feller wouldn't marry her, and I cowhided him—all but killed him. He went to Texas, and was blowed up in a steamboat, and she went off, the Lord knows where. I thought I'd found her. You see, it was a good many years ago, and I'd had a chance to forget her. I vow I never'll speak to another girl till I've been introduced to her, as long as I live."

Now Mr. Dan Buck could not but be conscious that Mrs. Ruggles and her daughter thought he was lying. He knew that he was not self-possessed, according to his habit, and felt that they received his words with incredulity.

"What made her look up to you so?" inquired Leonora, who had been quite impressed with that part of the scene.

"Why, you see, I told her that she needn't try to make me think that she wasn't Jane Buck, and that Jenny had a mole under her left eye, which I should know anywhere. Then she lifted up her face, and I knew it was all day with me—face as smooth as the back of your hand. Did you see how she blushed to have me look at her? Gad! I wouldn't have had it happen for the world; and there was all Crampton looking on, and seeing me talking to her, and everybody will think that she's some acquaintance of mine. Just my luck, always getting into some such a scrape as that. I felt just as sure when I went to church that something would happen; knew I should drop down dead in some way or other."

Leonora leaned over to Mr. Dan Buck, and whispered in his ear, "You—lie—*sir*."

Then Dan Buck began to swear. He called upon himself the most terrific judgments, and renounced all hope of a happy hereafter, if he had ever seen the woman before, or ever heard her name until he had heard it in Crampton. From this condition of overwhelming indignation, he came down, at last, by an artful gradation to one of injured innocence. This was his last resort, and it was successful. When he began to talk about turning his back upon Hucklebury Run forever, and leaving friends who had become inexpressibly dear to him, because they doubted his word of honor, mother and daughter surrendered without conditions; and before they drove up to the door of the family mansion, the young man had entirely recovered his spirits.

Others had noticed this interview between Dan Buck

and Mary Hammett, of course ; and she, in her truthfulness, was almost defenceless, when inquired of concerning her relations to him. She could not deny that she had seen him before. She only begged those who questioned her not to insist on her answering them ; and as all saw that the matter distressed her, they were well-bred enough to drop the subject. Whatever may have been their relations to each other, the meeting filled her with pain, and a vague apprehension of approaching evil. It seemed to her that her calamities would have no end. Her experience with Dr. Gilbert had left upon her a sad impression, and had disturbed the current of her life. She felt at no liberty to look to him for further counsel. She could not but be aware, in some degree, of the absorbing affection which Arthur entertained for her, and this troubled her more than her unpleasant passage with Dr. Gilbert. To be greeted at last by one who knew her, and who had her in his power, quite overwhelmed her.

Mary went to her room, and, with such calmness as she could assume, recalled the words that Mr. Dan Buck had spoken to her. "Mary," he had said with offensive familiarity, "you see that I know you. Mum's the word with me, of course. Very easy to write and post the old man—thousand dollars in my pocket—but Dan Buck knows a trick worth two of that. We'll have a laugh in our sleeves off here by ourselves. Perhaps you'll be able to speak to me now—know where you live, and will call round. When will it be most convenient ? "

These little sentences he had dropped into her ear as a man would drop pebbles into a pool, waiting to see them strike the bottom, and marking the ripples they awoke upon the surface. In all his language, there was something intended beyond its literal interpretation. The impression upon her was precisely as if he had said : " Mary, you see that I know you, and that you are in my power. I will take my revenge for your contempt of me in other years, in some way, either by discovering you to those who wish to find you, and whom you wish to avoid, or you shall favor me—Dan Buck—with your society." There was something that went further than this—that came to her from his hot breath, voiceless and inarticulate, but more dreadful than all.

As for Dan Buck, he could not rid himself of the presence of Mrs. Ruggles and Leonora quickly enough to meet his impatient wishes. The moment the horse was out of his hands, he took his cane for a stroll. He was excited and exultant. Crampton, which had begun to grow very tiresome to him, had suddenly become a very interesting place. He found a woman in his power—the woman of all the world whom he would have chosen. Coolly he recalled the scene of the morning, and then as coolly he undertook to calculate how he could make the most of the knowledge he had acquired.

The conclusions at which the young man arrived during his Sunday afternoon reflections, will be made apparent in the interview which he had determined upon having with Miss Hammett. A few days passed away, during which, by ardent devotion to Leonora and her mother, he succeeded in driving away the cloud with which the events of the Sabbath had shadowed their spirits. One night he announced his intention of walking to Crampton to see his tailor, hoping " by all that was good and holy " that he shouldn't run against a schoolma'am, or any of that sort of cattle, and asking Leonora to pray for him.

Mr. Dan Buck was undertaking, as he felt, rather a hazardous experiment—at least one of doubtful issue. It summoned into action all the bad boldness of his nature, and required all the hardness and insensitiveness he had acquired in years of unprincipled and unbridled living. He knocked at Mrs. Blague's door, boldly announced his name, and requested to see Miss Hammett. Now Mrs. Blague had already been directed by Mary to refuse her to Mr. Dan Buck, if he should ever call. Further than this, she had made Mrs. Blague promise that if he should ever find his way into the house and into her presence, she (Miss Hammett) should not be left alone with him. Mrs. Blague had agreed faithfully to do as Mary desired, but when she met Dan Buck face to face, her determination faded at once. There was that in his eye and manner which showed that he had no idea of being denied. He was in the hall and in the parlor, before poor, stammering Mrs. Blague could command her tongue at all. She felt that she could do nothing with such a man as he, and, instead of turning him out of her house as, in imagination, she had been doing all the week, with certain very lively and uncomfortable fleas in his ear, she went directly to Mary Hammett's room, and told her with almost a breathless fright that Mr. Buck was in the parlor, and wished to see her.

"I can't go down—I will not go down," exclaimed Mary, in great excitement. "You must tell him, Mrs. Blague, that I am sick, and cannot see him—that he must excuse me."

Mrs. Blague left Mary very hesitatingly, and descended the stairs, but before she reached them, she heard steps retreating through the hall, and knew that Dan Buck had been listening. She found him, however, coolly whipping his trousers with his cane, and devoutly regarding a picture of the Holy Family upon the wall.

"Miss Hammett wishes me to say," said Mrs. Blague tremblingly, "that she is sick, and that you must excuse her to-night."

Dan Buck laughed. "That's good, now—excellent!" exclaimed he. "Why, madam," he continued, "she would not miss seeing me to-night for any money. We are old friends, we are ; and she's only fooling you. You go straight back to her, and tell her that I haven't any time to-night for jokes, or I would indulge her. Tell her, too, that I have something very important to say to her. She'll understand it."

All this Mr. Dan Buck spoke in a loud tone, conscious, apparently, that Mary Hammett was listening above, and desirous that she should hear every word. Mary knew that the material of which Mrs. Blague was made, could not withstand him, and by a desperate impulse—before the lady could start on her way back—she flew to the head of the stairs, slid down the steps as if she had been a sprite, and stood before her persecutor, her eyes flashing with anger.

" What have you to say to me, sir ? " she inquired, standing before him, every fibre of her frame quivering with excitement.

Dan Buck answered not a word, but coolly pointed to Mrs. Blague.

" Mrs. Blague will remain with me," said Miss Hammett firmly.

" It makes very little difference with me whether she stays or goes," said he, coolly. " I rather think you wouldn't like to have her hear all that will pass between you and me. I'm sure if you can stand it, I can." And then he whipped his trousers again, and walked off with the pointer's head between his lips, and took another view of the Holy Family.

Miss Hammett grasped Mrs. Blague's hand, drew her to the sofa, and both sat down. Mr. Buck turned around, and looked at them for a moment, and said with a sneer, " It won't work."

" If you are a gentleman, Mr. Buck," said Mary Hammett, " you will have nothing to say to me that Mrs. Blague should not hear ; and now, if you have any business with me, I beg you to despatch it, and leave me."

The young man drew a chair deliberately in front of the women, and sat down. "Now I'm going to tell you a story—one of the funniest things you ever heard," said he. "Once there was an old man who had a great deal of money, and lived in a splendid house, and kept a splendid store, full of clerks and porters, and all that sort of thing, but his clerks and porters weren't good enough for him to tread on. Well, this old man had a splendid daughter, who had her favors for some folks, and for some she hadn't any. This daughter's name was——"

"Mr. Buck," interposed Mary, hurriedly, "if you are a gentleman——"

"But I'm not a gentleman," said Mr. Buck. "I never was a gentleman—don't pretend, you know, to anything of the kind. Well, as I was saying, this daughter's name was——"

"Mr. Buck!"

"What?"

"Have you no pity?"

"None to speak of—mean to get some next time I go to market—put it down on memorandum." Dan Buck coolly drew out a pencil and paper, and wrote down and read aloud, "Pity, one pint."

"Have you a sister, Mr. Buck?"

"Nary sister—do little something for you in the way of brothers, if you want."

"Have you a mother?"

"All out of mother—sorry, but stock exhausted."

"Have you any honor?" said Miss Hammett, angry at the insolent irony with which he had met her efforts to find some sensitive point in his nature, to which she might effectually appeal.

"You might as well stop that kind of dodge," responded Dan Buck. "You won't make any thing out of it, and I shall not get through with my story. As I was saying, the old man had a daughter, whose name—was—Mary——"

Mary lifted both her hands in deprecation of further progress.

"I see," said the young man maliciously, "that you do not want this woman to hear the next word, but I swear I'll speak it if you don't send her out of the room, and worse words than that, too."

To this purpose of the adroit villain, Mary was at length subdued; and she bade Mrs. Blague retire. Mr. Dan Buck followed her to the door, shut it after her, turned the key in the lock, and then withdrew it, and put it into his pocket. "Now," said he, "nobody can disturb us, and we shall have a charming time."

Mary rose to her feet alarmed. "What do you want of me?" she inquired.

"Oh! sit down, sit down. Allow me to conduct you to a better seat than that." And the scoundrel tried to put his arm around the frightened girl. In an instant she eluded him, and ran to raise the window. He followed, and held it down.

"What do you want of me?" she repeated.

"A kiss."

"Dan Buck," said Mary fiercely, "I understand you; and now you must understand me. There are things in this world that I dread more than discovery. You know what they are, and now if you do not desist from your purpose to insult me, I will scream so that all Crampton shall hear me. Your silence will never be purchased by me at the price of dishonor. I will not even allow you the privileges of a friend. Now what have you to say?"

"Of course, I understand all this. I understood it before I came here; and now you must understand that

Dan Buck looks out for number one, and is bound to make his pile. It's kisses or cash with Dan Buck—Mary or money. You know that I could get a thousand dollars out of the old man for tipping him the wink, and I can't afford to lose the rhino. You are nothing to me. You hate me, and think I'm the devil and all, and I shan't do any thing to change your opinion. You always had favors enough for you know who, but nothing for this child. Now what can you do for a feller?"

Mary was angry and disgusted with the mercenary scoundrel, but she was relieved. "You know that I am poor," said she, "and labor for every dollar I receive?"

"That's not my look-out," responded Dan Buck. "I know that you have only to say the word to have all the money you want; but if you won't say it, why, I can't help it. It doesn't seem to be just the cheese for Dan Buck to pocket your change, I know; but he knows where you can get more, whenever you care more about the money than you do about your own will."

Dan Buck said all this leaning forward in his chair with his elbows on his knees, and his hands employed in beating a tattoo upon his front teeth with the pointer's head. Such cool, imperturbable impudence Mary had never seen. After a few moments of thought she said: "How much money must I give you to secure your silence, and free myself from your importunities?"

"All you've got."

"And what security will you give me that your part of the bargain will be fulfilled?"

"The word of a man of honor," replied Dan Buck, with special unction, "provided you've saved up any thing handsome."

Mary smiled in spite of her vexation. "You have no honor, Dan Buck," said she.

Dan Buck's temper was entirely unruffled by this very uncomplimentary statement. "Wrong," said he, "got considerable.　Any quantity left over when I failed, you know—give you a mortgage on the lot."

"Then you are really in earnest in wishing to take this money from me?" said Miss Hammett.

"I'd rather it would come out of the old man, of course," said he. "Now you don't consider that I'm really making a great sacrifice in consenting to take up with what you've got to give me, for the sake of accommodating you."

Mary reflected for a minute, then rose and said : "Excuse me for a moment."

"Where are you going?"

"Up-stairs for my money."

Dan Buck drew the parlor key from his pocket, put it into the lock, and turning the bolt, said, "All fair now, no dodges," and then he opened the door and let her out.

The moment she retired, he went to the centre-table, turned over the cards and billet-doux, and among them found a note in Mary's hand-writing. This he carefully placed in his pocket-book, and was engaged in another critical examination of the Holy Family when the young woman returned. Mary handed him a roll of bank-notes, the result mainly of her year's earnings, and said : "Here is all the money I have in the world. If you choose to take the whole of it, be it so. Whatever you do, I wish you to understand that I consider you the blackest villain I ever saw."

Dan Buck took the notes, unfolded them upon his knee, counted them over, pocketed them, and, rising to his feet, said : "You've got off cheap ; and now, if you ever blow on me, I'll have the old man on your track in thirty-six hours. I wish you a good evening."

Then Dan Buck stuck his jockey cap upon his head, walked out of the house with a careless whistle upon his lips, and took his way back to Hucklebury Run.

When, at the end of the week, Arthur came home to spend the Sabbath, his mother told him the whole story of Dan Buck's visit so far as she knew it. Arthur raved with indignation. The thought that his angel, his impersonation of all earthly and heavenly graces, should be subjected to the insolence of so low and unprincipled a man as Dan Buck, aroused everything fierce in his nature. There was nothing in the way of retribution or revenge that he did not feel ready to undertake. He determined to call the villain to an account, and so informed his mother. Nothing could have alarmed Mrs. Blague more than this declaration. She immediately saw before her imagination the mangled corpse of her son, and tried words and tears in vain to dissuade him from his purpose. She did not see the secret spring of her son's ungovernable wrath, and was frightened at its manifestations. Accordingly, on the first opportunity, she sought Miss Hammett's room, and communicated to her the condition of her son's mind, and besought her good offices in pacifying him. Under the circumstances, Miss Hammett was alarmed, and begged for an immediate private interview with him in the parlor.

Seated there before him, she told him how necessary to her peace it was that Arthur should take no notice whatever of Mr. Dan Buck's insults. She could not tell him why it was so, but she assured him that no one could interfere between the young scoundrel and herself without doing her an essential unkindness. On that occasion, and on all future occasions, she must be left absolutely alone in the management of her relations to Mr. Dan Buck. If she should ever need assistance, the first one to whom she should look for aid would be Arthur Blague. Arthur was softened and conciliated by this latter assurance, but the close of the interview left him mystified and uncomfortable. What had Mary

Hammett been—what had she done—to make her the
subject of Dan Buck's persecutions? Why should she
be unwilling to have her cause espoused by a man who
was ready and anxious to protect her? What right
had a man of Dan Buck's character to force himself into
her society? By what means had he been able to do
this with impunity? These questions made him very
miserable, and his Sabbath was a day of moody abstrac-
tion, which all of Mary's delicate and cordial attentions
failed to alleviate.

CHAPTER XIV.

TRISTRAM TREVANION GETS REVIEWED, AND MISS GIL-
BERT GETS DISGUSTED.

WHEN Fanny Gilbert fully realized that she was
about to appear before the world as an authoress, the
hours were many in which her heart sank within her.
When the path to publicity was difficult or doubtful,
the goal was crowned with a golden glory. Now that
it had become easy and certain, clouds came dubiously
down and filled her with fear. She had been at work
for fame : what if, instead of fame, she should only win
disgrace? What if she should fail to arrest the attention of the world for a moment, and her book should
be carelessly kicked into oblivion? Through her conversations with Mary Hammett, she had learned that
the world really owed her nothing. She had not written her book from love of the world, or a desire to
benefit the world. She was conscious that there was
nothing in her motives, or her intentions, upon which
she could establish a claim to the world's charitable
judgments. She had selfishly labored all winter for
the sole purpose of gathering a harvest of praise, and

she knew that if she should fail to reap according to her hope, her labor would be lost without recourse. She could not fall back upon her motives and her aims for consolation, nor could she look forward to another generation for appreciation and vindication.

Many times did Miss Gilbert wish that she could be like the careless girls who called upon her—content with the little life they were living. She despised their devotion to dress, and their delight with trifles. She scorned the petty gossip of beaux and belles that busied their tongues; but she doubted whether she were as really happy as they; and sometimes she shrank from the gulf of active life and wearying thought into which she was plunging. She trembled when she thought that she was entering upon a life from which she could never retreat—that never in this world or the next could she be satisfied with the simple fact of being. She looked on, on, on; and there rose before her no high table-land of rest. The laborer passed her window, his hoe upon his shoulder, returning from his work in the fields. She watched him as he approached his dwelling, saw the little ones run out to welcome him, and the humble wife smiling at the door, and felt that in his insignificant life and unambitious aims there was indeed a charm worth sighing for—a charm which she was painfully conscious that she could not even choose to endow her own life with. She had burst the shell that enclosed the world around her, and had caught glimpses of the stars above her, and the great ocean of life that stretched around; and while she looked, her wings had grown, and she could never enter the shell again. Like thousands who lived before her, and millions that will come after her, for the first time conscious of the same condition, she sighed " Alas!" and turned to her work.

As nothing particularly worthy of note occurred at Crampton or the Run during the summer, among the other characters engaged in our story, there will be abundant opportunity to tell of Fanny Gilbert's work, and its results. It will be remembered that Mr. Frank Sargent had recommended certain changes to be made in her novel. She had given the subject a good deal of thought, and had finally concluded to act upon Mary Hammett's suggestion—to marry Grace Beaumont to Tristram Trevanion, in order that the public demand for poetic justice should be satisfied, and, further to compass the same end, to secure the violent death of the Jewish dwarf at the hand of her hero. Further than this she would not go. The title of her novel should remain as it was—" Tristram Trevanion, or the Hounds of the Whippoorwill Hills," forever!

As she knew her manuscript by rote, it was not necessary for her to procure its return from the publisher, in order to make the proposed changes. So, in the charming sovereignty of authorship, she coolly sat down, and decreed and executed the marriage and the murder. Not only this, but she dressed the bride in exquisite array, and crowned her with orange blossoms, and made a great feast, and (shall it be said?) created a family of beautiful children, who filled the hearts of their parents with unalloyed happiness through a very long term of years, and brought honor to the already glorious name of Trevanion. The dwarf died as he had lived—a miscreant; but in his last moments he confessed the justice of his doom, in that he had been the author of various murders in his vicinity, which had hitherto been shrouded in mystery. In consequence of this fact, Trevanion was able to escape all regrets for his violence, and complacently to regard himself as an instrument in the hands of Providence for punishing the guilty.

These alterations having been carefully executed, they were enclosed by mail to the publisher, and Fanny subsided into thoughtful inactivity, to wait for further developments. She did not wait long. At the end of two weeks she received a few sheets of proof—hardly more than specimen pages—to show her how the work would look, but enough to excite her, and bring to her a fresh instalment of dreams of the future. Ah! the first bliss of being in type! Nothing, in the most triumphant career of authorship, equals the exultant happiness of that precious moment. No event, but the morning of the resurrection, can bring a repetition of that emotion that pervades the soul when one's corruptible manuscript first puts on incorruptible letter-press, and the loose, uncertain mortality of running-hand rises into the immortality of print. Fanny Gilbert's age and temperament were abundantly susceptible to this charming experience, and she enjoyed it keenly. She shut herself into her room, and read, and re-read, the charming pages. She saw that the book was going to be a new one to her. The thoughts were crowded nearer together; their relations became more apparent to herself. She carried them to Mary Hammett, and the two young women read them in company. Dr. Gilbert read them; Aunt Catharine read them; and even little Fred was allowed to share in his sister's happiness.

It was well that the young authoress should be happy for her little moment. It was well that the world should be transfigured in the light of her new emotions. June, the month of roses, was at flood-tide. As Fanny sat at her window dreaming, she saw the green sea of foliage tossing in billowy unrest, and sparkling with myriad flowers, and foaming in the beds of its uneasy abysses with sheeted bloom. Out upon that beautiful sea all her sensibilities pushed their sails, to dance and float and fly, under the light of the great, slumbrous sun. What rare sea-birds were those that plied their cease-

14

less wings and sang their marvellous songs among the
waves!—orioles, like coals of fire, plunging in, and
coming out unquenched; automatic humming-birds,
stopping here and there, and sipping and sliding away
with a whirr, as if revolving upon, and following, an invisible wire; chimney swallows paying out from imper-
ceptible reels broad nets of music to catch flies with;
bobolinks, diving into the swaying masses of green, and
coming out with a thousand tough bubbles bursting in
their metallic throats; broad-winged hawks, slowly sailing above all, far up in the breathless ether, ripening
their feathery silver in the sun, and watching the play
beneath! And then what musical spray of insect-life
swept through the balmy atmosphere!—bees sprinkling
themselves upon the fresh blush-roses at the door, or
humming by, loaded with plunder; flies industriously
doing nothing; whole generations of motes sliding up
and down shadow-piercing sunbeams! Into this beautiful scene, and half-creating it, went Fanny's happy
fancy, dreaming, and dreaming, and dreaming, through
hours of intoxication.

The proofs came in slowly. There was evidently no
haste on the part of the publisher in completing the
volume. In fact, he had informed the young authoress
that he only aimed to have it in readiness for the fall
trade. The time, however, seemed very long; for
Fanny could do nothing while the grand event of her
life was in expectation. She had done her work, and
had no heart for further enterprise until she had received payment for the past. Miss Hammett, too,
seemed to be quite as much interested in the receipt
of the proofs as if the book were her own, for with
each instalment there invariably came a good-natured, sportive letter from the publisher, which she
was in the habit of borrowing and reading at her leisure.

The weary summer wore away at last, and September brought the long-wished-for volume, and in its company a most disgusting disappointment. Instead of the massive book which the massive manuscript and the multiplied proofs had prophesied, it was a dwarfed little volume, that indicated equal scarcity of brains and paper. The typographical aspect of the book showed that the printer had spread out into the largest space an incompetent mass of material, and had failed, at last, to make anything of pretentious magnitude. Poor Fanny looked over the books in her father's library, saw what other brains had done, and was driven into self-contempt—almost into despair. " Tristram Trevanion " made no show in the world at all! Why, it was no bigger than a Sunday-school book ; and it seemed to the writer so unaccountable that anybody could ever have spent as much time on a Sunday-school book as she had spent on that ! What possible object could they have had ! How could they have lived through it !

After all the dreams of the summer came a great reaction. The book was born, but it was a very insignificant child indeed, and was made quite ridiculous by the disproportion between its swollen and sonorous name and its gross weight. She conceived a new respect for the gentleman who had suggested " Shucks " as a fitting title, and wondered that he had been so generous as even to think of "Rhododendron." She laid it down upon the table, and looked at it with other books, and even went so far as to wonder whether, if it should secure the praise of the public, she should not be so much disgusted with the public for praising it, that the praise would lose its value.

Poor child! —for she was but a child—she had not learned that an achievement, to him who achieves, is dead—that it is only a block upon which he stands, that he may wreathe crowns about the brows of higher deeds.

She had not learned that to each great effort of a soul which God has informed with genius there comes an influx of new power, advancing its possibilities so far, that all it has done becomes contemptible to itself. She had not learned that the more genius glories in the results of its labor, the more does it show itself impoverished by its labor, and the more does it demonstrate the shallowness of its resources and the weakness of its vitality.

But the book was out. What should be its fate ? Dr. Gilbert had his own opinion of the volume, and some very well-founded apprehensions of its destiny. Since its enthusiastic reception by the pastor and his wife, he had thought about it a great deal more than he had ever done before. The reflections to which his visit to New York had given rise, had carried him into a juster estimate of his daughter's powers as a writer, and the world's needs and demands, than he had entertained before. In truth, the relations of his daughter's life to the life of the great world, had come to look to him very like the relations of Crampton to the great world of production and trade. But he had an interest in the book which Fanny had not. He had agreed to share the loss on its publication in case that publication should be a failure. He was pledged to all proper and practicable efforts, therefore, for its financial success.

A small package of the books had been sent to him for distribution among the local press. He made an errand to Littleton, and left a copy with the editor of the Littleton *Examiner.* He sent a copy by mail to the editor of the Londonderry *Gazette*, and another to the North Yerrington *Courier.* More distant members of the great newspaper fraternity were equally favored. Fanny was aware of these operations, and gradually came out of the condition of half-indifferent disgust into which the completed volume had thrown her, into one of painful anxiety. Now that public condemnation or public approval was imminent, her fears quite outweighed her hopes, and she could hardly sleep during the period that she awaited the decision of the local presses to which so peculiarly her fate had been committed. The Littleton *Examiner* had pretensions to literary character very much in advance of its neighbors. Rev. J. Desilver Newman, a young clergyman not altogether unknown in these pages, was supposed to have some mysterious connection with this press. The editor himself was a profound theorist, and delighted more in speculation than in matters of fact. It was very difficult, indeed, to obtain the news from his sheet, except in an incidental manner, for the events of the world were so accustomed to suggest new trains of thought, and to keep him busy among philosophical causes, that he had all he could do to present what he delighted to call " the rationale of current life."

The position of the Littleton *Examiner* was considered by the press of the region very enviable. That sheet was, in fact, quite the standard. All waited, before expressing an opinion, to see what the *Examiner* said. On some subjects they always took the liberty " to differ with brother Highway of the Littleton *Examiner*," simply because, in all matters of politics and religion, it was expected of them by their subscribers that they should differ with brother Highway. In literary matters, however, it was always delightful for them to add their humble testimony to that of brother Highway, in favor or in condemnation of any man, scheme, or opinion that might be under discussion. Besides, it was an easy way of making a paragraph to say, " We do not agree with brother Highway of the *Examiner*, when he says that," etc., etc., quoting brother Highway's paragraph without the disfiguration of quotation marks ; or to say, " Though differing with brother Highway of the *Examiner*, on a wide range of subjects discussed in these pages, it always gives us pleasure, when we can do it conscientiously, to bestow upon his sentiments our cordial approval, as we do when he remarks that," etc., etc., quoting a whole article, and leaving out the quotation marks, of course.

In this way, brother Highway was flattered and kept good-natured, and his " valued contemporaries," using his brains and words to fill their pages with, nursed their self-complacency by a dignified censorship of all brother Highway's utterances. So brother Highway wrote paragraphs and leaders and disquisitions for all of them, and all they had to do was, in editorial sovereignty, to approve of, or dissent from, brother Highway.

The Littleton *Examiner* came at last—wet and doubtfully fragrant from the press—and was received from the hand of the weekly post-rider by Fanny herself. She took it privately to her room to read it alone—her heart throbbing violently with apprehension. She opened the important sheet, and read, first, a long advertisement of the " Matchless Sanative," and, as if this were a fitting preparation for the catalogue of deaths, she then went through the mortuary record of the week. She had, of course, no interest in these things. The notice of her book was the first article that arrested her eye when she opened the paper, but she was not ready for it. Her eye ran around it, and then ran away— came up to it, and dodged—descended upon it like a bird upon a pool, and sprang up again, frightened at sight of its own feathers. At length, by a sort of spiritual endosmosis, the character and quality of the critique made its way into her consciousness, and she came gradually to its literal perusal.

Now brother Highway of the Littleton *Examiner*, never noticed a book, at any length, without giving his theory of the class of books to which the one in hand belonged. After his theory had had exposition, it mattered very little what was said about the book—in fact, it mattered very little whether he had read the book at all. He threw out his theory as that by which the book was to stand or fall ; and was often so considerate as to let the public decide whether it could abide the test of the theory or not. In this case, he had sacrificed an unusually extended space to the review, five-sixths of which were devoted to an exposition of his theory of novel-writing, and one-sixth to the book itself. The single paragraph on " Tristram Trevanion " seemed to be written to prove that the author recognized the *Examiner's* theory, and had constructed the book with sole reference to it. Fanny's quick insight immediately detected the fact that the editor had not read her book at all—or, rather, that he had done no more than to dip here and there into its pages. The degree of disgust with which she read the following paragraph relating to her volume, can be imagined :

" ' Tristram Trevanion,' tried by this test, and made to confront these great fundamental and eternal principles, betrays the ring of the genuine metal. The style of the writer is sparkling without being intense, flowing without looseness, and pure as the mountain brook without the stones and rocks and abysses which obstruct its flow, and throw its bounding waters into inextricable confusion. As we wade with heart absorbed, through its pellucid pages, in fancy's quickened ear we can hear the baying of the hounds upon the Whippoorwill Hills, the distant winding of the horn of the gallant Trevanion, the frenzied shriek of the perjured Jew, and all the varied music of that great song of life whose notes fall so forcibly upon the appreciative ear. The book is, of course, written by a woman. No man, living or dead, could have dressed Grace Beaumont for her nuptials with Trevanion with such precision and propriety, and we may add, with such gorgeous simplicity, if we may be allowed to use so suggestive a solecism. The writer, if we mistake not, is not altogether unknown in Littleton. We would not invade the secret of the musical masculine pseudonym she has assumed; but in its revelation, if it shall ever be unfolded, we are much mistaken if it is not found to invade the precincts of our stirring little neighbor, Crampton. The book cannot fail to have a million readers, who, we are certain, will bear us out in the assertion that this firs' offspring of the fair writer's muse, must introduce her to a career which will satisfy her most daring ambition."

"And this is the stuff that public praise is made of!" exclaimed Miss Gilbert, as the Littleton *Examiner* fell from her hands to the floor. It was praise, certainly, but it was praise that she despised, and was written that the editor might glorify himself, not her—written to prove that if she had not, by great good fortune, pitched upon the editor's theory of novel-writing as the basis of her work, she must inevitably and disastrously have failed. Aunt Catharine was more easily pleased, and thought Fanny had every reason to be satisfied with it. For her part, she could not see what could have been asked for better than that. Dr. Gilbert was not altogether displeased with it. At least, he thought the effect of it would be to help the sale of the book.

A week after this, Dr. Gilbert received by mail copies of the papers whose editors he had favored with the volume. These Fanny had looked forward to with greedy expectation, but she was more disgusted with their notices of her book than with that of the *Examiner*. The Londonderry *Gazette* " owing to the crowded state of its columns " (which columns were occupied largely with dead advertisements), had only space to repeat the very judicious remarks of brother Highway of the Littleton *Examiner*, which it was glad to do, because it was so rare that any thing appeared in that sheet worthy of unqualified approval. It then copied the closing paragraph entire, with the exception of the opening sentence. The editor of the North Yerrington *Courier* had not, up to the time of going to press, been in the

enjoyment of sufficient leisure to give the book such a
perusal as would enable him to do justice to the fair
writer. In the meantime, that his numerous readers
might get an inkling of what a treat was in store for
them, he would present the opinion of brother Highway
of the Littleton *Examiner*, who was admitted, "*by the
ladies*," to be a judge of such matters, and who was evidently thinking about "*them trout*" when he spoke of
the "*mountain brook*." This last suggestion Fanny did
not understand; but it was a habit of the editor to
carry on a private correspondence with his friends by
toothsome allusions to matters from which the envious
public was shut out altogether. The dodge by which
the editor escaped noticing her book, Fanny understood
very well. He was always pressed for time, and was
always promising to do something the next week, relying
upon the public to forget his promise, and upon himself to break it.

All the fragrance presented to Fanny's fastidious nostrils by the "local press" was exhausted. It had said
no word against her book—it had, in reality, praised it
very highly—but it had given her no satisfaction. Newspaper immortality never had seemed so hollow to her.
Other papers came in slowly. One spoke of Tristram
Trevanion as a sprightly juvenile, which all the children
would insist on having; and parents and guardians
might as well purchase the volume first as last. Another, without having read the book, presumed that it
was not mistaken in stating that the volume treated of
the times of the Crusades. There was a chivalric smack
to the title of the book which was quite attractive, though
the writer had drawn her inspiration, doubtless, from
Walter Scott.

In accordance with the directions of Mr. Frank Sargent, all these papers were sent to him, that he might
know what reception his adventure as a publisher was

meeting with.   In the meantime, Fanny sought for city
papers on every hand.   Very few were taken in Crampton, and none seemed to be conscious of her and her
volume.   A few weeks passed away, when she received
from her publisher a New York paper, with a long advertisement, marked to attract her attention.   The testimonials to the excellencies of "Tristram Trevanion,"
copied from various papers and periodicals, surprised
and delighted her.   It was better than she had believed
possible.   First in the list of testimonials was the following :

"The style of the writer is sparkling, flowing, and pure as the
mountain brook."—*Lit. Examiner.*

Then followed closely :

" Betrays the ring of the genuine metal."—*N. Y. Courier.*

" In fancy's quickened ear we can hear the baying of the hounds
upon the Whippoorwill Hills, the distant winding of the horn of
the gallant Trevanion, the frenzied shriek of the perjured Jew,"
etc.—*Lon. Gazette.*

" Parents and guardians may as well purchase the
volume first as last ; " " drawn her inspiration from
Walter Scott ; " and similar spirited and inspiring sentences and phrases, footed by the authority quoted, in
italics, filled up a long half-column.

Strangely enough, Fanny did not remember to have
seen these sentences before.   That she should have been
thus splendidly noticed in the *Literary Examiner*, the
New York *Courier*, and the London *Gazette*, seemed
like the realization of her most ambitious dreams.   She
longed to get hold of the papers themselves, that she
might swallow full goblets of the nectar with which her
enterprising publisher had only allowed her to moisten
her thirsty lips.   One thing seemed, for the moment,
blissfully certain—that a book which had not only re-

ceived the praise of the metropolitan journals of her own country, but compelled the reluctant applause of a high transatlantic authority, could not be considered a failure, even should it prove to be an unprofitable venture financially.

Full of her new delight, Fanny's first thought was to visit Mary Hammett, and allow her to share in her pleasure. The thought was executed at once, and Mary met the young authoress with genuine gladness, for she seemed happier than she had been for many weeks. "Now what?" said the schoolmistress, as they sat down together.

"Oh! I'm so happy!" exclaimed Fanny, expiring a long breath, as if her bosom were overloaded.

"Now what again, then?" said Miss Hammett, with a smile, bending to Fanny, and kissing her flushed forehead.

"I think Mr. Sargent is very kind," said Fanny.

Miss Hammett laughed. "Do you state that as an independent proposition, or has it some relation to you and your book?" she inquired.

"I think," responded Fanny, "that he has taken a great deal of pains in circulating my book, and collecting and publishing the notices of it. Then he is so thoughtful to send these notices to me. I suppose he thinks that I am a poor, anxious girl up here in the country, who needs comfort, so he tries to comfort me. I have a great inclination to fall in love with him."

"Don't, I pray you," said Miss Hammett. "It might break the heart of some poor girl. But come, Fanny, you have not told me what makes you so happy."

"Oh! I'm keeping it from you, to excite your curiosity. You will borrow it, as you do Mr. Sargent's letters, if I show it."

Fanny held the paper in her hands, and indicated

that the secret of her happiness was in its pages. Then she slowly unfolded it, and finding the advertisement, handed it to Miss Hammett to peruse in silence. Then she sat back and watched the face of her sympathetic companion, that she might gather new satisfaction from its expressions of surprise and pleasure.

Miss Hammett read the advertisement from beginning to end; but, for some reason, Fanny failed to find in her face the expression she anticipated. On the contrary, Miss Hammett's hand began to tremble, her cheeks and forehead grew hot and flushed, and it seemed as if she could never finish reading, and lift her eyes to those of the expectant authoress.

"Mary Hammett, what is the matter?" inquired Fanny, with genuine concern.

The schoolmistress lifted her eyes at this inquiry, with a costly effort of self-composure, and said : "My dear girl, I am afraid you have deceived yourself."

"What can you mean?" inquired Fanny.

"Have you never seen these sentences before ? " said Miss Hammett.

"Never. Have you?"

"I think I have," replied Mary, sadly; and going to her table, she took from a pile of papers a copy of the Littleton *Examiner*. Unfolding it, as she returned to her seat, she pointed Fanny to the notice of her volume in that sheet, and said : "You will see that it was the Littleton, and not the *Literary Examiner* that your publisher has quoted."

"But the extract is different to the original," said Fanny, in alarm.

"The words are all there," replied Mary, quietly.

"But what is this from the New York *Courier?*"

"You mistake again," said Mary. "That is the North Yerrington *Courier*. You remember that that paper adopted the *Examiner's* notice."

Fanny read in the London *Gazette's* notice the words, " in fancy's quickened ear," and then, as the truth burst fully upon her, her bosom heaved heavily, and the tears filled her eyes.

Miss Hammett took the poor girl's head upon her shoulder, where for a few minutes she sobbed in silence. Then Miss Gilbert rose to her feet, and wiped her eyes. After the first shock of disappointment, came anger. " Mr. Sargent is not the man I supposed him to be," said she. " He has intended to deceive the public, and to deceive me. These contemptible abbreviations are coolly calculated to mislead. It is mean ; it is outrageous ; it is a fraud upon the public. Does Mr. Frank Sargent suppose that I will allow a book of mine to be pushed by such paltry lies as these ? I will write him a letter that will make his cheeks tingle. I will tell him what I think of him, and his accursed publishing machinery."

Fanny walked the room with flashing eyes, and delivered her words with fiery vehemence, while Miss Hammett sat and watched her with such calmness as she could command. At length the excitement was exhausted, and the schoolmistress pointed to a chair, and said : " There, Fanny, sit down ! Let me beg you to do nothing while you are angry, for you will be sorry."

" Well, don't *you* think it was mean in him to try to deceive the public in this way ? " said Fanny, taking her seat.

" Possibly some clerk may have done it. Possibly the printer made the changes on his own responsibility. Possibly Mr. Sargent, in his haste, for he must be a very busy man, may have written these abbreviations without noticing the coincidences that we have detected at all. There are a hundred possibilities, either of which would relieve him from all blame in the matter."

Fanny was staggered, but still declared her belief that it was an intentional deception.

"Then you think," said Miss Hammett, "that a person who, for purposes of gain, tries to mislead the public by attributing to one name that for which another is responsible, is very blameworthy, do you?"

"I do, indeed. What a question!"

"Then if my friend, Miss Fanny Gilbert—a young woman—writes a book, and, for any selfish purpose whatever, says to the public upon her title-page that her book was written by a gentleman, bearing the name of Everard Everest, I am to suppose that she is unworthy of my friendship, and legitimately the subject of her publisher's execration, am I?"

"How ridiculous! That is not like you at all, Miss Hammett," exclaimed Fanny with a sneer.

"We can very easily imagine circumstances in which it would not be ridiculous," responded Mary, entirely unruffled; "at least, I know that authors have tricks, and I have no doubt that publishers have also—tricks whose essential nature and character are hidden to both by the veil of long usage, or the long veil of usage—which you please. My only wish is to have you act carefully and charitably. You are disappointed and angry, because you have been deceived, and because you imagine your publisher intended to deceive the public. You do not know that he intended to do any such thing, or that he personally saw the advertisement before its publication."

Fanny smiled sadly. She was not convinced that her anger had been without cause; but the schoolmistress, in her earnest endeavor to vindicate the excellent intentions and character of Mr. Frank Sargent, had outwitted and silenced her. "I have a good mind to be angry with you, Mary Hammett," said Fanny.

"Why, my dear?"

" Because you will never allow that Mr. Sargent can do wrong, and are always making me ashamed of myself."

The schoolmistress consciously blushed, and with a peculiarly expressive smile, said that she had heard a great deal in her life of quarrels between authors and publishers, and was determined to do what she could to lessen their number. Fanny then took the New York journal, which had so gratified and so disappointed her, and, tearing it in pieces, threw it upon the fire with a sigh, saying : " My father shall never see this."

As the young authoress walked thoughtfully homeward, some bird among the maples, or some spirit of the air, whispered in her ear an unwelcome truth. Where it came from, what wings bore it, she never knew ; but she received it as authentic. Her book was a failure, and her publisher, poorly able to suffer loss, had resorted to a violent advertising struggle to save it from falling dead at the threshold of the market. All her winter's labor, all her anxiety, all her doubts and fears, had availed her nothing. She had toiled and hoped for fame, but she had reaped only disappointment and mortification. " I'm a fool," she said to herself, " to care for the praise of a public that proves itself so utterly stupid. I'm a fool to permit myself to be miserable, because fools do not know the difference between that which is valuable and that which is trash."

This was an outburst of spite and spleen, and after it came a quiet flow of common-sense. Fanny felt that she was making herself ridiculous, for she knew that if the public had praised and patronized her, it would not have seemed foolish to her at all. On the contrary, it would have proved itself to be a very discriminating and just public indeed, whose praise outweighed the value of gold. She was very glad she had not expressed her spite in the hearing of the schoolmistress, for then she would have had this consideration thrust upon her in the peculiarly decisive style of that young woman.

When she entered her home, she encountered her father, looking grave and depressed. He spoke to her with a compassionate tone, quite unusual with him, and after they had sat down in the parlor, he told her that he had carried a periodical in his pocket for several days, which contained a review of her book. He had hesitated to show it to her, knowing that it would give her pain ; but he had concluded, as it was written in a kind spirit, that she ought to see it. The doctor's eyes were moist with sympathy for his daughter, and, as he handed her the journal, so heavily freighted with pain for her, he put his hand upon her shoulder with unwonted tenderness, and said : "You must not let it trouble you, Fanny. Rise above it—rise above it."

Fanny took the heavy pamphlet, and, without saying a word, retired to read it alone. If she had not risen above it, she had risen to it. Disappointment had been piled upon her so heavily, that she felt herself growing desperately strong. It was a review of several pages— discriminating, kind and conscientious. The writer professed to have been attracted to the volume by the music of its title, and then to have read it with no small degree of interest because of its genuine enthusiasm. It was evidently the product of a girl quite young, who had the materials of a noble womanhood in her, but who should not think of touching pen to paper again until the suns of a luster or a decade had ripened her. It quoted passages descriptive of natural scenery, to show how well she could write of that which she had observed, and then copied sketches of life to prove that she knew nothing of life whatever. Passages that Fanny had regarded as the choicest in her book she had the pain to see pointed out as the evidences of her youthful immaturity, or of her youthful tendency toward extravagance.

It spoke of her book as a "school-girl performance," and told the writer that she must not hope to win the ear and heart of the world, until, by genuine contact and sympathy with the world, she had learned its wants, experienced in herself its hopes and disappointments, its fears and its aspirations, and could speak from a heart rendered tenderly humane to the heart of humanity. Under the careful but faithful touch of the critic's pen, dream and delusion were dissolved, and when she had concluded the perusal of his article, "Tristram Trevanion" lay before her riddled, disembowelled, and hacked so terribly, that the manes of the Jewish dwarf, if it had been present, would have considered itself sufficiently avenged, even if it had been as exacting as Old Shylock himself.

Fanny closed the pamphlet, raised it higher than her head, and, dashing it to the floor with all her force, said : "I thank you, sir! After this, I care for nothing. I know the worst."

This violence to the review was not the result of anger, but of powerfully excited feeling, that blindly sought for some adequate mode of expression. She was relieved. She felt that she had read the truth, and that, whatever the critical world might have to say further, she had nothing to dread. She looked upon the prostrate and sprawling pamphlet, and nodded her head, and pressed her lips together, and said, " I thank you, sir," a great many times.

The mental storm passed off with abundant lightning, thunder, and wind, but no rain. Discipline had done Miss Gilbert momentary good, at least ; but she sighed when she thought that her career was hardly begun. What! must she wait for long years before she could hope to do any thing worthy of public consideration? Then hurrah for life !

The spell that had so long held her in thrall was dis-
15

sipated. The fate of her book was sealed. She had no
worthy praise to hope for in connection with it, and had
given up all idea of reward. A thousand schemes were
started in her active brain, and she was surprised to find
that her desire for praise had been essentially a terrible
bondage to her best life, and a bar to her best happiness. She had not, it is true, fully comprehended the
fact that she had been subject to the most disgusting
and demoralizing slavery, next to the slavery of appetite,
to which the soul can voluntarily bow its neck ; but she
was conscious, for the time, of a new sense of freedom,
and felt her soul expanding and strengthening in its influence.

But what could she see of life in Crampton ? She
would be mistress of the little life there was there, and
get away as soon as possible where it was better, and
more abundant. The change came at last, in a way she
little anticipated ; but meantime, she never relinquished
the project of having a career.

CHAPTER XV.

ARTHUR BLAGUE AWAKES FROM A PLEASANT DREAM. SO DO MR. AND MRS. RUGGLES.

It will be seen that there was a good deal of discipline going on among the better characters engaged in
our story, during the season. Dr. Gilbert had received
a very decided shock, and was taught that a strong will
is not omnipotent. The struggle was not so nearly finished as it appeared when he closed his memorable interview with Mary Hammett, but it was covered from
observation. He visited her school as usual, insisted on
her appearing at his table, met her in the street, and,

by dint of dogged determination, wore out his disappointment—compelled himself to bow to the decision that forever placed her beyond his possession. It hurt him, but it humanized him.

Mary Hammett herself was not without trials. It was a trial to meet Dr. Gilbert, and it had become so much a trial to encounter Arthur Blague, that she endeavored to shun him. She would give him no private opportunity to speak to her. She constantly feared the introduction of a subject that could result only in pain to him and to her. Her quiet had been disturbed more than once during this summer by the intrusion of Mr. Dan Buck, who insisted on her paying him more money. He had drawn around him a circle of dissolute companions in the village, with whom he spent whole nights of carousal, and, by threats of an exposure which Mary could not face, succeeded in compelling from her all her hard earnings.

Fanny Gilbert's discipline did not entirely cease with the disappointment consequent upon the failure of her book. When she had decided for the time to relinquish her schemes for the acquisition of fame, and to mingle with the life around her, she did not find that life ready to receive and minister to her. Her old companions had become offended with her protracted exclusiveness, and, conceiving that she felt herself above them, shunned her. Many of them had read her book, and, with the meanness characteristic of their small natures, had ridiculed it—adopted in irony its phrases —talked and laughed about it on every occasion of their meeting. They received the volume as an assertion, on the part of the authoress, of superiority. They felt that they had no defence but by combining, either to put her down, or to set themselves up, by ignoring her altogether. She was not invited to their social gatherings. Many passed her in the street without seeing her. While she was engaged in her labor, she had voluntarily isolated herself from them; now that she was ready for their society, and longed for their sympathy, they avoided her as if she were a tainted woman. This was one of the penalties of seeking for public praise which she had not anticipated at all. She had expected to be courted by those who knew her, and was disappointed. Their unreasonable jealousy made her angry, and, alas! hardened her. Many an evening Fanny walked her chamber alone, and revolved her trials. "They *shall* court me," said Miss Gilbert, stamping her slippered foot upon the floor. "I'll make them. It's in me, and I'll make them. I'm not a bankrupt yet, thank God!"

The life of Arthur Blague, after Mrs. Ruggles' "valuable accusation" to the society of Hucklebury Run made his appearance, was one of hard labor and constant annoyance. The proprietor and his family, and the plausible villain who had obtained a sort of mastery over all of them, lost no opportunity to insult him. Oftentimes he was tempted to angry resentment, but self-control gave him victory as often over them and his own indignant spirit. Had he not been at work for others—had he not subordinated his life to the comfort and support of those whom Providence had placed in his care—he would have fled. For himself, he would have endured nothing; but evermore there rose before his eyes the pale face of his dependent mother, and the helpless little hands of his brother, and he said to himself, "For these, I endure."

Besides, Arthur had one all-absorbing subject of thought. It pervaded, purified, and elevated his whole nature. When he opened his eyes in the morning, one sweet face and form seemed hovering over his pillow. When he closed them at night, the same angel came to comfort him, and to walk with him into the realm of dreams. In the full possession of one pure spirit, his life seemed to himself a charmed one. He felt released from the power of temptation, lifted above all low aims, and mean resentments, stimulated to faithful and unremitting toil, softened into sympathy with all the sorrow and trouble around him.

As he became more thoroughly absorbed by his passion for Mary Hammett, did he become more afraid of her. Her presence was almost painful to him. He detected this tendency in himself, and felt urged to almost desperate efforts to counteract it. The more he loved her—the more essential to his life she seemed to him—the more unapproachable did she appear. He could not love her more without plunging himself into absolute despair. At length, he came to feel that it was wrong for him to indulge in a passion that must wreck him forever, if its object could not be won ; and he summoned all the strength of his nature to meet the decision of the great question before it should be too late.

What should he do ? He could not go to Mary Hammett, and tell her to her face that he loved her. He could not fall upon his knees, and confess that his life and happiness were in her hands. He was deeply conscious that his fate was doubtful, and he could never take denial from her lips. He would write her a letter —resort of timid lovers from time immemorial. Oh ! blessed pen, that will not stammer ! Oh ! brave ink, that will not faint and fade in the critical moment of destiny ! Oh ! happy paper, that cannot blush ! Oh ! faithful cup, that bears one's heart's blood to the lips one loves, and spills no precious drop !

Of the letters Arthur wrote and tore in pieces, we present no record. One was too cool and self-contained, and so was sacrificed. One was too warm and demonstrative, and that was destroyed. But, on a certain Monday morning, as he was leaving his home for a week of labor at the Run, he thrust a note into Mary's hand without a word, and left her. In it he had poured out, like wine upon an altar of sacrifice, his whole heart. He told her how, from the first moment of their meeting, he had begun to love her; how from that time onward she had grown upon his heart, until he felt that life without her would become not only valueless, but miserable ; how she had absorbed his thoughts, become an inspiring power in his life, grown to be his purifier ; how, for her, he was willing to brave toil and poverty, and even death itself. He deplored his own unworthiness of her, and pledged himself to a whole life—nay, a whole eternity— of effort, to make himself one whom she would not be ashamed to call her lover and her husband.

During the week which followed the delivery of his letter, Arthur walked and worked like one in a dream. Abstracted, he saw and heard nothing that was going on about him. He went mechanically through his labor, ate his meals as if he were a machine, and retired to bed at night and rose in the morning in obedience to blind routine. When Mrs. Joslyn gave her signal, " Sh-h-h-h ! " he repeated it, under a vague impression that she was scaring chickens out of the house. When Cheek inquired what time it was, he replied that he was very well indeed—never better, in fact. He surprised the proprietor one morning by shaking his hand, and in- quiring, with great apparent interest, for his health. On being told testily that he was half-dead, Arthur thanked him for the information, and declared further that he was very happy to hear it—hoped he would continue so.

Saturday night came again, and he started as usual for Crampton.. He had received no reply to his letter, but he knew that before he should return to the Run, his fate would be decided. He dreaded to enter his home, for he felt that it held, and would soon reveal, the secret of his fate. He looked haggard and pale, as if he had worked and watched for a month. His mother met him with many anxious inquiries—wondered what had wrought such a change in him, and wept to think that her boy was killing himself for her. Miss Hammett was frightened when she read the lines which one long week of anxiety had engraved upon his face. She was calm, sober, and reserved. She had a sisterly affection for the young man, such as she felt for no other, and it pained her beyond expression to be deprived of the privilege of sympathizing with him. She felt almost guilty for being the cause of his pain. She would have been glad to throw herself upon her knees before him, and ask him to forgive her for something—she knew not what—to lay her hand upon his forehead, and whisper words of consolation to him.

The Sabbath passed away, and Arthur received no reply to his letter. She hardly spoke to him during the day, but confined herself to her room. His mother was conscious that there was some momentous secret between them, but did not guess its nature. On Monday morning, just as Arthur was opening the door to leave his home for another week, he heard steps upon the stairs, and, turning around, saw Mary Hammett descending. He stood, uttered no word, received from her hand a folded note, and left the house.

Did he open the note the moment he was out of the village? Not at all. He felt that he had a great work to do before it would be proper for him to read one word. As he trod the accustomed walk, there was a voice in his soul that said : " Young man, the decision of your destiny is in the hand of no woman, however angelic. It is in your own. If your life is lost, it will be lost because you are weak."

Straightway, he felt every power within him summoned to a great effort. His head was as clear as the heaven above him ; his heart as calm as the early morning landscape. Out before his imagination ran two paths. In one, he saw himself walking alone. Thorns were under his feet, clouds were over his head; feeble men and women and children were begging on either side for help; great hills and rocks rose in the distance; but far off the path climbed to the sky, and faded into a heavenly light. In the other, he walked with an angel in sweet converse, forgetful, in his bliss, of all the woes beneath the sun. Broad trees stretched their shadows over him, silver brooks murmured in the sunshine, and birds filled all the air with music. But the path was level, and by its side sat a feeble woman, with a babe upon her knee, imploring him not to forget her and the little one left to his protection. At the parting of the paths stood two figures with folded hands, waiting to hear the decision which the letter contained, and ready to conduct him—Duty and Inclination—equally eager to be his escort.

All this seemed to Arthur like a heavenly vision. Perhaps it was—perhaps it was no more than the result of a profoundly moved imagination. The task to which he felt summoned had called in the aid of every external spiritual force around him. Shall we doubt that toward an insufficient soul, that, in a great emergency, throws itself wide open to God's spiritual universe, spiritual forces rush, as a million miles of conscious atmosphere leap to fill a vacuum?

From whatever source the vision came, it impressed Arthur like a reality. He saw these two paths as distinctly as if they had been presented in very materiality to his vision; and he stopped where they parted from each other. Then he drew forth the letter, broke the seal, kissed it as if there were a soul in it, and read it through, every word. He kissed the name that subscribed the revelation, and two big tears bathed the page while he did it. Then he commenced at one side of the sheet, and slowly tore the whole into ribbons, then tore the ribbons into squares, and sowed them upon the wind. He stood for a minute like one entranced, gazing into vacancy, and then the sound of a distant bell recalled him to consciousness. He turned, as if expecting to see the two paths still, and ready to give his hand to Duty, but only the old familiar path to the Run lay before him—marvellously like the rugged passage of his vision, with the glorious morning sun blazing upon the mountain-top that stood far off against the sky.

He could not account for the strange strength that filled him—the strange joy that thrilled him. Uncertainty, that had brooded with uneasy and harassing wings over his heart, had flown. Doubt, that like a heavy cloud had clung around his head, had been drunk up by the morning light. Fear, that had haunted him night and day like a ghost, had fled. It was a relief to know that all his precious hopes were blasted. He realized, for the first time, how his blind love had debilitated—almost paralyzed him; how, forgetful of God and men, and all his useful purposes and aims, he had allowed his passion to quench the fire of his young manhood. He walked onward to recommence his daily labor, feeling that a great burden had been lifted from his shoulders, content that the question had been decided against him. The possibilities of his life had never seemed so great as now. He had never felt so free. If there was sorrow in his cup, there was exultation also.

One by one the expressions of Mary's letter came up, and passed before his mind, and he gained new strength from each. "Arthur Blague, I admire you. Would God I could tell you with how strong a sisterly affection I love you. Be a man. Overcome this passion of your youth. Do not let me be disappointed in you. Do not compel me to sacrifice my admiration and love for you, by any weak repinings over your disappointment. Deal in a manly way with the trials of the present, and the future will not fail to be generous to you." Then there were other words, that gave him deeper thought than these, words burnt into his memory, legible then not only, but through all his after-life ; words, too, into whose full meaning his after-life introduced him. " You tell me that I, a poor, imperfect woman, obliged to kneel and beg daily for the pardon of my sins, have become to you a purifier—nay, you use that higher word which you should not use in such an unworthy connection—your sanctifier. You tell me that your love for me has given you freedom from temptation, and compelled you to look with aversion and disgust upon all sordid and sensual things--that it has softened your heart, and elevated your life. If this is all true—and I will not doubt you, though what you say sadly humbles me, conscious, as I must be, of my own unworthiness—what would as strong a love for One who is altogether lovely do for you ? If I have had this influence upon you, through your love for me, what shall be the influence of Him who has room in his heart for all the hearts that have ever throbbed, or ever shall throb, in the world ? I would not obtrude upon you a thought like this, in a letter like this, did I not feel that in it lies the cure of greater disappointments, if such there be, than that which this letter will give you. Receive it, Arthur Blague. Think upon it, and God grant that it may lead you into a wealth of blessedness such as earthly love can never bestow !"

Busy with his thoughts, and revolving the words of the wonderful letter he had read, Arthur had nearly reached the hill that overlooked the factory at Hucklebury Run, when a horse's head made its appearance over the brow, and, following it, the familiar travelling establishment of the proprietor. As he met the carriage, he raised his eyes to see who could be setting out so early, and recognized Mr. Dan Buck and the proprietor's daughter, Leonora. From the evening of his parting with Leonora, she had not recognized him as an acquaintance, and he and Dan Buck were on no friendly terms of intercourse. He expected some insult, and was greatly surprised when that young man drew rein, and greeted him with a very polite " good morning."

" I wish you would look round and see to things a little to-day," said Dan Buck. " The old man is under the weather."

" What is the matter with him ? " inquired Arthur.

" Well, between you and me, I think he's got the pip," replied Dan Buck, nudging Leonora with his elbow, and thereby setting her to giggling.

Arthur did not smile. He was in no mood for it. Neither the man nor his weak and vain companion had ever seemed so contemptible to him before. So, without noticing his reply, he asked him where he was going.

" Oh! we are only going to have a little drive over to Littleton. I've got some business to do there, and Leonora thought she'd take a ride with me. We are going to make a day of it, and if the old man raises a row, you can tell him that we shall not be back till late." Then Mr. Buck turned to the horse, hit him a stinging blow with the whip, and yelling, " Let out the links," drove off at a furious rate.

Arthur paused, and looked after the departing pair. There had been something in Dan Buck's manner and in Leonora's appearance, that impressed him with peculiar apprehension. Something, he was sure, was not right. He tried to analyze his impressions, but they were too vague for analysis. He was only conscious of a conviction that there was mischief on foot, and that there was a mutual understanding of its nature between Dan Buck and Leonora. Arriving at the factory, he went about his labor as usual, and nothing occurred until mid-afternoon to recall the meeting of the morning. At that time the wife of the proprietor came sailing into the mill, carrying her usual quantity of canvas and bunting, and meeting Arthur, inquired with a great deal of dignity whether Dan Buck had returned. On being answered in the negative, she asked if he had informed any one before leaving how long he should be gone. Arthur told her of his meeting Buck and her daughter on the hill, and of the statement of the former that they should make a day of it.

"Father'll be awful pervoked," said Mrs. Ruggles, with a very solemn look.

"Mr. Ruggles is not well, I believe?" said Arthur interrogatively.

"No; he's been kind o' down t' the heel for some time—it's a rising of the vitals, I tell him. He was dreadful bad in the night, and Mr. Buck said he'd got some stuff that would settle his stomach for him, but it didn't seem to work the way he wanted to have it, and he can't keep nothin' down at all now."

"You can tell Mr. Ruggles that every thing is going on right in the mill," said Arthur; and the ponderous lady set her sails for the voyage homeward. She had proceeded but a short distance when she turned back, to inquire of Arthur if Mr. Buck had informed him where he was going. Arthur replied that he spoke of going to Littleton on business. "What business can he have at Littleton!" exclaimed Mrs. Ruggles, and then she moved off again.

Evening came, but Mr. Buck did not come with it. Again and again did the wife of the proprietor visit the mill, to inquire if any thing had been seen or heard of him. The hours of labor closed, and one after another the lights of the village were extinguished, yet no sound of horse's feet upon the bridge brought relief to the anxiously waiting ears in the house of the proprietor. On the following morning, at the break of day, there came a violent rapping at the door of Big Joslyn. Arthur heard it, and hearing his own name pronounced, dressed hurriedly, and found awaiting him the anxious face of Mrs. Ruggles.

"Arthur, you must come right up to the house, just as quick as you can," said the breathless woman. "We're afraid something dreadful has happened to Leonora. We haven't seen hide nor hair of neither of 'em yet, and they must have tipped over coming home in the night. Oh! I'm so worried that it seems as if I should die. If Leonora should be brung home a corpse, it would just about finish me off. Oh! I'm so phthys-icky!" The poor woman sat down on the door-step, and held her hands against her heart in genuine distress.

Arthur seized his cap, and ran for the house, leaving Mrs. Ruggles to come at her convenience. Arriving at the door of the proprietor, he knocked, and was told feebly to "come in." Before him, half-dressed, and looking terribly haggard and miserable, sat Mr. Rug-gles. Apprehension and anger struggled for predomi-nance in the expression of his jaundiced features.

"Do you remember where the key of the safe used to be kept?" inquired Mr. Ruggles of Arthur.

"Certainly."

"Do you remember my little tin trunk, with a pad-lock on it?"

"Certainly."

"Open the safe, take out the trunk, lock the safe again, and bring the key to me—quick!"

There was something in this speech so full of sus-picious impatience, that Arthur sprang to do the old man's bidding as if it had stung him. He was gone but a minute, when he returned, and informed the propri-etor that the key was neither in its accustomed place of deposit, nor in the lock of the safe. The veins swelled rigidly and painfully upon the brow of the proprietor, and notwithstanding his feebleness, he rose and walked the room, his lips pressed together, and every muscle of his face as tense as if braced to master a terrific spasm of pain.

"Look for that key again," said Mr. Ruggles fiercely, "and if you cannot find it, get a crowbar and open the safe, if you have to break it in pieces. Don't come back here without the trunk."

Off sprang Arthur again, fully possessed now of the master's impatient spirit. He sought for the key, but he could not find it. At this time the workmen were beginning to come into the mill. The machinist of the establishment was among them, and Arthur bade him bring his strongest tools and open the safe in the quickest way, even if he should ruin it. It was a difficult task. Bars and chisels and sledges were called into active requisition. The operatives gathered round in wonder to watch the strange movements, and were full of speculations as to their cause. At length an impression was made. A plate was loosened—bolt-heads were knocked off—a huge bar had got a bite at some vulnerable point—hinges were burst, and the contents of the safe were revealed. Bidding a man to keep guard over the contents of the safe, Arthur seized the little trunk in which the manufacturer kept his most important papers, and was about to start upon a run with it to the house, where he was awaited so anxiously, when he discovered that the hasp was broken. A closer examination showed that it had been carefully filed off. He called those around him to witness the fact, and then ran to the house of the proprietor as swiftly as his feet could carry him. The moment he opened the door, old Ruggles yelled, "What the devil have you been doing all this time?"

" Breaking the safe in pieces, as you bade me," replied Arthur, upon whose face the beaded perspiration hung plentifully.

" You didn't look for the key, you hound ! " said old Ruggles savagely, fumbling at the same time in his pocket for the key of the trunk.

" I think you'll be able to open that without any key," replied Arthur with bitterness. The old man took hold of the parted hasp, and lifting it, said, " Who did this ? "

" I don't know, sir."

" You lie ! "

" Half the hands in the mill are witnesses that the trunk was broken when the safe was opened."

" You lie ! " growled the old man, hesitating to lift the lid of the trunk, and striving to resist his convictions of the truth by abusing Arthur.

" Mr. Ruggles," said Arthur, with such calmness as he could command, " you are in trouble. If you want any help from me, you must not treat me like a dog. If others have been untrue to you, it is no reason why you should abuse me."

The old man looked up into Arthur's face vacantly, still hesitating to open the trunk. Finally he lifted the lid, moaning, " My God ! my God ! If he has done it ! " He took up paper after paper, and file after file, and ran them over and examined them. Then he examined them again, as if unwilling to admit, even to himself, that he had been robbed. At length he leaned back in the chair, and groaned, and wrung his hands in agony. After giving vent to his feelings, his excitement faded, and he said : " Arthur, don't be mad with me. You must stick to me now, and help me through. This damnable villain has poisoned me and robbed me. Now you must take one of the team-horses, and drive to the Littleton Bank, and inquire if a draft of mine for five thousand dollars has been cashed there. If it has, Dan

Buck is a robber, and has run away. Find Leonora, and bring her back. She has plenty of friends in Littleton, and very likely you will meet her on the way home."

These directions were given with comparative calmness, but it was the calmness of weakness—the speaker gasping at every sentence. His excitement had been too much for him, and he leaned back in the chair utterly overcome. Arthur left him with his wife, who, only half-comprehending the state of affairs, was busying herself with arranging the breakfast-table.

Without stopping for breakfast or change of apparel, Arthur harnessed a horse, and drove him to the Littleton Bank, a distance of five or six miles, and reached it as the clerk was taking down the shutters. Arthur made his inquiry concerning the draft, and found that the fears of the proprietor were realized. It had been cashed nearly twenty-four hours before, at the moment of opening the bank, and Dan Buck, with the proprietor's daughter, had immediately driven out of the village. Of this latter fact, Arthur took further means of satisfying himself. Dan Buck and Leonora, both, were known to many people in Littleton, and several of the villagers had seen them on their leaving the town. The horse, they testified, had been cruelly driven ; but as they knew the young man to be " fast," they had not thought of the matter further. The road by which they left was that leading to the Connecticut River, and as there was no considerable town upon the way, Arthur suspected at once that they had taken the shortest road to the New York stage-lines, and that they were already far on their way to the city.

The young man lost no time, but drove directly back to Hucklebury Run, as rapidly as his clumsy horse could carry him. During his absence, Mr. Ruggles and his wife had made some discoveries. They found that, by some means, Leonora had managed to take away with

her her choicest dresses, all her jewelry, and such necessary articles of apparel as it was possible to carry in a
small space. The horrible suspicion that she was a par-
ticipator in the robber's guilt, and had fled with him, had
fastened itself upon both father and mother ; and bitter
were the maledictions which the former visited upon the
head of the latter. In his terror he raved like a man
insane ; and in his anger he cursed his wife for the encouragement she had given not only Dan Buck, but every
young man who had visited the house.

Arthur drove up to the door, almost as deeply excited
as those who awaited his coming. There were but few
questions asked. Both the proprietor and his wife showed
in their faces the terrible anguish and apprehension that
held them in possession. Arthur gave a simple detail
of what he had heard—the fact that the draft had been
cashed, that both Buck and Leonora left Littleton together on the road leading to the river, and that the
horse had been cruelly driven.

The confirmation of the old man's fears was accompanied by demonstrations of feeling the most pitiful that
can be conceived. The theft of his money, by the ungrateful hands of his clerk, was a great trial, but it was
accompanied by a calamity so much greater, that it was
lost sight of altogether. That his petted Leonora, his
only child, on whom he had lavished all the affection
there was in his nature—whose desires had been his law,
and whose indulgence his delight—should become either
the mistress or the wife of a wretch like Dan Buck, was
more than he could bear. He wept, he whined, he
cursed by turns. He blasphemously called upon God
to tell him what he had done, that he must be thus for-
saken to disgrace and madness. Arthur listened in
horror, till he saw that the proprietor's emotions were
such as to destroy his power of action, and then he suggested that there should be a pursuit.

16

The old man rose from his chair, and tottering on his way across the room, came up to Arthur and leaned heavily upon his shoulder. The young man felt awkward under this demonstration of dependence, and still more embarrassed when the weak and half-crazed proprietor put his arms around him, and sobbed and whined in his helpless grief.

"Arthur, I've been hard on you, but you musn't mind it. You're the best friend I've got in the world," said he, in his whimpering voice. "Do what you can to get Leonora back. Oh! if you'll only bring her back safe, I'll give a thousand dollars; and just as soon as you're twenty-one, I'll make you a partner in my business."

Arthur shrank from the embrace of the proprietor, as if he had been a snake. He pitied him certainly, but he despised him still. The idea that money, or advancement in business, would be a more powerful motive than simple humanity, or neighborly kindness, in securing his good offices in the emergency of the hour, disgusted him. He put off the old man's hands, and standing away from him, said: "What I do for you, I do for a man in trouble, Mr. Ruggles. My good will is not in the market. Keep your offers for other times."

"Well, do what you can, Arthur—do it your own way;" and the proprietor sank into his chair again, with a groan.

Arthur departed, telling the disconsolate pair that he should probably be back at night. Going to his boarding-house, he snatched a hasty meal, and procuring a horse from a neighbor, he mounted him, and rode rapidly off to the nearest stage-line station. It was a ride of twenty miles, and it was mid-afternoon before he reached it. On his way he met Dr. Gilbert, who was out on a professional trip. Making known to him the nature of his errand, and informing him of the condition of Mr. Ruggles, he suggested that on his way home he should call upon him, and do something for his relief.

Arriving at the stage-house, he rode his horse directly into the stable, and saw before him, standing in a stall, the proprietor's horse with which Dan Buck had absconded. Throwing his bridle to the hostler, and giving him directions to feed and groom his horse, he sought in the shed for the familiar wagon, and found it at once. He had little doubt that Dan Buck had left the house, but deemed it a proper precaution, before claiming the horse and wagon, to make inquiries. At the office, he learned that Dan Buck and Miss Ruggles had arrived there the day before, just in time to take the downward day-coach, and had gone to New York, leaving word to have the horse and wagon taken care of until they should return. The office clerk informed Arthur that the horse had evidently been driven at the top of his speed, and that he came in wet, trembling, and staggering. In fact, the hostler had worked over him half of the night. Arthur informed him of the facts in the case, paid him for the keeping of the horse, and having fully satisfied himself that Dan Buck and Leonora had fled together, turned homeward, driving the lamed and jaded horse of the proprietor, and leading the one he had ridden, behind the wagon.

His passage homeward was slow, and he did not reach the Run until nine o'clock. As he drove up to the house, Mrs. Ruggles made her appearance, and came out to the wagon. "Don't make any noise, Arthur," said the woman, "for father has made out to get to sleep. The doctor has been here, and got down a portion of laudlum, and says he musn't be disturbed."

Arthur had left his saddle-horse on the way, where he procured it in the morning, and driving on to the barn, he took the harness from the much-abused animal he had reclaimed, and put him in the stable. On his way back he found Mrs. Ruggles still at the door, with a handkerchief over her head; and in a low tone he imparted to her the particulars of his journey, and its results.

Mrs. Ruggles had her words of penitence to breathe into the ear of the young man, and, further, she had various matters to impart to him in confidence. She had noticed for some time that Dan and Leonora had been "uncommon thick," but she supposed they were going to be married—in fact, she had no doubt of that, as it was. She wasn't, on the whole, inclined to regard the case so hopelessly as her husband did. She had no doubt that they would be back before a great while, and she knew father would forgive Dan Buck, if he would bring back Leonora. She was generous enough to say to Arthur that she did not believe that Dan Buck would make her daughter so good a husband as the young man who stood before her, and was obliging enough to inform him further that she shouldn't cry if there should be a change now.

Arthur marvelled that the mother could be so obtuse, as not to comprehend the fact that her daughter was a hopelessly ruined woman, and left her, tired, sick, and disgusted, with the promise to call early in the morning.

Morning came, and Arthur was admitted at the proprietor's door. To his surprise, he found Mr. Ruggles up, and dressed for a journey. He was weak and haggard, but the medicine and the sleep had restored to him a measure of strength, and a degree of composure and self-control. The old determination was in his face, and his eye burned fiercely.

He put to Arthur a few questions, and then told him he should follow the fugitives. He had already fed his horse, and he bade Arthur throw the harness upon him, and bring him to the door. When Arthur drove up, he found the proprietor waiting, with his portmanteau at his feet, and then received from him directions concerning the management of affairs in the mill during his absence.

"God only knows where I'm going, or when I shall come back," said the old man, as he feebly mounted the wagon, and drove away without a word of farewell to his wife, or even a passing look at his mill.

CHAPTER XVI.

ARTHUR'S DREAMS, AND HUCKLEBURY RUN AND ITS PROPRIETOR, COME TO DISSOLUTION.

WITH a start of forty-eight hours, it will readily be seen that Dan Buck had all the advantage over his pursuer that he could desire. Familiar with travel, and familiar not only with New York, but with its blindest retreats, he had abundant time to dispose of his money and of himself before Mr. Ruggles drove away from his own door. It is therefore needless to give the particulars of the pursuit. Mr. Ruggles found traces of the guilty pair, who had registered themselves by assumed names as man and wife, at different points along the route. He even learned of their passage on the same boat which bore him from Hartford. After arriving in New York, however, every track appeared to be covered. He secured the offices of the police, but they could not aid him. None of Dan's old friends had seen him. His former haunts were visited in vain. The most probable theory was that the villain had arrived in the night, and immediately taken some one of the outgoing lines of travel, and sought for other and more distant hiding-places. This supposition rose into a strong probability, when it was learned that a pair closely corresponding with their description had crossed to Jersey City, and taken passage in the Philadelphia coach.

Still the fugitives were forty-eight hours ahead of their pursuer—nay, more ; for considerable time had been wasted in New York. Mr. Ruggles knew too much to be deceived with regard to the relations that existed between his daughter and the man who had enticed her from home ; and in the hours of quiet into which his weakness compelled him, the whole subject was measured in all its bearings. Doubtless, at that moment, all Crampton was talking about the flight of his daughter, and the robbery committed by her paramour. The proprietor asked himself what Leonora could ever be to him, even should he secure her return. Could he have pride in her again ? Would not the presence of the tainted and ruined girl be a perpetual curse to him ? Would it be any satisfaction to have a daughter of whom he would be ashamed—a daughter to hide from all pure eyes ?

It could not be expected of a man like Mr. Ruggles, that he should be actuated by any higher views than these. He had for her no love that prompted him, for her sake, to save her from a life of infamy. When he saw that in Crampton, where all his interests lay—where his active life had been and would continue to be—she could never again be what she had been—could never again be the object of his pride and the source of his pleasure—his zeal for the pursuit of the guilty pair was extinguished. It is true that he thought how desolate his home would be without her, and how little there was left for him to live and labor for ; but as there were comfort and consolation for him in no direction, there was but little choice.

Poor lord of Hucklebury Run ! Hundreds had had

hard fare at his hands, but few of them all would have withheld their pity from him, could they have looked into his heart during those sad hours.

Immediately on the departure of Mr. Ruggles from home, Arthur, by coming more into contact with the operatives than he had done for several months, found an element of insubordination and mischief among them, to which the mill, under the direct rule of the proprietor, had been always a stranger. He knew that Dan Buck had insulted many of the men and women, especially the older and more sedate ; but it was not with these that the disorder seemed to lie. It was with half a dozen young fellows, who had been intense admirers of the fast New Yorker, who had aped him in his dress, learned and practised his slang, grown profane by his example, laughed at his vulgar drollery, and been participants in those carousals which he had delighted to call " conference meetings."

They took particular delight in abusing Arthur. They gathered in the mill, and had long conversations. It was not difficult to see that they sympathized thoroughly with the robber, and that they were anxious that he should escape from the clutches of the old man. Openly they would not justify him in the robbery of his employer, but they professed themselves to be quite satisfied with the fact that the latter had been " bled " a little. They admired the boldness of the fellow in stealing the proprietor's daughter from under his nose, and hoped he would get off with her. The moment factory hours were over, they either went away from the mill, to confer with other cronies of the robber, or went to some private room to consult with one another. In what direction all this was tending, Arthur could not judge. He had not been accustomed to regard the set as a very brave or dangerous one. It was one that Dan Buck could lead into any mischief, but not one, he thought, that would be apt to act very boldly on its own account. Cheek delighted in being Arthur's right-hand man, and brought to him reports of such movements of these young fellows as he became acquainted with. Cheek was very much their superior in natural shrewdness, and they had few meetings that he did not know of. In fact, by conversations with them separately, he had learned that if Dan Buck should be brought back a prisoner, they should " rescue him, or die."

Arthur and Cheek had, of course, a good laugh over this. It was a harmless kind of braggardism, that would do nobody harm, and would help to amuse the valiant young men who indulged in it. They, on the other hand, evidently attached great importance to it. They were mysterious. They conversed with each other by signs. Had the destinies of the world been upon their shoulders, they could not have felt the responsibility more keenly than they did that of being the champions of the honor, and defenders of the person, of their old leader, Mr. Dan Buck.

Cheek had seen and heard so much of this, that, at the end of a week after Mr. Ruggles left the Run for New York, he determined to play a joke upon the doughty young gentlemen. Arthur had sent him to a neighboring village on an errand, and returning in the evening, just as the hands were dismissed from the mill, he came driving down the hill at a furious rate, and pulled up before the door of the boarding-house. Calling Arthur to him, he mysteriously whispered, sufficiently loud for all around to hear, " He's got him." At the same time, he gave Arthur a wink, which the company did not see, or seeing, did not understand. Arthur understood it perfectly, and walked off to his room at the house of Big Joslyn.

The moment Arthur disappeared, Cheek was taken bodily by half a dozen fellows, and led to the trunk-room of the lodging-hall, and after the key was turned, was told to reveal all he knew of the matter, or they would "get it out of his hide"—an alternative which the set kept constantly on hand for all occasions. Check did not dare to tell them—they would do something, he was afraid, that they would be sorry for. After receiving from them a very comprehensive variety of threats, curses, and promises, he, with great apparent reluctance, divulged the rumor that he had heard, viz., that the old man had been seen at the stage-house, with Dan Buck in irons, and Leonora in tears, and that all hands would be at the Run that night.

The group of conspirators was evidently very much excited by this intelligence ; and though the idea of bringing Dan Buck back to Hucklebury Run in irons was ridiculous enough to make them suspicious of the character of the rumor, they were in no mood to reason on the subject. It seemed very probable to them that old Ruggles, whom every one believed to be capable of any thing when roused, would not only succeed in arresting the robber, but would delight in showing him up among his old acquaintances. The great wonder was that Dan Buck should have allowed himself to be taken alive. They questioned and cross-questioned their saucy informant, who found himself obliged to invent more lies than he had originally calculated for, but he was equal to the occasion. They at last dismissed him, threatening vengeance if he should ever report the interview.

Check was glad to be released. His joke somehow looked serious to him. He did not like the appearance of the fellows at all. A bottle was passed around in his presence, and he noticed that they drank deeply ; and, even before he left them, betrayed the first effects of their potation. Check did not know but they might give Arthur trouble, so he sought for him, and related to him the events of the trunk-room. Arthur was not alarmed, and retired to bed.

Cheek did not dream that Mr. Ruggles was really at the stage-house, as he had said ; but that was the fact. He had given up his pursuit of the fugitives after two or three days spent in New York, and feeling very ill and miserable, had committed the matter to the police, and started on his way home. Arriving at the stage-house, where he had left his horse, he lay down a few hours for rest, preferring to reach his home in the evening. He could not bear to meet the inquiring gaze and words of neighbors. He shrank from the hundred eyes that would peer out upon him from his mill, and witness his disgrace and defeat. The light distressed him. Darkness alone accorded with his depression—his helpless degradation.

As the sun went down, he called for his horse, and started for the Run. The animal was fresh with his week of rest and careful grooming, and went off briskly on his way home. The old man, haunted by his great trial, and feebly cursing his hard fate, wished that he were a horse—any thing but the man he was. He was going back, he knew not why. The charm of life was gone. In his weak-minded and vulgar wife, he had no refuge. In the love and sympathy of others, he knew that he had no right and no place. His life had been selfish and greedy. For many years his heart had gone out in affection toward only one object, and that one was not only taken away from him, but it was forever ruined.

The distance rapidly diminished that divided him from a home that had no attractions for him and no meaning—from duties that had lost their significance and their charm. At length he arrived upon a hill some five miles distant from the Run, from which, in the day-time, he could see the tall chimney of the mill. He pulled up his horse for a moment's rest, and for such calm reflection as the motion of the wagon denied him. There was no star to be seen. The sky was all obscured by low, dark clouds. As he sat with his eyes in the direction of his home, whither his thoughts had gone, he saw a faint light, as if, through the clouds, he caught reflection of a rising moon. As he gazed, the light grew brighter, then died away, then grew again. It was a strange light—not diffused over a large space—not soft and steady, but fitful—sometimes red, sometimes yellow. He watched it like a man entranced, and wondered, questioned in fact, whether it were not the figment of his own disordered brain. He wiped his eyes, and gazed again ; and dimly, but certainly, he caught sight of a tall shaft, and other familiar objects near it.

The pause and the trance were over. He struck his horse a heavy blow, and started down the long hill at a break-neck pace. He relinquished all thought of guiding the animal. The reins hung loosely in his hands, but the whip was grasped firmly, and used freely.

The horse was left to find his own way, while the eye of the driver was fastened upon the distant light that every minute grew broader and brighter. The low clouds before him had all changed to a deep, bloody red. Then little tongues of flame leaped and faded. Then a broad shaft of flame rose, quivered, and fell. Then a great spire of fire shot up, and swayed for a moment, and burst in myriad stars of fire, that were swept away, and fell in a crimson rain.

The long declivity was passed, yet the proprietor knew not how. His horse was running fiercely, and breathing heavily, with a short, quick snort at every straining leap. The wagon reeled from side to side of the road, but the rider, with every muscle rigid, seemed to have grown to it, and unconsciously to manage to keep it from overthrow. Soon he began to hear outcries from the farm-houses, and to pass men running toward the light, that flamed more and still more intensely. He passed dim faces that stopped and stood still with horror as he rushed wildly past them through the darkness, and rained, with constantly increasing madness, his blows upon the infuriated horse. Bridges, hills, rocks—all were alike unminded in that terrible ride.

One mile only remained to be passed over, and then the whole country around was alight. Chimneys sprang out of the darkness like ghosts in the reflection of the flames. Trees glowed like gold upon one side, and were wrapped in pitchy darkness on the other. The air was wild with yells, and full of falling cinders, swept off upon the wind. As the proprietor rushed on, growing still more intensely excited, half a dozen men leaped from the bushes before him, with the intention to stop his horse. Riding toward the light, both the animal and his driver were seen as distinctly as if the sun had been shining. The men caught a quick glimpse of the flying animal and the single ghostly passenger, and leaped back into the cover, just in time to save themselves from the resistless wheels, and the vehicle rushed on.

As the proprietor came to the summit of the hill that overlooked the mill, he saw that structure, which he had worn out a life to build, enveloped in flames in every part. The horse, as he rushed down the hill, caught early attention from the mass of men and women that crowded the road, and with frenzied shouts they rushed in every direction to escape him. The hill was descended with the same furious speed that had been maintained from the time the first burst of light was discovered.

Blinded by the blaze, and frightened by the heat, the horse came opposite to the burning mass, and stopped so suddenly as almost to throw the crazed proprietor from his seat. Then he stood a moment, trembling and smoking, in the fiery heat, then staggered, and fell heavily upon the road, stone-dead.

The moment the horse fell, his driver rose to his feet in the wagon, and faced the fire. The tumult all around him ceased. Every eye was turned to where he stood in the blinding glare, his pale face lit up by the roaring flames, and his garments smoking in the heat. Every tongue was silent. The proprietor's sudden and almost miraculous appearance, his wild ride down the hill, the fall of the overdriven animal, and the statue-like, unblinking gaze of those eyes into the glowing furnace, tended to impress them with almost a superstitious terror. His rigid attitude made them rigid; his silence hushed them. They expected to see him fall dead like his horse, or that some chimney would reel over and crush him.

At length, one man broke the spell which rested upon the crowd, and ran down the road, shielding his face from the heat with his cap. As he came up to the wagon, he shouted to the proprietor to run for his life. The old man, startled into action, leaped directly for the flames, evidently bent on self-destruction. Arthur Blague, for it was he, leaped after him, and grasping him around the body, dragged him away to where he could gather a single breath, and then lifted him to his feet, and led him like a child to his dwelling. Mrs. Ruggles was at the door weeping and praying, but the proprietor did not recognize her. He allowed himself to be led to his room, and laid upon the bed. His face already was a mass of blisters, and he moaned piteously. Arthur then left him for an hour, in the care of his almost helpless wife, and ran off to do what he could to save the property in the vicinity of the mill. In that brief hour, that massive structure, with all its wealth of cunning machinery, dissolved into air, and nothing was left but a heap of red and smoking ruins, and the tall chimney, standing stark against the wall of darkness that moved in as the flames went down, and surrounded the ghastly desolation.

Groups of bareheaded girls were gathered here and there without shelter. Men, whose bread was taken from them by the calamity, stood bitterly apart, and thought of the future. Careless young fellows jested and laughed, or went up to the ruins, and lit their pipes with a brand.

Having arranged for a watch, Arthur returned to the house of the proprietor, and found him in a raving delirium. Soon afterward, Dr. Gilbert, who had been off upon one of his night trips, came in, and administered a powerful opiate. The poor proprietor raved about Arthur as the cause of all his trials and reverses, and then talked wildly of his daughter and her seducer. At length, the dose took effect, and he slept. Arthur, utterly exhausted by the excitements and labors of the evening, dropped upon a sofa in the room, and in a moment was locked in slumber.

How long he slept he did not know; but before his eyes, in all his troubled dreams, the conflagration still raged on. The voices of a great multitude were ringing in his ears. At last, in the centre of the flames which rose and roared so wildly before his dream, there swelled a grand column of fire, following an explosion that seemed to shake the very ground, and to stun his ears to deafness. He was awake in an instant, but the room was perfectly dark. For a moment, he did not know where he was. There was a strange sound in his ears—a gurgling, difficult breathing, like that of a man bestridden by an incubus. He rose to his feet, and groped his way to an adjoining room, where he found a light burning, and where were gathered a dozen young women who had come in for shelter. They had heard

a noise, and were frightened into speechlessness. He
took the lamp in his hand, and quickly retracing his
steps, found the proprietor lying upon the floor, a sheet
of blood covering his face, and a pistol lying at his side.
He had waked, and drank in one draught the cup of woe
which the events of the week had mixed for him, and,
maddened by the mixture, had deliberately risen, and
with the weapon which his fears had for years kept at
his bedside, had blown out his brains. He was quite
unconscious, and a few long-drawn, stertorous respira-
tions finished the life of the proprietor of Hucklebury
Run.

It is needless to enter into a detail of the events immediately following the tragic end of this series of calamities—to tell of the coroner's jury, which found that Mr.
Ruggles died by his own hand, while temporarily insane ;
of the arrest of the young conspirators on a charge of in-
cendiarism, and their discharge, for lack of sufficient
evidence to hold them ; of the funeral, which called together a crowd from twenty miles around—a funeral with
but one mourner, and she not comfortless ; of the scattering of the operatives in all directions in search of
work ; of a generous subscription gathered in all the region to aid those poor people who had lost their all ; of
a brace of sermons at the Crampton church, suggested
by the events that had been described.

A few weeks passed away, and the cloud was lifted.
People ceased to think about the great event of the region and the time. The stream flowed by unused. The
tall chimney stood like a monument over dead hopes ;
over scattered life ; over ruined property ; over vanished
industry. The widow sat in her weeds in her little cottage on the hill, and dreamed of the past and the future.
It would be an outrage upon human nature to say that
she did not care for what had befallen her ; yet she felt
that life had something for her yet.

Long years before, she had ceased to love her husband, and long had she felt the galling slavery of his presence as a curse upon her. For her daughter she mourned. She wanted her society. She could forgive every thing, if the faithless girl would return. That she dreamed of the future, Dr. Gilbert ascertained early. She had never in her life called for so much medical attendance as in the first month after the death of her husband; and Dr. Gilbert always received a message from her with a wry face, and staid in her house but a short time. Exactly what she used to say to him will never be known; but he, by some means, ascertained that whatever might be the fate of the estate, she held, in her own right, an amount of bank-stock that would make her very comfortable under any circumstances.

Arthur, of all the operatives, was alone left with work to do. Of all of them, he only had a knowledge of the proprietor's business, and, under legal supervision, it was his task to settle the estate. There were multitudinous accounts to be adjusted, and in the settlement of these complicated affairs there stretched before him a whole year of remunerative labor.

CHAPTER XVII.

PHILOSOPHICAL, BUT IMPORTANT TO THE STORY, AND THEREFORE TO BE READ.

To the long winter which followed these startling and closely crowded disasters, Arthur, in after years, always looked back as the most delightful and fruitful of his early life. He was called upon to contrive for those who could not contrive for themselves—to find work for those who, tied to the Run by dependent families, could not go away freely to seek their fortunes elsewhere. He won to himself the gratitude and the prayers of the helpless. Joslyn and Cheek were provided for in Crampton, the latter obtaining the much-coveted situation of driver of the Crampton coach. Others were furnished with situations in distant villages.

Bound no longer to the vicinity of the mill, he again took up his lodgings at home. There, in the daily presence of her to whom he had once given his idolatrous love, he learned how stronger than the strongest will is the power of submission. It was by almost a fiercely persistent power of will that Dr. Gilbert overcame his passion for Mary Hammett; and, though he accomplished his object, he never met her without feeling that he had been wounded and terribly tried. Arthur, with no conscious exercise of will, submitted—accepted the decision made against him—and was at peace. From her high position in his imagination, Mary Hammett never fell. On the contrary, she was advanced to a still higher plane, where his dreams of possession did not venture to intrude. He was her disciple. She became to him an inspirer and a guide. In the atmosphere of her noble womanhood, his own best manhood found nourishment and growth. Never, for one moment, allowing his old passion for her to rise, his reserve in her presence all wore away, and she, instinctively apprehending the condition of his mind, became to him the elder sister that he needed.

She led him out into new fields of thought. They read books together, and talked about them. Gradually he felt himself advancing into a larger realm of life. His powers, under so genial a sun, developed themselves grandly, often surprising, by their scope and style of demonstration, the fair minister who, with earnest purpose, was striving to feed the fountain whence they sprang. It was her constant aim to bring his mind into

17

contact with the minds of others, that new avenues might be established through which nutriment might reach him, and that he might gain not only a juster estimate of his own powers, but of his own deficiencies.

Under this happy nurture, his old thoughts of doing something in the world, and something for the world, began to revive. He felt stirring within him prophecies of a future not altogether like the past. He felt his nature spreading into broader sympathies with humanity, and was conscious of enlarging power to follow in the track of those sympathies with a hearty ministry of good.

The earth sees no spectacle more beautiful than that of a completed womanhood, looking, by its delicate insight, into the depths of a half-developed manhood, and striving to stimulate, and nourish, and harmonize powers, that it knows and feels will some time rise above itself, and become, in return, its source of inspiration. Mary Hammett had a thorough comprehension of the material she had in hand. She saw its high possibilities —saw and knew that they were beyond her own. She thoroughly apprehended the nature and the limits of her mission. She felt that her work would be short, but believed that it would be fruitful.

There was one subject discussed by this amiable pair, that always touched Arthur profoundly. It was one proposed in a passage of the letter of the young woman to him, already in the reader's possession. Those words —" If I have had this influence upon you, through your love for me, what shall be the influence of Him who has room in His heart for all the hearts that have ever throbbed, or ever shall throb in the world!"—came often to Arthur in his hours of leisure, as if some angel had recorded them upon a scroll, and waited always to read them to him when he could hear. It was a subject which, in their conversations, was never thrust upon the young man by his Christian-hearted mentor; but it was one which so interfused her whole life, that all her thought was colored by it.

It was through these conversations that Arthur caught his first glimpses of the beauty and the loveliness of a divine life—a life parallel to, and, in its measure, identical with, the life of God—a life above the plane of selfishness, radiant from a heart indued and informed with love for God and man. Toward this life his discipline had led him. He had schooled his powers and passions to self-control. He had subordinated his own life to the life of others, by motives of natural affection and manly duty. He had submitted to a decision that placed forever beyond his possession the object of his fondest worship. All this had led him heavenward; it was for his companion to point him to the door. It was for her to speak to him of the duty of consecration, and of the charm of that life whose gracious issues are beneficence, and healing, and everlasting happiness.

Let the veil be dropped upon those experiences of a great, strong heart, adjusting itself, through prayerful scrutiny and careful thought, to a scheme of life above itself—a scheme brought down from heaven by Jesus Christ! Let no intrusion be made upon the calm joy of a soul when first it determines to give its life forever to God and men, to law and love, and feels itself in harmony with the spirit and economy of the universe, and knows that its life can only tend, in this world and in coming worlds, to blessed consummations!

Miss Fanny Gilbert was, of course, frequently a member of the social circle in Mrs. Blague's quiet dwelling; and though Arthur had been throughout most of her girl's life her beau-ideal of young manhood, she never lost occasion, when alone with Mary Hammett, very good naturedly, though very perversely, to quarrel about him. She professed herself unable to understand how a young man who was truly manly could fail to be ambitious, and how, being ambitious, he could patiently subject himself and subordinate his life to those who were beneath him. If she were a man, she was sure that she should die, if obliged to do what Arthur Blague had done, and was still doing. If she were a young man like him, she would not remain in Crampton a day. It seemed to her that Arthur was very much more like a woman than a man.

Miss Hammett's line of defence was, that Arthur was acquiring his education, under a master whose name was Necessity; that like all decent young men, he was tractable and patient under authority; that out of honorable subjection and self-control springs always the highest power to subject and control others, and that he had not got his growth. It was her theory, that a soul in its development needed time as much as nutriment—that its growth could never be hurried to its advantage. Trees live alike upon the earth and upon the atmosphere, and cannot be too much forced at the root, without destroying the proper relations between those visible and invisible influences which contribute to feed it. There is an atmosphere around each soul, as there is around each tree, and this God takes care of as he does the air, and only in a measured time can the soul gather from it what it contains of nourishment. The soul, therefore, must have time for growth, or grow unsoundly. The soul's sympathies are the soul's foliage, and only when the just relations exist between sympathetic absorption and the direct imbibition of the nutrient juices, does the soul grow strongly and healthily. The prime condition of such a growth as this is time. Storms must wrestle with it. Winds must breathe through it. Rains must descend upon it, year after year. In darkness and in light it must stand and absorb, even though it be unconsciously, those elements

that minister to its forces and its fibre. A soul thus growing will become larger and more beautiful than when
forced at the root, beyond the power of absorption in
the leaves.

Fanny admitted the ingenuity of the reasoning, and
believed in its soundness more thoroughly than she was
willing to confess; but it was directly opposite to the
theory of education she had received from her father.
With him, education consisted in the acquisition from
books, of the accepted facts of science and philosophy.
The quicker this could be done, the better. That stu-
dent who should the most readily and the most expedi-
tiously acquire the knowledge contained in a given number and variety of books was, in his estimate, the best
scholar; and he only could be an educated man who
should secure the particular knowledge prescribed by
the schools. It was in this way that his daughter Fanny
had been educated. With a mind that acquired with
wonderful facility, she had distanced all her associates,
and exhausted the resources of her schools before she
had arrived at full womanhood. The idea that sound
growth required time, had never occurred to him at all;
and he had determined upon putting his little boy
through the same course that his daughter had pursued.
He was to be urged, fired, and fretted with ambition,
taught to labor for the prizes and honors of scholarship,
and brought into life as soon as possible.

Notwithstanding this clash of theories, and Miss Gilbert's respect for that of her father, there was something
in that of the schoolmistress which gave her serious
thought. It somehow united itself with the words of the
reviewer which had so deeply impressed her. She felt
more than ever that she needed more life—that she
needed time—that there was something which time would
give her that she could obtain by no means within her
province and power to institute. She did not understand

how she could grow without direct feeding ; but she saw before her a woman, evidently her superior through the ministry of time. She did not recognize in Mary Hammett powers and acquisitions that outreached her own, but she apprehended a harmony, maturity, and poise, to which she could lay no claim. So, as she said when she finished reading the review of Tristram Trevanion, " Hurrah for life ! " she concluded her reflections upon Mary Hammett's theories by the exclamation, " More time, then ! "

There was one influence in Arthur's quiet home-life that his expanding nature drank as a flower drinks the dew. Little Jamie, his brother, a bright and beautiful little boy, was a constant source of delight to the young man. When the little fellow had reached his second birth-day, there was not a more precious and charming specimen of childhood in Crampton. Arthur carried him out in his limited walks, took care of him at night, and with even more than motherly patience bore with his petulance when ill, and his natural restlessness when well. The attachment between those two brothers, so widely divided by years, was the theme of general remark. Miss Hammett saw it with delight, and Miss Gilbert looked on with astonishment, admitting that it was all very beautiful, but very unaccountable. It seemed more womanly than anything she had seen in Arthur, and she saw few things that did not bear that complexion.

To Arthur, the opening of that little soul upon the realities of existence, the unfolding of its budding affections, the fresh simplicity of a nature newly from the Creating Hand, the perfect faith and trust of a heart that had never been deceived, the artless prattle of lips that knew no guile, the wonderful questions born of childish wonder, were like angels' food. Out of that little cup of life he drank daily nectar. He never tired of its flavor—never thrust it rudely away from him. The child almost forsook its mother in its love for the strong arms and great heart of its brother. In this sweet affection and wonderful intimacy, there was a prophecy of the future which Arthur could not read. Could he have done it, he would have sunk on the threshold of life, and prayed to die. Ah! blessed darkness, that rests upon each step that lies before us in the future! Ah! blessed faith, that frankly gives its hand to Providence, and walks undoubting on!

It was impossible for Miss Hammett to mingle so freely in the society of Arthur and Fanny, without thinking of them sometimes in the relation of lovers. She knew both sufficiently well to see that they did not understand each other. She knew that Fanny was far more accomplished than Arthur; yet she knew that Arthur had powers under whose shadow even Fanny would at some future day delight to sit. When Mary talked with Arthur about his ambitious friend, he always had quite as many objections to her as she was in the habit of expressing in regard to him. He could not love a woman who wanted the praise of the world. Such a woman could only be fit for the world's wife. He pitied any man who would consent to be known to the world as the husband of an ambitious and bepraised notability. Mother Hubbard's dog was a very insignificant individual. Besides, he disliked a " blue," and not only disliked her, but was afraid of her.

Mary Hammett tried to argue Arthur out of notions like these, not because she was anxious to contrive a match between her friends, but because she felt that Arthur was doing Fanny injustice; but she could make no impression on him. He declined to reason on the subject, and declared he had no prejudices upon it. He could only say that he felt as he did because he could not help it. There was something in her position and in her aims that offended him. He thought her a woman of genius, admired her powers, delighted in the vivacity of her conversation, and felt himself stimulated by her presence ; but the idea of loving and wedding her was repulsive to him.

Throughout this season of active and productive social life, Mary Hammett was haunted by a single fear—a fear that obtruded itself upon all her hours of retirement, and often came upon her with a pang when in the presence of her friends. She knew that the villain who had defrauded her of her earnings, and who had wound up his career in Crampton by the wholesale robbery of his employer and the seduction of his daughter, would exhaust his money. She knew, too, that even the large sum he had on hand would furnish him with food for his vices but a short time. She felt certain that his first resort would be the price of her betrayal. She had no doubt that her father would give him any reasonable sum he might claim for discovering to him her retreat. She felt, therefore, that her stay in Crampton was limited, and that any week might bring events that would cut her off forever from the companionships that had become so pleasant and precious to her.

She had fully contrived her plan of operations in the event which she so much feared, and when, at last, it came, she carried it into execution with better success than she had dared to expect.

CHAPTER XVIII.

MARY HAMMETT'S FATHER HAS A VERY EXCITING TIME IN CRAMPTON.

IT was a pleasant Saturday night in August, when, as Mary Hammett sat at her window, she caught a glimpse of the Crampton coach as it drove into the village, raising its usual cloud of dust, and bearing its usual covering of the same material. On its back seat sat an elderly gentleman with his head down, and an altogether superfluous amount of material around his face. Mary could see but little, and saw that only for a moment, but she was convinced that her day of trial had come. She could not be mistaken in the stout shoulders, the short neck, and the heavy eyebrows. She passed out of her room to get a better view of the passenger while he alighted at the hotel, and, though it was almost twilight, and the house at a considerable distance across the common, she was certain that her first impressions were correct.

She immediately returned to her room, and wrote a note to Dr. Gilbert, Aunt Catharine, and Fanny, and despatched it by the hand of Arthur, requesting those friends to call upon her so soon as it should be dark. They came accordingly, wondering much at the singular form of the invitation, and curious to ascertain what it could mean. Mary met them in the parlor, and calling in Arthur Blague and his mother, closed the door, and sat down before them, pale, faint, and trembling. There was an expression of painful embarrassment upon her face, and Fanny, anxious to do something to relieve her, rose, and crossing the room, took a seat beside her on the sofa, and handed her a fan. Mary put the fan aside with a quiet " Thank you," and said : " My friends, I am sure that trouble lies just before me, and I want your advice."

"Certainly," responded Dr. Gilbert promptly. "I'm sure we are all at your service."

"You have all been very kind to me," continued Mary, "for you have trusted me without knowing me, and received me as a friend without inquiring into my history. I wish to thank you for this, and to assure you that, whatever may be the events of the next few days, I shall remember you with gratitude as long as I live."

There was a pause. Dr. Gilbert, exceedingly puzzled, sat and drummed upon the arms of his chair. It was all a mystery to him—her solemnity, her apprehension, and her allusion to imminent events of an unpleasant character. "Miss Hammett," said the doctor, "what do you mean? Who menaces you? Are you going to leave us?"

"I may be obliged to leave you for a time, at least," replied Mary, her eyes filling with tears.

"Who or what can drive you from Crampton?" said Dr. Gilbert, bringing his hand excitedly down upon the arm of his chair. "Let them deal with me. Unless there is some one who has a legal right to control you, I will stand between you and all harm."

"Dr. Gilbert," said Mary, trembling, "my father is in Crampton."

"Your father!" exclaimed all her auditors in concert.

"My father is in Crampton, and he is very, very angry with me."

"What is he angry with you for?" inquired Dr. Gilbert, that being the first question that rose to his lips.

"Because," said Mary with strong feeling, "because I will not perjure myself."

"Let him lay his hand on you at his peril," said the doctor fiercely, again bringing his hand down upon the arm of his chair with a will.

"No, doctor, no; there must be no violence. I must get out of his way."

"Because you will not perjure yourself!" exclaimed the doctor, coming back to the cause of the difference between the young woman and her father. "I'm sure some explanation should go with that. I don't understand it."

"Dr. Gilbert," said Mary, "my father insisted upon my breaking the most sacred pledge of my life, and breaking two hearts with it; and on my refusal to do it, he bade me never enter his presence again. That is the reason I am here in Crampton to-night. That is the reason you found me in the mill at Hucklebury Run. I took his alternative, glad in my choice; and he is here to force me, if possible, back to my home."

"You don't know that," said the doctor, thoughtfully.

"You don't know my father," said Mary.

"But how did he learn that you were in Crampton? That's what puzzles me," said the doctor.

Then Mary told him of Dan Buck, and all the persecutions of which she had been the subject at his hands, and of her conviction, from the first, that this would be the result. Dan Buck had been a salesman in her father's store, had seen and known her then, had been discharged for his dissolute habits, and had now sold the secret of her hiding-place for money.

"Miss Hammett," said the doctor, rising to his feet, "I propose to manage this matter myself. You are not going to leave Crampton at all. If Dan Buck has told your father that you are in this town, he has told him what house you are in. Now just pack your trunks, and Arthur and I will take them over to my house. Aunt Catharine and Fanny will look after you; and if he gets an interview with you, he will get it because he is a stronger man than I am."

The doctor looked as if he thought that entirely settled the matter of her safety from all intrusion.

Aunt Catharine and Fanny very earnestly seconded this project of Dr. Gilbert. Aunt Catharine even went so far as to declare her intention to give the gentleman a piece of her mind if he should ever darken the door of the Gilbert mansion, at which the owner of that mansion smiled, and shrugged his shoulders. Fanny was delighted. This was life. She would lay away in memory every incident of this affair, and some time it should be woven into a romance. Mrs. Blague and Arthur objected, but the majority were against them; and when Sunday morning came, it found Mary Hammett the occupant of a room in Dr. Gilbert's dwelling, which overlooked the common and the hotel on the opposite side of it.

Through the half-closed blind, Mary Hammett was an earnest watcher of every movement at the hotel. For half of the day her father sat at his window, looking at the people as they walked or drove past on their way to and from church. He had his reasons for not showing himself in the street, and so had his daughter. The day wore away, and night descended again. In the evening, Mary for the first time revealed the story of her life to her companion, Fanny Gilbert, all of which Fanny carefully remembered, that she might have abundant materials for her future romance. The doctor and Aunt Catharine dropped into her room in the course of the evening to talk over affairs, and contrive for the emergencies that would develop themselves, without doubt, on the following day.

It was Mary's opinion, that her father, having learned her business and the habits of her charge, would keep himself out of her sight and knowledge, so far as possible, until she was within her school-room and alone with her little flock. This would give him his best opportunity to meet her without the intrusion of Dr. Gilbert, of whose strength of will and whose local power and influence, she had no doubt, he had been abundantly informed by Dan Buck. So it was determined that Mary should remain a prisoner in her chamber, and that Fanny should go over, and perform her duties as teacher.

This arrangement Fanny agreed to gladly. It would give her an opportunity to meet the old gentleman alone, and possibly furnish her with further materials for the great romance.

On Monday morning, there was a good deal of excitement in the family circle that gathered around the breakfast table in Dr. Gilbert's dwelling. All were possessed with the feeling that exciting and not altogether pleasant events were before them. Mary Hammett could eat nothing; and even Dr. Gilbert made very severe work of pretending to an appetite. It was deemed a matter of prudence to keep little Fred at home as company for his teacher. She would hear his lessons, and the plan delighted him. Fanny feared that she could not control his tongue, if the visitor whom she expected should ask any questions about the absent schoolmistress.

At nine o'clock, Fanny left the house, dressed to disguise her form and cover her face as much as possible; and soon the wondering children responded to the little school-bell, and vanished from the street to meet their new mistress. Fanny explained to them that it was not convenient for Miss Hammett to be with them, and that she should act as their teacher until their mistress should be ready to resume her duties. Her exercises had not proceeded half an hour, when she caught a glimpse of a figure passing the window. Her heart leaped to her mouth, and she turned instinctively toward the door, expecting at the next moment to hear a rap. Instead of this polite summons, the door was flung wide open, and an elderly gentlemen, red in the face—red to the very summit of his bald crown—stood before her. The first expression which Fanny caught upon his face was one of fierce exultation. This passed off, or passed into a look of vexation—a puzzled stare—that showed he was quite disappointed, and somewhat abashed. Fanny uttered not a word, but stood regarding him with well-feigned indignation and wonder.

As soon as the intruder could recover from his surprise, he said : " Excuse me for coming in without warning. I—I—expected to see some one else. This is not Miss Hammett. Is she in ? "

" She is not, sir," replied Fanny, with excessive frigidity.

" Are you the mistress of this school ? "

" I am, sir."

" Is Miss Hammett your assistant ? "

" She is not, sir."

The man looked still more puzzled. " There must be some mistake," said he. " How long have you been in this school ? "

" Twenty minutes."

" I do not refer to this morning, particularly. How long have you been mistress of the school ? "

" Twenty minutes."

A mingled expression of anger and alarm came upon the old man's face, as he walked rapidly and excitedly forward, shaking his cane in Fanny's face, and saying : " Young woman, you must not deceive me. You must tell me the truth. I am in no mood to be trifled with. Is the woman you call Mary Hammett in this house ? "

Fanny did not stir—did not wink—but, looking imperiously in his face, said : " Will you put down your cane, sir ? "

" There, damn it ! my cane is down," exclaimed the choleric gentleman, bringing it sharply to the floor. " Now answer my question."

" John," said Fanny to one of the boys, " will you

run over, and tell Dr. Gilbert that there is a strange gentleman in the school-room, who came in without knocking, and is using profane language before the children ? "

" John," said the old man, shaking his cane in his face, " you stir an inch, and I knock your head off." At this the little fellow began to cry, and when he began his little sister began, and one by one the scared children fell into line, and set up a very dismal howl indeed.

" Will you retire, sir ? " inquired Fanny, coolly.

" Will you tell me whether Mary Hammett is in this building ? "

" I have told you, sir."

The old man looked up and around, apparently taking the gauge of the structure, to see if there could be any hiding-place. He advanced to the door of a little recitation-room, opened it, and looked in. Then he looked into a wood-closet, at which some of the children, reassured by the calmness of their new mistress, began to titter. Then he came back to Fanny, who had not stirred, and said in an altered tone : " Will you tell me where Miss Hammett is ? "

" I will not, sir."

The man wheeled upon his heel without making any reply, and walked out of the house. Fanny was delighted with the interview. She had thought of such scenes a great many times—of " drawing her queenly form up to its full height," and saying extremely cool and imperious things—of " withering " some impertinent man by her " quiet and determined eye." She had tried the experiment and succeeded. She would like to try it again.

Fanny had not much heart for the school exercises after this. She was in the heroic mood, and did not perceive how her duties could help on her projects.

She watched the stout gentleman as he walked off, swinging his cane, and making long reaches with it, as if there were some power in the motion to lengthen out his legs. She saw that he made directly for the house of Mrs. Blague, and thither we will follow him.

Arriving at the door, he hesitated, as if to determine what should be his mode of entrance. Then he tried the knob, and finding the door locked, gave the knocker a strong treble blow. The door was not opened immediately, because Arthur had not completed his instructions to his mother. After she and Jamie had removed themselves to a distant room, Arthur started to answer the summons, just as the caller, in his impatience, had repeated it. Arthur opened the door, and stood coolly fronting the irascible gentleman, who was evidently disturbed by meeting a man. "Will you walk in, sir?" said Arthur, who had waited a moment in vain for the man to make known his errand.

The man walked in and entered the parlor, but did not take a seat. Arthur stepped up to him with a smile, and taking his hand, inquired: "To whom am I indebted for the honor of this call?"

"My name is—no matter about my name, sir. I called to see a young woman who boards in this family. Her name is—that is, the name by which you know her —is Hammett—Mary Hammett, I believe. Will you be kind enough to say to her that an old acquaintance would like an interview with her? Passing through the town—thought I would call—known her from a baby— very pleasant little village, this Crampton." The man said this, walking uneasily back and forth, and attempting to be very careless and composed.

"There is no woman of the name in this house, sir. You allude to Miss Hammett, the school teacher, I presume."

The old man bit his lips; but having assumed a false

character, he still affected carelessness. " She formerly boarded here, I think—I was informed so, at least," said he.

" Yes, she formerly boarded here."

" And you say she does not board here now? "

" She does not board here now."

" How long since she left you ? "

" Thirty-six hours."

" Where has she gone, sir? Where shall I be likely to find her ? "

" I cannot tell, sir."

The bald head grew very red, as its owner, puzzled and baffled, walked up and down the apartment. Then, as if he had forgotten the presence of Arthur, he said : " Twenty minutes out of school—thirty-six hours out of boarding-house—damned conspiracy ! " Then turning to Arthur suddenly, he said : " Young man, do you want money ? "

" Any money that I could get honestly," said Arthur, with a smile, " would do me a great deal of good."

" Look you, then ! " said the man, coming up to him closely. " Tell me where I can see this Mary Hammett, and I'll give you a sum that will make your heart jump. You see I wish to surprise her."

" I do not answer questions for money," said Arthur, " and as I have no talent for deception, or double-dealing, I may as well tell you, sir, that your relations to Mary Hammett are known to her friends here, and that your presence in Crampton is known to her. She has taken such measures as her friends have thought proper for keeping out of your way, and you will probably be obliged to leave Crampton without seeing her."

All this was said very calmly, but its effect upon the old man was to excite him to uncontrollable anger. He grasped Arthur by the collar, and exclaimed : " By ——, young man, you don't get off from me in this way.

18

Tell me where this runaway girl is, or I'll cane you." Arthur grasped the cane with one hand and wrenched it from his grasp, and with the other, by a violent movement, released himself from the hold upon his collar.

"There is your cane, sir," said Arthur, extending it to him. "You see I am not to be frightened, and that violence will do you no good."

The man looked at him fiercely for a moment, as if he would like to kill him; but he saw that he had to deal with one who was physically more than a match for him. Finally he said : "Young man, I have a right to know where this girl is. I am her natural protector, and I demand that you tell me where she is."

"I would not tell you for all the money you are worth," replied Arthur; "and you may be sure that you have learned every thing about her that you can learn in this house."

"Very well! very well!" said the man, stamping his cane upon the floor with such spite as to show that he meant any thing but "very well." "I am here for a purpose; and I do not propose to leave till I have accomplished it. I'm no boy—I'm no boy, sir; and if you are one of this girl's friends, you will do her a service by not provoking me too far. I may be obliged to see you, or you may be obliged to see me, again. Now tell me where this committee-man lives—this Dr. Gilbert."

Arthur walked to the window with some hesitation, and pointed out Dr. Gilbert's house to him. "We shall see—we shall see!" said he, as he covered his fiery poll with his hat, and walked off without the courtesy of a formal "good morning."

All these movements, so far as they were out of doors, had been carefully observed from the windows of Dr. Gilbert's house. Dr. Gilbert had made very early professional calls, and returned, anticipating an interview with the angry New Yorker; and he, with Aunt Catharine and Mary Hammett, had seen him enter and emerge from the school-house, and then call at the house of Mrs. Blague, and retire. When Mary saw him turning his footsteps resolutely in the direction of her refuge, she grew sick at heart, and almost fainted. She felt the relations which she sustained toward her father to be most unnatural, and it was quite as much from this consideration as any other that she was so sadly distressed. Nothing but a sense of outrage could ever have placed her in antagonism toward one to whom she owed the duties of a daughter. Nothing but what she deemed to be the forfeiture of his paternal character, could have induced her to break away from him, and from her motherless home. From the first she had shielded him. She had never told her story till she felt compelled to do it for her own safety and protection; and, had she been differently situated, her father's sin against her would never have been mentioned to any one but him to whom she had pledged herself.

The doctor saw him approach; and as he came near the dwelling, looking up and around, the former exclaimed: " Good Heaven! I've seen that man before."

Down the stairs Dr. Gilbert ran, as nimbly as his sturdy physique would permit, very highly excited with his discovery. He had never doubted that he should see a gentleman bearing the name of Hammett, whenever Mary's father should present himself. There flashed upon him the memory of a scene that he had recalled a thousand times; and now that the central figure of that scene was at his door, under such strange circumstances, his excitement was mingled with awe. It seemed as if the hand of Providence had revealed itself, and that, by ways all unknown and undreamed of, he was to be made instrumental in effecting its designs.

The door-bell rang, and the doctor answered it,

throwing the door wide open. The moment the visitor looked in Dr. Gilbert's face, the stern, angry expression which he bore changed to one of bewilderment and wonder.

"This is Dr. Gilbert, I believe," said he, extending his hand to that gentleman, who, in a brief moment, had determined upon changing the tactics arranged for the occasion.

"Mr. Kilgore, how do you do?" said the doctor, heartily shaking his hand. "What could have brought you to Crampton, sir? I had not the remotest thought that you would remember me. Come in, sir; come in. Why, you must have spent the Sabbath in the village, and this is the first time you have come near me. I should have been happy to take you to church. Our hotel is a very small affair, and you must have had a lonely time."

Dr. Gilbert said this with his hand still grasping that of Mr. Kilgore, and leading him slowly into the parlor. Then, still talking rapidly, he took from his hand his hat and his cane, and urged him into a chair, departing for a moment to carry the relinquished articles into the hall.

"I suppose I have met you before, sir," said Mr. Kilgore, of the great firm of Kilgore Brothers. "In fact, I know I have met you, for I never forget faces, but I cannot recall the circumstances of our meeting."

"That is not to be wondered at," replied the doctor, heartily; "but, really, I was flattering myself that you had called for the sake of old acquaintance."

Mr. Kilgore looked vexed. He had not played his cards discreetly; but the trick was lost, and he must look out for the next one. So he said : "Dr. Gilbert, be kind enough to recall our interview. I have certainly conversed with you."

"I called upon you one morning, in New York, to

endeavor to get you to publish a novel written by my daughter. Perhaps you will remember that there was an insane man in at the same time, who had a manuscript on the millennium, which he was anxious to get published."

Mr. Kilgore was still in the fog. Matters of that kind were of every-day occurrence in the little counting-room.

"Do you not remember," pursued the doctor, "sending your man Ruddock out of the room, and calling me back to ask me whether my daughter was obedient or not? Do you not remember getting excited about disobedient daughters?"

It was evident from Mr. Kilgore's face, that he remembered the scene very well. It was not a pleasant recollection at all. It came to him accompanied by a vague impression that he had not treated Dr. Gilbert with much consideration, and that Dr. Gilbert's present cordiality might not be so genuine as it seemed.

"We all have our ways, doctor," said Mr. Kilgore, by way of apology for whatever the doctor might recall from that interview of an offensive character. "We all have our ways. I suppose I'm a little sharp and hard sometimes, but my business has the tendency to make me so."

"Never mind about what passed on that occasion," said the doctor, laughing heartily. "If everybody who meets you on similar business, is as stupid and simple as I was, it would not be strange if it should make you sharp and hard. It is enough that we know each other, and that you are in Crampton. Now what can I do for you? By the way, you are not interested in the Ruggles estate, are you?"

The face grew red again, and the florid tint rose and re-enveloped the bald crown. "I was passing through Crampton," said Mr. Kilgore, hesitatingly, and turning from Dr. Gilbert's fixed gaze, "and learning that an old acquaintance of mine was here—a young woman—I thought I would call upon her. I came to you to inquire about her."

"Aha!" exclaimed the doctor, with a very significant smile. "That is the way the wind lies, is it? Upon my word, you New Yorkers hold out against age right gallantly."

Mr. Kilgore tried to smile, but made very sorry work of it. "You misapprehend me entirely," said he. "I —I—"

"Upon my word!" exclaimed the doctor, with another burst of laughter. "Sixty—a New Yorker—and modest! Why, it's the most natural thing in the world to love a woman at any age, but it's only the boys that are shy about it. Excuse me, Mr. Kilgore, but it's my way; we all have our ways, you know. Ha! ha! ha!"

Mr. Kilgore thought the doctor had very queer ways, and his opinion was agreed to by Aunt Catharine and Mary, who were listening to the conversation at the head of the stairs. They had never heard him go on so, and they wondered what he was driving at. Mr. Kilgore rose and walked to the window, to hide his vexation; and then Dr. Gilbert said: "By the way, Mr. Kilgore, who is this woman?"

Mr. Kilgore returned, and resumed his seat with an air of suffering but polite and patient dignity. "Her name is Hammett—Mary Hammett," said he.

"A very excellent person," said the doctor. "I know her well. She has been a teacher here, and if you have any serious designs with relation to her, I have only to say that you may go the world all over without finding her superior. Everybody loves her in Crampton. I hope you have no intention of taking her away from us at once. Eh?"

Mr. Kilgore's tongue would not move. His throat was

dry, and he tried to swallow something which would not go down.

"By the way," continued the imperturbable doctor, "there is some mystery about this young woman. She carries purity and truth in her face, but we know very little about her. There is a story that her father is very cruel, and will not permit her to marry the man of her choice ; but it seems very strange that any man can drive so good a daughter as she must be from home, simply because she chooses to marry the man she loves."

Mr. Kilgore's face and head fired up again. He looked Dr. Gilbert almost fiercely in the eye, to see if he was making game of him ; but that gentleman's front bore the scrutiny with obstinate unconsciousness.

"That's a lie, sir—a lie ! I know her father well," said Mr. Kilgore. "I know all about this matter. She wanted to marry her father's understrapper—a sneaking clerk, who took advantage of his position to cheat her out of her heart. I know him well, sir. He is not worth a cent—he could not support a wife, if he had one."

"Good fellow, though, isn't he ? " said the doctor, interrogatively.

"He don't know his place, sir—he don't know his place," responded Mr. Kilgore.

"Well, there are two things in his favor, at least." said Dr. Gilbert, decidedly. "He has had the taste to select one of the best women in the world, and has manifested qualities that evidently have secured the love of this woman. I would take that evidence before the certificate of any man living."

"You don't know the circumstances, doctor," said Mr. Kilgore.

"Well, I perceive that you are evidently not the man she has chosen, so that my rallying has all been wild.

I hope you will pardon my levity, for I really feel very much interested in Miss Hammett, and now that I meet one who knows her father, I wish to secure his good offices on her behalf. Just think of it now, Mr. Kilgore. Here is a young woman who has given her heart to a man—never mind whether he be young or old. That man may be poor. I was poor once, and so were you, if I have heard correctly. Now you are rich, and I am comfortable ; and if this man is as industrious as we have been, he may be as prosperous. Suppose you, when young, had been placed in his circumstances : what would you have said of the man who should deny to you his daughter, because you were poor? What would you have thought of a man who, after his daughter had pledged her troth to you, should drive her from his home because she would not renounce her pledge, and lose that which was more valuable to her than all the world besides? I say it would be brutal, and you would say that it was damnable. Now, if you know this woman's father, you can make yourself happy for a life-time by bringing about a reconciliation between them. It is really too bad for them to live so. It's a shame and a disgrace to him. I would not stand in his shoes, and take his responsibilities, for his wealth ten times told."

Dr. Gilbert said all this impetuously, without giving Mr. Kilgore an opportunity to get in a word. When he got a chance to speak, his face was almost purple with his pent-up excitement. "This woman's father, sir, has been disobeyed, and there is nothing that enrages him like disobedience. I know him well—well, sir— well. That daughter can have as good a home with him as ever daughter had, but her will must come under, sir—come under. He will not tolerate disobedience in his dependents."

"She has arrived at her majority, I believe," suggested the doctor.

" But she is a daughter, and a dependent."

" No, thank God! she is not a dependent. She takes care of herself, and earns her own living. If I were to offer her a living to-day, as a companion of my daughter, she would not accept it, because she will be independent. No, no! Thank God, she is not a dependent!"

" Well," said Mr. Kilgore, swallowing intently to get rid of his rage, " we cannot discuss this matter. Will you be kind enough to inform me where Miss Hammett is ? I have visited the school-house and her lodgings, in vain. She seems to have disappeared suddenly. Do you know where she is ? "

" I do, sir."

" Will you direct me to her ? "

" She is in my house."

" Will you lead me to her room ? "

" She does not receive calls in her room. I will tell her, if you wish, that Mr. Kilgore waits in the parlor to see her."

" No, no, for God's sake! don't tell her I am here. I wish to take her by surprise."

There was a rustle at the head of the stairs, and Aunt Catharine slid down, and came directly into the parlor, her black eyes flashing with excitement, and a bright red spot glowing on either cheek. " Miss Hammett will not see her father," said Aunt Catharine; " and if he's half of a man, he will clear out and let her alone."

" Catharine! Why, Catharine! " exclaimed the doctor.

" I don't care a bit—not a single bit. A man that talks and acts as he does, ought not to have any daughter."

Mr. Kilgore turned away from Aunt Catharine in disgust, and then rose and stood before Dr. Gilbert, so excited that he shook in every fibre of his frame. " Her father! eh?　Did you know that woman to be my daughter?"

Dr. Gilbert rose at the question, and answered very decidedly, "I did, sir."

"Do you call this courteous treatment?"

"I will call it what I choose.　I beg you to take the same liberty."

"Well, then, sir, I call it damned uncourteous treatment."

"Your language is less polite than emphatic, but it harms nobody."

Mr. Kilgore started to leave the room.　Dr. Gilbert passed out before him, and arrested him at the foot of the stairs.

"Will you allow me to see my daughter, sir?" said Mr. Kilgore, savagely.

"No, sir, I will not;" and Dr. Gilbert planted himself firmly before the enraged father, and waved him back.

Mr. Kilgore stood a moment with his hand uplifted, as if about to strike.　The doctor watched his eye, which suddenly grew bloodshot, while a purple tinge spread over his features and forehead.　The man was evidently arrested by a strange feeling in his head, for he suddenly slapped his hand upon his forehead, as if to dissipate an attack of dizziness; then he staggered, and fell to the floor like a log.

Mr. Kilgore was in a fit.

CHAPTER XIX.

MR. KILGORE RECOVERS HIS HEALTH, AND HIS DAUGHTER RECOVERS SOMETHING BETTER.

WHEN Fanny returned, full of anxiety and curiosity, from her school at noon, she found the family with disturbed and solemn faces, actively engaged in ministering to their unexpected patient. Mary, intensely excited, was busy with such offices for her father as she could perform without entering his presence, though her caution was unnecessary, for he was unconscious. Dr. Gilbert had bled him after his removal to a bed. This had relieved his more urgent symptoms ; but there followed long fits of fainting, and these, in turn, had been succeeded by a violent reaction, accompanied by a hot delirium. He raved about his daughter, alternately cursing her for her disobedience, and piteously pleading with her to return to her home. Much of this incoherent language Mary overheard ; and it was the cause of a profound revulsion in her feelings. It called back the old love which she once had cherished for her father, and in her sensitive spirit awakened questions as to the propriety of what she had done. How far was she guiltily responsible for this catastrophe ? Had she not been selfish ? Had she not been hasty ? If her father should die, would not the blame of his death be at her charge ?

Her father had seemed to her like an iron man—a man without a heart. She had never dreamed that any event could throw him from his balance—that any excitement that he might feel on her account could proceed to such a crisis as that which had prostrated him. As he lay, helpless and moaning, away from home and friends, a fountain of long frozen and pent-up tenderness in her heart gushed forth. The hard, imperious, defiant father had repulsed not only herself, but her sympathy and affection ; the helpless and friendless father melted her.

It was natural, of course, that, in this hour of her darkness and trial, she should call upon Arthur Blague for assistance. Accordingly, all the time he could spare from his business, he spent at the bedside of the patient, ministering to his wants, and controlling him in the more violent demonstrations of his disease.

Days came and went, Fanny still attending to the duties of the schoolmistress, and the latter doing every thing which she could do for her father. The fever and the delirium passed away at last, and they threatened to leave him in the arms of death. Through all these weary days and nights, Mary had wept and prayed—wept for the pain she had caused, and prayed for the forgiveness of all that God had seen of wrong in her treatment of her father—prayed that he might recover, and that then, while his hands were weak, and the eye of the world, which he so much regarded, was removed from him, the great Spirit which moulds and moves the hearts of men, would turn his heart toward her and the man whom her love had made sacred to her.

On the evening when the fever reached its crisis, Dr. Gilbert came down-stairs, and taking his seat in the parlor by Mary, told her that the night would probably decide her father's fate. She gathered from the expression of his face and the tone of his voice, that, in his judgment, the event was problematical. Up to this time she had not consented that his New York friends should be made aware of his illness, and she felt that there was another terrible responsibility upon her. She learned that he was lying in entire unconsciousness, his excitement all gone, and his pulse but feebly fluttering with life. Her reserve was laid aside in a moment. She rose to her feet, struggling to control the convulsions of her grief, ascended the stairs, and, for the first time, entered the chamber where her father lay. Arthur was there, endeavoring to compel the patient to swallow a stimulating draught. She quietly took the cup from his hand, and indicated her wish that he should retire. The moment the door was closed, she sank upon her knees, and, pressing her lips to her father's cold and clammy hand, burst into an uncontrollable fit of weeping.

As the first gust of her sorrow subsided, she began to pray. At the beginning, her words were earnest and importunate whispers ; but soon her voice, in the stress of her passion, joined in the utterance, and the very walls of the room seemed to listen to, and drink in, the language of her plaint and her petition. She prayed that God, the All-Loving, the All-Merciful, the All-Powerful, would restore her father to health—that then and there He would reveal Himself to succor and to save. She prayed for her own pardon, and for grace to bear the blow, if her father should be taken from her. She prayed that, if the life which was become so precious to her should be spared, out of this great trial and great danger might spring precious fruits of good to her and all who were dear to her. Often pausing, she kissed the hand she held, and exclaimed : " Alas ! that I should be the cause of this ! "

At length she rose, and placed her hand upon her father's damp brow, and smoothed back the thin, white hair upon his temples, and listened to his breathing. Then she sank upon her knees again, and bathed his hand with tears.

Precious ministry of filial love !—bruised and trodden under feet for many long and cruel months, yet still vigorous at the root, and full of perfume in its broken branches ! She felt the feeble pulse, and there was a new thrill in it. She looked upon the impassive face, and the pinched, deathly look had passed away. As she gazed, trembling with excitement and hope, it seemed, to her sharpened apprehensions, as if a voice had whispered to her soul : " Your prayer is answered." So real was the assurance, that she exclaimed: " My Heavenly Father, I thank thee !"

As she watched and wept, and kissed the hand which she still held, and gazed in her father's face, she saw tears form beneath the closed lids, and creep down the pale cheeks, and leave their track of healing where she had not seen tears before for many years. She grasped the hand she held with the fervor of her joy, and with such emphasis that it seemed as if an electric thrill had been shot through the sick man's frame. " Do you know me ? " she exclaimed. " Do you know your Mary ? "

The feeble lips tried to utter a reply, but the tide of life had not yet risen to them. A gentle return of the pressure which she had maintained upon his hand was his response.

" And do you—can you—forgive me ? Tell me so ; " and the hand, as it responded, was covered with kisses.

Then came to the excited and grateful daughter another gush of tears. Why does she weep now ? Ah ! there is another question which she longs to ask ! She hesitates. On that question hang the equivalents of life and death to her. She had become aware that behind the veil of weak and powerless flesh before her, there was a spirit whose eyes and ears had been open during all her presence in the chamber. She knew, when those tears slid out upon her father's cheek, from eyes that seemed asleep, that there was a wakeful soul behind them, in calm consciousness all the while. She knew that he had been touched by her presence and her prayers. She felt that somehow God had made her a minister of life to him. She shaped her question. It was brief, and as she breathed it to her earthly father,

her thoughts went upward, far above that powerless form, to Him who was feeding the springs of its returning life, with the prayer for favor.

" And him ? "

A shadow of pain gathered upon those pale features—a spasm of distress—indicative of the struggle which that little question caused in his feeble mind. Mary watched him with trembling anxiety, condemning herself for her haste in putting him to such a trial in such a condition. A tremor passed over his frame, as if he had summoned himself to a great decision. Mary rose suddenly to her feet in alarm, and bent her face close to his. Slowly the long-sealed eyelids opened, and father and daughter gazed into each other's eyes. The struggle was over, and a feeble smile, full of kindness, lighted for a moment the old man's face, and then the eyes closed again.

To this moment of perfect reconciliation with her father, Mary in after years looked back as the happiest of her life. It translated her at once from the realm of doubts and darkness in which she had walked since she left her home, into the realm of her fondest dreams —from realities of the sternest mould, into probabilities of life that seemed impossible of realization from the supernal charm with which her loving imagination had invested them. Broad and bright before her opened the pathway of the future. In a moment, her heart had travelled over the distance that interposed between her and him to whom for many weary months she had been lost, in anticipation of the meeting which should repay for all anxiety and all suffering. During the rapid passage of thoughts that crowded through her mind, her thanks went upward all the time to Him to whose overruling providence she traced all the blessedness of the moment, as incense rises heavenward from censers swung by unregarding children.

As the smile faded from her father's lips, she stooped and imprinted a kiss upon them, full of tenderness and gratitude, saying : "Father, you will get well, and we shall be very, very happy again. Now I must write some letters, and you must sleep. I shall sit with you to-night, and no hand but mine shall nurse you hereafter." She then administered the cordial that Arthur had left, and retired from the room.

As she came again into the presence of the family, her countenance beamed as if she had stood upon the Mount of Transfiguration. She shook the doctor's hand in her joy, and kissed Aunt Catharine and Fanny. "O my friends! I am happier that I can tell you," she said. "My father's crisis is past—he will get well—and we are friends." All were glad in her happiness, but their sympathy was accompanied by a pang which all experienced alike. That which brought joy to her, separated her from them.

Leaving her to write her letters to her New York friends, informing them of the illness of her father and his apparent amendment, we will pass over two or three days, and look in upon one of these friends.

The hours of business were over in Mr. Frank Sargent's modest establishment, and its enterprising proprietor had withdrawn into his little counting-room, and shut to the door. For a while, he thought of his business; and there came to him, strangely, thoughts about Miss Fanny Gilbert's novel. It had not succeeded—would not sell. He must write to the doctor, and claim the fulfilment of that gentleman's pledge to share the loss which the publication of the book had occasioned. He thought of the doctor, and tried to imagine the features of his daughter. He could not get them out of his mind. They and the book haunted him. If his thoughts strayed away, or were forced away into other matters, they came back immediately to them.

He tired of this at last, and, unlocking a little drawer at his side, he drew forth a letter that he had read a thousand times before, but one which always gave him an impetus into reveries that drove business out of his mind. He opened and read :

"My Dear Frank:

"This night I take one of the most important steps of my life. My father and I have had a long conversation about you, in which he has endeavored, by promises and threats, to make me renounce you, and break my pledge to you. I have reasoned with him, besought him, on my knees begged of him to relent, but all to no purpose. He forbids you the house, and commands me to renounce you forever, or to renounce him. He was very angry, and is implacable. I have taken the alternative he offers me. I shall leave New York to-night. I leave without seeing you, because I fear that an interview would shake my determination ; but I am yours—yours now, and yours forever. I shall go where you will not find me, and, if you love me—ah! Frank, I know you do—you will make no search for me. I shall not write to you, because money will buy the interception and miscarriage of letters, but I shall think of you, and pray for you every day, nay, all the time.

"This may seem strange and unwarrantable to you, but, Frank, be true to me, go into the work of life, and demonstrate to my father and the world the manhood there is in you ; and God will take care of the rest. I go, trusting in that Providence which never forsakes the trusting—with a firm faith that out of this great trial will spring the choicest blessings of our lives. Have no fears for me. If any great trial befall me, you shall know it ; and when the time shall come for the realization of our wishes and the redemption of our pledges, it will declare itself. Never doubt me. I cannot be untrue to you. Remember that I leave my home for you. We may not marry now. You are not ready for marriage.

"Forgive my seeming coolness, for my heart is bleeding for you. Do not be unhappy. Cast your care upon Him who cares for you. God bless you, Frank, and keep you! Your own

"Mary."

The closing words of this letter he read, and read again. The abrupt sentences and the marks of tears, not yet obliterated, showed in what a passion of tenderness they were written. Nearly three years had passed away since that letter was received, and its words were the last he had seen from her hand. Where on the earth's face she wandered or sojourned, he knew not. Whether she were still in the land of the living, he knew not. It had cost him the daily exercise of all his faith in her and in God to maintain his courage and equanimity. Her father had visited him in anger, demanding the hiding-place of his daughter; and when he had stated the substance of this letter, and the fact that he absolutely knew nothing of her, he was told that he lied.

The letter lingered in his hands. It was indued with a new charm. There was a strange vitality in its utterances that took hold of his heart with a fresh power. As he sat regarding it, it seemed as if the spirit of Mary was at his side, looking over his shoulder. In the twilight, he hardly dared to stir; and a superstitious fear crept over him—a fear that his Mary was indeed dead, and was present with him in a form which he could not see.

He was startled from these imaginations at last, by the entrance of his errand-boy, with a package of letters from the post-office. The first upon which he laid his hand had upon it the post-mark, "Crampton, N. H." The hand was the same that he had been perusing. He opened it and read :

"DEAR FRANK :

"Come !

"MARY."

He sprang to his feet transformed. The listlessness was gone, and every nerve in his frame thrilled with excitement. The night-boat had left, and, though impatient beyond expression, he was obliged to wait until morning before setting out. In the meantime, he had a world of business to attend to. He sent for his principal clerk, told him that he should be absent for several days—how long he could not tell—and gave him all the necessary directions for carrying on the business. He replied to his letters, laid out work for his clerks, and in three hours had transacted more business than an ordinary man would have done in as many days. He looked forward and provided for the payment of his notes ; and, arranging for a daily interchange of letters between himself and his establishment, retired to his boarding-house to prepare for his journey.

Now that we are to see more of Mr. Frank Sargent, we should know more about him. It will be seen readily enough that he was not a great man. Why did so good and so noble a woman love him ? Simply because he was true, and had life in him. Wherever he went, there went gladness and vivacity. Frank Sargent was always wide awake. He only needed the presence of half a dozen people to stimulate him into the most delightful drolleries. People loved to hear him talk, whether he uttered sense or nonsense. He could sit down by the side of an old woman and charm her by his tide of small talk, or frolic with a band of merry children, until his coat-tails were in danger. He was a great man in small parties, an indispensable man at picnics, the superintendent of a Sabbath-school, a " bloody Whig " in politics, as he delighted to call himself, and the most zealous and earnest of his circle in a revival of religion. He was a man who stirred up every circle he entered, and was welcome everywhere except at the house of the elder Kilgore.

The reader has already learned incidentally, that he had been a clerk in the house of the Kilgore Brothers. In this house, he had made himself very popular, both at home and away, for he had travelled for the house quite extensively. The old man had once greatly delighted in Frank Sargent. When he came back from his long trips, it was the highest entertainment the elder Kilgore had at his command, to invite Frank home to dine with him, and hear him relate his adventures by the way, and tell of his ingenious methods for entrapping "lame ducks," a kind of game which the house, in its large and widely extended operations, had a good deal to do with. Many were the hours which the vivacious traveller helped Mr. Kilgore to pass pleasantly away, and great was Mr. Kilgore's admiration of, and confidence in him. Fertile, volatile, voluble, with a great capacity for business, a thorough devotion to the interests of his employer, and a sense of Christian honor which always manifested itself as the basis of his character, he was, indeed, no mean companion for an old man like Mr. Kilgore.

Still, Mr. Kilgore always regarded him as an inferior —a man to be patronized and encouraged, particularly so long as he was an efficient minister to the prosperity of the house, and aided in the digestion of a good dinner. Frank Sargent knew the old man, and humored him by always "keeping his place"—going no further than he was led. This, Mr. Kilgore appreciated; and he regarded the young man with great complacency. Of course, when the clerk visited Mr. Kilgore's house, he met Mr. Kilgore's daughter; but Mr. Kilgore's estimate of his own position and that of his family, and his confidence in Frank Sargent as a young man who knew his place, forbade the suspicion that between the young people there could be more than the common interchanges of politeness. In fact, he had, on more than one occasion, apologized to his daughter for bringing Mr. Frank Sargent home with him.

After Mr. Kilgore had finished his heavy dinner, and had become too dull to listen to the conversation of his talkative clerk, the young man felt at liberty to devote himself to the daughter, and she, in turn, felt bound to entertain him. We are not aware that there is any philosophy that will satisfactorily account for two people, totally unlike, falling in love with each other. It is a matter of every-day occurrence, as all know. At any rate, Frank Sargent and Mary Kilgore met but a few times in friendly intercourse, before, by steps which they did not mark in the passage, they became lovers. Thus the matter went on for weeks and months, the old man, in his purse-proud blindness, seeing nothing of the state of affairs. Mary occasionally dropped in at the store, and it was there, in her conversations with the young man, that the jealousy of the other clerks was aroused, Mr. Dan Buck's among the rest.

At last, Frank Sargent began to think that if he was to become the husband of Mary Kilgore, he must be something more than a clerk, and have more than a clerk's income. Both he and Mary supposed that the old man knew, or suspected, their attachment for each other ; and furthermore believed, from his cordiality to the young man, that he looked upon the matter with favor. So Frank Sargent, on one occasion, proposed to Mr. Kilgore the subject of going into business on his own account. The old gentleman expressed surprise and regret, but would not interfere. He knew that the young man's personal popularity would take custom from his own house, but he was too proud to admit, for an instant, that anybody was essential to the house of the Kilgore Brothers but himself.

Frank Sargent then set up for himself, and made a good beginning. Mr. Kilgore's old customers, many of them, came to him, and he had the good-will of all his associates. But his love matters would have to come to a crisis sooner or later, and so it was agreed between the lovers that he should make to the father of the young woman a formal proposition for her hand. Great was the surprise, and greater the wrath, of the great Kilgore, when the audacious young bookseller submitted his confession of love, and his request for the bestowal of its object upon him by its nominal owner. The old man was at first thunder-struck, then indignant, then angry. He drove him out of his counting-room, forbade him his house, and, from that moment, was his enemy ; losing no opportunity to injure him in his business, and striving by all allowable means to crush him.

The rest of this long story is sufficiently in the reader's possession. Mutual friends contrived meetings for the lovers, and at last, after a painful scene between father and daughter, the latter fled, leaving only the letter which Frank Sargent had perused every day for three years before he received another from the same hand.

Bright and early on the morning succeeding the events in the young publisher's counting-room, that gentleman, having passed a sleepless night, stepped on board the good steamer Bunker Hill, and set out on his journey to Crampton.

Alas ! for the impatient feet that trod the deck of the industriously toiling steamer ! If Frank Sargent could have increased her speed by the application of that fraction of a one-horse power that was in him, he would contentedly have labored at the crank all the way. When, at last, he landed, and commenced the passage up the valley as " a deck passenger " of the slow coach —for he always rode where he could see the horses, and talk with the driver—it seemed as if the long miles had surpassed the statute to a criminal degree. But all journeys have an end, and, still sleepless, he found himself at length seated with Cheek upon the box of the little Crampton coach.

Frank Sargent could not have fallen in with any one better informed than Cheek, of the points upon which he needed light. So, by a process which a thorough-bred New Yorker understands in an eminent degree, he "pumped" him all the way; praised his horses, and managed to get out of him Mary's history since he had known her. He learned also of the presence of Mr. Kilgore in Crampton, of the dangerous sickness he had survived at the house of Dr. Gilbert, and of the rumor, current in the village, that father and daughter had "made up," and that "the whole thing had been straightened."

"I tell you," said Cheek with emphasis, as a general summing up of his revelations, "that any man who takes Mary Kilgore out of Crampton against her will, will kick up the greatest row that ever was started in this place."

Now it did not occur to Cheek at all, that the lively gentleman who sat upon the box with him, and begged the privilege of driving his horses, was Mary's lover; so, after Frank Sargent had succeeded in getting all the information he wanted from the driver, the latter undertook to obtain fitting repayment. "I reckon, perhaps, you know Mary Hammett, as we used to call her, pretty well, don't you?" said Cheek.

"Know her? I think I do," responded his passenger.

"Brother, perhaps?"

"No."

"Cousin, may be?"

"Not a bit of it."

"Some sort of relation, I s'pose?"

"Well, no—not exactly."

"Neighbor?"

"Yes, neighbor—old neighbor—old friend—knew her years ago—known her ever so long."

"Well, I guess she'll be glad to see you, now. You don't know the feller she's engaged to, do you?"

"Oh! yes; I know him very well; he's a particular friend of mine."

"I vow! I should like to see him," said Cheek; "he's punkins, ain't he?"

"Some," replied Frank Sargent, with a laugh he could not repress. Then he added: "What kind of a man do you suppose he is? How do you think he looks?"

"Well, I don't know," replied the driver. "My mind's always running on one thing and another when I'm driving along, and I've thought him up a good many times. I reckon I should know him if I should see him."

"Just describe him, then. I can tell you whether you are right or not."

"Well, I reckon," said Cheek, squinting across the top of a tall pine-tree they were passing, "that he's a tall feller, with black whiskers and black clothes, and an eye that kind o' looks into you. It don't seem to me that he ever says much, but he has an easy swing, that makes people think he knows everything, and isn't afraid. I've always had a notion, too, that he wears a thundering big gold watch-chain, and a seal with a kind of red stone in it. I ain't certain about the stone, but it's red or yellow, I'll bet my head." Then Cheek scratched the head that he was so willing to risk, and added, "I don't know—you can't tell about these women. Sometimes the best of 'em will take a shine to a little, flirtin', fiddlin' snip, and be so tickled with him, they don't know nothing what to do with themselves."

Frank Sargent laughed with a " haw-haw," that made the woods ring. "Capital hit!" said he. "Capital hit!" Then he laughed again.

"What are you laughing at?" inquired Cheek, dubiously.

"Oh! nothing. I—I was wondering whether I could guess as nearly the appearance of a girl in Crampton, or on the road, that swears by the driver of this coach."

"Well, go in!" said Cheek, taking a squint across the top of a maple.

Mr. Frank Sargent very good-naturedly "went in," in these words : "She's a long girl, with blue eyes, about a head taller than you are ; sings in the choir without opening her teeth ; writes verses about flowers and clouds, and children that die with the measles, and works samplers."

"Now, what's the use of running a feller?" said Cheek. "You know you ain't within gun-shot."

"Well, tell me all about her, then," said the publisher, who was willing to do any thing to pass away the time.

"She's no such kind of a bird as you've been talking about, I tell you. She's right—she is. You can't hardly tally how she's coming out, because she isn't exactly a woman yet. She's kind o' betwixt hay and grass, you know—got on long dresses, but looks odd in 'em."

"She must be very young," remarked Cheek's much-amused auditor.

"Young, but not green," said Cheek. "She's got an eye that snaps like that," and he illustrated her visual peculiarity by cracking his whip in the immediate vicinity of his horses' ears. "She's waiting for me, you know," continued the communicative lover, "and I'm beauing her round, and sort o' bringing her up. If I hadn't taken her young, I never should do any thing with her in the world. It's just with women as it is with colts. You want to halter-break 'em when they're little, and get 'em kind o' wonted to the feel of the harness, and then, when they're grown up, they're all ready to drive. She's one of them high-strung creatures—all full of fuss and steel springs—that'll take a taut rein, I tell you, when her blood's up. She's just like her mother."

"Got a smart mother, has she?"

"Yes, *sir*. No mistake about that. Oh! she's just as full of *jasm*.'"

Frank Sargent laughed again. " You've got the start of me," said he. " Now tell me what ' jasm ' is."

" Well, that's a sort of word, I guess, that made itself," said Cheek. " It's a good one, though—jasm is. If you'll take thunder and lightning, and a steamboat and a buzz-saw, and mix 'em up, and put 'em into a woman, that's jasm. Now my girl is just like her mother, and it's a real providence that I got hold of her as I did, for if she'd run five years longer without any halter, she'd have been too much for me—yes, *sir*."

At this point of the conversation, the spire of the Crampton church came boldly into sight, and the laugh that rose to the young publisher's lips died away as if his mouth had been smitten. A great crisis in his life was doubtless before him. A great question was to be decided. He was to meet again one whom he loved almost idolatrously—one whom circumstances had hidden from his vision and withheld from his embrace with threats of eternal separation. He felt his heart thumping heavily against its walls, and trembled with excitement.

" Stop at the hotel ? " inquired Cheek, who had been struck with his passenger's sudden silence.

" Take my baggage there, and me to Dr. Gilbert's," was the reply.

Then Cheek took from its pocket the little horn which daily proclaimed to the people of Crampton that the mail was in, or coming in, and blew a most ingenious refrain—the instrument leaping out into various angular flourishes, as if a fish-horn had got above its business, and were ambitious of the reputation of a key-bugle.

" That's Dr. Gilbert's house," said Cheek, putting his horses into a run. Mr. Frank Sargent was pale. He looked at the house. He saw the door partly open, and caught a glimpse of a woman's face and form. The horses were pulled up at the gate with a grand flourish, and the passenger leaped from the box; but before he had advanced a rod, Mary was on her way to meet him. They rushed into each other's arms, and stood for a minute weeping, without a thought of the eyes that were upon them. Aunt Catharine was at the window, crying like a child. Fanny was wild with excitement, and ran down the walk to meet the lovers.

During all this scene, the Crampton coach stood very still, and its driver's eyes were very wide open. He sat and watched all parties until they entered the house; then, turning to his horses, and reining them homeward, he gave vent to his astonishment by the double-shotted exclamation—" Christopher Jerusalem ! "

CHAPTER XX.

WHICH CONTAINS A VERY PLEASANT WEDDING, AND A VERY SAD ACCIDENT.

AFTER Mr. Frank Sargent had been introduced to the Gilbert family, and had renewed his acquaintance with Dr. Gilbert by the most extravagant demonstrations of cordiality, the reunited lovers were left for a whole blessed hour in one another's society. In that hour, a great deal of talking was accomplished, and a great deal of happiness experienced. Mary communicated to her lover the outlines of her own story, already narrated, and informed him concerning the condition of her father. Since his reconciliation to her, she had hardly left his bedside, and had had the satisfaction to see him daily mending under her assiduous nursing and her loving ministrations. That afternoon she had informed him of the expected arrival of her lover, and, though the matter was painful to him, she was sure that his mind was decided upon it, and that he would interpose no further obstacles to their union. He was still very weak, and would be unable to see his old clerk for some days, and probably would not be strong enough to leave Crampton for a fortnight.

After tea, Mary insisted that Frank should leave her, and get the sleep which he needed. He had never been more wide awake than at this time, but he loyally obeyed, and taking his leave, crossed over to the Crampton Hotel, and selected his lodgings. The little, yellow-breasted piazza was full of people when he arrived, not one of whom was not aware of his relations to the schoolmistress. In fact, all the village was gossiping about his arrival, and everybody was anxious to get a look at him.

The next day he spent, of course, at the Gilbert mansion; and if he had been a resident of it for a twelvemonth, he could not have been more at home. He first elected Fanny to be his sister, by a " unanimous vote." Then he conciliated Fred by giving him a ride upon his shoulders, and telling him half a dozen funny stories; and wound up the achievements of the day by kissing Aunt Catharine, who pretended to be terribly offended, but who finally acknowledged to Mary that he was an excellent fellow, though a " perfect witch-cat." It was very pleasant and amusing to see how quietly Mary took all these demonstrations. Confident in the good heart that shone through his extravagances, and confident in the power of others to see it, she gave herself up to the entertainment as if he were a stranger to her. Sometimes, indeed, she checked him with a good-natured " Frank!" and established herself as a kind of regulator, to indicate when his mill was going too fast.

Dr. Gilbert was amused, but Frank Sargent had other entertainment for him; and long and very interesting

were his communications upon various matters of public
interest. He talked of politics, of business, of religion,
of literature ; and added more to the doctor's stock of
current information than he could have gathered from
all his newspapers. On the whole, the family were
much pleased with the lover of their friend Mary. He
brought life into so many departments of their life, and
adapted himself so readily to their tastes and tempera-
ments, that they felt his presence to be a sudden accession to their wealth. Mary relinquished him to them
in the kindness of her heart. He was hers for a lifetime.
She would lend him to them while she could.

The following day was the Sabbath—always a welcome day to Frank Sargent, because it was usually a
day of very agreeable business. At home, besides attending to his own charge as superintendent of a Sabbath-school, he was usually out at one or more mission
schools during the day, and joined with others in seeking for the neglected and uninstructed. These things
gave him an opportunity to talk, and to one who was always full, this was a great privilege.

It was customary with the superintendent of the
Crampton school to invite every stranger who made his
appearance to address the children. The gift of public
speech was rare in Crampton, and a talking stranger
was a Godsend. Accordingly, when Frank Sargent remained after the benediction was pronounced at noon,
and stood up, smiling pleasantly upon the children as
they gathered into the pews, the superintendent came to
him, and having been introduced by Dr. Gilbert, requested him to open the school with some " remarks."

Very memorable were those " remarks," made with
rare and racy freedom, for they awakened many smiles,
and were the occasion of many tears. He told the
school about the poor children in New York—how he
had found them in rags, and filth, and wretchedness,

and washed their faces with his own hands, and taught them to read. He told how a sweet little girl had been taught to love her Saviour, and how, afterward, she had died in her little garret, and said she was going home to her Father in heaven, where they had beautiful carpets on the floor, and red curtains at the windows, and chairs as soft as the grass. Then he told them about a good little boy who said he was one of Jesus Christ's little lambs, and when he went to heaven he was going to have a bell on his neck. The first story made the children cry, and the second one made them smile ; and then Mr. Frank Sargent said that all the little children were Jesus Christ's lambs, at which one little boy giggled. Then the speaker asked the boy what he was laughing at, and the boy told him he laughed because his name was Charley Mutton, and all the other little boys called him Charley Lamb. Then Mr. Frank Sargent smiled, and the doctor and Fanny smiled, and all the school came as nearly up to an outburst of mirth as they dared to.

Then the speaker told them how so much had been accomplished for the poor children in New York. It was done by co-operation. Everybody interested in the work did something ; and, to show them what miracles could be wrought by co-operation, he told them a story of a man who had no legs forming a partnership with a man who had no arms, and both together taking and carrying on a farm. The man who had no legs got upon the shoulders of the man who had no arms, and the man who had legs carried the man who had arms all about, the latter sowing the grain and hoeing the vegetables, and picking fruit from the trees. Neither could do anything alone, but co-operating, they were able to carry on a large business, and made a pile of money. The vivid colors in which the speaker painted this brace of farmers made a decided impression, and awoke many smiles. But these were banished by his closing words, which were solemn, earnest, and touching. The children had never heard such talk before, and were very much impressed.

At the conclusion of his " remarks," he was invited to instruct a class of young women, and here he became so much interested and absorbed, that he talked loudly enough to be heard in all parts of the house, and talked quite beyond the tinkling of the little bell that announced the close of the hour.

On Fanny's return, she gave a glowing account of Frank's hit as a speaker to Mary, who had remained with her father. Mary received the announcement of his success with the same quiet smile with which she regarded all his performances. Knowing that he did strange, and often ludicrous things, she also knew that his heart was right, his apprehensions keen, and his ability equal to any task he might see fit to undertake. As for the young man himself, he had the satisfaction of seeing the boys all about Crampton common, for a week afterward, riding on one another's shoulders, and sowing dirt in illustration of his illustration of co-operation. He also received a well-executed pencil drawing, representing his heroes of the farm, from the hand of a smart young man, just home from college.

Mr. Kilgore mended rapidly. A week after the safely surmounted crisis of his fever, he sat up in his chair for an hour. But he was not without his mental burden. He had regained possession of his daughter, but it had been done at a great sacrifice of feeling. For once in his life, he had been conquered. His plans for a splendid matrimonial alliance for his daughter had been thwarted, and it was a great humiliation for him to think of swallowing all his words, and receiving as a son the young man whom he had so thoroughly hated and persistently abused. But the step had been taken, and could not be retraced ; and his old pride, though galled and humbled, came to his aid at last. Could not he, the great Kilgore, do as he would with his own ? If he chose to confer his daughter upon Frank Sargent, he could carry the matter through in splendid style, and who would presume to question him?

When he became sufficiently strong he consented to receive his future son-in-law. He greeted him with no demonstration of feeling, and Frank took the hint at once. The past was to be buried, and not alluded to at all. They talked about business, and Frank was soon running on in his usual entertaining style. His inquiries for the old man's health were made self-respectfully, but with such a genuine interest that the invalid felt ashamed of himself. He could not help feeling that if the young man should wish he were dead, it would be the most natural thing in the world.

As the days came and went, Frank became more and more the companion of Mr. Kilgore. The attachment existing between the young people was never alluded to upon either side. Frank dutifully and respectfully assumed and performed the offices of a son, but neither asked questions nor made communications. Mary, in calm confidence, was sure that Frank could make his way if he had an opportunity, and never embarrassed their intercourse by her presence. There were abundant invitations for Frank to go fishing, and riding, and gunning ; but he sacrificed everything, for the sake of ministering to Mr. Kilgore's comfort and recovery. The old man felt, in the depths of his heart, that Mary had made a good choice for herself and for him ; and both Frank and she saw that time alone was needed for her father's wounded pride to heal, in order to reconcile him entirely to the match.

Toward Dr. Gilbert, Arthur Blague, and Fanny, Mr. Kilgore pursued the same course that he followed in respect to Frank Sargent : he ignored the past. The somewhat bitter passages that had occurred between him and them, individually, were never alluded to by him. Each, in turn, had tried to explain, but he would hear nothing. One evening, after he had sufficiently recovered to be able to sit in his chair the most of the day, he sent for Dr. Gilbert, and held with him a long interview, the results of which made themselves apparent the next day, when the doctor called Frank and Mary into his office, and, having closed the door, informed them that it was Mr. Kilgore's desire that they should be married before leaving Crampton. Mr. Kilgore himself did not wish to have any conversation with them at that time, nor at any future time, on the subject. He accepted the facts as they existed, as facts for which he was not responsible, and with which he saw fit not to quarrel.

As soon as Mr. Kilgore's wish regarding the marriage was known in the family, all were in a flutter of excitement—all but Mary. In her calm faith, she had never seriously doubted that the time would come for her union with the man whom she loved. When it came, it did not surprise her. Nothing surprises a truly trusting heart.

As Frank and Mary looked into the future, beyond the event which excited so much interest in all around them, the first plan that shaped itself was one for taking Fanny with them to New York. This they talked over at length, and with this Mary ventured to approach her father. He made no objection to the plan—in reality, it was a pleasant one to him. He was anxious to see his large house populated once more—to hear again in it the sound of happy voices, and especially the happy voices of young women. He looked forward to the time when—the first questions and surprises over, and the new order of things adjusted to the stereotyped facts of his business life—he could throw off his reserve, and be cheerful, and even merry once more.

Mr. and Mrs. Wilton were called in to a grand council, Dr. Gilbert in the chair, to assist in deciding upon the character of the coming wedding. Mary wanted no wedding that would not either admit everybody or exclude everybody ; and it was determined at last that the ceremony should be performed in the church, in the morning, and that all who should choose to do so, might call upon the bride at the house of Dr. Gilbert afterward. This plan having been definitely settled upon, was reported throughout the village within twenty-four hours. In the meantime, Dr. Gilbert had consented to his daughter's visit to New York, and had secured a new teacher for the centre school. Fanny was in her glory. The excitement attending the preparations for the wedding and her journey, was delightful. It brought into operation her administrative faculties, and gave full employment to all her energies. Mr. Kilgore looked on with admiration. Her style of character was much more to his liking than that of his daughter. It was more after what seemed to him the true Kilgore pattern. It was more queenly, more ambitious, more exclusive. In fact, Mr. Kilgore, as he grew stronger, grew gallant, and took Fanny into his confidence and under his patronage, all of which pleased Mary very much.

The morning of the wedding came at length, and it found the Crampton church better filled with an expectant throng than it had been since the memorable exhibition of the Crampton Light Infantry. It brought forth, too, as on that occasion, a fine procession from the centre school-house—a procession of Mary Kilgore's pupils, for whom seats were reserved in front. The celebration of a marriage within the walls of the Crampton church was a great event—the first of its kind ever known in the village—and everybody was out.

At the appointed hour, Dr. Gilbert walked into the church with Aunt Catharine, followed by the great Kilgore with Fanny on his arm. Then came Mr. Frank Sargent with Mary, the latter in a gray travelling dress, and, following them, came Arthur Blague and his mother. It was not a very gay-looking party, it must be confessed, but, as it came in front of the children, and the bridegroom and the bride separated themselves, and walked before the pastor, Mary could not refrain from looking out upon her old charge with her accustomed smile. Instantly all the children rose to their feet, and stood while the words were pronounced which made a wife of their old teacher.

Mary could hardly wait to receive the congratulations of the friends immediately about her before she turned to her children, and received their kisses. It was a very pretty sight indeed—one which moistened the eyes of the crowd of spectators, and upon which even the dignified Mr. Kilgore looked with a degree of complacent satisfaction. As for delighted Frank Sargent, he could not keep his eyes away from the touching spectacle, and finally seized and kissed half a dozen of the little girls, as a slight demonstration of the condition of his feelings, at which the audience laughed, and the little boys clapped their hands.

Mary had a great deal of difficulty in getting out of the church. There were so many to take her hand and to wish her joy, that she was quite weary before the gauntlet of the broad aisle was run. On returning to the house, the party entered the parlor, and formally received and entertained their friends. Among these, all were astonished to see the widow Ruggles. She greeted Mary with a great deal of cordiality, and immediately begged to be introduced to her father. Him she seized (metaphorically) by the button, and in her own vulgar style told, so that all around could hear, of

Mary's former connection with "father's mill." She went so far as to express the hope that Mary had laid up a little something, and, furthermore, enjoined it upon Mr. Kilgore to see that she held it in her own right; so that if her husband should ever be "took away," she could have something to comfort her. She informed Mr. Kilgore of her trials, and particularly of her consolations under the strokes of Providence, and was glad to meet with one who had lost his "pardner," because he could feel for her.

At last, Dr. Gilbert took pity on Mr. Kilgore, and actually pulled Mrs. Ruggles away, to introduce her to Mr. Frank Sargent, who had previously begged the privilege of disposing of her.

Mr. and Mrs. Joslyn were among those who came in to pay their compliments—Mr. Joslyn with his hair very nicely braided over his head, his arm dangling through that of his wife, and his heavy frame sustained by his toes, in the apprehension that in some corner of the room there was a baby asleep. Mrs. Joslyn's face was flushed with the excitement of the unusual presence and occasion, and the task of managing her husband; but she had a few straightforward words of congratulation to say, and these she said, while Mr. Joslyn said nothing. As they fell back before the incoming tide of friends, Mrs. Joslyn encountered her daughter and Cheek in the passage. The bow of her daughter's bonnet not being exactly what it should be, she tied it again; then took hold of the front with both hands, and gave the wire a cleaner arch; and, after bestowing a twitch or two upon the skirt of her gown, dismissed her with the injunction to behave like a woman, and keep her mouth shut.

Cheek, since his accession to the dignity of stage driver, had grown a little foppish, and affected gay colors about his neck. A red-checked waistcoat and a sky-blue cravat did flaming duty with a coat of invisible green, which had great square pocket-lids on the skirts, and very large brass buttons. The moment Frank Sargent caught a glimpse of this pair, and received Cheek's good-natured wink at a distance, he sprang to meet them, and pulled them directly into the centre of the noisy group.

"Yours respectfully," said Cheek, by way of response to the bridegroom's greeting, and also by way of congratulation. Then turning to the bride, he gave her his hand, and with a bow which made his square coat-tails stand out very straight, said, "Here's hoping!" Having paid his own personal respects, he waited until Mary had bestowed a kiss upon his "girl," and then presented the latter to Frank Sargent, as "The Aforesaid." Frank shook her hand very cordially, and told her what an excellent time he had enjoyed with Cheek on his way to Crampton. The dear little creature could do nothing but courtesy, and say, "Yes, sir." Cheek looked on in admiration, and finally beckoned the bridegroom aside. When he had succeeded in getting him into a corner, he said quietly, with a nod at "The Aforesaid," "What do you think of her?"

"She's a nice little thing, Cheek, and does you honor," responded Frank Sargent heartily.

"Little dumpy about the waist yet," said Cheek, "but you know they kind o' spindle up after a while."

"She's good enough for anybody," said Frank Sargent.

"Now that ain't so," said Cheek, "and you know it. She will be, when she's done; but she ain't ripened off yet. You saw her mother, didn't you? Great woman. The little one has got her points, but she wants age. I'll show you something that'll cure sore eyes at thirty paces, if you'll come round in about three years."

The bridegroom was much amused, for Cheek said all this with his eyes upon his hopeful prize, scanning her

" points " as critically as if she were a filly that he was
anxious to sell.

" There is everything in taking them young," continued Cheek, " for then they improve on your hands.
Now you've just married a finished-up girl. I don't
s'pose mine will ever come up to your'n, but your'n won't
grow any better, and mine will. All the fellers try to
run rigs on me, and ask me how my baby gets along,
and what's the price of bibs ; but they've all got mortgages on property that won't rise, and when their girls
begin to get rings round their eyes, and lose their front
teeth, we'll see who'll talk about bibs." Cheek nodded
his head very decidedly, as if his plan were one which
did not admit of serious question from any quarter.

The crowd of friends was too great to allow of the
further extension of this conversation ; and for full two
hours the parlor was the scene of a social eddy in
Crampton life, which streamed in at one door, and out
at another, until all had paid their compliments to the
bridal pair and the dignified Mr. Kilgore.

It was generally understood at what time the party
were to leave, and at length the house was cleared. Of
all the observers of this lively scene, there was no one
who looked on with so much sadness as Arthur Blague.
He felt that he was soon to be bereft of his most precious wealth. He had schooled himself to look upon
Mary Kilgore as the possession of another; so that his
feelings were neither selfish nor mean ; but she had been
so much to him—she had inspired him with so much
courage, and had led him to the adoption of such fresh
and fruitful motives of life—that her departure seemed
like the setting of a sun—like the withdrawal of the heat
that warmed and the light that cheered him. He thought
of the brilliant scenes that lay before the retiring party,
and the humdrum, barren existence that was left to him,
till his own life grew tasteless and insignificant. Though

pressed to remain at the house of Dr. Gilbert until the bridal party should take their leave, he excused himself, and retired to his home.

The regular Crampton stage did not go out that morning. A wagon was despatched with the mail; but the coach and Cheek were detained as "an extra," to take over the bridal party. Trunks were deposited on the door-steps of the Gilbert mansion, busy feet traversed the house, and all was excitement. A hasty lunch was taken by the family, which was hardly concluded when Cheek's horn sounded across the common, with a flourish little short of miraculous, and soon the rattle of the wheels announced that the coach and the time for departure had arrived.

All went to the door. Cheek, out of respect to the party, had not changed his clothes, but shone upon the box like a fire, of which his red waistcoat formed the body of the flame, and his sky-blue cravat the smoke. Before descending from the box, he removed his coat, and, in obedience to his old habit, rolled up his shirt-sleeves, as a preparation for the labor of loading the baggage. The last trunk and bandbox were at length in their places, and the last strap was fastened. Then followed the leave-taking, in which everybody cried, except Mr. Kilgore, who stood apart, and who, after all the others had made their adieux, shook the hands of Dr. Gilbert, Aunt Catharine, and little Fred, took out his big gold watch, looked around upon Crampton common, apparently to see if he had left any thing there, examined the sky to see whether the weather suited him, then took his seat in the coach by the side of Miss Fanny Gilbert, and then said, "All ready."

Kisses were tossed back and forth as the horses were reined into the street, and then there came a loud crack of the whip, and, following this, extravagant efforts upon the driver's horn, that awakened all the echoes, and brought faces to all the windows along the street. Among the faces were those of Arthur Blague and his little brother Jamie, the latter of whom was in an ecstasy of delight. Mary leaned out of the coach to get the last glimpse of the pair. As she receded, she saw the little boy, by a sudden movement, release himself from his brother's grasp, and fall out of the window into the yard. She screamed, still gazing, and as she turned a corner, she saw the little one picked up limp and lifeless; and Arthur was left alone with the great trial out of which he was to work his destiny.

CHAPTER XXI.

BEING A BRIDGE LONGER THAN THE VICTORIA, AND HAVING ONLY TEN PIERS.

OFTEN, as we move through an interesting landscape, crowned with copse and rock and forest, and crossed by streams and strips of pasture and tilth, we catch a glimpse of some green hill in the far distance, and forget the beauty which throngs the passage, in our desire to reach the eminence that overlooks it, and the world of beauty in which it lies. We long to drink, at a single draught, the nectar that hangs on bush and rock, and vine and tree—to embrace in one emotion the effect of that exquisite combination of light and shade, of green and gray, of hill and vale, of stone and stream, that go to form a completed landscape. We tire with details; we seek for results.

As in landscapes, so in stories—we come to points, sometimes, when we long to overleap the incidents of the life through which we move, and, planting ourselves upon some sun-crowned year that rises in the distance, survey at a glance the path we have trod. We are in haste for events, and do not care to watch the machinery by which they are evolved.

Precisely at this point has this story now arrived ; and in this brief chapter we propose to take a stand upon a green hill-top ten years away, and thence look backward upon the life whose characteristics and whose issues have interested us so deeply.

We take the ten-years' flight, and here we are ! How easy the imaginary passage, and how soft and bright the landscape, as we turn to gaze upon it ! Yet these years have been crowded to their brims, every one, with change, and their contents poured upon the world!

This is Crampton ! Would you know it ? Ten years have revolutionized it. Within that time, a track of iron has been laid along its border, over which the engine drags its ponderous burdens. Even now, the whistle sounds, and the people—a new and peculiar people—rush to catch the daily papers. Where once stood the little hotel, so distinguishing a feature of the social life of the village, stands now a large brick structure, with a flag run up from its observatory, and a Chinese gong in the hall. Ten years ago, Crampton had but one church ; now it has five. The railroad has introduced " the foreign element ; " and there is a new structure, with a cross upon the top, as the result. The Methodists and Baptists and Episcopalians have all built churches, for which they are very deeply in debt, and for which " children yet unborn " will be obliged to pay. There are new streets cut in all directions, and there is a flaming row of stores, in which financial ruin is imminent, if we may judge by the placards in the windows. One is " selling off to close the concern ; " one is " selling off at less than cost ; " one advertises " goods to be given away ; " and another, after denouncing all its competitors as " slow," declares its determination to undersell them to such a degree as to drive them from the place, the whole of them being, even now, on the verge of suicidal despair. The smart and smiling young men behind the counters are evidently not fully aware of the fate that awaits them, but that only makes the matter worse.

Hucklebury Run has not been allowed to lie in ruins, but has passed into the hands of a Boston company, and many of the old operatives are back in the old place—the old place made new and comfortable. The widow Ruggles still resides in her little cottage, in the enjoyment of the income from her bank stock, which has been considerably increased by the amount saved from the wreck of the old proprietor's fortune. The enterprising woman has failed in her persistent efforts to secure a man to take the place of her departed " pardner," but is by no means discouraged.

Dr. Gilbert and Aunt Catharine are greatly changed. The little black pony died years ago, and the old gig passed out of sight with him. The rheumatism has dealt harshly with the old doctor, but has not so severely injured his feelings as the young physicians, assisted by certain homœopathists and eclectics, and Thompsonians, and Indian doctors, who cut his practice in a great many pieces, and vex his righteous soul by their innovations. Still he stumps about upon his farm ; but his hair is gray, and he carries a cane, not as a matter of habit, but of necessity. He has fought against his calamities bravely, and the children will tell you where he has cut a hole in the ice in the winter, for the bath by which he has tried to rouse his failing constitution into new vigor. As his strength has declined, and his business died away, he has turned his thoughts more and more upon his children, and particularly upon his boy Fred, now a young man and in college. To see him shine as the leader of his class, and the star of his pride, is now his great ambition. Through all his boyhood and young manhood, he has pushed this favorite child to the most exhausting effort, and finds his exceeding great reward in a degree of progress that secures the enthusiastic praise of the college faculty. The letters which he receives from the college, he exhibits to his old friends and neighbors, on all occasions, for he carries them in his pocket all the time.

Big Joslyn has become quite bald, and there is no longer any hair to braid upon his temples. His children are grown up around him. One or two are away at school. Others are in the employ of the railroad company. Others still are gone to work upon farms, where they are to remain until twenty-one. Mr. Joslyn himself tends the switches at the Crampton station, and, in his movements among the rails, takes good care never to waken a sleeping locomotive, always rising to his toes at the " sh-h-h-h " of the hissing steam. Mrs. Joslyn has become a smart and well-dressed woman, and takes care of a snug little house which is the envy of her neighbors. The family generally has been getting thrifty in the world. Mr. Joslyn's wages have improved, the children are earning more than the cost of their living, and a pair of genteel boarders occupy a suite of rooms in their modest dwelling. These latter are no other than Mr. and Mrs. Thomas Lampson. Mr. Lampson carries a gold watch, with a gold chain, wears upon his bosom a diamond pin, and ornaments the third finger of his left hand with an immense seal-ring. Mr. Lampson is " the popular and gentlemanly conductor of the Crampton and Londonderry Railroad," and was once known familiarly to the reader as " Check." Before the dawn of this gentleman's popularity and importance, the old sobriquet has gradually faded out. The president and superintendent of the road call him " Tom," but few approach him with so much familiarity. Everybody likes him, and everybody admits his claim to the possession of the handsomest wife "on the road." Mrs. Lampson has "ripened" according to his expectations. She is now twenty-five, has been married only two years, and is learning to play upon the piano. She always goes out to the platform when the train comes in, and the passengers ask Mr. Lampson who she is; and he takes a great deal of pride in informing them indefinitely, but very significantly, that she belongs to a man "about his size."

In that neat little dwelling across the common still reside Mrs. Blague and her two sons, Arthur and Jamie. We hesitate to unveil the changes that have occurred there. The widow has become a shadow even of her former self. She takes a degree of pride in Arthur, but leans upon him like a child. His will is her law, and she knows no other—desires to know no other. Ten years of pain and anxiety and watching have broken her to the earth, though they have strengthened and purified her manly son. The sprightly child that sprang from the window when we last saw him, has, by that accident, become a helpless, emaciated creature, without the power to speak a word or move a limb. The neighbors, as they pass the door, hear the sound of gurgling, painful breathing—hear it at any time in the day, and at any time in the night—hear Arthur's words of cheer and endearment—and say, "Poor boy! Noble man!" But none go in to see the poor boy and help the noble man. The noble man does not wish it, and they shrink from the pain which they know their sympathy would excite.

Still subordinate, still nursing, still doing woman's work! Still the life of Arthur Blague is devoted to the weak and the suffering. His mates have won their early honors, established themselves in their callings and professions, married their wives, and still he lingers behind, bound by the ties of nature and Christian duty to those he loves. Yet on the basis of this self-sacrifice has he been building, almost unconsciously, a character so sound, so sweet, so symmetrical, that every one who knows him regards him with a tender respect that verges upon veneration. Days and weeks and months and years, has he spent with the invalid brother on his knee, and a book in his hand. He has seen no college ; but he is educated. He has had no discipline, according to the formularies of the schools ; but he has a mind which, slowly compacted in its powers, and trained to labor, by necessity, amid a thousand distractions, is the marvel of all who come into contact with him. The years as they have passed over him have added to his growth. Patiently doing his daily duty, and accomplishing his daily work, he has left results in the hand of his Master, and waited for the mission toward which he has felt for many years that his discipline was leading him.

Since first, under the influence of the good angel whom Providence brought into his mother's dwelling, he devoted himself to Heaven, he has entertained the desire to preach the Gospel of Jesus Christ—the noblest and most glorious function of a consecrated human life. This desire shaped itself, as time passed on, into determination, and determination was merged at length into definite project. He has seen no theological school ; he has won no laurels ; he has embraced no system. With him, Christianity is a life. It has grown up in him, it has possessed him. In daily study of the Bible, and daily contact with human want, as seen in his own life and in the life around him, he has learned the secret of religion, and the power of the sacred office he has chosen. He has learned that the power of preaching resides not in the defence of creeds and the maintenance of dogmas, but in the presentation of motives to purity, and truth, and self-abnegation. He has learned that the office of Christianity is to import divine life into human life ; and, as a minister of Christianity, he has learned that sympathy with the suffering, and service for the weak, and knowledge and love of the common human life that surrounds him, place him where he can deal out the Bread of Life as it is needed, to hearts that recognize his credentials. With a heart full of charity, and with sympathies that embrace all the forms of humanity around him—sympathies won by participation in their trials—every word that falls from his lips bears the stamp of sincerity, and is redolent of the true life of which it is the issue.

Already is Arthur Blague licensed to preach. Already has he preached in Crampton. Already is he talked about in vacant parishes, as the most promising man of the region. But still he lingers at home. His work is not done there yet ; and his first duty is for those who are in his care. The feeble mother is to be supported, and the poor, misshapen brother is to be attended. Day and night he watches, yet when he walks abroad, the smile of a heart at peace with itself, with God, and with the world, sits upon his countenance. Up through contumely and suffering and disappointment, this vigorous life has pushed its way, and they have fallen to its feet and fed its growth ; and henceforth there is nothing in contumely and suffering and disappointment to do it harm. Whatever of base material this life touches, it transforms into nutriment, and assimilates to the elements of its own vitality.

If we look in upon a New York household, situated in the most opulent and fashionable quarter of the city, we shall find in the brown-stone dwelling of Mr. Kilgore not only Mr. Frank Sargent and his wife, but three beautiful children, who cling to their grandfather's knee, or engage in rare frolics with their still boyish father ;

while the sweet mother, to whom maternity, and a satisfied love, have only added a broader, deeper, and tenderer charm, looks on and smiles in her old delightful way. Nominally, Mr. Kilgore is still at the head of his business. He has the seat of honor in the counting-room, and to him, in terms of respect, Mr. Frank Sargent, who is his partner as well as his son, always appeals; and Mr. Kilgore imagines that he manages every thing as in the old times, when he tells his son to do just as he thinks best. He walks back and forth to his place of business, when he does not ride, leaning upon Frank Sargent's arm. Not a word about the past has ever been exchanged between them; but gradually, by respectful assiduity, has the young man won upon the old man, until he has become the very staff of his life. The new blood introduced into the firm has increased its business, and all are very prosperous.

In a little recess, apart from these, sits a queenly young woman with a pile of newspapers and periodicals in her lap—Miss Fanny Gilbert—whom ten years have lifted into the grand beauty and maturity of twenty-seven. The broad plaits of dark hair sweep back from her brow, and her full form is rich with the blood of womanhood. She sees nothing of the pleasant family group upon which the young mother is gazing so happily and contentedly. She does not hear the voices of the children; for before her lie the critiques upon her last book, which, in memory of her publisher's old suggestion, she has entitled "Rhododendron." She has mingled with life. She has patiently waited until, in the strength of her powers, she has felt competent to make the trial which should decide her fate as an authoress. She has tried, and has abundantly and gloriously succeeded. She takes up one paper after another, and all are crowded with praise. Beauties are indicated that she had not even suspected. Quotations are made, which, in the light of popular appreciation, glow with new meaning to her. Her long-thirsting heart is surfeited with praise. She is famous—she is a notoriety. She knows that in twenty thousand homes "Rhododendron" is passed impatiently from hand to hand, and that in twenty thousand circles her name is spoken. Every mail brings in applications for her autograph. Parties are made by lion-lovers, where she may be exhibited. She is gazed at in church; she is pointed at in the street; clerks whisper her name to one another whenever she enters a shop; her name and praise are the current change of social life.

Miss Fanny Gilbert gathers her papers and pamphlets in her hand with a sigh; and, bidding the family group a good evening, ascends to her chamber. She throws open the blinds of her window, and looks out upon the street. Carriages with happy freights of men and women are rolling homeward from their twilight drives. Lovers are loitering arm in arm along the sidewalks. She looks abroad over the city, and thinks that in multitudes of dwellings "Rhododendron" is being read—that thousands are speaking her name with praise, and that no one of all those thousands loves her. She feels, in her innermost consciousness, that she has drunk every sweet that popular praise can give her—honest, high-flavored, redundant praise—yet her heart yearns toward some unattainable good—yearns, and is unsatisfied. The fruit, that shone like gold high up upon the boughs, is plucked at last, but it turns to ashes upon her tongue.

She looks back upon the last ten years of her life, and traces in memory the outlines of her career. She has moved in fashionable circles; has been courted and admired as a brilliant woman; she has clung to the home of her New York friends, and been rather a visitor than a resident of her own; she has sought for admiration, and, with it, has won the ill-will of her own sex; she has imperiously compelled the attentions of men who were afraid of her; she has been received as a belle in gay saloons, and won a multitude of heartless conquests; yet, in all this time, among all favoring circumstances, no honest man has come to her with a modest confession of love, and a manly offer of his hand.

As she thinks of all this, and of the sorry results that attend the perfect triumph of her plans, there come back to her words spoken by Mary Kilgore years and years ago—"Miss Gilbert, the time will come when even one soul will be more than all the world to you—when you would give all the praises of the world's thousand millions—when you would give the sun, moon, and stars, if they were yours, to monopolize the admiration, the love, and the praise of one man." Then she thinks of those further words —" The great world is fickle, and must be so. It lifts its idols to their pedestals, and worships them for an hour; then kicks them off, and grinds them into ruin, that other and fresher objects of worship may take their places." She sees herself the idol of the hour, and feels in her sad and sickening soul, that in a year her name will begin to vanish from the public mind, and another name will be uppermost. The prize so long toiled for and waited for, not only fails to content her now, but melts away, even in her hands, and passes to others.

Never in her life has Fanny Gilbert felt so lonely as now. The triumph of her life is the great defeat of her life. She has achieved all she has labored for, and gained nothing that she really desired. She looks forward, and her life is a blank. How can it be filled? What shall she labor for hereafter? Is her life to be a waste? Is this longing for some satisfying good forever to remain unrealized? Ah! how the gray, fixed eyes grow soft and blue once more! How the woman's nature, kept so long in abeyance, asserts itself! How ambition fades away, and love of freedom dies in the desire for bondage, and self-sufficient independence longs to lean upon, and hide its head, in some great nature! She begins to comprehend the magnitude of a manly soul, and the worth of a permanent, never-dying affection that survives all changes, and blossoms sweetest when the fickle world frowns darkest. She gets a glimpse of that world of the affections in which one heart outgrows a world and outweighs a universe.

The newspapers and reviews fall from her hands. They have ceased, for the time at least, to be of value. She descends the stairs again, and, in her altered mood, the queenly Fanny seats herself upon a bench by the side of Mary, and lays her head upon her lap. She comes back to her whose life has been a daily lesson of satisfied love and Christian duty. The children are gone to bed. Mr. Kilgore has retired to his room, and Mr. Frank Sargent is out upon an errand. Mary says not a word, but leans over and kisses Miss Gilbert's cheek, and is startled to find tears upon it. Then they rise, and, with their arms around each other, as in the old times in Mary's little chamber in Crampton, they walk the spacious parlor and talk. Somehow, in this embrace and the interchanges of affection that accompany it, Fanny is soothed, and she retires to her bed at last, thinking that there is something left to live for, after all.

If we walk down Broadway, where the crowd is thickest and the Babel voices are loudest, we shall, in passing a certain door, hear a loud, harsh voice, going on in a sing-song, professional way—uttering something, we know not what—a coarse " blab-blab-blab," that arrests us, because we imagine we have heard the voice before. We look in, and a square, red-faced man stands upon a bench behind a counter, in a little box of a room that is large enough to contain hardly more than the half-dozen loafers assembled around the speaker. In one hand the master of ceremonies holds elevated a little gavel, and in the other a showy gold watch, which he is making extraordinary efforts to dispose of at auction. He engages our attention and addresses himself to us; and, as we catch the wink of his eye, and read the puffy outlines of his brazen face, we recognize our old acquaintance, Mr. Dan Buck—the most notorious Peter Funk in the city.

As we do not care to renew our acquaintance with the reprobate, we turn and retrace our steps. The hotels and saloons are ablaze with light, and here and there we meet the painted creatures that prowl for prey at this hour. On a corner, under the light of a street-lamp, we see one of these, chatting with two or three sailors. She is intoxicated, and is saying that which makes her brutal audience laugh. As we come to where the light falls full upon her face, we behold the wreck of what was once the pride of the old proprietor of Hucklebury Run. Poor Leonora!

Do you care to go back to the country and look further? We have met others, but they have little interest for us. Rev. Dr. Bloomer has been "settled" three times since we saw him, but that is not remarkable. Rev. Jonas Sliter has injured his voice, and become an agent for a society which he started himself, and which contemplates nothing less than the restoration of the Jews to Jerusalem. In this way he proposes to usher in the millennium. Thus far, he has only been able to support himself upon his collections, but thinks there is "great encouragement for prayer." Rev. J. Desilver Newman is not yet married. He has always been a beau, but somehow none of the young women love him. He has the name of being a fortune-hunter, so that all the rich shun him from fear, and the poor from spite.

He dresses very well indeed, and is supposed to be vain.

Thus we have our characters again. Some of them we have seen for the last time, and we bid them farewell without regret, glad to drop the burden, and commune alone with those whom we love.

CHAPTER XXII.

MISS GILBERT GIVES AND RECEIVES VERY DECIDED IMPRESSIONS.

MR. KILGORE's carriage stands before Mr. Kilgore's door. There are affectionate leave-takings in Mr. Kilgore's hall. Miss Fanny Gilbert, in her travelling dress, is kissing her farewells upon the rosy lips of Mary's little ones, and shedding tears as she parts from their mother. Mr. Kilgore, in a fit of gallantry, claims a kiss for himself, which Miss Gilbert not unwillingly accords to him. The trunks have already been sent to the boat, and Frank Sargent gives the young woman his arm, and they descend to the street. They take their seats, the steps are put up, handkerchiefs are waved as telegraphs of affection by the separated groups, and the carriage rolls off down the street, and turns a corner, and is lost in the din and whirl of the great city.

After the publication of " Rhododendron," and the discovery on the part of Fanny that there was no satisfaction in her new fame, she began to pine for the old faces. She was tired for the first time of her New York life. Its round of gayety, its excitements, its pursuit of admiration, became a weariness to her. She felt self-condemned for so long forsaking her father, and for taking so little interest in her brother Fred. Especially, now that she had achieved her objects, did she desire to taste the love of those who took pride in her. If they would only love her better for her fame, it would do her good. Her heart craved love now. This she must have, or life would lose all its meaning to her. She turned her back on her New York associations with little pain, anxious only, in her altered feelings, to nestle once more at the heart of home.

There was another event that hastened her departure. Her brother was soon to graduate, and he had already received the honor of the highest appointment in his class. This honor had always been accorded to him by the students themselves ; so, when he received it, there was no surprise. Dr. Gilbert had written to his daughter a glowing account of Fred's progress, and concluded with an earnest request that she would return and witness the coronation of his long-cherished hope. There was something in her father's exclusive devotion to his son that piqued the daughter, but she felt, in her conscience, that he had treated her quite as well as she had treated him. There was only a passing allusion to her new book in the letter, and this half-offended her ; but she determined to return, and to try Crampton life once more.

The ten years that had matured her had built railroads, and her passage homeward was not the painful and tedious one of former years. Coffee in New York and tea in Crampton, on the same day, did not involve great fatigue ; and it was hardly past mid-afternoon when Miss Gilbert made her last change of cars, and found herself upon a train of the Crampton and Londonderry Railroad, in the care of " the popular and gentlemanly conductor," Mr. Thomas Lampson. As Mr. Lampson came along to collect the tickets, he recognized Miss Gilbert by a slight touch of the forefinger upon the very small visor of his blue cap, and a smile that illuminated his whole face.

"Why, Cheek! Is that you?"

"Well, Fanny, 'tis. Glad to see you. How have you been?" and Cheek took Miss Gilbert's hand, and shook it as if it were a wild animal that he wanted to shake the life out of. "Back in a minute," said he, as he passed along, and shouted "Tickets!" in his professional way.

Now, Miss Fanny Gilbert was slightly shocked by this familiarity; but her joy at seeing an old face had betrayed her into undue cordiality, and she was obliged to abide the consequences. She was shocked but not displeased. There was genuine friendship in that shake of the hand—a personal interest beyond the desire to see and speak to a notoriety. So when Mr. Thomas Lampson came back, shuffling his tickets in his hand, in a way that showed his familiarity with "old sledge," and touched his visor again with his forefinger, she made a place for him upon her own seat, and the conductor and the authoress were soon engaged in conversation.

"I've read Rhody," said Mr. Lampson, "and it's a tall thing."

"You mean Rhododendron?" said Miss Gilbert, with a smile.

"Right again," responded the conductor, rasping his thumb-nail across the end of his package of tickets.

"I am glad that you like it," said Miss Gilbert.

"Well, I do like it—I like it first-rate. It's a tall thing—it's a trump. Yes, I like it first-rate. I vow, I wonder where you picked it all up. I told my wife it was the strangest thing how a woman could spin such a story right out of her head, and make everything come in right and come out right. She says it only happened so; but I know better. Now, how—how d'ye go to work to begin? I couldn't any more do it than I could —a—a—well, what's the use talking?"

Miss Gilbert was much amused by this humble trib-ute to her transcendent powers, and simply replied that it was easy enough to write a novel when one knew how.

"After all," continued Mr. Lampson, "we don't care half so much about the book up here in Crampton as we do about you. I tell you we feel pretty crank about having a book-writer in Crampton. The fact is, Miss Gilbert, that we are just about as proud of you as if we owned you, and when we see the papers talking about you, and making a great fuss about your book, we just say to ourselves : 'That's a woman we raised. It takes Crampton to set the world going.' Now I don't s'pose you ever thought of such a thing, and, very likely, it's ridiculous ; but I'm just as proud of you—I am, upon my word—as if I had a mortgage on you."

Fanny Gilbert smiled, but her lip quivered, and she turned her head toward the window, while two big tears formed in her eyes, and dropped from her cheek. There was something in this simple praise that touched her more than all the reviews she had read.

Still Mr. Thomas Lampson, in the abundance of his genial nature, went on. "I s'pose you've been living among grand folks down to the city, and think Crampton people are green ; but they don't care half so much about you there as we do, and it kind o' seems to me that if I could write a book that would make my own folks happy, it would do me more good than it would to be purred over by a snarl of people that didn't care any-thing about me."

"You are right—entirely right," responded Miss Gil-bert, emphatically.

"Well, I guess I am," said the conductor. "I know how it is with me, now. You couldn't hire me to go away from Crampton, for I was raised here, and every-body knows me, and everybody is glad to see me get along. If I was to go on to another road, I should be like any other conductor ; not but what I could make friends, but I shouldn't care what they said about me. Now, when a feller that has always known me comes along, and slaps me on the shoulder, kind o' familiar, and says, ' Hullo ! Tom ; what's the state of your vitals ? ' I know what it means, and it makes me feel good all over. I s'pose all of us have a kind of hankering after people's good words ; but I tell you it makes a mighty sight of difference with me who gets 'em off. When that little wife of mine says, ' Tom, you're a good feller, God bless you,' it goes right in where I live. Well, it does ! O Lord ! what's the use talking ? "

The concluding exclamation of the conductor's little speech was produced by his finding Miss Gilbert's eyes fastened full upon him, and an indistinct apprehension that he was getting silly.

" Tell me about your wife," said Miss Gilbert.

" Oh ! shoh ! you don't want to hear anything about her."

" Indeed I do," replied Fanny, with a heartiness that the conductor felt to be genuine.

" Well, you must see her, and make up your own mind about her. All I can say is, she suits me. I tell you," and the conductor lowered his voice to an exceedingly confidential tone, " we have mighty good times. When I am through my trips at night, and we get into our room together, and the curtains are down, and nobody round to bother, I look at her sometimes by the hour when she sits sewing, and I say to myself, ' Tom Lampson, that property is yours. That little live woman thinks more of you than she does of all creation besides. You're a king, Tom !' Oh ! I tell you I have seen that little room grow and grow, till all the world outside looked mighty small—so small, that I wouldn't give the skip of a tree-toad for the whole of it. Now,

you've had good luck, and done a splendid thing, and
everybody's talking about you, and I s'pose you take
real solid comfort in it ; but if I'd got to choose between
writing Rhody, and owning that little woman at home,
I should say—oh! well—what's the use talking ? We
are different, you know. One has his likes, and another
has his likes, and what is one man's meat is another
man's poison, and so it goes."

Here the conductor rose to his feet, gave a sharp
scrape upon the end of his package of tickets, and
shouted " Littleton ! "

Fanny Gilbert felt that she was indeed approaching
home, but home, with all its newly awakened charms,
did not interest her so deeply as the conversation she
had had with the simple-hearted Tom Lampson. She
had been weighing vital values in new scales. Now
that her long hallucination relating to the value of popularity and fame was dissolved, her mind was open to
the reception of truth—nay, she was thirsty for truth,
and was ready to drink it from the humblest fountains.
She comprehended what the honest conductor meant
when he told her that his wife's praise " went right in
where he lived ; " for she felt that the praise she had
sought for and found did not go in where she lived.   It
did not touch the deep places of her life.

There is never a train of cars with a notoriety upon
it whom somebody does not detect ; and, entirely without Miss Gilbert's consciousness, it became known to all
upon the train that the writer of " Rhododendron "—
old Dr. Gilbert's famous daughter—had been enjoying
a cosy chat with the conductor.   On the arrival of the
train at Littleton, it was whispered upon the platform
that Miss Gilbert was in a certain car.   The train
paused for some minutes, as it was an important station, and at length Fanny became aware that curious
eyes were looking at her, not only from the seats

around, but from the platform outside. Young men with canes in their hands and cigars in their mouths loitered by with affected carelessness, and gave her a brazen stare; and others stood at a distance and made their comments. Straight out of her woman's nature there sprang a sense of shame and indignation, and by almost an involuntary movement she drew her veil down before her face.

Yet precisely this notoriety had she sought. Not a page of " Rhododendron " had been written in which she had not indulged in dreams of this kind of reward. Nay, she had imagined herself in precisely these circumstances, with assumed unconsciousness receiving the homage of the curious crowd. Once behind her veil, she analyzed her feelings. Having weighed the value of her newly found fame with relation to her truer life, it became in a degree offensive to her. The moment the woman's heart within her became dominant, she shrank from the demonstrations which her long-sought position so naturally evoked. Those curious eyes invaded the sanctity of her womanhood. She felt them as a degradation.

The whistle sounded, the bell rang, and the train moved on. Tom Lampson hurried through and collected his tickets, and then respectfully resumed his seat by the side of Miss Gilbert. " I s'pose you hear all the news from Crampton ? " said the conductor, interrogatively.

" I hear very little," replied Miss Gilbert.

" Mr. Blague has had a pretty hard life of it," said her interlocutor.

" I suppose he has; tell me what you know about him."

" Well, he sticks to that little boy as if he were his mother; and he has done it for years and years. There isn't another man in the world that would do as he has done ; yet he doesn't seem to mind it, but keeps right along. Well, there's no use talking, he's a great man, and is bound to make his mark. I've known Arthur Blague a good while, and I used to be kind of intimate with him, you know, but he's got ahead of my time. Now I think I don't know anything, and ain't anybody, when he's round—if you know what sort of a feeling that is. I don't pretend to be a very good man, *you* know, and I'm always spilling my nonsense around ; but I never see that man walking through the street, so sort o' splendid, and kind, and good, but what I think of Jesus Christ. I vow I never do. Now that's a fact."

"I have been told that he has commenced preaching," said Miss Gilbert, quietly.

"Yes, and you ought to hear him. I don't know how he does it, but he gets hold of me awful. If I ever get pious and join the church, Arthur Blague is the man that'll bring me to it. I tell you, when a man gets in front of him on Sunday, he catches it—no use dodging —might as well cave."

"I shall hear him, I hope," said Miss Gilbert. "By the way," she added, with affected indifference, "Mr. Blague is to be married, I believe."

"Is he ?"

Fanny blushed in spite of herself ; and to evade the responsibility of starting a report she had never heard, asked the conductor if he had not heard it before.

"No," said he, decidedly, "and—no disrespect to you—I don't know a woman in the world good enough for him."

Fanny made a low bow, looking archly in blushing Tom Lampson's face, and said : "I thank you."

"Well, now, you needn't take a feller up so ; you know what I mean. I don't say but what you're handsome enough, and smart enough, and genteel enough, and good company, and all that ; but you ain't one of

his kind ; you ain't—a—well, you know what I mean—
you ain't—a—you sort o' look out for number one, you
know, and kind o' like to have a good many strings to
your bow, and wouldn't love to buckle into such a life as
he's chalked out for himself."

Tom Lampson grew redder in the face from the time
he commenced his apology, or explanation, until he
closed—an embarrassment which Miss Gilbert, in some
moods, would have enjoyed excessively. As it was, she
could not avoid the consciousness that she was regarded,
even by her humbler friends, as a selfish woman. She
could not be offended with Tom Lampson ; for, while
he blurted out the most humiliating truths, it seemed to
be done under protest, and with a tone that deprecated
her displeasure. She, the gifted and famous Fanny Gilbert, was not good enough to be the wife of a humble
minister of the Gospel !

If Tom Lampson had a simple nature, it was also a
sensitive one, and he was not slow to recognize the fact
that Miss Gilbert did not wish to extend the conversation. So he excused himself, and visited another part
of his train. Fanny had looked from her window but a
few minutes when familiar objects began to show themselves, and soon the spires of Crampton were in sight.
The whistle sounded, the train slacked its speed, and
soon came up to the Crampton station. On the platform, awaiting her arrival, she saw her father and her
slender, fair-haired brother. The old doctor greeted
his daughter with unusual demonstrations of joy as she
alighted, and she kissed her tall and bashful brother so
heartily that he blushed to the tips of his ears. Leaving Fred to see to her luggage, she took her father's
arm, and walked homeward to the old mansion. One
would naturally suppose that a parent, with such a specimen of womanhood upon his arm as Fanny Gilbert,
would have been very proudly conscious of the fact, as

he promenaded the fresh brick sidewalks of Crampton. The truth was, however, that Dr. Gilbert was not thinking of his daughter at all. He was glad to see her for her own sake, always; but he was specially rejoiced at this juncture, because she had an interested pair of ears into which he could pour his talk about that prodigy of scholarship, Fred Gilbert. All the way from the station to the house, he entertained his daughter with what the president of the college had told him; and what a certain professor had written to him; and how certain gentlemen, who had talented sons in the class, were piqued at Fred's triumph, and what he proposed to do with Fred as soon as he got out of college, all of which interested Fanny not a little, and grieved her a good deal.

She had felt this exclusive devotion of her father to the son of his hope many times, but never so keenly as now. She now wanted love—her father's love. She wanted to warm her heart in the same paternal interest with which her brother was indued.

Aunt Catharine's greeting was one that did her good. She kissed her a dozen times at the first onset, and called her " dear heart," and helped her off with her hat, and went to her chamber with her, and was " so glad she had come home." " Your father," said Aunt Catharine, " is just about crazy over Fred: and he won't see that the poor boy is killing himself, and ruining his constitution besides."

Fanny could not help smiling at the order of dissolution which the good woman suggested; but her own impressions from Fred's appearance coincided essentially with those of her affectionate aunt.

Not a word had thus far been spoken about " Rhododendron," and Fanny realized more and more how much the world of affection overshadowed the world in which she had had so much of her life. After dressing for tea, she descended to the drawing-room, and found

Arthur Blague, whom Aunt Catharine had invited to meet her, in conversation with the doctor. As usual, Dr. Gilbert was pouring into Arthur's ear the praises of his boy. As the queenly girl made her advent, Arthur rose, and greeted her with such easy grace and thorough self-respect and self-possession, that Fanny, almost hackneyed in the forms of polite life, found herself dumb. Arthur took her hand, and did not relinquish it at once, but looked down into her face, and told her how glad he was to see her, and, more than all, spoke of " Rhododendron," and thanked her for writing it. He had read it, every word ; and had read not only the book, but the most important reviews of it that had appeared.

In the collision of these fresh, strong natures, the other elements of the family circle fell back into commonplace. Fanny was tired, but there was something in Arthur's presence which stimulated her, and, without design or effort, the reunited old friends found themselves at once in the most animated and delightful conversation. Arthur gave his arm to Fanny, as they passed out to the tea-table, in a way so courtly and unembarrassed that Fanny could not help wondering where the recluse had learned all this. She had seen nothing of Arthur for years. She remembered him as the bright particular star of her girlish dreams, but supposed that he had become bashful, and, in a degree, timid. It did not occur to her that his old reserve had passed away, not by the development of the element of self-esteem in his character, but by the actual measurement of himself with relation to the personalities among which he moved. He had modestly weighed his own character and gauged his own power. He had risen into the self-assertion of his own manhood. He was not, in reality, versed in the conventionalisms of society; but he was a law unto himself. Out of a sense of propriety, which he had learned to trust, and a heart of earnest good-will, his actions in society all sprang ; and it was not in his nature to do a good thing ungracefully. What Fanny had learned in society as the result of cultured habit, he had learned at home, and comprehended intuitively.

It quite astonished the doctor and Aunt Catharine, and the slender collegian, to see Arthur Blague so much at home with the polished young woman. He talked as they had never heard him talk before. He unveiled a life which they had never suspected. He had found a mind well versed in current literature, and it was a luxury that he had not enjoyed in Crampton for many a day. They talked of authors and of books, and finally of the reviews that had been written of Miss Gilbert's book. These the young clergyman took up, one after another, and pointed out their excellencies and their mistakes, betraying the most thorough insight into the aims of the authoress, and showing that he had not only read her book, but comprehended its whole scope and aim.

The consciousness that a single sound, good mind had actually dissected and carefully estimated the pet product of her brain and heart, gave Fanny a fresh happiness. Was it unmaidenly in her to think how, in the companionship of such a nature as that of Arthur Blague, she could develop both her heart and her mind ? Was it unnatural for her, in her new mood, to feel what a blessed thing it would be to be overshadowed by such a mind — how sweet it would be to sit beneath its branches, and scan the heaven of thought as their sway unveiled it ? If so, she had not greatly sinned, for it was the first time she had ever been similarly moved. She comprehended, for the first time, how sweet a thing it is to develop, reveal, express one's self in the presence of a great soul that measures with an appreciative, admiring, and loving eye, every utterance and every power.

The meal was unusually prolonged. Here and there

a suggestive fact or a seminal thought was uttered, leading the vivacious pair into fresh fields of conversation and discussion, in which they seemed to revel, while the remainder of the family listened in delighted silence. Occasionally, Arthur Blague turned to Fred for his opinion, or to ask a question, or to drop a suggestion that would bring him into the circle of conversation. But Fred only spoke in monosyllables, and seemed to be utterly unacquainted with the realm of thought through which the talk of the hour was leading him.

The doctor noticed the embarrassed silence of his son, and did what he could to draw him out ; but, in truth, there was nothing to draw out that had relation to the things discussed. From his youngest childhood he had been forced into a receptive attitude and habit of mind. Acquisition from text-books had been the single work of his life. Use, demonstration, action—these he knew nothing of whatever. Words, forms, rules, processes—these he had gorged himself with ; but he had been allowed no time for their digestion, and they had in no way become disciplinary of those powers which are the legitimate measure of every man's manhood. Of the questions that touched the heart and life of society, he knew nothing ; and he sat before Arthur Blague and his accomplished sister as weak, and impassive, and dumb as the babe of a day. He was, too, painfully conscious of his deficiencies. Among students, measured by the standard of the college faculty, he was at home—the peer of his associates. In the life of the world, he was lost.

Dr. Gilbert looked on and listened in wonder. In Arthur Blague, he apprehended a mind bubbling and brimming with wealth. In his pet child—the brilliant collegian—he saw nothing but an intellectual stripling, entirely overshadowed by the robust nature, and varied culture, and demonstrative powers, of the home-grown man. One had become an intellectual pigmy on his advantages ; the other an intellectual giant on his disadvantages.

Arthur Blague took early leave of the family, after rising from the tea-table, from consideration of Miss Gilbert's fatigue. As he left the door, and slowly walked homeward, where the accustomed night of watching awaited him, he felt that he had met with one of the most refreshing passages of his life. For long years he had, whenever he met Fanny Gilbert, been aware of something in her character which was repulsive to his sense of that which is best in womanhood. She had always appeared heartless and selfish. There was a certain boldness — a certain masculine forwardness— that impressed him most unpleasantly. What had produced the change ? He felt that he had found his way into her nature and character through a different avenue, or that he had found a new side to her character, or that she had changed. He felt, indeed, that it would not be wise for him to see very much of her. Such society would not only tend to divert him from the aims of his life, but it might endanger his peace. He could not think of Fanny Gilbert as the wife of a minister. He would not think of her as the wife of Arthur Blague.

As for Fanny herself, she went to her bed delighted and satisfied. She felt that she had been talking with a man, and that that which was best in her had been seen and appreciated by him. She had received from him no vapid compliments, uttered for the purpose of pleasing her. Not one word of flattery had been breathed by him ; but, out of a sound judgment and a true conscience, he had uttered that which nourished her self-respect, and gave her an impetus toward those nobler ends of life that were dawning upon her. He had met her as an intellectual equal. He had probed her mind with question and suggestion ; and under the

22

stimulus of his genial presence it had abundantly responded to their research.   Moreover, she saw that the
peerless boy of her early dreams—so long forgotten and
so long slighted—might easily become the peerless man
of her maturer judgment.   But he was a minister, and
she was not good enough for him!   She and Mr. Thomas
Lampson had the mutual honor that night of agreeing in
opinion upon this point.

A few days passed away, bringing no opportunity
for enlarging the acquaintance so happily renewed between the young minister and Miss Gilbert.   It seemed
to the young woman that he shunned her, as, indeed, he
did.   They met occasionally on the street, and she always detected in him an air of restraint, very unlike
the easy and happy manner in which he had carried
himself on the evening of their meeting—an air which
equally mystified and piqued her.

As soon as Fanny's old acquaintances found that
her heart was open to them, they flocked around her,
invited her to their dwellings, vied with each other in
their cordial attentions to her, and were happy in her
society.   At every fresh fountain of love thus opened
to her, she drank with delight.   Softened by every
day's experience, and rejoicing in the grateful aliment
which her new life brought to her, and the humble love
that paid her tribute, she could only wonder at the long
delusion that had enthralled her.

In the meantime, the young valedictorian had returned to college, to make ready for the approaching
anniversary, which was to witness his triumph, and set
him free from the bondage of his college life.   In the
few days he spent with his sister, she found that the
triumph which lay before him would in all probability
be the last of his life.   He had overtasked himself, and
had well-nigh expended the stock of vitality with which
nature had endowed him.

CHAPTER XXIII.

THE CRAMPTON COMET REAPPEARS, PASSES ITS PERI-HELION AGAIN, AND FADES OUT.

"COMMENCEMENT" at old Dartmouth! Day memorable to incoming freshmen and outgoing graduates! Annual epoch in the life of Hanover, on one side or the other of which all events respectfully arrange themselves! Holiday for all the region round about, for which small boys save their money, and on which strings of rustic lovers, in Concord wagons, make pilgrimages to the shrines of learning! Day of the reunion of long-separated classmates, who parted with beardless faces and meet with bald heads! Day of black coats, pale faces, and white cravats! Day of rosettes, and badges, and blue ribbons, and adolescent oratory, and processions, and imported brass bands! Carnival of hawkers and peddlers! Advent of sweet cider, and funeral of oysters, dead with summer travel! Great day of the State of New Hampshire!

Commencement day came at old Dartmouth, and found Dr. Gilbert and Fanny in the occupation of the best rooms in the old Dartmouth Hotel. Booths and tents had been erected in every part of the village where they were permitted, and early in the morning, before the good people of Hanover had kindled their kitchen fires, or the barkeeper of the hotel had swept off his foot-worn piazza, the throng of peddlers and boys began to pour into the village.

Dr. Gilbert's zeal in educational matters, and Dr. Gilbert's reputed wealth, were appreciated at Dartmouth. He had, a few years before, been appointed to a place upon the board of trustees of that venerable institution, and had annually exhibited his portly form and intelligent old face upon the platform during its anniversaries. He enjoyed the occasion and the distinction always; but he had never visited his alma mater with such anticipations of pleasure as warmed him when he rose on the morning we have introduced, and threw open the shutters to let in the sunlight of a cloudless "Commencement Day." Dr. Gilbert shaved himself very carefully that morning. Then he enveloped himself in a suit of black broadcloth, that had never spent on the Sabbath air its original bloom. Then he brushed his heavy white hair back from his high forehead; and it is possible that he indulged in some justifiable reflections upon the grandeur of his personal appearance.

There were several reasons for the delightful character of Dr. Gilbert's anticipations. The central reason was, of course, the gratification he would have of seeing the son of his love honored in the presence of a cloud of witnesses. Another was the pleasure of appearing with a daughter who had made herself famous. Another was the expectation of meeting his surviving classmates. To these it would be his pride to appear as a patron and trustee of the college; as a man who had been successful in his profession, and in the accumulation of wealth; and as the father of the valedictorian, and a celebrated authoress. In fact, as Dr. Gilbert stood that morning, looking at himself in his mirror, and thinking of what he was, and what the day had in store for him, he could not help feeling that it was, indeed, the great day of his life.

The breakfast bell rang its cheery summons, and the doctor knocked at his daughter's door. She would be ready in a moment. So he paced slowly up and down the hall, swinging his hands, and giving courtly greeting to the rabble that poured by him in their anxiety to get seats at the board. The long stare that some of them gave him, he took as a tribute to his venerable and striking appearance, as, in fact, it was. At length Fanny appeared ; and taking the stylish woman upon his arm, he descended to the breakfast-room, where fifty men and women were feeding at a long table, at the head of which were two vacant chairs, reserved for Dr. Gilbert and his daughter. In an instant all eyes were upon the distinguished pair. Then neighboring heads were brought together, and, in whispers, the personal appearance of the authoress was discussed. Old men looked over their spectacles, and young men in white cravats looked through theirs. Fanny could not but be conscious that she was the object of many eyes, and, holding her own fixed upon her plate, she breakfasted in awkward silence.

She thought the company would never finish their meal. The truth was, they were all waiting to see her retire ; and when she and her father rose to leave the table, there was a general shoving back of chairs, and two or three old gentlemen came around to exchange a cordial " good-morning " with Dr. Gilbert, and get an introduction to his daughter. Busily engaged in conversation, they naturally took their way to the parlor ; and, before Fanny could get away, she found herself holding a levee, with a crowd of persons around, pressing forward to be introduced. A fine old doctor of divinity had assumed the privileges of a friend, and while Dr. Gilbert was, with happy volubility, pouring into the ears of an old classmate the praises and successes of his son, his daughter was coolly receiving the homage of the assembly. There were a dozen young men who had come back to get their " master's degree." Some of them had their hair stuck up very straight, like bristles, and some of them wore their hair very long, and brushed behind their ears. Some were very carefully dressed, and none more so than those who were seedy. Some were prematurely fat, and others were prematurely lean ;

but in all this wide variety and contrariety, there were some things in which they were all alike. They had all read "Rhododendron," they all admired it, they were all happy to meet its author, they were all desirous of making an impression, and were all secretly anxious of winning the special favor of Miss Gilbert.

Thus forced into prominence, Fanny exerted herself to converse as became her with those about her; but always, as the smiling gentlemen appeared and retired, she could not resist the feeling that they were beneath her—that they were immature—that they wanted age and character. There was an element of insipidity—something unsatisfying—in all they said. Often the figure of Arthur Blague, who had no part in this festival, came before her imagination—the tall form, the noble presence, the deep dark eye, the rich voice, revealing the rich thought and the rich nature—and the chattering and smiling throng seemed like dwarfs to her.

At length her brother appeared, and taking his arm she left the room, and ascended with him to her parlor. The poor boy was pale, and trembling with nervous apprehension. A bright, red spot was burning upon either cheek, his dark eye was unnaturally bright, and the exertion of ascending the stairs had quite disturbed his breathing. He had worked up to this point with courage; but now, that he was about to grasp the prize for which he had so faithfully struggled, not only his courage, but his strength, failed him. Fanny was very sadly impressed by the appearance of her brother. Her eyes were full of tears as she put her hand upon his shoulder, and said: "Ah, Fred! If I could only give you some of my strength to-day!"

Then the doctor came in, but there was something before his eyes that blinded him to the real condition of his son. He was brimful of happiness. He had been praised, and congratulated, and flattered, until he was as happy as he could be. The young man saw it all ; pressed his feverish lips together in determination, and spoke no word to dampen his father's ardor. In that father's heart was the spring of his own ambition. To gratify him—to accomplish that upon which his father had hung many years of fond hopes—he had labored, night and day, in health and sickness. Now he was determined that the soul within him, upon which the frail body had lived for months, should eke out his strength, and carry him through the trial of the day. Fanny saw it all, pressed his hand, and said, "God help you, Fred!" and the young man went out, to act his part with his associates.

At this time the village was becoming more and more crowded ; and word was brought to the doctor that he had better secure a seat for his daughter in the church, in which the exercises of the day were to be held. So Fanny dressed early, and was taken over by a smart boy with a blue ribbon in his buttonhole, while the doctor remained behind to add dignity to the procession.

At ten o'clock, there was a sound of martial music in Hanover; and a company of bearded men in military uniform, preceded by a marshal, and followed by a large company of students, marched to the Dartmouth Hotel, and announced by trumpet and drum their readiness to conduct Dr. Gilbert and his associate dignitaries to the church.

Down the steps, through a crowd of eager boys, and rosy-cheeked country belles, and their brown-faced lovers, Dr. Gilbert, arm in arm with an old classmate, made his way, and took his place of honor in the procession. Word was given to march, and the village rang again with the blare of brass, and the boom of drums, and the din of cymbals ; and the marshal, and the band in beards, and the corps of students, took a circuit around the common, and, reaching the church at last, where a great crushing crowd was assembled upon the steps, the students divided their lines, and the guests and the men of honor passed through with uncovered heads, and disappeared within.

In five minutes more, every seat and aisle in the church was filled. It was ten minutes before order could be secured. Then music was called for, and the overture to Tancredi was played as a prelude to a prayer not quite so long as the opera ; which, in turn, was followed by " Blue-eyed Mary," introducing a lively march, called " Wood-up," which introduced the ambitious leader of the band as the performer of a preposterous key-bugle solo.

Then came the " Salutatory " in very transparent Latin, in which everybody was " saluted "—the President of the college, the professors, the trustees, and the people. The beautiful women present received special attention from the gallant young gentleman, and the cordial terms of this portion of the salutation drew forth marked demonstrations of applause. It was noticed, however, that when the trustees were greeted, the young man addressed himself particularly to Dr. Gilbert, who received the address with graceful dignity ; and that when feminine beauty came in for its share of attention, the young man's eyes were fastened upon Miss Gilbert, who occupied a seat upon a retiring portion of the stage. It really seemed to the doctor as if all the events of the day took him for a pivot, and revolved around him.

As the exercises progressed, Fanny Gilbert found herself strangely interested. There was nothing of special attraction and brilliancy in the orations ; but there was something in the subjects treated, and in the names pronounced, that called back to her a scene of the past, which occupied a position quite at the other end of her career. " The Poetry of the Heavens " brought back to her the chalk planetarium of many years before, on which that poetry was illustrated under her special direction. "Napoleon," and "Cæsar," and "Joan of Arc," all figured upon the Dartmouth stage, and she could not help smiling as Rev. Jonas Sliter returned to her memory. So, through all that tedious day, Dartmouth and Crampton were curiously mixed together, as if in fact, no less than in imagination, there were a connection between them. There sat her father before her, as he had sat a dozen years ago—pleased, eager, interested. There was she, occupying the same relative place upon the platform. There was the green baize carpet; there was the throng before it. Again and again rang out the cheers, as they rang on the day of the exhibition of the Crampton Light Infantry. There was she, awaiting, as on that occasion, the appearance of her brother—a comet to come forth from the hidden space behind the curtain, and then to retire.

The vividness with which this old experience was recalled to her imagination by the scenes and events around her, impressed Fanny almost superstitiously. The day and its incidents seemed like one of those passages known to be strange to our observation, yet impressing us with their familiarity—glimpses caught through some rent in the oblivious veil that hides from us a previous existence. The doctor saw nothing of this. It was fitting that there should be this introduction to the performance of his son. Every glory won by those who came upon the stage, and retired, was added to the crown of his boy, for he had distanced all of them. Not a good word was spoken, not a worthy success was achieved, that did not minister to the splendor of his son's triumph.

Orations and music were finished at last, and only the Valedictory of Fred Gilbert remained to be pronounced. Around this performance and around him, was concentrated the keenest interest of the occasion. His devotion to study, his personal beauty, his excellent character, his well-known gifts, and his achievement of the highest honors of his class, brought to him universal sympathy, and directed to his part in the day's programme the most grateful attention.

His name was pronounced, and the moment he appeared he was greeted with a general outburst of applause. The doctor forgot himself, lost his self-possession, and leaned forward upon his cane with an eager smile. Quick before Fanny came again the old planetarium; but alas! the golden-haired boy was gone, and a pale, fragile young man, with chestnut curls, was in his place. The house was still, and the feeble voice went out upon the congregation like the wail of a sick child. He had evidently summoned all his strength; and, as he proceeded, his tones became rounder and more musical; but the whole address seemed more like a farewell to the world than a farewell to the college. Tears gathered in all eyes under the spell of his plaintive cadences, and all seemed to hold their breath, that he might expend no more upon them than was necessary.

The last words were said, and then there rang out over the whole assembly cheer upon cheer. Bouquets were thrown upon the stage by fair hands in the galleries, and handkerchiefs were waved at the tips of jewelled fingers. The doctor's eyes are wet with delight, but Fanny sits and watches the young man in alarm. There is a strange, convulsive movement of his chest, as he stoops to gather the bouquets at his feet. He carries his handkerchief to his mouth, and holds it there while he bows his acknowledgments to the galleries. As he retires from the stage, Fanny catches a glimpse of the handkerchief, and it is bright with the blood of his heart! Ah! the comet has come and gone out into the unknown spaces—sunned itself in public applause for the last time—gone to shine feebler and feebler in the firmament of life, until, in an unknown heaven, it passes from human sight.

This fancy flies swiftly through Fanny's brain—this thought pierces her heart—as she rises to her feet, walks quickly across the stage, and whispers a few words in her father's ear. He looks up into her face with a vague, incredulous stare, and shakes his head. She takes him firmly by the arm, and leads him wondering to the curtain behind which Fred has retired. She parts the hanging folds, and both enter. The movement is little noticed by the assembly, for some have already turned to leave the house, and others are listening to the music, or making their comments to each other upon the address.

As the doctor and Fanny entered the little curtained corner, they saw Fred sitting in a chair, freely spitting blood upon his handkerchief, and surrounded by a little company of frightened associates. Dr. Gilbert, though he had been accustomed through a long professional life to disease and calamity in their most terrible forms, stood before this case as helpless as a child. Beyond the most obvious directions, he could say and do nothing; and an eminent physician of the village, at that moment seated upon the platform, was sent for. By Fanny's order, Fred was removed to the hotel, where she could nurse him; and all the events of the day were forgotten in this new and most unlooked-for trial.

This seemed to be the one event of Dr. Gilbert's life for which he had no preparation. It took from him all his strength and all his self-possession. He stood before it in utter helplessness, offering no opinion, assuming no responsibility, hardly able to perform the simplest office of attendance, taking Fanny's will as law, and relying upon the professional skill of others. As the more serious features of the attack passed away, and Fred was allowed to whisper his feelings and desires into the ear of his sister, he expressed a decided wish that his father might be kept from his bedside. The affliction of his father pained him more than his own disease, and he could not bear to look at him.

The composure and happiness of her brother astonished Fanny beyond measure. As he lay upon his bed, day after day, with his pleasant eyes upon her, and her hand in his, he seemed more like a child that had lain down to rest, than like a young man suddenly snatched from active life and enterprise and hope. "Oh! it's so sweet to rest, Fanny," he would say, "so sweet to rest."

The multitude had departed, and the hotel and the street were pervaded by almost a Sabbath stillness. Days passed away. Sympathizing friends called and made inquiries, and offered unaccepted services, and retired. The doctor lounged upon the piazza, or walked listlessly about the halls, or engaged his friends in conversations, of which his poor boy was always the theme. Every word of encouragement given by the professional attendant was repeated by the doctor to every man he met. Once or twice, he entered his son's room, and began, in the old way, to talk of what he should next undertake, under a vague impression that a contemplation of possible triumphs in the future would stimulate and encourage him. But the young man turned his face away in distress, and Fanny interfered in his behalf.

Fred Gilbert was not only a child again, but he wished to be one. Manhood's great struggle with the world had come upon him too early. He had been forced away from home—driven to the seclusion of study—stimulated to efforts that necessarily crucified his social sympathies—and now, when he was disabled, and the great prize secured, he was only too happy to become helpless, and to give himself up to the care and attention of others. A sick girl could not have been more gentle, more affectionate, more submissive. He rejoiced in subjection, and was as happy under Fanny's brooding care as a babe upon its mother's bosom.

A fortnight passed away, and the young man became able to occupy his chair for the greater portion of every day. September was creeping on, and, though the earth still looked fresh and green, the murmurous hush of autumn was settling upon the landscape. The dreamy, sibilant breath of insect life, unintermittent, but heard rather by the listening soul than the listening sense, pervaded the atmosphere, as if it were the aspiration of a seething sea of silence. Industrious relays of crickets made music all day and all night. Here and there upon the tops of the maples, bright leaves of carmine or vermilion showed themselves. The maize in the fields displayed its tokens of maturity; and the apple-orchards were bending beneath their burden of crimson and gold.

On one of the loveliest days of this charming season, Dr. Gilbert and his family set out upon their return to Crampton. An easy carriage had been secured, and two days of slow driving and frequent resting were occupied by the journey. Dr. Gilbert entered his dwelling a strangely altered man. His thoughts had flowed in one channel so long, and he had lost in the passage of life so much of his native elasticity, that he could carve out no new enterprises and discover no new fields of interest. His mind had travelled eagerly on with his boy, until the current of his boy's life was checked, and then he neither knew which way to turn, nor cared to turn at all. Fanny studied carefully, not only the case of her brother, but that of her father; and the more thoroughly she became acquainted with both, the more was she convinced that new and peculiar cares were coming upon her.

While Fred was in immediate danger, her fears and

her sympathies, added to her active duties, kept her mind engaged. The moment home was reached, and Aunt Catharine's ministry secured, she began to grow uneasy, and to long for something to engage her powers. The further pursuit of literature did not enlist her thoughts at all. She had had enough of that, and felt that she could never undertake it again, unless under the impulse of some new motive. But Fanny was not left to seek for labor ; it came to her. Her father wanted writing done and business transacted ; and, by degrees, she found herself absorbed in an employment entirely new to her. Gradually assuming the responsibilities of her new position, she became accountant, farmer, and general manager of the estate. This new life pleased her well, and the success which attended her administration of affairs was the marvel of all who knew her.

The invalid brother grew stronger, but he was broken-spirited. He had not a particle of ambition for anything higher than he had achieved ; and it was evident to his friends that his stock of vitality was too far reduced by premature expenditures to allow him to accomplish anything further in the world. If he rode out, Fanny always drove. If any business was to be done, it was put upon Fanny. She assumed the reins of authority in the household—gracefully, and with sufficient consideration for her father—and became " the man of the house." All this pleased her not a little. When not otherwise engaged, she was in the farm-yard, among the horses, the cattle, and the sheep. Her dominion there had a strange fascination for her. The dumb creatures all learned to love her. They ran toward her when she appeared, took food at her hand, obeyed her will, She drove horses that were no more than half-tamed, and took delight in the dangerous play. People talked about her, and only a single autumn, filled with these pursuits, made her rather unpleasantly notorious.

Out of this life, so greedy a nature as hers could not draw food always, and was not destined to draw food long. Yet she was trying to be more unselfish than she had ever been. She was exercising more patience and forbearance in her relations to her family than she had ever exercised before. Her brother could not read ; so, many a long evening she read to him ; but she felt the task to be irksome. Often, when engaged in these offices, she thought of her patient neighbor, Arthur Blague, and wondered where his strength, patience, and equanimity had their source. When she mixed with the world, and came into contact with the rough natures around her, she felt strong ; but when she came to this patient, humble ministry, she felt that she was but a weak and wilful child.

Arthur had been an interested—sometimes a painfully interested—observer of all her movements. He had, however, little of her society, because he chose to keep away from her. He had been pleased with her efficiency in the service of her father, but there were displays of masculine tastes that troubled him more than he would have been willing to confess.

CHAPTER XXIV.

MISS GILBERT RECEIVES A LESSON WHICH SHE NEVER FORGETS, AND WHICH DOES HER GOOD ALL THE DAYS OF HER LIFE.

THE winter that followed these events was a severe one, and restrained the occupants of the Gilbert mansion within the walls of home. Fanny missed the variety and vivacity of her old New York life. The same duties, the same amusements, the same faces, the unvarying, dreary scene, tired her. Never in her life had she indulged so deeply in reverie. It seemed to her that she had lived her life out—that she had either come to its end, or had exhausted all its grateful significance. She looked backward, and saw that the freshness of youth was gone, and that she had achieved the highest good she had labored for. She examined the present, and found herself in the maturity and full strength of her powers without an object of life that laid hold upon the coming years, and without satisfying companionship. She looked forward, and the future spread itself before her, a dark and meaningless blank.

A nature like hers could not sleep. Vitality is a restless principle, and she had it in abundance. Sometimes she would issue forth in the wildest storms, simply for the pleasure of excitement—the excitement of struggling with fierce winds and overcoming obstacles. Occasionally she and Arthur were thrown into one another's society, always accidentally. By some strange influence, they found it impossible to maintain a distant reserve in one another's presence. There was no disguising the hearty pleasure with which they took each the other's hand on every unsought opportunity. Fanny wondered why Arthur did not oftener call upon her. She was piqued by his apparent desire to shun her, for her woman's heart told her that he was happy in her presence, and her woman's heart longed for his manly society.

There had been a long winter storm—not the storm of a day or a night, but of a week—not heavy, covering fences and filling the highway with drifted piles—but intermittent, coming down in sleet and snow, from low, gray clouds that hid the mountain-tops, and hung chill and hard, with discouraging persistency, over the valleys. Morning after morning had broken upon the inmates of the Gilbert mansion in dismal gloom, and day after day twilight had descended upon mid-afternoon. The same bleak landscape, the same muffled sleigh-riders—their heads bent to break the blast—the same gray sky, the same dull life from day to day, had wearied and chafed Fanny Gilbert until she began to feel that winter life in Crampton was unendurable. At last, the storm broke up. In the night, the wind chopped about, and came down from the northwest in a long, hard blow, that bellowed in the chimneys, and slammed the blinds, and whistled through the leafless maples, and roared on the distant hills, as if it were rejoicing in its own rough way over the great victory it had won from the grim spirit of the storm.

As the sun rose, the wind fell ; and very blue was the sky, and very dazzling and inspiring the light, that greeted the eyes of the Crampton people, as they looked out of their windows that morning. Fanny Gilbert declared at the breakfast-table that she would have a sleigh-ride, and that Fred should accompany her. The doctor informed her that the family horse would be in use for other and more necessary purposes. Then she would take the colt. She had already driven him, and would be delighted to drive him again. Her father expostulated, and Aunt Catharine prophesied evil ; but they made no impression on Fanny, who had deter-mined upon her ride.

Accordingly word was sent to the stable, immediately after breakfast, to have the colt and sleigh brought to the door ; and Fred was muffled in the warmest clothing by Aunt Catharine, while Fanny rigged herself for the drive. The colt was led around, and seemed to be in quite as good spirits, under the influence of the bracing morning air, as his mistress. She went out, patted him upon the head, caressed him, and kept him quiet while Fred was taking his seat, and then quietly stepped into the sleigh and took the reins. His head was re-

23

leased by the groom, word was given to go, and off flew
the spirited creature like a bird.

Arthur Blague stood at his window while this scene
was in progress, and witnessed it with vague uneasiness
and apprehension. As the gay turn-out passed his window, he felt moved to take his hat and go forth to see
the progress of the riders as they passed out of the village. He followed them with his feet and his eye, as
they rapidly vanished in the distance, and then walked
on for his own quiet enjoyment.

Wrapped in his thoughts, and exhilarated by the influences of the morning, he had left the village half a
mile behind, when he caught a view upon a distant hill
of a horse flying toward him at a frantic pace. He stood
still, and as it approached, he felt sure that it was no
other than the half-broken creature that Fanny had
driven off with. He heard no outcry, but he saw people
run out, after the horse and sleigh had passed, and lift
their hands in helpless fright.

Already the running horse was near him. He saw, in
a moment, that it would be impossible to stop him by
standing before him; so he chose the only practicable
alternative for helping and saving his friends. The colt
dashed madly toward him, while he kept his eye fixed
upon the sleigh. As it came up, he grasped the dasher
by a motion quick as lightning, and threw himself by
desperate force into the vehicle. A vague impression
that he was hurt upon the head, and a wild sensation of
flying through the air, were the subjects of his first consciousness. The next moment he was upon his feet, the
reins were jerked out of Fanny's hands, and then the
frightened colt felt the strength of a man upon his
mouth. Fanny said not a word : not a word was spoken
by any one. The animal struggled desperately, but
tired at last under the steady powerful check, and subsided into a short, broken canter, then came down to a

trot, and then stopped, trembling and reeking, before Dr. Gilbert's door.

Arthur stepped out of the sleigh, while the stable-boy, who was near, took the colt by the head ; and then he lifted Fanny to the ground, so weak and faint that she could hardly stand.

When both had seen Fred safely on his way to the house, they looked in each other's eyes. She could not speak. She gazed in the face of her preserver, down which, from beneath his hat, the blood was flowing freely, and was as dumb as if her lips were frozen. ·

" Fanny Gilbert," said Arthur, with a firm voice, " do not be guilty of this foolhardy business again ! Allow me to conduct you to the house."

She answered not a word, turned upon her heel, and left him. Arthur then went to his home and attended to his wound—his two wounds, in fact—the wound upon his head, and the wound upon his feelings. He knew he had spoken strongly ; but he felt that the risk of his life had given him warrant for it.

Fanny entered the house, mortified and offended. She was but a woman, with a woman's strength after all. It had been demonstrated to her by one whose strength, presence of mind, and courage had humiliated her, and shown to her her inferiority. Not only this, but he had assumed toward her a tone of command, such as no man—not even her father—had assumed for many years.

In the course of the morning, these thoughts passed away. Then came shame for her lack of consideration for one whose flowing blood testified to her how much she was indebted to him. She had shown neither magnanimity nor gratitude. She had not even exhibited good breeding. She knew that she must make amends ; and, though her pride restrained her, she determined that she would. The doctor had already walked over, and ascertained that Arthur's wound was a superficial one ; but that could not satisfy Fanny. Her personal duty in the matter must be done, or she could never meet him again without shame.

In the afternoon, Fanny dressed herself with more than her accustomed care, for a formal call upon the young clergyman. It was such a visit as she had never undertaken before. It was a visit to which she felt urged by every sentiment of honor and of self-respect. She knew that Arthur could misconstrue no call from her that would cost her humiliation and a confession of wrong. She even went so far as to con the phrases of her confession and her prayer. The feeling of a culprit destroyed her self-possession, and her heart beat heavily with excitement as she lifted the knocker at Mrs. Blague's door.

The smile of glad surprise with which Mrs. Blague greeted her, assured her, at once, that Arthur had not mentioned the unpleasant manner in which they had parted from each other in the morning; and the fact made her still more ashamed of herself. Mrs. Blague was so happy to think that no one had been hurt. Arthur's injury was nothing. It would heal in a few days. After a few minutes' chat, Fanny inquired for Arthur, and expressed a wish to see him.

Mrs. Blague left the room, and Fanny was alone. The doors were left ajar as the mistress of the house went upon her errand ; and coming down through the silence Fanny heard the terrible breathing of little Jamie—heard it until every sympathy of her nature was bleeding. Mrs. Blague was absent for some minutes, and, in the meantime, Fanny grew nervous and sick at heart. It seemed to her as if she could not remain in the house. She rose and closed the parlor door, but still that same stertorous respiration pierced her ears, and haunted her impatient consciousness.

At length Mrs. Blague descended the stairs and reappeared. She brought a troubled expression upon her features, and an embarrassed manner. Arthur, she said, nervously and blushing, would see Fanny in his study. Fanny hesitated—then said, "Very well ; " and rose and followed Mrs. Blague up-stairs. The latter led the way to a distant door in the back part of the house, opened it, turned Fanny in, and retired.

Fanny found herself in a strange place. There was a small library upon one side of the room, in an open case, and upon another a couch of singular construction. A bright fire was burning upon the hearth, and there was an air of quiet comfort in the apartment ; but the sound of that terrible breathing pierced her very soul.

Arthur was seated at a window with something in his lap—something that had the face of a human being on which were traced deep lines of distress, but the form and proportions of nothing that she had ever seen. She knew it must be Jamie ; but it seemed impossible that it could be. He was dressed like a girl ; but from the bottom of his skirt protruded a pair of feet, misshapen, dwarfed, and stiff, hanging to ankles that were no larger than her two fingers. One emaciated hand and arm hung at his side, as loose and lifeless as the sleeve that half hid it. The other was swaying wildly in the air with its curled fingers and stiff joints, under the excitement produced by the presence of a stranger. Nothing half so sickening—nothing half so revolting—had ever met her eyes before.

She nerved herself to meet the repulsive vision, and approached nearer, trembling with excitement. The little fellow's head, or, rather, his neck, lay upon his brother's arm, and not a breath filled his chest that was not drawn into it by a spasm that thrilled Fanny with sympathetic pain. She did not see Arthur's look and smile of greeting at all. Absorbed by the vision of the afflicted child, and harrowed in all her sensibilities by its efforts for the vital air upon which its terrible existence fed, she could not remove her eyes from the sad and distressed little face. Her eyes filled with tears, and she wiped them, and wiped them again. Her bosom heaved with convulsive sobs which only her most powerful efforts could control.

" Is he dying ? " whispered she at length.

" Oh, no ! " replied Arthur ; " he is very well to-day, and enjoying the sunlight very much."

" Very well ? Why ! how long has he been like this ? "

" Ten years."

" Breathing like this ? "

" Oh ! no. He has breathed like this only five years."

" Five years ! My God ! My God ! " and Fanny sat and looked into Arthur's eyes with vague incredulity ; her face as pale as that of the poor child before her.

At this moment the child indicated by a motion of his lips that he wished to change his position, and Arthur brought him forward so that he could lean upon his hand.

" What did you mean, when you said that he was enjoying the sunlight very much to-day ? " Fanny inquired. " Do you mean to say that he really enjoys anything ? "

" Certainly he does," replied Arthur, with a full, cheery tone, that went straight to the heart of the little boy, and straight from his heart into his face, illuminating it with a smile as full of love and heaven as earthly smile can be.

Arthur put him back upon his arm again, and looked fondly into his eyes. The emaciated chest struggled on for its coveted breath, but the heart looked up through those soft, dark eyes with unutterable love and gratitude.

" He knows his friends," said Arthur, in his strong, cheerful way ; and the words called out the same sweet smile, and the same look of unutterable gratitude—certainly unutterable by him, for his lips had never spoken a word since the accident which befell him ten years before.

" He's one of the happiest little fellows in all Crampton," Arthur continued. "He sits here with his brother, and looks out of the window, and sees the horses go by and the children at play, and keeps me in the house, and makes me study, and warms my heart with his precious smiles, and pays me ten thousand times for all I do for him. He's one of the noblest and happiest little fellows in the world."

As Arthur said this, the boy repeated the old smile—his sole return for all the care that brotherly or motherly love could lavish upon him. Fanny looked on with wonder—almost with awe. No such unselfish love—no such devotion—had she ever seen or dreamed of.

"He is more quiet at night?" said Fanny, interrogatively.

"No."

"Who takes care of him?"

"I do."

"How can you? How can you sleep?"

"Miss Gilbert, I have not slept more than an hour at a time for ten years."

"Arthur Blague!"

"Not more than an hour at a time for ten years."

"And yet you are cheerful and happy."

"So happy that it seems to me sometimes that I must be dreaming, and that, by and by, I shall wake to life's sterner realities."

The proud woman sits before the humble man vanquished. She can imagine how, in the din and heat of battle, even she could face death at the cannon's mouth. She can imagine how, for a great cause, strong men can suffer hardships for many years—for a whole lifetime; but this patient subjection of a great life to the wants of a suffering child, for a whole decade, away from the eye of the world, not only uncomplaining but abundantly happy, rises in her apprehension into an unapproachable heroism. She thinks of her own impatience with the dull realities of her Crampton home, of all the selfish pursuits of her life, and she sinks down into a sickening self-contempt.

It was easy now for her to ask Arthur to forgive her for the rudeness of the morning ; and she did it, forgetting all her nicely trimmed phrases, and losing all her reluctant shame. She thanked Arthur for the lesson he had taught her, and in the fulness and impulsiveness of her heart she told the young man how much she respected and admired his self-abnegation.

As she spoke, Arthur's eyes sank to the floor, and tears filled them. When she closed, he lifted them to her face, and said : " I thank God for giving me the discipline with which he favors almost exclusively your sex. I do not wonder that women are so much purer and better than men. They have opportunities which few men have. Of all the heroisms this world has ever known, those wrought out in rooms like this are the greatest and the noblest—wrought out by patient, self-denying women. God has singularly favored me from my birth. He has kept my heart close to the suffering always, and my hands busy in humble service ; and before Him, to-day, I declare that I would not exchange what I have won in this sympathy and service for the wealth of a thousand worlds like this. This cup, of which I have been drinking daily and almost hourly for many years, and which seems so bitter to you, has become inexpressibly sweet to me. God help me when I shall be called to put it away from my lips forever ! Always, in the presence of this little painful life, my heart is melted down into the tenderest love and pity. I take it to my arms ; and all my resentments, all my pride, all my own little trials, fade out ; for I know that in this little suffering boy—this pure and patient spirit—I hold against my heart the form of Jesus Christ—of Jesus Christ ! Oh my God ! what a privilege ! "

As Arthur said this, his eyes were full of the light of a dawning heaven in his soul. Fanny looked at him in awe and wonder. She had caught a glimpse of something divine. The glories of great secrets shone out upon her. Transcendent motives of life revealed themselves dimly to her quickened moral vision. The sublime melody of another sphere breathed in the young man's voice; and she faintly apprehended the immortal harmonies into which the discords of time were swiftly resolving themselves. In the strange excitement of the moment, she dropped upon her knees before Arthur and the child, buried her face in her hands, and sobbed convulsively. The gifted, the famous, the courted, the imperious Fanny Gilbert bowed humbly in the presence of a consecrated life, under the shadow of great thoughts that seemed to be let down from the heaven above her.

Jamie's little misshapen arm waved wildly back and forth as he looked up into Arthur's face, with an anxious, inquiring gaze; and his breath came harder under the strange excitement. Arthur could have wept like a child over the scene before him. He longed to drop at her side, and pour out his soul in prayer. His firm lips quivered, and there rose to them, from a soul profoundly moved, the words: " Father in Heaven! Our hearts, and the issues of our lives, are in Thy hands. Make us children whom Thou shalt delight in; engage our hearts and our hands in Thy service, eradicate from us all our selfishness, and lead us into Thy perfect peace!"

The room was silent. The little boy's breath came easier for the moment, and then there rose from Fanny's lips a whispered " Amen!"

There was a sound of feet in the passage, and Fanny rose, and resumed her seat. Mrs. Blague came in. She saw the marks of excitement and of tears upon the faces before her, and started back. The question—" What, mother?" from Arthur, arrested her. Mrs. Blague had a story of destitution to tell. There were two little boys down-stairs —children of a widow who had only managed to live through the long storm—and the little boys had trudged through the snow three miles for help.

" Go," said Miss Gilbert.

" Give them something to eat, and tell them to wait for me," said Arthur. Then he added : " It is almost time for Jamie to sleep, and then I can go."

Fanny sat for a moment thinking. Then she rose, removed her hat and cloak, drew off her gloves, and, coming forward to Arthur, handed him a bank note as her portion of the afternoon's charity. " Little Jamie," said Fanny, " will sit with me while you are absent."

Little Jamie seemed to understand it all, and looked up into her face with that old precious smile, which had repaid so many kindnesses rendered him by others, and which went straight to her heart with its freight of pleasure. Arthur saw the smile, and it pleased him, but he had at the moment a pleasure that rose above even that. He uttered no expostulation, and made no objection. There was something in this prompt adoption of a painful task on the part of Miss Gilbert that thrilled him with a new and strange delight.

Fanny took her seat, and Jamie, heavier than she had supposed, was laid in her arms. Arthur received Fanny's direction to call and inform her family that she should not be at home until evening, and then departed upon his long walk and his errand of mercy.

Mrs. Blague took a hint from Arthur, and retired from the room, leaving Fanny and the poor little patient to each other's society. The painful respiration of little Jamie made her heart bleed. The door was closed, and she was alone with the little one whom God for some great purpose had smitten—alone—how the thought thrilled her !—with Jesus Christ, in the person of that sick child. Inasmuch as she gave her sympathy and her service to this little one—this little unknown one—the least important of all the children around her—she served and sympathized with him! The Lord of Heaven and Earth was in her arms! The place where she sat was holy.

The little boy lay gasping upon her lap, looking wonderingly into her face, but was evidently happy. He had seen her pass the window, doubtless, many times, and thought of her as a grand woman to whom he was nothing. As he found himself in her arms—the subject of her kind and compassionate smiles and her tender care—there was a delighted expression upon his face whenever she looked at him. She did not know how far he understood her, but she told him long and beautiful stories that she had repeated many times to the happy little children in the far-off New York home. Then she sang to him—low, dreamy tunes that soothed his poor brain and nerves, and at last he went to sleep upon her bosom.

Fanny looked around the room, and thought of the weary, weary years that had been spent there by Arthur Blague, while she was away, courting the flatteries of the vulgar, mingling with the rich and the gay, or working impatiently to win the applause of the public; and her life shrank into contemptible proportions. Working for herself, absorbed in the pursuit of a career which should give significance to her and to her life, she had run through life into nothingness; while Arthur, with his heart turned from himself toward others, doing his first duty with patience and active purpose, stood fronting God and all God's universe, with a life before him as rich as heaven, and as broad and long as eternity.

Of the silent prayers breathed that afternoon, of the resolutions formed, and the projects conceived, her after-life betrayed the results.

It was dark before Arthur returned. Several times

during the afternoon Mrs. Blague went in and insisted upon relieving Fanny of her burden, but the proffered relief was refused. She longed to be tired. She was happy in her weariness. She desired, above everything, that there might, through the ministry of this invalid boy, come into her heart a meek spirit—a spirit of patient self-sacrifice. Not till Arthur entered the room, did she release the little form she had tended so gently during that long afternoon. Then she gave Jamie to his mother, resumed her hat and cloak, and, taking Arthur's arm at the door, walked home, talking of the happy afternoon she had spent, inquiring for the poor family whom Arthur had visited, and giving him no opportunity to utter a word.

That night she was full of her new thoughts, and so was Arthur, though they were very different from hers. Ah! if he could see that strong nature and that rich culture of hers all subordinated and devoted to the purposes which ruled him, what a companion would she be for him! Since the memorable evening he spent with her on the occasion of her return from New York, he had felt compelled, for the sake of his own peace, to avoid her society. She had opened to him a mind so full of treasure—so facile and bright—that he left her fascinated; but when he calmly remembered that, in the motives and purposes of his life, she had no sympathy, he felt compelled to repress his rising interest in her, and to trample his new thoughts of her under feet. The moment, however, that her heart was toned up to the key-note of his own, he was conscious of a sympathy that thrilled every fibre of his nature. He held little Jamie all that evening in a dream.

When Fanny entered her home, Fred had gone to bed, and the doctor and Aunt Catharine were sitting before the deep wood fire after their usual custom— Aunt Catharine knitting, and the doctor trying to read a newspaper and punching the forestick. Fanny sat down with an exceedingly happy face, and related the story of her afternoon's experience—bringing tears to Aunt Catharine's eyes, and interesting her father very deeply. Neither had seen Jamie Blague for years. He was felt to be so painful a sight, that he had been persistently kept from visitors ; and they felt that Arthur had had no idle motive in bringing Fanny into contact with him.

As she closed her story, the long, shrill whistle of the locomotive announced the incoming train, and the delayed mail. The train, owing to the storm, had been late for several days. Dr. Gilbert fretted with the thought that he could not get his letters and papers until the next morning, and Fanny declared her readiness to go for the mail. This she accordingly did, and did so quickly, that she returned with her cheeks glowing with the influence of the air and the exercise. She handed to her father the letters directed to him, and, retaining one for herself, bearing the familiar New York post-mark, sat down to read it.

" Frank Sargent is coming here to spend the next Sabbath ! Good ! " exclaimed Fanny with a burst of delight. " What can bring him here at this time of year ? " she continued. " There are none of his lame ducks, that he talks so much about, here, I know, for bookstores are not abundant. What can bring him here ? " and Fanny laid down her letter and said again, " What can bring him here ? "

" Coming to see you," suggested Aunt Catharine.

" Not he. He never goes anywhere except on business, and is never from home on Sunday if he can help it. Something is in the wind."

Then Fanny read the remainder of the letter, and a postscript written by Mary, and pondered and wondered until she went to bed. The doctor knew all about it, and chuckled over his secret comfortably after Fanny retired.

CHAPTER XXV.

IN WHICH ARTHUR MAKES A GREAT MANY NEW FRIENDS, AND LOSES THE MOST PRECIOUS FRIEND HE HAS.

SATURDAY night brought the expected visitor, and the expected visitor brought with him his accustomed fund of talk and high animal spirits, besides a couple of friends, whom he left at the hotel, and whom he did not speak of to Fanny. Fanny questioned him about his family, inquired after Mr. Kilgore, and finally spoke of "Rhododendron." It had been a great success, and continued to be. Then Fanny wanted to know what brought him to Crampton. He had come, he said, to pay to her her copyright on the books thus far sold, and to urge her to write another book. Any thing she would write now, the public would read. A wild sweep of the old ambition passed through her soul, but it died as the new motives which had found foothold there asserted themselves. No—she should write no more books—at least, not now, nor soon. Frank Sargent affected great disappointment ; he was " sorry to lose his journey," and so on, through a large amount of innocent dissembling.

" By the way," said the doctor, with an air of affected chagrin and disappointment, " I understand that Arthur Blague is to preach to-morrow. Sorry you can't hear our regular minister."

" What a pity ! " exclaimed Mr. Sargent.

Fanny bit her lip. " I think you will have no reason to regret the change," said she.

" Does he amount to any thing ? " inquired Frank Sargent.

"If you wish to know my opinion of him," replied Fanny, "it is that he amounts to more than all the Wiltons there are in the world. I certainly know of no man in New York whom I consider his equal in natural gifts, in natural eloquence, or"—and Fanny's lips hesitated to pronounce judgment on a subject not long used to them—"in Christian piety."

"That is your candid opinion, is it?" said Mr. Sargent, with a shrewd twinkle of the eye.

"That is my candid opinion. What do you look at me in that way for?"

"Nothing;" and then Frank Sargent looked in the doctor's face, and they both indulged in a hearty laugh, which left Fanny very deeply puzzled.

Then Mr. Sargent went on plying Fanny with questions with relation to the young minister; drawing her out in regard to his social qualities; exciting her into defending him from some disparaging remark, and keeping her engaged in talking about him. At last, she went into his history, and closed with the narrative of her experience in the study. Then he inquired about Jamie, and asked whether it was thought that he could live long, and manifested such a marked interest in the young man and his affairs, that Fanny became still more puzzled over the matter. He explained himself by remarking that he had heard Mary talk so much about Arthur that he felt quite interested in him. In fact, he was glad, on the whole, he was going to preach on the morrow. Mary would be glad to hear from Arthur, and to learn what kind of a figure he made in the pulpit. Then Mr. Sargent and the doctor looked one another in the face again, and laughed as before.

Fanny was much inclined to be offended. "Excellent joke! isn't it, now?" said she.

As Mr. Sargent had pushed matters far enough, he changed the subject, and spent the remainder of the evening in a rattling conversation on a great variety of topics, and, at last, went to bed.

After breakfast and family devotions the next morning, Mr. Sargent announced his determination to go over to the hotel, and see if there were not somebody there whom he knew, promising to return in season to accompany Fanny to church. He found at the hotel his brace of New York friends—saints of his own pattern—specimens of young America sanctified—one of them a flashy gentleman, with a moustache on his lip, and a cigar under it, and the other an overworked, lean, wiry little man of thirty-five, prefaced by a violent diamond breastpin.

"Made any discoveries?" inquired Mr. Frank Sargent.

"Yes, we've been pumping some—all right as far as it goes—very popular—must draw, according to all accounts," replied the little man with the breastpin.

"Messenger breed," responded the moustache and cigar—strong, rangy, large, good bottom, handsome, speed enough for all practical purposes, and kind. Found out anything, Sargent?"

"Well," said Mr. Sargent, "I have had a talk with the smartest woman in New Hampshire—with the writer of 'Rhododendron.' I would give a hundred dollars to have you hear, as she told it to me, the story of this man's life." Then Frank Sargent went on in his most eloquent style, to repeat the story, and it certainly lost very little in passing through his lips.

Let no profane person suppose that these men— talking so lightly, so jocularly, in fact, about the young minister—were men who held his office in low esteem, or regarded his work with indifference. They were business men—Christian business men—whose efficiency and practical devotion in pushing on all Christian enterprises in their city home, had secured for them the appointment to the mission in which we find them engaged. They were workers and givers, with busy hands and tongues, and open purses. Relieved from the cares of business for the time, and thrown together under such pleasant circumstances away from home, their hearts were light, indeed, but they were prepared to attend the ministrations of the day with tractable hearts, and to judge of them with minds rendered keen and catholic by large intercourse with the world and a practical knowledge of its wants. A saint in a moustache had never been seen in Crampton, and lively religious people, in smart overcoats and good boots, were by no means common, so that the errand of this trio was not likely to be suspected by the multitude.

"Is he matched?" inquired Moustache, intent on keeping up his equine figure. (Moustache drove a very fine horse at home, and loved him.)

"Well—doubtful," replied Mr. Frank Sargent.

"Ought to be. Girls will all be after him. Besides, it will take a double team to do our work."

"Never mind that," responded the breastpin, very decidedly. "All decent men get married, of course; and any man who is good enough to be a minister will attend to all his Christian duties, in time." (Breastpin married young, and was the father of six children.)

"The old man had got it all fixed, had he?" inquired Moustache.

"Everything arranged," replied Mr. Sargent, "and nobody suspects any thing. If we don't like him, all we've got to do is to go back, and take a new trail; and nobody here will be the wiser for our visit. If we do like him, why, then we'll try to make him like us—that's all."

After an hour spent with his New York associates, the first morning bells rang out from the church belfries, and Frank Sargent walked back to the house of Dr.

24

Gilbert, to fulfil his pledge to Fanny. When Arthur Blague mounted the pulpit that morning, there were three strangers in the church, who not only measured his form and gait, but who noticed the manner in which his hair was parted, examined his neck-tie, scanned his linen, and criticised the squeak of his boots. These strangers did not sit together, but were distributed in different parts of the church—one at the extreme rear, for the better measurement of the power of his voice.

Arthur rose, and invoked the divine blessing in calm words that seemed to come from the depths of his soul, as if—conscious of his weakness and his dependence at all times—he could absolutely do nothing then and there without aid. When he pronounced his "Amen" over the hushed assembly, Moustache looked at Breastpin and gave a slow wink, and Breastpin responded with a little nod. Arthur had made an impression. As for Frank Sargent, he forgot all about his mission and his New York associates, in his interest in the services of the morning; and Fanny, who sat by his side, was no less interested than he. The sermon was well calculated to make critics forget to criticise, because it was written to accomplish a purpose infinitely higher than the satisfaction of a critical judgment. It was a revelation of the great motives of a great life; and the audience was moved by it as a forest bows to the breath of a mighty wind. They felt its power, forgetting for the moment over what sea it came—on what cloud it rode—and conscious only that it was from heaven.

After the morning exercises were finished, the New Yorkers quietly took their way to the hotel without speaking to each other, and met in their common parlor. Moustache was in a state of profound excitement, which he undertook to modify in some degree by lighting a cigar. "I told you he was Messenger stock," said he— "Gospel Messenger, and no mistake."

"Well, on the whole, what do you think of him?" said Mr. Sargent, through whose influence entirely his friends on the "Committee of Supply" had visited Crampton.

"What's the use of asking?" said Breastpin. "What prayers!" Now that man prays for what he wants, and not for what he thinks he ought to want. What is a prayer good for that scatters all over Robin Hood's barn?"

"Well, now — that's so!" responded Moustache. "There are some prayers that seem to me like a man out with a lantern in the night, trying to find an ' Amen,' and looking into all the dark corners, and poking over the stones, and going up hills, and diving into valleys, and climbing up trees, and rummaging things miscellaneously, till he finds it, if it takes him a week. You can't follow such a prayer as that. You always go to looking after the ' Amen ' yourself, and find it first, sure."

"And then," said Breastpin, "those prayers that seem to be chapters out of the Cyclopedia of Useful Information."

"For the benefit of the Deity," suggested Mr. Frank Sargent.

"Now there is nothing of the kind in this fellow," resumed Moustache. "Straightforward talk—lifted right up from the lower shelf. I looked at him, and cried all the time. He's a—he's a magnificent man, and we might just as well make out a programme of exercises for his ordination, as any way. Sargent, draw up a call. What's the use of being lazy?"

Mr. Sargent and Breastpin laughed. "First catch your hare," said the former.

"Previously having your cooking utensils ready," responded Moustache.

"There's time enough for all these things," said Frank Sargent, and, taking up his hat, he left his companions in a very happy frame of mind, and walked over to dine with Dr. Gilbert.

The afternoon services passed off like those of the morning, confirming the good impression already produced, and convincing the New York "Committee of Supply" that if they could supply such material as they had discovered to their congregation at home, it would be the best thing in their power to do. In the evening, Frank Sargent asked liberty of Dr. Gilbert and Fanny to invite his New York friends over ; and they came, passing the evening in the discussion of the sermons and the young man who had preached them. Fanny had already begun to suspect the nature of their errand, and lent her tongue gladly in favor of her friend.

Before they retired, it was arranged that the whole party should dine with Dr. Gilbert the next day, and that Arthur should be invited to meet them, so that they could have an opportunity of judging of his social qualities.

At the appointed hour, on Monday, Arthur Blague walked into Dr. Gilbert's parlor, and was presented to the New Yorkers. Mr. Frank Sargent had already called upon him as an old acquaintance. Fanny, conscious of her power to engage the conversational faculties of her friend, quietly took the business into her own hands, while the New Yorkers, with a modesty quite unusual with them, became listeners, so far as possible. Ah, Fanny! She did not dream that those keen, quiet, critical eyes were examining her qualifications for a minister's wife, all the time. It did not enter her thought, at all, that above that dark moustache was an eye that was measuring her power to " match " that of Arthur. It was a very pretty exhibition, and abundantly satisfactory. A heartier, happier tableful of friends had never gathered about Dr. Gilbert's board.

Dessert came on, and then Dr. Gilbert, according to

previous arrangement, said : " Arthur, these gentlemen came from New York to hear you preach yesterday, with a view to giving you a call to a new church which they have been instrumental in gathering in their city. We have fairly entrapped you, and now I shall let them speak for themselves."

Arthur smiled. No shadow of surprise passed over his features. He was as cool and collected as possible.

" You receive the news as if it were an every-day affair," said Miss Gilbert.

" It is not news," Arthur replied.

" Who told you ? "

" My good friend Tom Lampson, the conductor, who said," continued Arthur, laughing, " that he could tell a pack of minister-hunters as readily as he could a bridal party."

There was a general laugh, at the expense of the " pack ; " the " pack " itself joining very heartily in it.

" Well," said Mr. Sargent, " as we understand one another, we may as well proceed to business." Then he revealed the nature of the enterprise in which he proposed to engage Arthur Blague. He and his companions had been members of an old, overgrown, lazy church, full of inert material, and so crowded with men and money that it could not stir. In fact, it had become a very slow institution—one in which they could not feel at home at all. They wanted more work, and had accordingly swarmed, with a large number of the younger portion of the church and congregation, and, " roping in " a goodly company of others, belonging to different societies, had built a new church edifice, organized, and got ready for operations. They had all " bled " profusely, and proposed to bleed to any desirable extent for the success of the enterprise. All they wanted was a minister. There were plenty of ministers in the market, but they were all slow. Mr. Sargent, for himself, and on behalf of his associates, wished to express his entire satisfaction with the young man who preached for them the previous day, and to institute some practicable measures for getting him to New York.

Thus the business was opened for discussion. There was no more levity among the members of the deeply interested group. The "Committee of Supply" had made its decision, and they were ready to talk in earnest. They did talk in earnest. Arthur presented the difficulties in the way of his leaving Crampton for the present, and they set themselves vigorously to work to bear them down. At last, he felt himself compelled to compromise with them. He would accept no call from them ; but if, in the course of the winter, he could leave his brother long enough, he would preach for them a few Sabbaths ; and then, if they did not change their mind, and the congregation seconded them, he would agree to consider a call.

Miss Gilbert was ready in a moment. "You can go any time when you will, and I will assist your mother in taking care of Jamie," said she.

At this, they all rose from the table, and returned to the parlor. There Mr. Sargent took Arthur by the button-hole, and enlarged upon the desirableness of the situation to which they invited him, and the field of usefulness that would be opened to him, assuring him that he would find in Moustache and Breastpin a pair of the most splendid workers in New York. Then Moustache took him by the button-hole, and assured him that he would look after his health, giving him an airing every day on the Avenue, if he liked it, after a horse that had constitutional objections to being passed on the way. He closed by assuring him that Frank Sargent and Breastpin were the most efficient and desirable men in a church that it was possible to conceive. When Moustache relinquished the young minister, the vacated button-hole was seized by Breastpin, who told him how reluctantly he had come to see him, how much and how happily he had been disappointed, how sorry he was to leave Crampton, how he could not go unless Arthur accompanied him, how he hoped at no distant day to make the acquaintance of Mrs. Arthur Blague—their new minister's wife—how he—Breastpin—must not be taken by Arthur as a fair specimen of the church, what a fine building they had to worship in, and how, had it not been for Frank Sargent and Moustache, the enterprise never could have succeeded in the world.

There was no escaping these importunities without a definite promise of some kind, and it was finally given. Fanny having agreed to share with Mrs. Blague the care of the invalid boy, Arthur promised to be in New York on the following Sabbath, and to spend a few weeks in the city, meeting the people, examining for himself the condition of their enterprise, and leaving all permanent arrangements for the future to the indications of Providence.

It lacked but a quarter of an hour of the time for the departure of the afternoon train. No sooner was the decision declared, than the New Yorkers, having accomplished their business, made their hasty adieus. Frank Sargent ran up-stairs, packed his valise, came down, kissed Fanny and Aunt Catharine, said " God bless you " to the doctor, and ran for the station-house. Moustache and Breastpin flew to the hotel, paid their bills, seized their carpet-bags and shawls, ran to the depot, swung themselves upon the last platform as the train moved off, greeted Frank Sargent with a cordial " hullo ! " as they took the seats he had reserved for them, and all commenced their homeward journey in high spirits. They talked all the way to New York, Moustache leaving the car several times on the road, and coming back from certain interesting conferences with the baggage-master, smelling of smoke ; and the next morning all were immersed in business, as if nothing unusual had occurred.

They left their acquaintances in Crampton—especially Arthur Blague—with sufficient food for reflection. To tell the truth, his heart leaped within him as he caught a glimpse of the work thus opened to him. To take his stand in the metropolis of the country, among the best minds of the age, where mental food and stimulus abounded, seemed to him a great privilege. But little Jamie! What could he do, if tied to him there ?

Arthur had seen enough of men to know himself. He had no misgivings touching his power to sustain himself among the competitions of city life. The only considerations that drew him back from entering the door thus invitingly thrown open to him related to his brother and his mother. He could do what he had agreed to do, at least, and God would take care of the rest.

Toward the last of the week, Arthur having made his arrangements, left Crampton for New York. He tried to explain to Jamie that he should be gone for a long, long time ; and Jamie either understood his language, or correctly interpreted his affectionate parting. The little fellow seemed to be sadly impressed, but tried to smile upon Fanny as she took him in her arms. He watched his brother from the window, as he walked to the station-house ; and when he disappeared, went into a paroxysm of difficult breathing that quite frightened Fanny.

It would be weary work to tell of the weary work of the following month, in the house of Mrs. Blague. As the days came and went, and Arthur did not return, the invalid boy seemed to sink into sick and hopeless discouragement. The voice of a man in the hall below— the sudden opening of a door—would excite his expectations for a moment, and then he would shut his eyes to hide his emotions. When the train came in, day after day, and he saw the passengers passing through the street, his straining, eager eyes would watch until all passed out of sight ; and then they would close again, and the breath that had been half-suspended would come with redoubled difficulty.

To Fanny, these weeks were weeks of trial. A single afternoon spent with the boy when she first saw him had tired her ; but when, day after day, she subjected herself to his service, the task often seemed unendurable. Yet she felt that the discipline was necessary to her. She desired, above all things, to seat herself within the secret of Arthur Blague's life and strength. She longed to forget herself in devotion to others, until benevolence should become the supreme expression of her life. As the days went by, she felt her task growing easier. She was with the invalid during the day, but at night she relinquished him to his mother, and she could not deny to herself the fact that, every evening, as she walked homeward, she had won peace and satisfaction from the toil of the day. She felt, too, springing up in her heart, a love for the afflicted boy which she had never expected to feel ; and learned how, out of compassion, and pity, and ministry, love for the forbidding is born.

At last, a letter was received from Arthur by Mrs. Blague, fixing the day for his return. They did not try to explain the matter to Jamie until the welcome morning, and then they told him that Arthur would be at home before night. The news wrought a great change in him. He was excited, and exceedingly happy. Smiles played upon his face all day, and his mother testified that he was more comfortable than he had been for years. His eyes were very bright, and when the long whistle of the incoming train reached his ear, he became almost hysterical with joy. As the passengers left the train, he caught a distant view of Arthur's form,

and the little, misshapen arm swung wildly to and fro
with his intense excitement. He watched him as he approached, his little chest laboring heavily for breath,
and when he heard his steps in the hall, he sank back
upon Fanny's arm to wait the coming of the form and
face for which he had pined so long. Arthur entered
the room, threw himself upon his knees by the side of
the boy, took him in his arms, and pressed his face to
his. There he held him for a moment, and then suddenly put him away. The cords of life—so long tense
—had snapped. A heavenly smile was on the face of
the child, but the laboring muscles were still. Jamie
had died of joy. Happy death ! Thrice happy in that
his mission to the earth was fulfilled !

When manhood, in the pride of its power, and in the
midst of its unfinished enterprises, is suddenly laid in
the arms of death, and loving women and little children
are left without a protector, grief and pity are called
to their profoundest exercise. When budding woman
fades like a flower, and is carried out to sleep with flowers upon her bosom, those among whom she grew are
touched with an ineffably tender sympathy and sorrow.
Grief and tears for such as these the world understands ;
yet when some poor sufferer—some patient bearer of
the cross, climbing painfully up the rising years—gives
up the ghost, no darkness comes upon the world, and
no veil is rent in the temple of the world's heart. Men
say, " We cannot weep. It would be wrong to weep.
We should rejoice that a life so full of pain is ended—
that suffering is swallowed up of everlasting peace and
joy."

This was what the people of Crampton said about
the death of Jamie Blague. A hundred pairs of lungs
breathed easier because his lungs had ceased to labor.
A hundred hearts beat more freely and happily because
his had stopped. Those who loved Arthur, were glad

little Jamie was dead—not because they were hard-hearted, but because they were tender-hearted.

But to Arthur the extinction of this painful little life was like the going down of the sun. It left him in darkness. In the first hour of his grief, he held him in his arms, kissing his lifeless lips, and breathing out upon him the wealth of his affection in endearing names and tender expressions. Mrs. Blague was helpless under this new calamity—the more so from the fact that Arthur was unmanned. Fanny regarded the scene with mingled awe and grief. She recognized, at once, the hand of Providence in the event. The boy had done his work for Arthur and for her; and when it was finished, God had taken him. What a teacher had he been to her!

Finding herself the only one able to perform the necessary offices relating to the child, she prepared his couch, and then, kneeling before Arthur, she gently disengaged the little body from his hands, and bore it to the pillow on which it had breathed out so many nights of pain. There she smoothed his hair, and composed his limbs, and left him, with the same sweet smile upon his features that lighted his passage into the land of rest. Returning to her home, she bore the sad news of the event to Aunt Catharine and the other members of the family. In a few minutes afterward, the facts had found their way into the village, and willing hands came in abundance to assist the family in their sad emergency.

When Fanny returned to the room of death, she found Arthur kneeling at his brother's bedside, gazing into the sweet, dead face. He rose to his feet as she approached, and said, " Let us go down."

The will that had submitted so long and so many times to the Will supreme, had bowed, and he was calm. The first shock past, there was to be no repining. He had gone down into the deep waters of grief, with the little foundered bark, but had risen and laid hold upon the life-boat. The sea still tossed beneath him ; and rent and broken affections were strewn upon its surface, but heaven was blue above him, and full of stars.

The next day a little coffin was brought into the house, and the day following that, there was a funeral. The house was filled in every part, and though the air was biting, and the snow was drifting outside, the yard was crowded with people. After a prayer was made and a hymn sung, Arthur himself read from Paul's letter to the Corinthians those wonderful revelations touching the resurrection of the body which have been repeated in the ears of so many Christian mourners. It was with a voice full of emotion that he pronounced the words : " It is sown in corruption, it is raised in incorruption ; it is sown in dishonor, it is raised in glory ; it is sown in weakness, it is raised in power."

" I thank God for little Jamie," said Arthur, as he closed the book. " His feet were taken from him here that mine might be trained to walk in the ways of righteousness. His hands were palsied that mine might be taught to give themselves in service to the weak and the helpless. His body was racked with pain that I might drink deeply of the cup of self-denial ; but the little body—so feeble and misshapen—which we sow to-day, shall rise in immortal power and beauty. Then shall I have him in my arms again, and then shall we, his lips unsealed, thank God together."

Arthur expressed his gratitude to the assembly for the sympathy that had been extended to his mother and to him, and for the multiplied acts of kindness rendered to the little sleeper during his painful life. He intimated that his continuance in Crampton would be of short duration—that the work of life for which he had been so long in preparation would soon be commenced in another home. The only obstacle to his removal God had taken out of the way, and he accepted the event as the indication of his duty.

The little boy was borne out to the graveyard, to take his place by the side of his father and the little brothers and sisters who had long been dust. The sand was shovelled back, and as the silent multitude moved away, and separated, the snow came down, and covered all the spot with its mantle of white.

Arthur walked into his still house, his mother leaning upon his arm, feeling, for the moment, as if the work of his life had been taken from his hands. He wandered through the silent rooms, and paced up and down his study, unable, in the strange circumstances in which he found himself, to take up a book, or to engage himself in any mental exercise. He sat down in his old seat, took up his Bible, opened it, and read the first passage upon which his eye fell—" Rise, let us be going."

He cast his eyes upward, and said : " Lord, I am ready."

CHAPTER XXVI.

DESCRIBING AN EVENT OF THE GREATEST INTEREST TO ARTHUR BLAGUE, FANNY GILBERT, AND THE READER.

ARTHUR thought he was ready to go ; but he was not. Both his circumstances and his feelings held him back. When he thought of dislocating himself from all the associations of his life—of selling off the old house, in which his whole life had been passed, of taking his mother to a new home, of leaving his early friends, and, particularly, of parting with one toward whom he felt himself attracted with constantly increasing power—his heart sank within him. Besides, the shock he had received staggered him more than he was aware. Under the strength of his first rebound from the blow that had laid him low, he thought he was ready for his work; but there came upon him a reaction from the other direction. His life had flowed in one channel too long to be suddenly diverted. He found that there was a certain preparation to be effected. He must get accustomed to his new outlook upon life. Before he could work with what strength there was in him, his powers and sympathies must be harmonized by a process which time could only complete.

It has been more than hinted that the first interview that Arthur enjoyed with Miss Gilbert, after her return from New York, made a profound impression upon him. For a long time, he feared to have that impression renewed. Years previously he had determined, in his own mind, that the brilliant woman would not be a suitable wife for a minister—nor for him. Her aims were not his; her motives were not his. But he had caught a view of the better side of her character, and it had charmed him. Afterward, he had been a quiet, deeply interested observer of her life, and the strong masculine traits that she often betrayed offended him, and produced a reaction in his feelings. Her fearlessness, her self-confidence, her love of masculine, out-of-door life, her daring drives, and the genuine business spirit with which she came into contact with men in the management of her father's affairs, gave him pain. It seemed as if she were one woman to him, and another to everybody else.

Yet the events of the study, and her ready service during his absence, had changed his mind; as she changed, his feelings changed; and he had begun to feel that there was something in her and in her society which he needed. He dwelt upon all her acts of kindness to little Jamie and his mother—upon the delicate sympathy she had extended to him—upon the faculty she had to stimulate and fructify his thoughts—and he felt his admiration of her merging into a sentiment that was deeper and more tender.

He had already apprised his New York friends of the death of his brother, and informed them that the event would probably defer somewhat a definite reply to their invitation. So, as he had pushed this decision further from his thought, and as the changes through which he had passed had, in a degree, unfitted him for study, he found himself, as the weeks passed on, irresistibly led into Fanny Gilbert's society. He studied her instead of his books—studied her, too, with entire absence of weariness ; for he found in process of development within her a new style of life. She had become his pupil. She sat before him like a child, asked him questions, led him by her strange tact out into the field where he had his best life, explored his motives and his sources of strength, searched him through and through for that which would give her food and guidance. Many precious hours did Arthur pass with her in these conversations ; and, as he was not unfrequently invited by Mr. Wilton to preach, many were the sermons which he preached to her.

The winter had broken up, and still Arthur lingered in Crampton, unable to speak the word that should cut him off from his old home, and transfer him to his new sphere of labor. Fanny, meantime, had conceived such a reverence for her friend, and had become so profoundly impressed with his superiority and her own unfitness to be his companion, that she fought against every suggestion that she could ever become his wife. She was his disciple. She was learning of him how to live worthily. She could not but think, at times, how sweet it would be to be the acknowledged mistress of such a heart as his, and to repose in the shadow of such a nature and such a character ; but, the more she thought of this the more unworthy she seemed to herself of occupying so precious a place.

Again came the still, bright days when nature, like an infant just awakened from a long, oblivious sleep, lay with open eyes, looking silently upward, and waiting the breezy footsteps and the sweet kisses of the motherly spring. Again Fanny Gilbert sat at her window, as on that spring day many years before, when " Tristram Trevanion " was in manuscript, and Mary Hammett was teaching the little children in the school-house across the common. She thought of the changes that had passed over her since then—not only over her, but over all who were dear to her. She recalled the feelings she had indulged in with relation to Arthur—feelings which she used to express to Mary. She had once, in her girlish pride and ignorance, despised the boy who could so easily subject himself to the lives of others. She had thought him girlish; but now she comprehended the fact that it had been through womanly offices that he had won the grandest characteristics of his manhood ; while she, having run through her life of ambition, achieved her aims, and had her career, had come back to learn of Arthur Blague how to be a woman, and how to be happy.

That night she received a call which surprised and puzzled her. Mr. Thomas Lampson, the conductor, was announced, with a request that he might see Miss Gilbert alone. He seemed to be a good deal embarrassed, and found himself obliged, at last, to draw forth from his pocket a package of railroad checks, and to reassure himself by rasping the end of it with his thumbnail.

"The fact is, Miss Gilbert," said he, desperately,

"that I have been feeling mighty mean over a little something I said to you once. I feel meaner and meaner the more I hear about you, and I've come here to-night to have it squared off. I can't go on so any longer. I got myself so worked up about it, that I lay awake half of last night thinking it over; and I told my wife if I lived to make another trip, I'd have the thing settled, if it killed me."

"Why! what can you mean?" said Fanny, with a smile of wonder.

"Haven't you got any thing laid up against me?" inquired the conductor.

"Nothing."

"Don't you remember the little chat we had when you came back from New York?"

"Very well; but there was nothing unpleasant in it to me."

"Well, there was to me," said Tom Lampson, "and I'm going to get rid of the whole of it. I told you there wasn't a woman in the world good enough for Arthur Blague, and you took it up. Well, I didn't mean to do any thing wrong, but when you turned on me. and I tried to paddle off, I meant you—inside you know—I saw you read me like a book."

"Oh! I never laid that up against you," said Miss Gilbert, good-naturedly. "Besides, what you said was true, as I have learned since."

"Well, I want to take the whole thing back. I've heard all about what you did for Widow Blague's little cripple when Arthur was gone—how you stuck to him, and tended him, and how kind you was to the old woman, and I felt meaner than beans about it. I spoke to Arthur about you the other day, and the tears came into his eyes as quick as wink. So says I to myself, if Fanny Gilbert has got hold of him, she's right. You know I swear by him straight through; and I came here to-

25

night for nothing under heavens but to tell you that I think there is one woman in the world good enough for him. Haven't you—ah—sort o' altered? Don't you think it's kind o' done you good to—O Lord! here I am, getting into hot water again!"

Fanny could not help laughing and shedding tears at the same time. "I hope I am altered somewhat," said she—"altered for the better—and I am not at all offended by your allusion to the fact."

"Well, people talk about it, you know," said Tom Lampson; "and I got it out before I thought what was coming. Don't you s'pose Arthur will go to New York?"

"I think he intends to go, though he has never told me so definitely."

"What is he waiting for?"

"I'm sure I cannot tell. He has business to close, I suppose, and you know he has been a good deal depressed by the death of the little boy."

Mr. Lampson sat half a minute rasping his cheeks. Then, looking Fanny innocently in the eyes, he said: "*I* think he means to get married before he goes. It's the general talk about town, I find. People have got the notion somehow. Do you know anything about it?"

"Nothing. How should I? Whom do people imagine he is going to marry?"

The conductor regarded her with a very shrewd, arch look, which was intended to bring a blush to her face, but which did not move her at all. "Well," said he, rising suddenly to his feet, "you are too much for me, Miss Gilbert; I can't hoe my row at all with you. All I've got to say is, that I want to be all right with both sides of the family. Whatever happens, I don't want to have any hard feelings toward Tom Lampson."

"You talk in enigmas."

"I presume I do. I'm always saying something out of the way, and it is time I was getting along."

Tom Lampson backed out of the room, bade Miss Gilbert good-night, then came back and shook hands with her, then expressed his regret for having given her so much trouble, and finally departed.

Fanny did not know what to make of all this, though it appeared that the people were talking about a match between her and Arthur, and that Tom Lampson, a devoted friend and admirer of Arthur, wished to intimate to her that he had no objection to it. While she was thinking of this, the door-bell rang, and immediately Arthur Blague was shown into the parlor. Fanny blushed crimson the moment she looked into his face, as if she supposed he could read her thoughts, and as if those thoughts were guilty. For several weeks she had felt self-distrustful in his presence, and now she was quite embarrassed. She could not talk, but listened to him as if she were a child, of whom no demonstration was expected.

Though oppressed by a degree of timidity, and suffering from that sense of insignificance very common among genuine lovers, Arthur could not but read her heart. He saw that a few weeks had wrought a great change in her, and he would have been very stupid had he failed to interpret it aright. As he looked upon her in her altered mood and bearing, he felt his own strong nature, so long held in check, going out to her with a fresh and hearty tenderness.

Fanny found her tongue at last. Taking up the subject suggested by Tom Lampson's visit, she inquired of Arthur when it was his intention to go to New York.

"I have not told you I should go at all," replied Arthur.

"I know—but you will go."

"I suppose I shall, but it is harder than I ever dreamed it would be, to leave Crampton."

"I hope you will go; I think you ought to go. They

want you so very much," said Miss Gilbert, in explanation of her decided opinion upon the subject. "Mary Sargent," she continued, "has written to me an account of all your successes there, and the strong desire of the church for your return."

"They are easily pleased," said Arthur vacantly.

"Then I am sure you ought to be."

"Since my friends here are so willing to have me leave them," said Arthur.

Miss Gilbert blushed, bit her lip, and dropped her eyes before the questioning gaze that Arthur gave them. "Your friends here," said she, "desire to see you in the place where you belong, engaged in doing the work which you are so well calculated and prepared to perform."

"Then you really wish to have me leave Crampton?"

"Mr. Blague," said Fanny earnestly, "you cannot misunderstand me, when I tell you most sincerely that I do. Your work is not here; and though you will take from my life that which I can poorly afford to spare, you will deprive thousands, by remaining, of that which will be of inestimable value to them."

Arthur's eyes grew luminous. "It is hard," said he, "to cut loose forever from this old retreat, and cast my life among strangers."

"They will soon cease to be strangers, and laboring for them, you will quickly learn to love them. Then think what a life lies before you!—great, it seems to me —great beyond comparison. Think of twenty-five years of labor in such a city as New York. Think of bringing your mind into contact with a hundred thousand minds in those twenty-five years, with the privilege of urging upon them the motives of your own life—of inculcating purity, and truth, and goodness—of pronouncing the name of God over the brows of multitudes of little children—of joining a whole generation of young men and women in marriage—of ministering consolation to the dying—of speaking words of comfort to a world of mourners—of quickening the intellects of masses of men—of emptying your own life, to the last drop, into the life of the world, flavoring your age and race, and enriching the blood of immortality itself. Think how, day after day, men in doubt and darkness, and women in fear, will come to you for guidance and for strength—how, Sabbath after Sabbath, they will throng to hear your voice, and go away the better for hearing it—how thousands of hearts will cling to yours by a myriad twining sympathies, rejoicing in your presence, and aching in your absence, and praying for you always."

Arthur's lip quivered, and he could hardly control his emotions as the eloquent woman unveiled her estimate of his office and its privileges. He knew that she did not see the other side of the picture, yet he knew that she saw one side of it correctly. But it was the revelation of her heart and mind which interested him the most deeply, for all that she had said had passed through his thoughts before. He had come to the conclusion that, personally, she was not altogether indifferent to him ; and when, in fervent and well-chosen words, she magnified his office, and betrayed her sympathy with the great aims of his life, he was thrilled with a new joy.

" Since you think this life so great and so desirable," said he, drawing his chair nearer to her, " how would you like to share it ? "

" What, sir ? " Miss Gilbert trembled and grew pale.

" How would you like to share it ? "

Fanny could not, or would not understand, but sat in dumb wonder, looking into the earnest face before her. Her eloquence was all gone ; her lips were sealed.

Arthur pitied her confusion, and reproached himself for his awkwardness and his stupid abruptness. He drew his chair still nearer to her, and took her unresisting hand. "Miss Gilbert," said he, "there is but one tie that binds me to this place. As you say, my life and my work are not here. I believe this, yet my heart is here. It has been here—been bound here—more than I was aware—more than I was willing to acknowledge to myself—since I first met you on your return home. This confession must be made, and it may as well be made now as ever, if you will hear it. I offer you not only a share in the work of my life, which you estimate so highly, but I offer you my heart and my hand. Will you take me? Will you become my companion? Will you walk this golden road with me? Will you be my wife, and go with me whither God leads me?"

Arthur said this strongly and impetuously, pressing her hand with unconscious ardor, and looking in her face as if he would read every thought and emotion that struggled upward for expression. The strong woman was weak. The blue eyes were suffused. She bowed before the will that looked through the eyes of the young minister, and the strength of the passion that breathed in his voice. There was a long minute of silence, in which they could hear the beat, and feel the jar, of one another's hearts. At last, she looked up tremblingly, with an expression of undissembled pain, and, saying, "I am so unworthy—so unworthy," burst into tears.

"So am I."

Both rose by a common impulse to their feet. There was no secret beyond. They were lovers. Fanny Gilbert, the ambitious Fanny Gilbert, the brilliant authoress, the courted and admired woman, now gentle, yielding, humble, grateful, and glad, was pressed to the strong man's heart. In that precious embrace, thrilled with satisfaction through all her gentler nature, she found herself at home. Henceforth there was nothing in fame for her. The little world around her, thronged with its pigmy millions, could not charm her out from that great world of the affections into which she had entered, and in which she reigned alone. A great man wholly hers! What had the world for her more than this? What had the world for any woman more than this? Like a ship long tossing on the ocean, driven hither and thither by fitful winds, now creeping among sunken rocks, and now careering proudly over the obedient waves, yet always restless, she furled her life's broad sails in this still haven, dropped anchor, and was at rest.

In the brief hour that followed this denouement, these richly-endowed natures and accordant hearts, that had been tending toward each other through such dissimilar and widely separated paths for many years, became one—one in affection, sympathy, purpose, and destiny. Arm in arm they stood, wrapped in present joy, and calmly fronting the life of labor and self-denial that lay before them. Each, self-relinquished to the other, and both to heaven, they received and appropriated heaven and each other in return, so that with the new influx of life, and love, and happiness, they felt ready for any work to which duty might call them. Into that sanctuary of love, and into that hour of love's first bliss, came no echo of the world's discordant voices. A noble man and a noble woman had received the choicest treasure the earth had for them. In the first consciousness of sudden wealth—in the first experience of possession— it seemed as if their joy and peace filled the earth—as if the great world of life into which they had entered had blotted out the world around them—or rather, as if they stood upon the pinnacle of life, and all beneath was commonplace and poor.

At length, by some accident that not unfrequently occurs in interviews of this character, Miss Gilbert's head leaned against the young minister's breast. It was a very pretty sight indeed, particularly if the observer definitely understood the relations of the parties. Aunt Catharine did not; and when, without being aware of Arthur's presence in the house, she came silently down stairs, and suddenly into the room, her eyes took in this very remarkable and unusual vision, she stood the impersonation of bewildered wonder.

"What—under—the—sun—moon—and—stars!" exclaimed Aunt Catharine, at length.

The lovers were both embarrassed, but Arthur first achieved self-control. Fanny blushed to the tips of her ears, while Arthur took her hand, and led her directly before the astonished intruder. Looking Aunt Catharine pleasantly in the face, he said: "Have you any objection?"

"Now you don't mean—"

"I do."

"That you have been—"

"Yes."

"And gone—"

"Certainly."

"And done that?"

"Just as true as you live."

Aunt Catharine threw herself into a rocking-chair, and rocked herself, and cried like a child. The lovers were somewhat puzzled by this demonstration, but they sat down near her, and the good old spinster soon found her tongue, and explained herself.

"I didn't believe—I never believed—that those prayers of your mother, Fanny, would be forgotten. I've always felt as if the Lord was looking after you, because I couldn't think he'd forget such a prayer as your mother offered with her very last breath. I've been praying for just exactly this thing for six weeks; but I didn't expect the Lord would answer me—I didn't;" and then Aunt Catharine buried her face in her handkerchief, and cried again.

" Then you've no objection ? " said Arthur.

" Objection !   Goodness !   If the Lord hasn't any objection on your account, I'm sure I haven't any on Fanny's."

Then, by a sudden revulsion in her feelings, she began to laugh half-hysterically, and then they all laughed together.

" Now," said Aunt Catharine, " you have got to go into the office, and see the doctor, and I am going with you."

Arthur hesitated and remonstrated.   This was no joke ; and it seemed a rude way of approaching so delicate a subject as asking for the person of a child.

But Aunt Catharine was excited, and could not understand how a great, joyful fact, such as this was to her, could call for delicate treatment—in that house, at least. So she put Fanny's arm in that of Arthur, took the other herself, and, listening to no remonstrances, led them into the office and into the presence of Dr. Gilbert.

" Here is a young man," said Aunt Catharine mercilessly, " who has been abusing his privileges in this house, and taking things that don't belong to him."

The doctor looked up from his newspaper, through his spectacles, with a questioning gaze, evidently conscious that something unusual was going on, but entirely at a loss as to its nature.   He rose from his chair, took Arthur's hand, inquired for his health, and invited him to be seated.   Arthur declined the seat, held to the doctor's hand, and said :

" I am hardly responsible, Dr. Gilbert, for appearing here on my present errand, with this apparent levity."

" Hem ! " from Aunt Catharine.

Arthur turned upon his tormentor an appealing look, but she was laughing behind her hand.

" Oh ! never mind her nonsense," said the doctor ; " but what is your errand ? "

"Did I ever ask many favors of you, doctor?"

"Never half enough: glad if I can do any thing for you. Tell me what it is, and you shall have it, even to the half of my kingdom."

"I want just half of your kingdom," replied Arthur; and, taking Fanny's hand, he led her forward, and said: "I want, I need, I love your daughter. Will you give her to me?"

"What does she say about it? Can't you speak, girl?"

"I think," said Arthur, smiling, "that if you have nothing to say against the transfer, she and I can arrange the rest."

The doctor took off his glasses and wiped them, and looked benignantly upon the pair before him. Then he turned, and walked away from them, and cleared his throat, and blew his nose. Then he came back, and his face became red, and his throat grew worse and worse. At last, he made an impatient gesture, and blurted out, "Oh! God bless you! God bless you! Go along;" and then turned and looked into the fire. Fanny, who had not uttered a word, went to his side, kissed him, and the group turned, and left him to master his new difficulty of the throat as he best might.

The next day the engagement was announced, and such a lively day of talk Crampton had never enjoyed before. There were many, of course, to find fault with the match, but, as the parties most interested were satisfied, that did not matter. The next day, too, Arthur wrote a letter to the "Committee of Supply" in New York, accepting the invitation to the pastorate of the new church. In a private note to Mr. Frank Sargent, Arthur informed him of his engagement to Miss Gilbert, at which there was great joy in the house of the Sargents, and among a multitude of Fanny's old acquaintances, who had become aware of the change in her character and purposes. In fact, the matter got into the New York papers, which, following the example of the Athenians, (ancient Athenians,) "spend their time in nothing else but either to tell or to hear some new thing." It was publicly stated that "Rev. Arthur Blague, a young man of the most promising genius, had accepted the call of —— Church," and that rumor had it that he was soon to be united in marriage to no less a personage than the brilliant writer of " Rhododendron."

Mr. Thomas Lampson, the popular and gentlemanly conductor, etc., etc., was probably quite as much delighted with the arrangement as any of his neighbors ; and, having had a hand (in his opinion) in bringing his friends together, he next procured a pair of passes to New York, from the president of the railroad corporation, and sent them to Arthur, as a slight inducement for him to reply favorably to his New York call.

CHAPTER XXVII.

WHICH CHANGES THE RELATIONS OF SOME OF OUR CHARACTERS, RELATES THE CHANGES OF OTHERS, AND CLOSES THE BOOK.

LIFE with our Crampton friends did not linger : why should its story be prolonged ?

Arthur felt and acted as if the power of another soul had been added to his own. He was in no mood for love's dalliance and dissipation. The sense of loneliness which once oppressed him, as he tried to front the life to which he had been called, was gone, and, with the companionship which had been pledged to him, he felt prepared for any labor and all sacrifice. The past was a long dream of toil and trial into which his memory flowed

with ineffable tenderness ; the future, a bright reality of
love, beneficence, and fruition.   He longed to immerse
himself in the life that was already dashing at his feet,
as a strong swimmer, standing upon the ocean's beach,
longs to plunge into the waves, and drown the restless
fever of his powers.   The long subordination of his being past, every faculty of his soul sprang into positive
life and demonstration.

Toward her new life, Fanny proceeded tremblingly.
Her self-confidence relinquished, she turned to him to
whom she had pledged herself, for guidance and encouragement.   It was a strange thing to her, that in her feeling of dependence there was no sense of humiliation—
no loss of self-respect—that in this feeling she found a
degree of joy, and rest, and strength, to which she had
hitherto been a stranger.   She had lost her habitual self-
seeking—lost her imperious will—gladly laid down her
proud self-reliance, and found her womanhood.   In after
months and years, she learned, through feeding the
springs of a man's power, enriching the food of his life,
purifying his motives, encouraging his efforts, and filling
his heart with love, what were her true relations to manhood.   She learned that man and woman are one—that
neither man nor woman can lead a manly life alone—
that the noblest manhood must draw its vital elements
from womanhood, and that all the strong and masculine
demonstrations of her own life had been bald and barren.   She learned that man holds in his constitution the
element of power—the basis of all demonstrative public
functions—and that, by the degree in which woman possesses this element, is she exceptional, even if she be
not abnormal.

She learned, too, that this characteristically masculine element of power, unsoftened, unregulated, unpuri-
fied, unfructified by the characteristic elements of womanhood, or the discipline of womanhood, is a blind,

selfish, unfruitful force, dissociated altogether from goodness, and lacking the essential qualities of humanity. She learned that the power of Arthur Blague was a good power through the womanly subordination of his early life, and that the noblest function of her life was to sit in the place of that early discipline, and inform and inspire the demonstrations of his manhood by her own ministry of womanly love and tenderness. When her life had become fully blended into unity with his, she learned that a woman's truest career is lived in love's serene retirement—lived in feeding the native forces of her other self—lived in the career of her husband.

But we are getting along faster than our lovers. Arthur's engagement to Fanny, and the changes which it involved, were not without very important relations to their respective families. The question as to what should become of Arthur's mother, though troubling her not a little, did not amount to a question with Arthur. The man was not a less dutiful son than the boy. He determined that, wherever he might go, his mother should accompany him ; and, as it was hard for her to think of parting with the house in which she had lived so many years, Dr. Gilbert generously provided for its retention in her possession. It would be a good summer house, he said, for them all to occupy during the annual vacations.

So, unobtrusively, and with a crushing sense of her uselessness in the world, Mrs. Blague accustomed herself to the thought of removing to New York. Her life was hid in Arthur. All her pride, all her love, and all her earthly hope were in him.

Dr. Gilbert, though cordially approving Fanny's match, was quite overcome with the thought of losing her. The failure of his son to fulfil his early promise, and the change that had been wrought in his daughter, had effected a revolution in his feelings. In truth, now that

Arthur had been brought into such peculiar relations to him, he began to dwell upon his prospects in the same way that he formerly did upon those of Fred. It was but a few days before he was ready to talk of his' prospective son-in-law with all the ardor of an old and over-fond father.

Poor Fred! All this affected him deeply. Rest had done much for him, and he felt his strength slowly mending, but the removal of his sister was to him like the loss of a right eye. When he saw that he was to be left alone, stranded upon a barren home ; when he saw how his father's interest in him was abated—how that interest had been transferred to others—he was very sad.

But this did not last. He saw how soon the care of his father's affairs must come into his hands, or pass into those of strangers, and the consideration awoke him to new life. Renouncing forever his studies and all ambition for distinction, he set himself about business— taking Fanny's place in doing his father's correspondence, and mingling in out-of-door life, as he became strong enough for it.

The gossips of Crampton, though busy with their inquiries, could find out nothing relating to the approaching wedding. Fanny herself was puzzled about it quite as much as they, and was helped to a decision, at last, by a suggestion from her New York friend, Mary Sargent.

About this time, Mr. Lampson, the conductor, called to see Arthur Blague upon business. The superintendent of the road had been invited to a more desirable post in another corporation, and the conductor wanted the vacant place, and considered himself competent to fill it. He was sure Arthur could get the appointment for him, and Arthur promised to do his best for that end. Through Arthur's influence, or by means of his own excellent reputation, " the popular and gentlemanly conductor" was, a few days afterward, transformed into " the obliging and efficient superintendent."

When Thomas Lampson, Esq., called upon Arthur to inform him of his good fortune, it occurred to the latter, that, as his friend's salary had been materially increased, it was possible that his wants had been enlarged in a corresponding degree. So he proposed that when he should remove to New York, the new superintendent should take his wife over to the vacated house, and set up housekeeping—using the family furniture, and taking care of it, with a view to ultimately purchasing the whole establishment. The proposition pleased Mr. Lampson exceedingly. To become the master of Arthur Blague's mansion was a new and very grateful dignity, and the matter was finally arranged to the satisfaction of all parties.

On a bright May morning following this arrangement, there was a huge collection of trunks and boxes upon the piazza of Dr. Gilbert's house, and another pile equally large in front of Mrs. Blague's dwelling. There was also, at the station-house that morning, an unusually large number of young men and women, unprepared for a journey. They had come to witness a departure, and they did not wait long. The trunks and boxes were brought over upon a truck, and they were soon followed by the members of both families entire—Arthur and his mother, Fanny and Fred, and the doctor and Aunt Catharine. They were all going down to witness Arthur's ordination, at the invitation of Mr. Frank Sargent and his family. The group of townspeople closed around Arthur to bid him farewell, and to offer him a thousand good wishes. Fanny was adjured not to think of getting married before she returned, which, for some reason, brought a bright blush to her face.

The new superintendent of the road took the occasion to run over his line that morning, and relieve the party of the care of the luggage they had taken, besides making himself generally agreeable all the way. No conductor was allowed to invade the sacredness of that group by the call for tickets. As they approached the trunk-road that would separate them from Mr. Lampson's care, the superintendent invited Arthur to a private interview. They therefore took a seat together.

"You know," said Tom Lampson, "that I sent you a couple of New York passes, a while ago."

"Yes, and I was very thankful for them."

"You know, too, that I went to you to get a good word for me with the directors, when I wanted to be superintendent."

"Yes, and I was very much obliged to you for that."

"The two things weren't a great ways apart, were they?"

"No—why?"

"Did you think, because I sent you those infernal, little, contemptible passes, that I wanted to hire you to work for me?"

"Never! of course not."

"All right, then," said Mr. Lampson. "I was thinking about you last night, and this thing came across me, and I just kicked the clothes off, and jumped out of bed, and frightened my wife all but to death. The fact is, that I didn't know anything about the superintendent matter when I sent those passes—not a thing."

"My dear fellow, I didn't suppose you did," said Arthur, with a hearty smile. "So you have had all your trouble for nothing."

"Well, I was bound not to let you go away thinking that Tom Lampson was a mean man—giving things to his friends for the sake of getting work out of them. All square, is it?"

"Oh! you know it is, Tom," responded Arthur.

"Ever think of old times, Mr. Blague?" inquired Mr. Lampson, changing the subject. "Remember about mowing bushes, up in Ruggles' pasture? Things have changed some, haven't they?"

"I have thought of these things a great deal lately. The Lord has been very kind to me, and to you, too, Tom. Just think how prosperously you are getting along."

"I know it," responded Mr. Lampson, "and it's a rotten shame that I ain't pious; but I don't get at it, somehow. I mean to be, though, and I think I shall be. I vow I'd give a pile if I was only all through with that thing."

"Where there's a will there's a way, in religion, as in other things," replied Arthur.

"To tell you the truth about it," said Mr. Lampson, "I've always been hoping I should get converted under you. It don't seem as if Daddy Wilton could do anything for me. He don't stir me up a particle. I thought you'd fetch me once, but somehow it didn't stick."

Arthur could not help smiling at the strange conception of Christianity which had possession of the mind of his friend, but felt that he had no time then to enlighten him.

"If I don't get along," said Mr. Lampson, "you'll see me in New York. I ain't going to drop this thing, any way. I believe if I'd begun back, when you did, I might be a preacher now, myself. I tell you, religion does lots for a feller. It kind o' nourishes him all over, and all through. I told my wife the other day—says I, It's just like manure in a bed of roses. It ain't very pleasant, perhaps, when you first get hold of it, but it makes a feller grow—it does—it's true."

Arthur only had time to respond to Mr. Lampson's opinions touching the fertilizing influence of religion, and to give him a cordial exhortation to carry his good resolutions into effect, when the train was stopped, and the passengers were directed to change cars. Arthur bade the superintendent an affectionate farewell. The latter

26

saw the baggage of the company safely shifted, and then went about, looking under the cars, and up to the sky—anywhere but in the faces of his departing friends. As the train was about starting, he ran into the car, shook hands with them all, laughed all the time, jumped off, and waved his handkerchief, and then went away wiping his nose with it, and pretending to have a very ugly cinder in his eye.

That night the party slept in the spacious Kilgore mansion, of which Mary Sargent was the mistress. Poor Mrs. Blague moved like one in a dream. She had hardly expected to live to reach New York; and to be entertained in such magnificent style by her old boarder—the mistress of the Crampton Centre School—under such peculiar circumstances, seemed so unreal—so miraculous—that it oppressed her quite superstitiously. A day or two, however, sufficed to give her command of her scattered senses, and she soon began to enjoy the change of scenery and circumstances to which her journey had introduced her.

Very interesting rumors were in circulation in the church to whose pastorate Arthur had been called—rumors which found their way out into the circles in which the popular authoress of " Rhododendron " had moved in former years. The audience that assembled to witness the ordination exercises was remarkably large. Many were at a loss to imagine why such a crowd should be collected, even in the great city, on such an occasion. The seats were not only all filled, but the aisles were crowded with patiently standing men and women.

There were, at least, three deeply interested witnesses of the simple and impressive ceremonials by which Arthur Blague was set apart to the office of the Christian ministry, and inaugurated as pastor of the new church—Mrs. Blague, Mary Sargent, and Fanny

Gilbert. As he stood before them, calm, and firm, and self-possessed, his eye bright with the full strength of manhood, a thousand sympathetic hearts beating around him, and a great career lying before him, tears filled their eyes, and all their sensibilities were flooded with excitement, as if they were moved by the inspiration of eloquence or poetry.

At the close of the exercises of the occasion, while the audience waited for the accustomed benediction, Arthur descended from the pulpit, and made his way, unattended, down the broad aisle to the pew where Fanny Gilbert sat with her friends. He opened the door, bowed with a pleasant smile to Fanny, who rose, took his arm, and advanced with him to the chancel, where a white-haired old pastor awaited them. There the career of Miss Gilbert ended, and the career of Mrs. Arthur Blague began. There, in the presence of Arthur's people, did she give herself to him and to them. The old pastor gave them and the congregation his benison, and a multitude of friends pressed forward to make the acquaintance of their new pastor and his wife. Among those who came around the interesting pair, were several of Fanny's old friends, who welcomed her back with abundant joy. Mr. Frank Sargent took the occasion to be very busy. There were several persons present whom he wanted in the church, and whom he had thus far failed to "rope in." These were brought forward and introduced to the Rev. Mr. Blague and his wife, and treated with all that consideration which their uncertain position demanded.

———

Thus, for the purification of the great city, was another rill of the healthful country life poured into it. Thus, in God's loving and far-seeing providence, was brought to its terminal link that long concatenation of trial and sorrow, of struggle and disappointment, of patient waiting and faithful working, of sickness and death, which has formed the staple of this story. Into these two lives, prepared for great purposes, had been poured abundant experiences. For them had others unconsciously lived. Even the proprietor of Huckle-bury Run, and the man who robbed him both of his money and his daughter, were made tributary to the grand result. With frames which only country breeding can build, with broad and fruitful natures, with power to labor, and with determined will and purpose, they gave themselves to the city—a contribution to those conservative and recuperative forces of city life, ever-more country-born, which make progress possible, and which alone save that life from fatal degradation and final extinction.

Thenceforward they became dispensers rather than receivers. Hitherto, events had ended in them—little rivulets of experience, running in from wide distances, had found in them their termination ; plans of life had exhausted their material on reaching them ; plots had unravelled themselves at their feet. Now, prepared for their destiny and their ministry, the stream of benefi-cence went out from them, and grew broader as it flowed. Crampton life, which had seemed so poor, in-significant, hard, and barren, blossomed in New York into consummate beauty, and shook with its burden of fruit like Lebanon. We shall hear of that fruit in the " harvest-home " of the angel-reapers.

There was a midsummer gathering but a few years ago at the old Gilbert mansion. Dr. Gilbert and Mrs. Blague were not there, for they had passed away. Dr. Gilbert had lain down to rest by the side of his wife, and Mrs. Blague had taken her place with her husband.

little Jamie, and the fair-haired children of her youth. The house has a new master and a new mistress. Fred Gilbert is a farmer, and Mrs. Fred Gilbert is a sister of Mrs. Thomas Lampson—in short, a Joslyn—not only a pretty woman, but every way a worthy one. So Arthur Blague and his wife, Thomas Lampson and his wife, and Mr. and Mrs. Fred Gilbert, are bound to each other by family ties no less than by the closest friendship.

The party talk of old times and old scenes. They walk over to the burial-ground, and, in silence, gather about the clumps of roses that hide their friends, and speak tenderly of the departed. Arthur leans upon the family monument, and, gazing upon the mound that rises above the breast of little Jamie, goes back in memory over his painful history, and weeps like a woman. At length, he calls to him his three children, and tells them where their little uncle lies, of whom they have heard so many times.

As they pass out they note a newly made grave by the side of that of Mr. Ruggles. "So the old woman is gone," is all the remark that is made. They call upon the Joslyn family—now one of the most thrifty and respectable families of the town—thanks to Mrs. Joslyn. The old man is past work, but the old woman looks as if she might last twenty years yet.

But the town generally is changed. Neither Arthur nor Fanny feels at home. They turn toward their newer friends and fresher associations—to the good five hundred hearts in which they have their dwelling-place; and as they turn to bid farewell to Crampton, we wave them our adieu!

THE END.